Nisi Shawl

Everfair

TOR

A TOM DOHERTY ASSOCIATES BOOK
NEW YORK

This is a work of fiction. All of the characters, organizations, and events portrayed in this novel are either products of the author's imagination or are used fictitiously.

EVERFAIR

Copyright © 2016 by Nisi Shawl

All rights reserved.

Map by Michael Gellatly

Designed by Jonathan Bennett

A Tor Book
Published by Tom Doherty Associates
175 Fifth Avenue
New York, NY 10010

www.tor-forge.com

Tor® is a registered trademark of Macmillan Publishing Group, LLC.

The Library of Congress has cataloged the hardcover edition as follows:

Shawl, Nisi, author.
    Everfair / Nisi Shawl.—First edition.
        p. cm.
    "A Tom Doherty Associates book."
    ISBN 978-0-7653-3805-1 (hardcover)
    ISBN 978-1-4668-3784-3 (ebook)
    1. Utopias—Fiction.   2. Steampunk fiction.   3. Congo (Democratic Republic)—Colonization—Fiction.   4. Belgium—Colonies—Africa—Fiction.   I. Title.
    PS3619.H3947 E94 2016
    813'.6—dc23

                                                            2016288352

ISBN 978-0-7653-3806-8 (trade paperback)

Our books may be purchased in bulk for promotional, educational, or business use. Please contact your local bookseller or the Macmillan Corporate and Premium Sales Department at 1-800-221-7945, extension 5442, or by email at MacmillanSpecialMarkets@macmillan.com.

First Edition: September 2016
First Trade Paperback Edition: September 2017

Printed in the United States of America

0 9 8 7 6 5 4 3 2 1

For Octavia, who knew this day would come

Historical Note

This novel derives from one of history's most notorious atrocities: King Leopold II's reign over the Congo Free State. The exact number of casualties is unknown, but conservative estimates admit that at least half of the populace disappeared in the period from 1895 to 1908. The area thus devastated was about a quarter of the size of the current continental United States. Millions of people died.

The steampunk genre often works as a form of alternate history, showing us how small changes to what actually happened might have resulted in momentous differences: clockwork Victorian-era computers, commercial transcontinental dirigible lines, and a host of other wonders. This is that kind of book.

I like to think that with a nudge or two events might have played out *much* more happily for the inhabitants of Equatorial Africa. They might have enjoyed a prosperous future filled with all the technology that delights current steampunk fans in stories of western Europe and North America. And more. In *Everfair* they do.

Of course steampunk is a form of fiction, a fantasy, and the events within these pages never happened. But they *could* have.

Some Notable Characters

European:

Lisette Toutournier, 1/28/1873–8/3/1954, author, nurse, and intelligence agent

Adelaide/Daisy Albin, 8/15/1858–5/4/1924, "The Poet," a founder of the Fabian Society, married to Laurence/Laurie Albin, mother of George and Lily Albin, foster mother of Rosalie Albin and Laurence/Laurie Albin, Jr.

Matthew/Matty Jamison, 5/19/1860–6/19/1937, playwright, knighted in 1912

John/Jackie Herbert Owen, 7/26/1856–8/13/1913, a founder of the Fabian Society

Laurence/Laurie Albin, a founder of the Fabian Society, married to Daisy Albin, father of George, Lily, Rosalie, and Laurence/Laurie Albin, Jr.

George Albin, son of Daisy and Laurie Albin, married to Martha Livia Hunter Albin in November 1897

Lily Albin, daughter of Daisy and Laurie Albin

Rosalie Albin, daughter of Laurie Albin and Ellen Main Albin

Laurence/Laurie Albin, Jr., son of Laurie Albin and Ellen Main Albin

Ellen Main Albin, a Fabian Society member, married to Laurie Albin in April 1897

Albert Dowson, an engineer and Fabian Society supporter

Christopher J. Thornhill, a British intelligence agent

USian:

Serenissima/Rima Bailey, 11/2/1894–3/7/1967, actress
Martha Livia Hunter Albin, 8/10/1858–2/27/1964, married
to George Albin in November 1897
Thomas Jefferson Wilson, 10/16/1849–8/2/1923, missionary
and military officer
Chester Hunter, engineer and inventor, Martha Livia Hunter
Albin's godson, brother of Winthrop Hunter
Winthrop Hunter, engineer and inventor, Martha Livia
Hunter Albin's godson, brother of Chester Hunter
The Lincolns, a Baltimore-based family of entrepreneurs

African:

Mwenda, 1875–6/22/1954, king of the territory sold to the
Fabian Society by Leopold II
Josina, 1865–12/2/1928, priest of Oxun, intelligence agent,
Mwenda's favorite wife and queen
Fwendi, 1888–9/16/1970, intelligence agent
Captain Renji, one of Mwenda's military leaders
Captain Tombo, one of Mwenda's military leaders, trained to
fly aircanoes in 1912 and 1913
Old Kanna, King Mwenda's chief counselor
Nenzima, a fighter, elder, and representative for the
Grand Mote
Mwadi, princess and intelligence agent, daughter of Josina
and Mwenda
Lembe, one of Josina's favorite attendants
Sifa, one of Josina's favorite attendants
Alonzo, an intelligence agent for Josina and Mwenda and
representative for the Grand Mote, cousin to Josina
Yoka, refugee, fighter, devotee and apprentice priest of
Loango
Loyiki, refugee, courier, representative for the Grand Mote
Great-Uncle Mkoi, the only other survivor of Fwendi's
village, brother of her grandmother

East Asian:

Ho Lin-Huang/Tink, 1/18/1881–7/18/1978, engineer and inventor, representative for the Grand Mote, brother to Bee-Lung

Ho Bee-Lung, pharmacist, sister to Tink

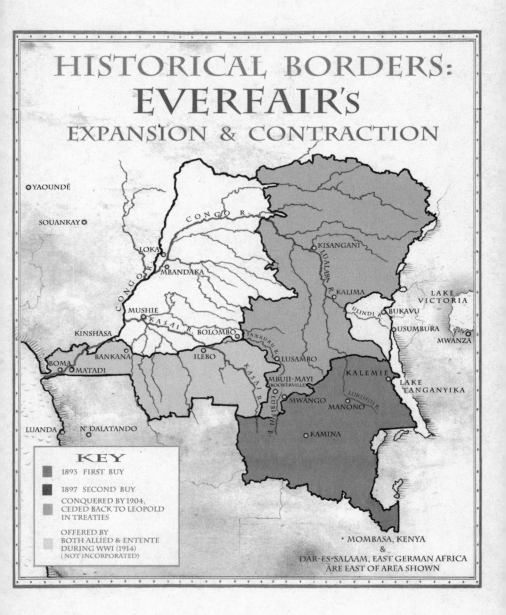

HISTORICAL BORDERS:
EVERFAIR's
EXPANSION & CONTRACTION

YAOUNDÉ

SOUANKAY

CONGO R.

LOKA

MBANDAKA

CONGO R.

MUSHIE

KASAI R.

KINSHASA

BOLOMBO

SANKURU R.

BANKANA

ILEBO

KASAI R.

BOMA

MATADI

KISANGANI

LUALABA R.

KALIMA

ULINDI R.

BUKAVU

LAKE VICTORIA

USUMBURA

MWANZA

LUSAMBO

MBUJI-MAYI
(ROOKERVILLE)

KALEMIE

LUKUSHI R.

MWANGO

MANONO

LAKE TANGANYIKA

LUBISH R.

LUANDA

N'DALATANDO

KAMINA

KEY

1893 FIRST BUY

1897 SECOND BUY

CONQUERED BY 1904,
CEDED BACK TO LEOPOLD
IN TREATIES

OFFERED BY
BOTH ALLIED & ENTENTE
DURING WWI (1914)
(NOT INCORPORATED)

MOMBASA, KENYA
&
DAR-ES-SALAAM, EAST GERMAN AFRICA
ARE EAST OF AREA SHOWN

*Look for a long time at that which pleases you,
and a longer time at that which gives you pain.*

—COLETTE

Part One

Burgundy, France, July 1889

Lisette Toutournier sighed. She breathed in again, out, in, the marvelous air smelling of crushed stems, green blood bruised and roused by her progress along this narrow forest path. Her progress, and that of her new mechanical friend. Commencing to walk again, she pushed it along through underbrush and creepers, woodbine and fern giving way before its wheels. Oh, how the insects buzzed about her exposed skin, her face and hands and wrists and ankles, waiting to bite. And the vexing heat bid fair to stifle her as she climbed the hillside slowly—but the scent—intoxicating! And soon, so soon, all this effort would be repaid.

There! The crest came in sight, the washed-out summer sky showing itself through the beech trees' old silver trunks. Now her path connected with the road, stony, rutted, but still better suited for riding. She stood a moment admiring the view: the valley, the blurred rows of cultivation curving away smaller and smaller in the bluing distance, the sky pale overhead, the perfect foil for the dark-leaved woods behind her and by her sides. Not far off a redwing sang, cold water trickling uphill.

She had the way of it now: gripping the rubber molded around the machine's metal handlebars, she leaned it toward her and swung one skirted leg over the drop frame. Upright again, she walked it a few more steps forward, aiming straight along the lane, the yellow-brown dust bright in the sun. The machine's glossy paint shone. Within the wheel's front rim its spokes were a revolving web of intricacy, shadows and light chasing one another. Tiny puffs of dust spurted from beneath the black rubber tires.

She raised her eyes. The vista opened wider, wider. The road laid itself down before her.

Up on the creaking leather seat. Legs drawn high, boots searching, scraping, finding their places . . . and pedal! Push! Feet turning circles like her machine's wheels, *with* those wheels. It was, at first, work. She pedaled and steered, wobbling just once and catching herself. Then going faster, faster! Flying! Freedom!

Saplings, walls, and vines whipped by, flashes of greenbrowngreengrey as Lisette on her machine sped down the road, down the hill. Wind rushed into her face, whistled in her ears, filled her nose, her lungs, tore her hair loose of its pins to stream behind her. She was a wild thing, laughing, jouncing over dry watercourses, hanging on for dear, dear life. Lower, now, and some few trees arched above, alternately blocking the hot glare and exposing her to it coolwarmcoolwarm, currents of sun and shade splashing over her as she careened by. Coasting, at last, spilling all velocity till she and the machine came to rest beside the river.

The river. The comforting smell and sound of it rushing away. Out on the Yonne's broad darkness a barge sailed, bound perhaps for Paris, the Seine, the sea beyond, carrying casks of wine and other valuables. Flushed from her ride, Lisette blushed yet more deeply, suddenly conscious of the curious stares of those around her: Mademoiselle Carduner, the schoolmistress; and Monsieur Lutterayne, the chemist, out for a promenade during his dinner hour or on some errand, seizing a chance to vacate his stuffy shop. Flustered, she attempted to restrain her hair into a proper chignon, but at only sixteen and with many pins missing, this was beyond her skill. She began furiously to plait her thick blond curls, and the others moved away.

At last she was alone on the riverbank with her mechanical friend. She tied her plaits together, though she knew that momentarily they would slither apart. She stroked the machine's still-gleaming handlebars, then leaned to fit her forehead at their center, so. "Dear one," whispered Lisette. "How can you ever know how much you mean to me? Who would not give all they could, everything they had, in exchange for such happiness as I have found with you?"

Sans words, the front tire's black arc responded to her whispers with visions. It preached to her of motion, of travel, of the mysteries dwelling beyond this sleepy, provincial village.

"Ah, yes, and one day, my dear, one day . . ." She raised her head and gazed out again at the river, at the barge now nearly gone from view. "One day we shall venture out and see for ourselves what it is the world holds for us."

Boma, Congo, December 1889

Horror.

The Reverend Lieutenant Thomas Jefferson Wilson could think of no other word to sum up what he had experienced on this trip. Even now, alone in the quiet, white-walled room provided him by his host, he heard their cries, he saw their wasted bodies, their eyes bulging large in their thin faces, pulsing with defeat, hopeless as marine creatures stranded on a desolate beach. He *smelled* them, their sores running with blood and infected matter where chafed by their chains at neck and wrist and waist and ankle. Smelled the sweat of their fear, the fear that made them lift up and carry burdens half their malnourished weight till released by death. Smelled their abundant corpses rotting by the trail in the tropic heat.

This land was to have been Heaven.

Restless as ever, he abandoned his seat on the narrow cot to unshutter the room's one window. A breeze brought some relief from the day's fierce temperatures. Even up here, on the capital's plateau, a Pennsylvanian such as himself found the Congo "Free" State's equatorial climate hard to withstand. But he should not complain.

Or not on his own behalf.

A tapping at the door. He opened it on a child of eleven, the household's primary servant—a boy named Mola, he recalled. "'Soir," the boy slurred in French. He entered, bearing with him a tray, the meal his master offered in lieu of the repast shared by Boma's white residents at the hotel near the river below.

The Reverend Lieutenant Thomas Jefferson Wilson would not be welcome at that hotel, for he was not white.

The dishes on the tray held vegetables, the ever-present manioc, and stewed meat of some sort—probably from a fowl or goat. No doubt this was what Mola himself would sup upon, and Thomas made sure to tender the boy his thanks as effusively as his limited French allowed. When he was alone again he placed the tray beneath his cot, the food untouched. His journey upriver to Stanley Falls and then back here to the port of Boma had entirely wrecked his appetite.

The wine he also set aside, to aid him later in seeking sleep. He drank instead a gobletful of water from a crystal decanter, then set that on the sill to cool and turned again to his work.

To the horror.

At forty a veteran of three wars, Thomas had seen and survived much. Though no more than a child at the American Civil War's onset, as soon as blacks were allowed to fight he had enlisted and seen action. That must be why his sojourn here in the Congo was affecting him so adversely, he told himself sternly. His reaction was not illness, not pain and anguish, but anger: righteous indignation that the evils of slavery, which he had staked his life to eradicate from the face of the Earth, had sprung up once again. Unprotested and, what was worse, unremarked, they had met him everywhere he journeyed in this supposed Utopia.

A pair of thin pillows lay over his traveling desk, incompletely concealing it. He retrieved it and drew forth the manuscript of his open letter to King Leopold, monarch of this realm and soi-disant benefactor of its benighted native population.

"Good and great friend," the salutation read. "I have the honor to submit for your Majesty's consideration some reflections respecting the Independent State of Congo, based upon a careful study and inspection of the country. . . ." So far, he had written five pages and not yet named a third of the atrocities he had been forced to witness. The whippings, the murders committed so casually as if a form of sport, innocents dismembered—Thomas's gorge rose, but he settled nonetheless to his self-appointed task.

Keeping his intended audience in mind, he aimed for a tone of forthrightness that yet maintained discreet silence on the more repulsive details of what he had discovered. The open letter would be published in his paper, *The Commoner,* and also as a stand-alone pamphlet; perhaps in boards as a small book, on the Continent. There he would find support for such an enterprise, translators . . .

The light dimmed rapidly, but not till he heard the clattering ratchet of the steam-driven trolley climbing Boma's cliffs did Thomas cease his efforts. That noise, he knew, presaged the arrival of his host, the Anglo-Flemish trader Roger Morel. Thomas didn't trust him, didn't trust anyone who profited from Leopold's reign. He packed away his open letter and went to meet the trolley at the platform mere yards from Morel's villa.

Four cars comprised the steam train's entire length. Their iron fuselages had been painted a brilliant yellow with gaudy red, blue, and green trim. This jaunty coloring and the fortuitous semblance of a face in the alignment of their doors and windows lent the cars a charming air much like the illustration in a children's book. Thomas at first had succumbed to this charm and to the undeniable romance of such a small machine so beautifully built—until his peregrinations brought home to him the human cost involved.

Beneath the leafy serrations of a grove of palms the cars disgorged themselves of their riders, black-clad white men replacing their hats and stepping carefully down the platform's wooden stairway. Morel bared his head again in salute to his visitor. Exchanging meaningless pleasantries, the two returned to Morel's home.

Mola took his master's hat and gloves at the door, handing him a glass half-filled with a greenish liquid. Thomas made as if to return to his room, considering his social obligations for the evening met, but Morel would have none of it. "No, no, my friend, I insist," he said, indicating with his drink the sitting room's best chair.

Ensconced perforce on its cushioned mahogany, Thomas accepted from Mola a second glass. He sipped the unknown beverage with his customary suspicion as the boy slipped from the room. It was faintly bitter and contained no alcohol he could detect.

"So." His host had assumed a seat on the divan, crossing his legs and clasping his hands over one knee. "You leave the day after the morrow?"

"Yes." There were other colonies to explore, perhaps more truly paradisiacal, more suited to providing his colored brethren a new home. The ship would stop for Accra and Dakar, and he intended to travel from there to Tunis, Cairo—"That is my plan."

"I advise you to change it."

Thomas looked at Morel inquiringly. His eyes held a warning gleam that overrode Thomas's mistrust of him. Thomas set the harmless glass down on the side table with a steady enough hand and spoke: "I fail to take your meaning, sir."

"Ah. You have no confidence in me. That is well." Morel nodded as if confirming a pet theory to himself, his chin doubling. "You are being watched. You must leave tonight and go—elsewhere. A different route, more direct."

A different route? "To where?" No use attempting any further to dissemble.

"To England."

Not home. "Not to America?"

"In England you will be safe—enough. But this continent—there are large stakes, and the holders of those stakes are at every hand. During supper this evening I overheard enough, my English being supposed more imperfect than it is, to warrant giving you this warning."

Morel stood. "As well, I have a—a commission of sorts— If you will allow me to retrieve certain papers I wish you to convey—" He left and returned with a sheaf of documents—bills of lading, figures in long columns, maps. Thomas read them in growing dismay. Here was proof, if such would be needed, of what he had witnessed. Proof and beyond proof . . . The scope of the problem far exceeded what he had seen with his own eyes. Not thousands but tens of thousands were doomed unless the abominations practiced so freely in the Congo Free State were to cease, and cease now.

Liverpool, England, October 1890

Grim brick walls, dark with dead smoke, crowded Jackie Owen's path. They huddled over him, blocking the grey clouds but not the icy rain. A drop ran beneath his collar. Another followed it. He shrugged irritably in his mackintosh but hurried on, pressing through a small group of workmen just freed from some nearby dock or warehouse.

It wasn't the buildings' fault. The narrowness of the ways between them, mere corridors, was what annoyed. So obviously outmoded. No room for machinery of any sort. Here was Victoria Street, a modern thoroughfare at last. Four lanes for carriages, business facades well set back but of more or less uniform height, meaning electric tramlines could easily be strung overhead between them. Striding rapidly along, an unconscious smile of contentment lurking behind his beard, Jackie saw only enough of his surroundings to avoid crashing into obstacles. He was lost, though continuing automatically on his course to St. George's Hall. Lost in time, rapt in visions of things to come.

In Jackie Owen's spectral Liverpool, the many layers of garments hampering females he passed gave way to sensible clothes allowing their limbs liberty of movement, their blood hygienic circulation. Prices disappeared from shop windows, beggars from corners and alley entrances, rendered obsolete by the benignities of the surprisingly successful Fabian movement's socialism. And though the sun broke suddenly through the storm he took no note. Its brilliance was quite eclipsed by the *eminence argent* of an immense dirigible filling his mind's sky.

Reaching the confluence of several broad avenues, Jackie entered St. John's Gardens, still dreaming. These verdant acres had but lately been reclaimed from a church building, a hundred-year-old edifice that had been overdue for destruction—much like, in Jackie's opinion, the institution it represented. In his imagination, the gardens' new statue of reformer William Rathbone would be joined by monuments to others more radical—to himself? Why not? If he, John Herbert Owen, should make such a mark on the world as he expected, it would naturally be acknowledged.

Perhaps, also, there would be a likeness of tonight's speaker. A black, yes, but by all reports a most distinguished man.

As he approached the steps climbing to the hall's northmost entry, that closest to the Small Concert Room, Jackie let his visions recede. He was interested in who else saw fit to attend this evening's performance.

The number surprised him. One or two damp placards held up by defenders of the regime confirmed that his opinions were not universally held. Yet dozens of people sharing them streamed ahead of him and fell behind—scores, hundreds. Wilson had appeared in Liverpool many times over the last few weeks, as attested by journalists here and in London. Of course his earlier venue had been a Baptist church. The church was abolitionist, but Jackie Owen, like other members of the dissident, socialist Fabian Society he had helped found, avoided such places. Perhaps they were not the only ones; perhaps more people were coming to their political senses.

Inside, only a faint odor assailed his nose. Kept in check by the hall's amazing draughtless ventilation system (Jackie had made an earlier visit simply to tour this innovation), the smell of wet wool and feathers and inexpensive *parfumerie* increased only a little as he entered the confines of the room itself.

The audience looked to include a fair number of his countrymen. By no means restricted to manual labor here, they engaged in every form of trade and had infiltrated all classes. Liverpool was home to one of the largest concentrations of Irishmen off the Emerald Isle. And Irishwomen, too. He heard their low, lovely accents as he took his seat, wives admonishing their men to have a care, that broadcloth cost more than a penny the yard, sure, and was never meant to be soaking up so much of the world's blessed moisture.

How he missed such talk in London, in the parlors, conservatories, and withdrawing rooms he frequented there.

A hush descended as the Reverend Lieutenant Thomas Jefferson Wilson took the podium. A dark, slim, upright man in dark dress, he stood out in the Small Concert Room's gleaming brightness like a wick in a brass lamp. His words were fire.

"I come before you on this evening to tell of an evil in a far-off land which is yet nonetheless present here in this room, in our very midst," the man began. Evidently a practiced orator, he nourished the flame he had lit without vain expenditure of air, without ever seeming to raise his voice. And still it filled that room, and the ears of his audience, at least eight hundred by Jackie's best estimate. Their ears, and their hearts as well. He accused none of them of committing this crime, as he termed it, against humanity. Accused none but implicated all.

"Yes, I repeat, a crime against humanity! Are we blacks not men? Our skin is dusky, but our blood runs as red and salt as that of any fairer race.

"Picture yourselves, then, in the circumstances of these poor Negroes of the Congo. You who toil here in Europe for wages which permit you a bare living, a bare hope of something more for your offspring, imagine if you were to receive *nothing*. Imagine if you were beaten, threatened with death, if your dear wives were ravished from your sides and kept in prison till you had satisfied your employers' impossible demands. Imagine, then, if you failed to meet them."

Here he stepped off the stage's left side, disappearing from the view of all but those seated at the extreme right edge of the room's spherical plan. It was a measure of the hold this man exercised over his listeners that the hush that had greeted his first words only deepened in expectancy at his absence. Perhaps they had seen or had word of prior presentations and knew what was coming.

Wilson returned quickly, bearing with him a very ordinary-looking basket. Deserting the podium, he placed it on the stage's edge, tipping it to expose its contents. Jackie beheld a mass of greyish lumps.

"Rubber," Wilson pronounced, in accents usually reserved for the vilest of epithets. "Raw rubber, a substance bidding fair to replace ivory as the Dark Continent's most profitable export." He lifted from the basket a single, uneven ball of the stuff and held it up as a Hamlet might hold his Yorick's skull. "A substance noteworthy for its strength, flexibility, and capacity to shed water. Vital to the production of tires for automobiles, bicycles, omnibuses—modes of transport to which I, and many of you also, owe *our presence here tonight*." Sounding now as if he choked on his barely contained fury, Wilson managed to continue. "Also used in waterproofing *boots* and *mackintoshes*"—here Jackie felt himself flush with guilt—"rubber is harvested in the wild at great effort. A basketful such as I here display for your edification is the result of many days of grueling and dangerous work performed by dozens of desperate men. Desperate, desperate men, driven by such inducements as I have already outlined for you. And if"—Wilson turned now to gaze upon his audience, offering them the grey lump on his open, outstretched palm—"if they fail, then God above must help them, He must show them mercy, for no man on Earth will do so. For the wives are *killed—strangled,* generally, as bullets are too dear to spend on such a task. And the empty baskets are then *filled,* filled to overflowing with their husbands' *severed hands*!"

Now the conflagration. Now the fires of outrage burnt freely as the audience rose to its feet, crying aloud for justice. Jackie stood with them. Marvelous! To be part of such a mob, to feel its unstoppable power for *good*. It must be for good . . .

But the fire Wilson had lit did not burn entirely beyond his control. When the crowd's bellows had crested, the dark figure on the stage lifted its arms as if supplicating Heaven. Quiet fell.

"I hear you," the speaker declared. "I hear your words clearly; you say with our Lord, 'As you have done unto the least of these, so have you done unto me.'"

Jackie would not have put it that way, but a chorus of "Aye"s and "Hear! hear!"s came in response. "How, then," Wilson asked, "shall we right this wrong?"

The reverend lieutenant explained his program and the fire flickered, died to embers. Letter-writing and petitions to Parliament was what he asked of them. A movement along the lines of Abolitionism. Which had been well and good in its time.

But Jackie had a better idea.

Brussels, Belgium, August 1891

Did she, Lisette Toutournier, actually love this man Laurie Albin? Or was it merely that she so hated this city that she welcomed the excuse his company gave her to leave it?

Under the hood of the barouche she regarded her newfound lover critically. Despite his blond hair Laurie was fully fourteen years her senior. Not that thirty-two was *old,* exactly . . . And his moustaches, so foolish! The ends turned up wildly, without gathering themselves into points first, like toothbrushes found at a sudden disadvantage. Now his hot, damp hand clasped hers in the darkness afforded by their conveyance. Hot, and eager, whatever conventional wisdom might say about the English.

"Having second thoughts?" His breath tickled her ear and she drew away.

"No," she answered, and that was not at all a lie. First thoughts, one ought to call them, for her decision to elope had had naught to do with thinking. Even now the caress of his soft fingers upon her naked neck brought with it an unwanted shiver of sensual delight. Oh, why had no one warned her?

The carriage wheels slowed. Lisette leaned forward and saw that they had reached the Gare du Nord. At last. She gathered her two meager boxes and let the coachman help her to the pavement, let Laurie pay his hire. They passed beneath one of several tall arches. Lisette loitered as obscurely as she might, her head down, facing a long and boring wall of polished marble while Laurie hurried to purchase their tickets. But here they confronted an obstacle: the train was delayed in its arrival. Laurie explained the problem in French rendered less intelligible even than usual by his nervousness: There would be a wait of nineteen minutes, no more, till they could board and leave this detestable town. He was taking her away with him, to England, to Kent, to a countryside far removed.

Lisette seated herself on the hard bench Laurie had selected for them, removed from the majority of other passengers. Nineteen minutes. Not enough time for her two uncles to find and rescue her from this rash venture. Enough time, however, for her to regret it.

Her lover was a married man. Had he admitted as much to her? No! And yet, inexperienced though she was, Lisette had a presentiment that this was so, despite his promises to take her to his home. How not? A gentleman; pleasant to look at, if she were to be honest; well-off enough that work had never marred his hands, softer than her mother's; with an affable and easy air that sought to ingratiate itself to women—and very nearly always succeeded.

She remembered the first time she had seen him, her Laurie, hovering at the front door of the journal's offices. Smiling and removing his so obviously English hat as she produced the key to unlock it, thanking her politely as she held it open but insisting that she proceed him. And then, realizing that they two were alone in the dusty, disordered offices, he *blushed*! His vulnerability had pierced her to her heart.

But what had absolutely won her was the honor he paid her by posing to her the questions he had come to investigate for essays he would write to appear in the newsletter of his Fabian Society: matters of state, international treaties, conventions and accords between the governments of Europe concerning the wealth of Africa—he had refrained from assuming her to be unimportant, setting aside her youth, her femininity—or so she had believed at the time.

So she had believed. But see him now, possessive, as passionate as one could show oneself in public. See with what difficulty he restrained himself from stroking her wrist as it lay beside him on the bench's arm.

No one else had taken her seriously. It was because of this that she had fallen for her lover's pretense of doing so.

On the breakup of her home, a dissolution her parents had seen fit to protect her from till the last possible minute, till the day the house and its contents were advertised as going on auction, there was the question of how to dispose of Lisette. A question she had no part in deciding, for her wishes had been consulted in nothing—nothing! They had even sold her beloved bicycle . . .

Her mother and Captain Toutournier, her father, were to be taken under the wing of her half-brother, Hermes. They and Lisette's older brother Jules resided now with Hermes and his wife in a village not far from where the family once had lived so happily.

Hermes was a doctor with a flourishing practice. Jules studied to become a chemist, so that was all right. But Lisette—who had attended Hermes on his rounds when he was just starting out!—should not be tempted to pursue such an unladylike career. A teacher, or better yet a housewife, that was what Lisette was meant to be, naturally . . . It was with great reluctance her family allowed itself to be persuaded of the suitability of sending her here, to stay with her maternal uncles, both journalists.

Yes, Lisette had begged, had cried and pleaded to come here, to this sty of a city! With its unlucky river penned beneath heavy cobblestones and fed unending streams of muck, Brussels had a sewer for its heart. And all *les Bruxellois* were pigs, and glad to feed from that trough.

But not she.

All this while Lisette's feet were throbbing. Out of sight, on the platforms to the station's rear, trains came and went. She felt their rhythms through her bootsoles, heard the hiss and thunder of their arrival above the din of her thoughts. Then it was time, and as in a trance she rose, Laurie linking his arm in hers and guiding her forward. A maze of tracks opened beyond a glassed partition. Engines of might! To left, to right—on all sides of her they gathered, but Laurie knew where to walk between their steel shoulders.

Then an empty stretch and she saw a ways ahead to where one

locomotive waited alone, steam wrapping him like a cape. A tall stack rose from his round black tank, a lantern blazing at the base like a jewel on a turban. A magician who would whisk them away from this ugliness, who would carry them on his broad, strong back to the land's end, to the very edge of this continent.

And then they would sail beyond, to England.

They were seated. Lisette's confusion dissipated and she realized that Laurie had paid for the accommodation of a sleeping coach. Touched, she smiled at him—but quickly understood that this was likely done for his own convenience.

Soon her understanding was confirmed. In the middle of the afternoon. Eager, yes, her Laurie; barely had they left Brussels before he importuned her to "take a little rest." On thin white sheets Lisette lost the last vestige of her girlhood. Then it was her lover who needed "a little rest." Lying awake in the last light stealing by the tops and bottoms of the blinds, she found comfort in the rocking motion of the train's carriage, so regular, and the lilting undersong of its wheels.

Kent, England, February 1893

Daisy Albin didn't object to Lisette Toutournier. To the contrary. It was Ellen who had sulked on her arrival and who still, almost two years later, seemed to chafe at the situation. Ironic, as Ellen was *not* dear Laurie's *legal* wife, as Daisy was.

But they all contrived to rub along together. Even in early February, with the days so brief and cold and wet, the nights so ridiculously lengthy. With the new, larger house nonetheless rather small for four adults and an equal number of children. Really, it was a blessing that Laurie had taken Ellen with him on this latest business trip, though it saddened little Lisette.

Daisy wrote the end of the last line and allowed herself a glance up from the verse-covered pages on her desk blotter. With a shock she saw that the dark had advanced enough to turn the window to a looking glass. Her lamp glowed bravely against the blackness. Her hair blent with it, framing her face in short curls that melted without fuss into the air. Her long nose, which she described to others as making her look like "a particularly sagacious sheepdog," was in good evidence.

But where were the children? It must be almost half five. Still out-of-doors with their *tante* Lisette?

As if she had wished upon a talisman for their presence she heard them come in by the side entrance: the clump of boots, the piping soprano of little Laurie Junior, Georgie's voice awkwardly seesawing, laughter rising from Lily and Rosalie. Lisette shushed them with reminders that "Mama wrote herself"—the dear girl's grasp of English had grown steadily, but it slipped when she became excited.

There was nothing more Daisy truly needed to accomplish here. She left her desk and opened her study's door, calling out, "Darlings! Is it time for tea already?"

"Mama!" The four children climbed the stairs as she descended and they met halfway in a joyous tangle. Daisy loved them all, the two youngest Ellen had borne just as well as their older siblings.

Lisette stood on the bottom step, having entrusted their wraps to one of the housemaids, probably Harriet, since this would be Thursday, Mary's afternoon off. "In the playroom, chérie?" Daisy half-asked, half-invited.

Those disconcertingly wide grey eyes smiled. "But of course," said Lisette, continuing up the stairs and catching Daisy by the hand. She laced their fingers and lifted their arms ceilingward. They danced a mock-solemn figure in the children's wake, curtseying to one another on the braided rag rug where they ended. It would puzzle anyone watching, Daisy knew, her evident pleasure in the company of a girl most would call her rival. So beautiful, and so young: a few weeks ago, in January, Lisette had turned a mere twenty years old.

While they arranged the children's blue-enameled chairs around the big circular table, Daisy heard the tale of the afternoon's walk: hare tracks sighted in the snow that yet remained along one stretch of privet; an owl spotted in the spinney behind the abandoned henhouse; a small pile of apples that must have fallen from a cart on its way to the cider mill and that "very well might still be good to eat!" as Rosalie pronounced with a six-year-old's optimism. The apples in question, produced from pockets and pinafores, looked and smelt as if they had started to ferment.

Nurse and Harriet entered then with milky tea and trays of sliced ginger cake and bread-and-butter. For a while Daisy was too busy pouring and serving to worry about the apples. As the hungry explorers feasted, Lisette lobbied for the apples to be "put out for the deer," a proposal attracting far more favor than would have attached to Daisy's first impulse of pitching them in the rubbish.

After assisting Nurse in preparing the children for bed, Daisy and Lisette returned to the playroom rather than waste the fire still burning there. Blessing the day she had stopped wearing her corsets, Daisy knelt on the hearth as easily as if she were her own daughter.

Lisette pulled a low stool up beside her. "When will they return?" She spoke French. Daisy and Lisette often did when alone together.

She sighed. "No word. What have you—"

"Me? I have heard nothing, chérie. He does not write." The firelight showed Lisette's touchingly stoic face.

"You would have liked to go?" Laurie had of course taken Ellen with him on this trip, because she was his secretary, as he was the Fabian Society's. That was why.

"To London?" Lisette shrugged. "Perhaps. It has been a few months since my last visit. There may be new things to see . . . But, no. It is better here. With you." One of her surprisingly large hands rested softly on Daisy's cropped curls. Her hair stirred gently. So gently. As if touched by the lightest breeze.

Daisy sighed and leaned back so her head rested in Lisette's lap. The luxury of silence surrounded them. Now Lisette stroked her temples, her forehead, smoothed her thick eyebrows. Now she swept the tips of her fingers along the semicircular edges of Daisy's ears.

All too soon the sound of Harriet's approaching feet ended the moment's peace. She brought a letter delivered with the last post, and Cook's request to serve them supper in the sitting room at eight. The usual time. Daisy nodded absently and opened the letter. It was from Laurie, finally. He had been gone a week. Only two pages; she read through them swiftly and swore in exasperation.

"What happens?" Lisette asked. "It is he?"

"Yes." She scanned the pages again, hoping to have missed something, to have misread them.

"What happens?"

"Donors are interested in the Society's new colonizing project. Mr. Owen has asked him to go to Brussels again."

"To see Leopold?"

"Yes. Here." Daisy wanted to ball the poor letter up and toss it in the fire, but she made herself fold it neatly and hand it to Lisette.

"He does not say when he means to return." Lisette stared at the two pages as if, upon longer inspection, more words might fade into visibility.

"No." She stood and pulled her watch free of her skirt pocket. Almost eight. For Lisette's sake she forced a cheerful expression. "But I'm sure he'll be back as soon as he can. It's Lily's birthday on the twenty-sixth, and St. Valentine's in less than a fortnight—"

"He may easily mail us red ribbons and paper lace from abroad, and perhaps a verse copied out of some book." Lisette folded the letter with an air of cool detachment Daisy knew to be assumed, and reinserted it in its envelope. "Shall we sup, chérie?" She took Daisy's arm in a formal clasp and they went down.

Harriet served. In her presence the subject was dropped. They discussed literature instead: Daisy's latest novels over the soup, then Lisette's own efforts with the ham and asparagus.

Lisette had become Daisy's secretary after conquering the Automatic Type Writer—Mr. Owen's attempt to get Daisy to resume producing columns for the Fabian Society's newsletter. The contraption had thoroughly intimidated her. Lisette, though, seemed immediately drawn to its shiny black finish and the insectlike complications of its inner workings. First she had helped with the overdue correspondence to Daisy's publishers and readers. Then came the girl's own manuscripts. They were . . . not like Daisy's ghost stories, nor like her adventures for children. Nor like anything else she could remember seeing.

The night before, Daisy had taken "The Creatures' Dialogue" to bed and read it as the candle guttered low. Now she tried to express to Lisette how strange it was, and how good.

"What made you think of talking animals?" she asked.

The girl raised her shoulders and tilted her head quizzically, fingers at her full lips. "But you, you do so all the time: your Phoenix?"

"Yes, but for children." The "Creatures'" diction was not what one would employ with young people, and some of the subjects these Pussies-in-Boots discussed among themselves challenged even Daisy's quite advanced principles. They would not be at all suitable for the nursery set. "Will you write more?"

"You believe I should?"

Daisy reassured her on that head as enthusiastically as possible. Though she hadn't the slightest idea where to find an audience for these tales of cats and dogs sailing the skies in balloons and discovering imaginary lands, lands whose inhabitants participated in the most daring of sexual adventures. Who wouldn't want to read them? But who would risk putting them into print?

Kisangani, Congo, October 1893

It could be that his decision to ban all whites from the country had been a mistake. Young King Mwenda stirred on the creaking leather of his throne bench, restless as always with self-doubt he should not show. He held the creased barkcloth message loosely in one hand. He had read it. The runner waited belly-down on the packed earth of the royal courtyard for his word on this matter. So also waited his wives and counselors and the spies in their midst.

How he longed for the simplicities of life in the bush. The scent of sap, the sinking of the soft soil beneath his steps. But at the tender age of thirty-six seasons his role as leader denied him those sorts of pleasures.

He let the message fall from his hand and Josina bent gracefully to retrieve it from the ground. He grasped the haft rising from the sheath slung upon his left shoulder.

"Hai!" Old Kanna cried out in alarm and pointed at the copper shongo shining in Mwenda's hand. The sharp curves of its edges glinted quietly in the courtyard's cloudy light. He held a weapon. No matter that this was a ceremonial knife, highly decorated. The king had drawn a weapon. Mwenda knew he would be expected to use it somehow before he returned it to its sheath.

Another ingot on his back. Why had it been necessary to pick up the burden of conquest? Why?

Because four seasons ago his spirit father had bid him do so. To turn aside from the joys of youth. No other, said his father's oracle, was so well suited to unify the nations' power. No other could satisfy the land's needs.

To satisfy his court's expectations would mean killing someone. Whom? Soft-armed Josina, still stooping with her head bowed and afraid now to move? Another wife—one less favored?

He had taken up his shongo to gaze upon the world's reflection in its surface. Metal had many uses besides killing the unjust. Let his watchers wait for death to be dealt.

In the shongo's largest copper blade he saw his face, skin reddened with the protective powder of the cam tree. He strove to make his mind quiet, to shift his focus deeper into the dull glare.

Had he misunderstood the directions that had brought him to his earlier decree? It could indeed be that his decision to ban whites from the country was a mistake. Those absent ones who honored his wishes were the very sort he would prefer to deal with, while the rest remained and behaved as written in the plea for help from his land's southwestern frontiers brought by the runner prone before him.

The terrible words on the barkcloth had turned in his mind to screams as he read them, keening now through the silence he sought within. "The whites have taken away all the women, and all children below the height of eight fingers," the message cried, "to be killed unless we deliver to their encampments huge quantities of the hardened tears of the vines-that-weep. By way of showing they truly mean to do this evil, they have sent to us, your captains, the severed heads, hands, and feet of our mothers."

Mwenda the warrior wanted only to fight and kill these barbarians. Mwenda the new king knew he must contain his raw heat. Months earlier, his spirit father had warned him there would be bad consequences to leading a direct conflict against the whites. Along that path lay sorrow.

At times his spirit father spoke in pictures shown upon the shongo's blades. Pictures for Mwenda's eyes alone, he understood. Never before had he attempted to see these visions in the company of other human beings as he now did. Was it even possible?

Perhaps. Perhaps the clouds parted. Perhaps the sun struck dazzling sparks from the copper's surface. Perhaps these sparks entered the silence and darkness within Mwenda's mind and lit fires there, flames that shaped themselves into answers. Not the answers he sought. But the answers he would need.

Mwenda lowered the knife and blinked. All was as it had been before he became blind to his surroundings. Josina still stooped, only the heaviness of her breath betraying the effort it took to remain in this position. The runner lay at Mwenda's feet, in Old Kanna's rapidly fading shadow.

The king stood. Cocked his strong right arm and threw the shongo as hard as he could, over the heads of the startled court. A heartbeat passed. Then he heard the *thok* of a sharp blade burying itself in the thick trunk of the tree planted beside the shelter of his ancestors. *Satisfactory,* he thought, but without a smile. The shongo's resting place indicated that the country's defense was in the ancestors' management. His heir-to-come would retrieve the ceremonial knife when this affair was over.

For now he would follow his spirit father's instructions. Aloud, he said, "We will surrender."

The shocked silence held, but fear and astonishment filled the royal courtyard like a cooking smell. "Bid the runner rise," Mwenda told Old Kanna. "Take him to your home and feed him and give him a place to rest. We will send another to our captains Renji and Tombo with full instructions, and to our other captains elsewhere."

He turned to Josina, who was erect now, as enticingly pretty as ever. "Your cousin."

"Alonzo?"

"Yes. He speaks the whites' language?"

"They have many, just as we do, and Alonzo is conversant in several." Josina couldn't help showing how proud she was. "The Portuguese, in which tongue I am alike fluent, naturally"—naturally, since she and her cousin both hailed from beyond the frontier, from Angola, a land the Portuguese tribe had settled in great concentrations—"and the French, too, of course, but also the Spanish, the Dutch, and the English."

"Good. He will go." His wife looked troubled, but didn't protest. "Find him and bring him here."

Mwenda dismissed most of the other courtiers, sending one to fetch back Old Kanna. When Josina returned with Alonzo, she knelt down a bit away from the circle gathered about the king's throne. She made no move to leave again. He let her stay. Mwenda knew she spied on him for her father. But what her father didn't know was that she also informed Mwenda about *his* doings. Understanding Josina and her ways made the king feel comfortable. He was judicious in what he allowed her to find out. This was a much better arrangement than one based on mere trust, in his opinion.

"Alonzo, you will bear our commands to the southwest."

His wife's cousin looked up from where he crouched. He had the face of a beautiful woman: high cheekbones, large eyes framed by thick-lashed lids. "Yes, my king."

"Renji and Tombo will tell those they protect to disappear."

One gently curved eyebrow arched higher than its mate. "To disappear?"

"To vanish as they did when we invaded. Abandon their crops and fields and homes. Even the towns, their workshops and markets. Disperse."

"Disappear. Yes." Alonzo nodded thoughtfully, gazing downward.

"Also, the terms of our surrender." At this, all in the courtyard looked alert. Even, despite herself, Josina. "There are to be none. No conditions. We will tell the whites our surrender is complete." Mwenda paused. None spoke, though Old Kanna hummed worriedly deep in his throat.

"And that it will go into effect"—Here he paused again. The images shown him by his spirit father required careful translation into the language of living humans—"when the dance of the sun and earth repeats the steps now taken."

Frowns all around him as Old Kanna and the other advisors attempted to understand why he had used these words. Only Josina met his gaze steadily. He nodded to her his permission to speak.

"The French mark the sun's movements also," she said. "They call one pair of seasons by the word 'ah-nay.'"

Mwenda nodded. He had not known the foreign term, but even whites must have a way to express a basic idea like a season pair. But why had his spirit father framed it so?

"Aha! *Sanza!*" Old Kanna proclaimed, and at once Mwenda saw him to be right. The counselor's aged wisdom illuminated the haze of the king's inexperience. He would engage in a game of *sanza* with the whites, a game the Europeans would fail to realize that they were playing.

To tell the truth in a manner that made it impossible for his enemies to comprehend it; to force them to believe what he had never said; this was *sanza*. The surrender he offered would be accepted, but viewed with suspicion, and rightly so, for his people would give up their lands by simply abandoning them. For a time.

Further, the wording of his stipulation for when the surrender commenced—repeated exactly as given by his spirit father—would be heard as a stupid child's poor attempt to understand their concept of ah-nay. Thus the whites would underestimate Mwenda's intelligence.

In reality, as most people knew from those who lived in the sky-watching countries to the north, the sun danced with other suns as well as with the earth, in complicated maneuverings never to be exactly repeated. The dance would proceed in this fashion till long, long after Mwenda's reign, till long after his life had ended, long after the ends of the reigns and lives of all his heirs. The next of whom would retrieve the shongo from the tree where Mwenda had buried its blade, after the sham truce had ended. After the war they would not need to fight was won.

He would make his surrender and it would be accepted, though Mwenda would still be safe to wage war from the bush without breaking his pledge. This was his spirit father's plan. Or all of it Mwenda needed to know for now.

Londonderry, Ireland, November 1893

"All right." The Reverend Lieutenant Thomas Jefferson Wilson laid his hands on the deal table between them and looked at Mr. Owen with a gaze as expressionless as he could manage. "Let us see the deed of sale, as you assure me the land is to be ours." He kept his hands flat so that the pine boards of the table stayed them from their trembling, trying his best to remain calmly seated in this workaday kitchen, though he felt himself to be at the gates of Heaven.

Liberia, a colony founded in violence and funded by Southern slaveholders, was at the moment the sole safe destination for Negroes returning to their ancestral home. The Fabian Society proposal Mr. Owen presented would change this. His people had a chance to save themselves—and simultaneously to uplift their savage kin. The sun of redemption would dawn soon over the Congo Free State. He would live to see it.

Mr. Owen looked much moved himself. He cleared his throat before speaking. "Yes. I—" He reached inside the grey wool coat he wore despite the kitchen's heat. "I have it in my pocket here." He drew forth a sheaf of paper softly folded in thirds and spread it open.

Thomas leant forward to examine it. The writing was all in French, and made only a little sense. But one paragraph seemed full of outlandish names coupled with the word "fleuve," which he knew to mean river. The numbers followed by the degree symbols must indicate latitude and longitude. Still, he shook his head.

Mr. Owen mistook that. "But the tract is vast!" he exclaimed.

"Thousands of square miles, and some of the richest croplands on the African continent—"

"No, no, it's not—"

"Do you tell me that my efforts were in vain? After the work I've done to ensure that our common dream—"

Thomas's landlady opened the door and stuck her head through. "Any trouble, Lieutenant Reverend, sir?"

"None, Mrs. Swain. Let us alone, if you please." No doubt due to his fame, Thomas had found lodging easily enough here in Ireland, and indeed in every place he went among the British Isles. Unlike at home. But the corollary effect of general public interest in all his endeavors had begun to wear on him after three years. He worried it would bring him to the notice of those against whom Morel had warned.

"It's only that your voices have risen a bit, though you may be unaware so, and I'm fearful you'll be disturbing our other tenants at their tea, and I know you was wishful not to, which is why you come in here, but if you'd rather invite your guest up to your rooms I'm certain it will—"

"My apologies." Mr. Owen bent in a sort of seated bow. "We became excited in our conversation. Momentarily. Excuse us to your boarders, and—have you a boy? Yes?" He held a coin out at the level of the door's knob and Mrs. Swain's hand emerged to take it. "If you don't mind asking him to procure some sort of treat to soothe their ruffled feelings—"

Thus dispatched, she closed the door. "With your permission?" Mr. Owen rose and opened it to reveal her already half the way along the passage. "Though if you're not interested after all, then there's no need for such stringent privacy."

"Mr. Owen, I am interested. Very much so. I only . . ." He only wished he were learned enough to have understood the map over which he'd shaken his head in confusion. Thomas hated to admit the irregularities in his education to a man who so obviously took his own more protected upbringing for granted. "I only wonder— if—wonder—how many I will be able to provide—" Nothing could be allowed to hinder his mission; his excuse for not immediately seizing on Owen's offer must make *sense*. "That is, how many other American Negroes I can persuade to join our enterprise."

In answer to these maunderings he received a rather sharpish look. Then a decisive nod. "I'm of the same mind. We must do our utmost not to repeat the errors of the past. Enforced transportation and settlement, as in Australia, or indenturement, servitude of any sort—the slightest hint of slavery! We must avoid them all.

"Which is why—" Owen stood and peered into the passageway. "Ah. If you will procure your topcoat I'll show you those works now, as I promised."

There'd been no such promise, but Thomas heard Mrs. Swain's flat-footed tread approaching over the rush mats covering the passage floor. He took the hint, and they left the kitchen on the tide of her thanks.

His Chesterfield hung on the rack by the front entry. He donned it as they descended the steps to the street. It was a new purchase and he felt childishly pleased with it. He berated himself silently for this as they walked beneath pink clouds and lamps recently lit. Pride goeth before a fall. He ought to think instead of his mission, the vow he'd made to rescue his brethren back home in America, who struggled just to put rags on their backs. Ought also to recall the salvation deserved by those poor heathens dying even now in the sweltering jungles of King Leopold's Congo. Their case had been beyond horrible three years ago, and since then he'd done no more than talk about it.

Yet his speeches must have made some difference, must have hindered the tyrant in his hellish designs to some extent. The outcry against Leopold had swelled measurably, and subscriptions to *The Commoner* had increased. The Benevolent Fund he and Mr. Owen's Fabian Society had established had helped, but now it would be spent up. He hoped those who had contributed would appreciate the use to which it was about to be put.

They turned down Police Court Street, accompanied only by ordinary passersby. Soon the Foyle flowed before them. Its broad waters lay for the most part in the shadow of the embankment on which they trod, only reflecting the sky's lingering brightness far out near the river's eastern shore.

They stood still a moment, then promenaded slowly north as if admiring the view while Owen laid forth the particulars of his plan. Leopold wanted to sell a far greater portion of his holdings than they had asked for. "About half is what it comes to, as you'll have deduced from the deed," Owen said. "Of course, now he wants more money than we've raised."

Thomas hid his traitor hands in the capacious pockets of his Chesterfield. Was the purchase not to go through, then?

"Which brings me to my proposal."

He kept his voice smooth. "And that is—"

"I have a rich donor. Anonymous. He will provide the complete sum necessary for the sale, leaving what we've collected to be used in buying equipment, supplies, hiring ships—and to be given as grants—small grants—to our settlers."

"Grants to—" Now even Thomas's well-trained voice failed. The fading clouds above rolled back in his vision to reveal fields of diamonds, paving stones of everlasting pearl—

The smell of tobacco recalled him to the stony earth. Owen was offering him a cigar. He accepted it—a bad habit, smoking, but one he'd never been able to rid himself of. Presently the two of them sent up grey clouds to mingle with the wisps of cirrus gradually disappearing into the darkness.

They continued walking and talking. At first Thomas had a hard time suppressing his elation. But there would be so much work. He soon sobered. Recruiting suitable families for the colony would be rendered both easier and more difficult by the funds to be disbursed. And on what would these grants' exact amounts be based: Skills? Need? The number of souls in a household? Ought they to be advertised openly, or would that attract too many adventurers? Should monies be advanced before recruits set foot in Africa so that they might pay their own passage there, or was this a sure invitation to fraud? Thomas's head fairly spun with questions. All the while he made out to Owen that he was calm, collected, and utterly assured of the next steps they would need to take.

"Unless we mean to walk all the way to Lisahally, it's time to head back." Owen sounded regretful about stopping, as if ready to proceed down to Loch Foyle at the slightest hint of willingness on Thomas's part. Turning to confirm this impression, Thomas realized with a shock he could barely see the pale blur of the white man's face. The night was moonless, and they'd arrived at a district of industrial docks and warehouses, poorly lighted. Peering about, Thomas found no obvious assassins lurking nearby. Ahead hulked a crane. Its huge iron hook dangled into the ruddy glare thrown through a window high in the black bulk of some otherwise featureless building. The wind carried scents of soot and rust and tar.

"Yes. No doubt." They reversed their course and sped up. He still held the cigar, which had ceased burning, unattended.

He could think of no way to find out other than asking. "Who is your anonymous backer?"

"Ah. That would be telling. And you *are* a journalist."

"And your partner." Silence answered him for long minutes.

"He's a member of the Society," Owen admitted at last. "Dedicated to our principles. He wanted to found a college, but this is better. It will have more impact."

Thomas hunched lower in his Chesterfield. All the problems of working with Owen came down to his Fabian Society and its so-called principles. The man was an avowed atheist, an advocate of free love and common property. As were all his closest associates.

Better, however, to consort with an honest atheist than that lying, murdering papist king. Mr. Owen had denied again and again having any desire to hinder the teaching of the Gospel. Thomas believed him. And he knew exactly who'd be capable of holding the man to his word.

On the pavement before his lodgings Thomas bade his partner a hasty farewell, agreeing hurriedly to meet with him again the next day and cross off more logistical details from a list that already seemed endless. Mrs. Swain lay in wait for him in the front parlor. She helped him out of his coat while talking gaily of nothing of consequence, but, noting his distraction, soon left. When he announced he had "something to write" she happily provided him with an extra candle and went off to her bed, probably congratulating herself on contributing her mite to the creation of a masterful speech or sermon.

But it was, again, a letter Thomas composed on his much-employed traveling desk, as in Boma. Not, this time, an open letter to a monarch to be published, but a private letter to a widow woman. A comrade in the armies of Christ.

"Dear Martha," he began, and went on for an hour, covering five pages and crossing them, explaining the situation in full. Telling her how and why their colonial enterprise had suddenly widened in scope, with their partner providing the additional funds this would necessitate. Asking her to undertake to manage their affairs so that this imbalance in the colony's financial underpinnings would not disadvantage them. Exhorting her to heighten her watchfulness in all to do with these new and worldly allies.

On Board White Bird, *June 1894*

Lisette Toutournier sailed with the Albins to their new African home as a matter of course, to outward appearances merely the children's governess. Her attachment to Laurie, never robust, had weakened over the years, but that to Daisy became ever stronger. And once aboard *White Bird* she found she also loved the ship: its stacks and railings, decks and companionways. Loved its deep, sleek secrets, black and shining with grease, throbbing with power.

On the long voyage to Freetown the sailors had come to respect Lisette and indulge her open admiration of *White Bird*, though at first, of course, she was suspect, being a woman, and young, and beautiful. But eventually—some time between Funchal and the Canary Islands, she believed—they came around. They accepted her. It helped that she was never in the slightest ill, and that she wore trousers, and shoes of sensibleness, or sometimes no footgear at all. That she tanned in the fierce sun instead of burning— thanks to her half-Negro *grand-père*, but they would not hear of him from her—did no harm either. Nor did she complain at any time of the warm, insistent rain.

Daisy had accompanied her husband Laurie Albin and his "secretary" Ellen ashore to meet with Mr. Owen, and she'd brought Laurie Junior along with her as his birthday treat. One would think that the older children would have tired by now of shipboard life and be aching also to disembark, but here they sat, ranged round her like so many pirates awaiting orders from their chief. George had even gone so far as to tie one of Lily's scarves around his head. Rosalie, who had earlier suffered much from the sun, had borrowed her mother's best hat, without, Lisette was certain, either Ellen's or Daisy's permission. As the near-constant equatorial rain had subsided for the afternoon the hat would not be hurt.

She would happily have taken pity on poor Rosalie's strawberry red cheeks and retired below to the library, for while there she could have surreptitiously composed a new chapter in her saga of the trouble-hungry sprites accompanying her to a new continent. But she anticipated sure protests from the older ones if they lost their view of the so-briefly blue sky and this famous Gold Coast: the gently climbing green gardens studded with houses like blocks of pastel chalk; the white beach where the bright waves came at last to rest. Above their crashing the damp air echoed with the cries of the barge crews ferrying coal for the ship's capacious fuel bunkers, the clang of loaded buckets being raised and lowered.

Could she bring her charges, somehow, to venture with her to see the end result of this process? But no, she herself had barely gotten permission to visit the bunkers, fierce with the heat of nearby furnaces. Occult clouds of black had swirled in their almost-emptiness; she had ruined a white blouse simply by wearing it in such an atmosphere. She treasured its dusky folds more than the silk chemise Laurie gave her at the voyage's outset, but the bunkers were no place for these well-brought-up infants. She sighed.

"It's not going to be a sad story, is it?" asked Lily.

"Sad stories are for girls," George opined. "Tell us an adventure."

"I have promised you not one story of any sort!" Lisette shook her blond head in denial. "And besides, you have been far too naughty for—"

"*I* have been good! *Very* good!" declared Rosalie. "And I don't want a story—" Over the expostulations of her siblings she continued, "*I* want a *pretend*."

The others agreed this would be an acceptable alternative, with George stipulating that there should be a good swordfight in it, and Lily pleading for something about their new home.

Lisette bent her creative powers to producing a "pretend." "You, George," she announced, "are a king—"

"Not that blighter Leopold!"

"No, no," she assured him. "An African king, who is plotting to rescue his sister and daughter—"

"Which one is the princess?" asked Rosalie.

"They are both princesses, and they have been stolen by—"

"But what about the queen? Will you play her?"

At thirteen George was just entering the phase of his growth when he might fall in love with an older woman. "The queen is dead," Lisette said firmly. "I will be the evil general who has stolen the princesses to be my hostages against the king."

"But you can't be a general—generals are men! You're—"

Lisette glowered under her eyebrows. "Do you dare to doubt my powers?" Of a sudden she stood, assuming a rigid stance, her aspect martial. She pointed at a sheltered companionway rising a little ways along the boat deck. "There is my fortress. I retire into it now with my captives." She took Lily and Rosalie each by the arm and prepared to march away with them.

"Wait—I say—" George hesitated as she turned back to face him. "I mean, how exactly am I to—you know, to overcome you? By myself, you know."

"Ah. You admit, then, that I am formidable enough as an enemy?"

"Yes! Of course—yes, hang it—but—what am I to do?"

"You must strive for a tactical advantage, and hope that my hostages have not totally been quelled to their fate." Lisette had intended to offer the boy more direction, but really! She led the smirking girls to the stairs' shedlike entrance, settled them several steps down, and returned to the top to keep watch.

Their brother *should* have gone below using the starboard companionway, then come back up by this one, attacking her from the rear and inciting his princesses to help. But no. Such an idea was too simple.

Loud banging, scuffling sounds, and the scraping and sliding of shoe soles over her head, accompanied by boyish epithets, told Lisette what his preferred course of action was: to climb the sloping shelter covering the companionway and fall on her from above. She clutched her forehead. What idiocy! How now would the girls understand when to—

"I say!" A thump from above, and George's head appeared in the door frame upside down. "There's another big liner coming alongside of us!"

The girls crowded past Lisette, their status as captive princesses abandoned with the rest of the pretend. "Where?" "Can we see it?" "Which side?" "How did you get up there?" "Can we?" they cried.

Looking with her sails unfurled more like a white bird than their own vessel, the new ship glided with increasing slowness past their port side, then stopped. She was a steamer too, but not so swift—Lisette spied one lone funnel between the fore and aft masts.

"V-e-r-o-n-a," Rosalie spelled out, her chin tipped up to rest on the side rail. "Vair-onn-ah?" Lisette corrected her pronunciation.

"Is this the ship from America we're waiting to meet up with?" asked Lily. "The one which is to sail beside us?" She lifted her arm to wave at several small figures standing facing them on *Verona*'s deck.

"'Course it is, you ninny," said George. "Can't you see how black they all are?"

"I only asked—"

"No bickering, children. George, you will see plenty blacker faces every day in our new home; you must accustom yourself and not make comments."

"Look! They're lowering a boat!" George sounded not the least abashed by this scolding. Lisette wondered who the boat's passengers were—one seemed to be a woman, but to tell more lay beyond her powers at this distance. Sailors began rowing and the boat progressed—toward *White Bird* rather than the shore. No need to speculate who arrived. Soon she would know.

She shooed the children ahead of her. Their suite lay between the cabin shared by her and Daisy, and the one occupied by Laurie and that conniver Ellen. In moments she had set them to washing their faces and found the comb. She managed to make all presentable before the steward knocked at her door. Sticking her head out into the passage she intercepted him as he turned to go. His message had been meant for Daisy, but none of *White Bird*'s crew were ignorant of the Albins' special arrangement. She instructed him to bring the guests down.

No servants had come with them from England, so Lisette admitted the visitors to the suite herself. Thank the heavens there were only three; with George, Lily, and Rosalie, the tiny sitting room was filled. She took their hats and gloves to rest on the folding washstand in the adjoining room, spreading the woman's light shawl on her and Daisy's bed.

The woman was named Martha Livia Hunter. Shorter than Lisette, she yet commanded the men accompanying her without effort. They were younger, perhaps lacking ten years of her apparent thirty-five—the woman's creamy brown complexion glowed not far off its peak, its smoothness barely wrinkling in the corners of her expressive eyes.

Mrs. Hunter—as she styled herself, explaining the absence of Mr. Hunter as due to the gentleman's long-ago death—told her escort where to stand—graciously, but in the manner of an order. George gazed up at her adoringly from a cushion on the floor. So very vulnerable at thirteen.

"These are my godsons, Chester and Winthrop." Mrs. Hunter made the introductions with a warm smile. "They have already begun training our passengers to make them ready for the Great Work. It will not be long now!"

Lisette smiled in return and nodded. Not that she knew in exact the date they were due in Boma, but it must be a week or less. From there, who knew how long till they reached Kasai Territory?

"I thought to bring them here to review with Mr. Owen what they've been teaching the other settlers—"

"Oh! He has yet to board—but I am sure he would wish you to wait . . ." As it seemed the only thing to do, she invited Mrs. Hunter and her godsons to lunch with her and the children, who remained on their best behavior throughout the proceedings. Mrs. Hunter called them charming right to their faces, thus completing her conquest of George.

Just as they finished with their pudding, the part of the family who had gone to shore returned. It transpired that Laurie Junior had not much enjoyed his birthday treat, so Daisy brought him back to the ship, with his mother and father as well. Mr. Owen, and the Reverend Lieutenant Wilson, whom Lisette now met for the first time, joined them.

This was too much for the little sitting room to accommodate; they retired to walk about the promenade deck. Lily and Rosalie clung to Daisy's hands as if she were the true mother of both. George remained in Mrs. Hunter's thrall; she, in turn, seemed captivated by Little Laurie and totally oblivious to the blandishments of Laurie Senior. It was all most interesting.

The two godsons, Chester and Winthrop, attempted to discuss with Mr. Owen their concerns over some machinery they'd fetched with them from Charleston; he responded by monopolizing the conversation, talking loudly of the differences between steerage and first class berths on the *White Bird*. Apparently these displeased him. Well, he had only to assign himself to the same quarters as his mechanicals and laborers, if that was the trouble. And the further from Daisy the—

"You needn't fear me telling."

Lisette started. Mrs. Hunter had spoken softly, but almost directly into her ear.

"Telling? Telling of what?"

"Of your race."

"My race? Burgundian? What has that to do—" She stopped. Grand-père. *Le Gorille* had been a mulatto. All the village knew, though it was never a topic of conversation. But how could this woman, a stranger—

"You see, yes. You've done well enough at keeping your secret hidden, though, and it's safe with me—for the moment."

"My secret?" Lisette laughed. She had to. Extortion was an expensive alternative. Mrs. Hunter smiled, but not as warmly as when they'd made their initial acquaintance.

Maybe a salting of fact. "I'm going to settle in an African country, in the company of socialists and American Negroes, and you think it will matter to them that I am one-sixteenth—"

"Oh, I'm sure the admixture is a bit more than that."

Lisette shook her head, made a face as if in sorrow at an enemy's mistake. But the woman was, of course, correct in her surmise. Who could have told her of the Toutourniers' shadowy connection to the peoples of the so-called Dark Continent? Daisy didn't know of it. Maman had mentioned it in one letter, but cryptically. True, the letter had vanished from Laurie's bedroom overnight—had that been the work of Ellen?

"In any case, one drop is enough to taint you in certain eyes. I have heard that some members of Mr. Owen's working class entertain quite stupid ideas on the subject of our race." The merest emphasis on that "our." "And, of course, no one likes to be lied to."

And about that this Hunter was right also. Which meant, therefore, that Lisette would need to make Daisy a confession.

Fifty Kilometers out of Matadi, Congo, July 1894

To Jackie Owen, the way seemed arduous and long. During this time—miscalled "the dry season"—the Congo sweltered in humidity comparable to the Gold Coast's. The wet air corroded everything. The rank vegetation smoked almost as much as it burned when fed into the expedition's small boilers.

Chester and Winthrop had had the right of it; their steam bicycles were destined for greatness. The traction engines did well enough over terrain recently cleared for construction of a railroad. But that would end. The broad way they traveled would narrow to a mere footpath ahead, up where the Mah-Kow coolies had their camp.

And for now, the ground continued to rise.

Jackie turned to look back along the procession following him. Line of sight ended after only a dozen men, but his elevation allowed him glimpses of those farther behind.

Beside the three heavy traction engines, the baker's dozen of bicycles valiantly pulled more than their own weight. English workers and natives took turns shepherding the narrow, wheeled baskets trundling in the bicycles' wakes. Clouds from their boilers diffused into the mist spiraling up from the jungle's relentless green.

But why was that last machine's plume so much thicker than the rest? Hurriedly he signaled a halt and went back down to investigate.

Winthrop was there ahead of him. "The regulator's faulty, Mr. Owen."

"Is it possible to repair—"

"It must be replaced. I'll take care of it."

"We have a spare one?"

The stocky Negro nodded at the first wheeled basket in the steam bicycle's train. "Several." He leaned forward and began to unpack a wooden chest. "I'll finish tonight."

Jackie continued to the end of the halted line, explaining the problem. As he had expected, the natives received the news with stoicism. Since the expedition didn't require them to kill themselves with the effort of hauling its luggage up to the river's navigable stretches, they found no fault in however else things were arranged.

The women were another matter. The Albins' governess, Mademoiselle Lisette Toutournier, still held the handlebars of the steam bicycle she had appropriated at the journey's outset. "How is this? We lack at least two hours till darkness and you call a stop?" For some reason that escaped him, the French girl challenged Jackie at every opportunity.

Daisy Albin's anxiety was understandable: she had left the children behind in Boma with their father, Laurie. The sooner the expedition reached their lands beyond the Kasai River, the sooner she would be able to establish a safe home for them there. "Are you sure you couldn't find a more inconvenient camping ground?" Her rueful grin took away her words' sting.

Jackie reconsidered their surroundings. The considerable slope was more than an engineering obstacle; it might indeed prove difficult to sleep or pitch a tent upon.

"If we proceed with less equipment should we not meet with a better location? Soon?" Mademoiselle Toutournier's wide grey eyes unnerved him with their steady gaze.

Jackie shuddered at the thought of the women striking out on their own, meeting with unmanageable dangers such as poisonous snakes or colonial police. He had opposed their presence on the expedition as strongly as it was possible to do without making a churl of himself or intimating that they were somehow inferior to men. That would be contrary to the principles upon which the Fabian Society was formed.

The third woman, Mrs. Hunter, approached, accompanied by Wilson and by Chester, the other of her godsons. "I would like to introduce a suggestion . . ."

Jackie steeled himself to reject an unreasonable demand of one sort or another—a night march? Several hours' retreat to a site earlier passed by?

"Perhaps we would do better not to sleep at all? Reverend Wilson and I have been thinking to hold a prayer meeting, a revival, and there is no time like the present. We might easily—"

Jackie paid no heed to the rest of the woman's argument. Yes; the idea had its merits. But proselytizing a religion?

"We are part of a socialist expedition." He could tell by Mrs. Hunter's expression that he had interrupted a sentence. He went on nonetheless. "If I put the issue to a vote, do you think a prayer meeting will be the choice of the majority?"

"I—I believe most of my countrymen to be decent, God-fearing Christians."

"*These* are your countrymen!" Jackie swung one arm wide to indicate everyone in their immediate vicinity and beyond. "Not only those who came with you from America, but all now on the expedition—Catholics! Skeptics! Atheists! Savages as well—do you not count your African brothers' opinions as mattering? Shall we canvass their number for a suitable spokesman to explain to us the spirits lodged in the trees and bushes?"

"I venture to—"

"Yes, you *venture,* you venture forth to a new life. A new home. A new country, and new countrymen." If only he could bring the colony's expedition to some sort of coherence, to unity; then the whites' sacrifice would mean so much more. What would that take?

Mrs. Hunter turned to Wilson. "But our aim is to build a sanctuary for the soul, isn't it? As well as for mere physical victims of the tyrant's cruelty?"

Wilson nodded. "Yes, we must consider all aspects of our peoples' well-being."

What had Jackie expected? The man was a minister, after all, though he had agreed to the Society's project of colonization as Jackie, their president, had extended it. In the end, the plan was for a series of gatherings up and down the trail. Mrs. Hunter decided she and Wilson would harangue all three parties in turn. Each was centered loosely around one of the traction engines' boiler furnaces.

They began with their "countrymen," the Negroes grouped together at the procession's rear (Jackie had done his utmost to integrate the expedition's various factions, but to no avail). The Christians' message, from all he could tell, contradicted none of the Fabian Society's ostensible reasons for crossing the Kasai River, only casting them in the light of a mandate from Heaven. He listened a short while to what Mrs. Hunter and Wilson preached. Then he preceded them to the British and Irish workmen clustered around the middle boiler, whose participation in the Society's experiment he'd insisted on—gambling that, in the eyes of the audience he had in mind, the workmen's race would trump white Europeans' objections to their class.

Though for many years an office-holder in the Fabian organization, Jackie Owen was no public speaker. As an author, the written word was what he normally relied on and, he hoped, what would soon attract the attention this project had been set up to generate.

Given the circumstances, he did his best. He made sure the firelight fell on his face. "Practical dreamers," he said. "That's what we are. Dreamers, but realistic about it. Heads in the clouds, but our feet on the ground." He saw their eyes glittering, but little else.

"You've come this far. Abandoned your homes, left your wives behind." Well, most of them had. "Trusting me. Trusting in your own right hands, the work you do. The work that has made the world and will now make it anew." He paused. What else was there to say? Nothing that could be said.

In the distance behind him he heard music. Church songs. In-voking primal reactions with pitch and rhythm—how could he fight that? He couldn't.

But the men listening: maybe they could. "If I stood here all night, I wouldn't be able to convey to you one half of what I aim for us to accomplish in our new home, liberated from the con-straints of capitalism and repressive governments. I know many of you are eager to share your own ambitions for our endeavour, and I invite you to do so—now is the time!" He called on a workman whose name he remembered from a recruitment meeting. "Albert, step up and tell your fellows about that flanging contraption you're wanting to rig up."

"Me?"

"Yes—yes, you, come here and talk a bit—"

Albert obliged, stepping into the furnace fire's ruddy glow with his jacket and shirt wide open to the heat and insects. Self-educated, of course. Still, he had some highly original ideas on how to revise manufacturing processes for an isolated colony . . . but as his eyes adjusted to the darkness beyond the boiler's imme-diate vicinity, Jackie saw the audience's interest was not much more than polite. Music exercised its all-too-potent charms. Heads nodded, hands tapped against thighs, necks and shoulders swayed, and he thought they'd be singing themselves at any moment. The song ended before that happened, though. Albert finished his discourse in silence and stood in the furnace's light without, evi-dently, any idea of what next to do.

"Thank you, Albert," said Jackie. This elicited light applause and gave Albert the impetus he needed to find and resume his old place among the onlookers.

Just as Jackie was wondering who next to impose upon for a testimonial, the music began again. No, not again, not the same music from the same source. This came from the other end of their impromptu encampment, from the head of the procession. Where the natives had gathered by the boiler furnace of the first traction engine. Where Mademoiselle Toutournier had insisted on remain-ing, with Mrs. Albin insisting on remaining with her.

A lyric soprano sang a song he'd never heard that was, somehow, hauntingly familiar from its opening notes:

> *"Ever fair, ever fair my home;*
> *Ever fair land, so sweet—"*

A simple melody, it was winning in its self-assurance, comforting, supportive, like a boat rowed on a smooth, reflective sea. Then it rose higher, plaintive in a way that made one want to satisfy the singer:

> *"Ever are you calling home your children;*
> *We hear and answer swiftly as thought, as fleet."*

A chorus of lower voices, altos, tenors, and baritones, repeated the whole thing. Then the earlier voice returned in a solo variation on the theme:

> *"Tyrants and cowards, we fear them no more;*
> *Behold, your power protects us from harm;*
> *We live in freedom by sharing all things equally—"*

The same yearning heights, supported by an inevitable foundation. A foundation that was repeated as the resolution necessary for the verse's last line:

> *"We live in peace within your loving arms."*

He was staring through the darkness at the little light piercing it ahead. So, he felt sure, were all those with him. The chorus repeated, graced this time by—bells? Gongs? Singing swelled around him now and he joined it. A second verse, and a third one, and by then he was on the edge of the circle with Daisy Albin and the lead engine at its center. She sang. She it must be who had penned the words, taught them by rote, composed the music in which the entire expedition now took part. The bells and gongs revealed themselves to be pieces of the traction engine, struck as ornament and accent to the anthem's grave and stately measures.

The anthem. This was it: their anthem. Before they'd even arrived home, they sang their nation's song. And knew its name: Everfairland. This would be what Leopold endangered, what could rouse all Europe to revenge it if it were lost.

Mrs. Albin had stopped. The chorus continued. Jackie made his way through the happy, singing throng to clasp and kiss her hands.

Mbuji-Mayi, Everfair, February 1895

Daisy quite doted on the little hut they'd built her. It had the air almost of a summer cottage. The dirt floor made her feel like a pioneer, uncivilized, but its surface was really very hard—Jackie had tamped it down with a stone weight lifted by one of the traction engines—and clean. And it stood several inches higher than the ground surrounding it, to forestall flooding in the rainy season to come.

Like a ring of clerestory windows, the gap between her house's high, thatched roof cone and the mats of her outer wall let in gentle, indirect light and a refreshing breeze. A red-tailed parrot came sometimes to the trees the builders had left growing by the front entrance. If Lisette lived here she'd want to tame it.

Surely the children would enjoy spending a year or two here, far from the horrors Leopold wrought upon the lowlands. She had written to her husband a month ago. He would bring them by Lily's birthday, before the start of the rainy season.

"I knock on your door." Lisette had become so formal since they ceased to share quarters. Or had the watershed been her nonsensical "confession"?

"Enter!" Daisy called from her new stool. The door was a bit beyond Lisette's reach, a few feet inside the doorway, leaning against the post from which it would later be hung, well before any danger of storms. For now the frame was filled by a fringe of raffia. Lisette pushed this aside, her down-drawn face expressing—what? Impatience? Frustration?

No table yet. "May I offer you some beer?"

"Water only. I must go back . . ."

Expressing exhaustion, Daisy decided. "Beer would be better for you." The Bah-Looba who had emigrated here with them said that fermentation got rid of certain parasites. Or that was one translation.

"Very well, then. Beer. But not so much as to make me drunk."

Daisy got up to go to the beer jar in the storage room. "Will you sit?"

"I mustn't stay." But Lisette collapsed onto the stool anyway. When Daisy returned with the beer-filled calabash, Lisette's head rested on cupped hands propped up by the elbows on her knees. Her white kerchief lay spread in her lap, exposing the coiling disarray of her plaits.

Daisy knelt on the mat-covered bed next to the stool, her only seat for her first week in her new home. She lifted the calabash cup. "Here."

Lisette took a long pull. "Ahh. Thank you." She offered the calabash back. Daisy accepted it and drank what was left. When she was finished, she set the empty cup on the mat.

Lisette looked around the hut's interior silently for a moment, taking in the carved posts, the prettily woven baskets hanging from them, the bare bench. "You have adjusted yourself quickly."

Daisy laughed. "Are you saying I've 'gone native'? I only accepted this place because it seemed easier than arguing."

"No, but it is beautiful. I don't find any fault." Not with where Daisy lived, but *how*. Alone.

"Nor I with you, chérie," Daisy responded gently. If her cottage—their colony's first private permanent structure—had been built to reward her for composing Everfair's national anthem, the infirmary had been built as a lure for Lisette. Who'd begun sleeping there before Daisy's hut was habitable, deserting their shared tent for its fresh-laid wooden floors.

Another silence. Longer and less comfortable. It stretched and stretched. Only the soft rustling of thatch brushed by the straying wind ruffled its awful smoothness. Then Daisy held out her hand.

Lisette took it. "I can't. Patients are waiting." But she let Daisy slide her palm up along her brown-skinned arm and tug till she followed the pull downward and fell beside her on the bed. "Chérie, my dear . . ." They kissed.

"You don't know—"

"Shush. Of course I do." Daisy had helped out, bathing and bandaging wounds, boiling water, straining broths. Miles and miles now from the nearest collection points, and still Leopold's victims poured in, half-starved, half-strangled, shot, limping, fevered, slashed with knives . . .

Those who made it this far generally lived. Generally. And joined the colony.

"There are always more." Lisette sat up, rebuttoning the light cotton shirt on which Daisy had just begun making headway. "Always. It is wicked to leave them . . ."

"Yes. But you must sleep"—without hope, she rose to sit herself—"so why not here?" She couldn't help stroking the back of Lisette's neck, the tender, sweat-damp curls hidden beneath her coronet of plaits. She felt the girl softening like honey in the sun.

Then she straightened, crystallized. "No. I belong with the other blacks."

Stung, Daisy drew back. "It isn't— You *aren't*!"

"Some would say I am." Lisette retrieved her kerchief and stood, tying it back in place. "And who are you to decide?"

When Lisette had confessed her Negro blood, Daisy had vowed it would make no difference between them. But she must have said or done something wrong: a word misspoken, a glance misunderstood.

She followed Lisette to the doorway. "Is that it? Is that what keeps you away? What can I do?"

"Nothing." Lisette turned to face her. Disconcertingly, she smiled. "Try not to think it is what you do which will make things better." This time it was she who reached for Daisy's hand. Daisy gave it. "If you are sure you want—" Lisette stopped. Her face— what did it express now? She cocked her head as if listening. One undecipherable look and she was gone, vanished with a whisk of the raffia fringe.

A second later Daisy stepped after her to see Lisette scurry off along the path to the infirmary. Before she could run and catch her and tell her yes, yes, she was sure, Jackie appeared from the opposite direction, calling her name.

"Daisy! Hello! The best of news—they're almost here! I hurried ahead to tell you!"

"Who? What—" Someone was coming? But why had Lisette left so suddenly?

"'Who'? Why, your family, woman, the ones you've been *waiting* for." He had her shoulders in his strong grip. He shook them once for emphasis.

Had Lisette heard his approach somehow from inside Daisy's hut? Still, why depart so dramatically—why not simply—

"Or, some of them, anyway, I'm afraid—look here, it's the most rotten thing imaginable, but Laurie Junior . . . that is to say, Ellen had to return to Bristol—her health—and naturally Laurie Senior was needed to escort her and they took him, but I kept them from bringing away the other three—"

Think, she told herself. Logic. She had to think. About what was most important. The children—the "other three"—were coming—soon—now—Jackie had "hurried" to tell her. The children—but not Little Laurie? No, that must be wrong. He needed her. "So when will they be back? With the baby?"

Jackie frowned and bit his lip. Hadn't he understood her questions? "You'll want to be sitting down, Daisy." He tried to steer her through the raffia-filled doorway.

She resisted. "No. Tell me."

"He's deserted you."

Daisy felt calm descend over her like a cold wave. Washing away panic and confusion. Helping her think. "For Ellen."

"There's to be a divorce."

"They're gone." Saying made it so. "They've taken the—" Her voice failed, but not her logic. The "baby," Laurie Junior, now four and no longer a total infant, was Ellen's son, as the world reckoned these things. Though really they were all Daisy's. All four hers.

"He wanted the other three as well, but I stopped him."

The other three. Lily, George, and—"Rosalie, too?" Ellen's daughter. As the world reckoned these things. "Rosalie and Lily and George are—are coming? Here? But he—" She had to make it make sense. Never much interested in the girls, Laurie'd always taken great pride in fathering his two boys. "He would want George. So why? Why—"

"George refused to go back."

Which would hardly have been an impediment. There must be more. The red-tailed parrot scolded them from a high, safe branch. She caught a glimpse of leaves rustling as it hopped from one perch to another. Then her eyes went back to Jackie's face, seeing it clearly now: jaw held grimly square beneath his brown beard. Eyes glazed with tears under brows jutting low like protecting bluffs.

The parrot squawked indignantly. It disliked having to roost near the trees' tops, but wouldn't descend any lower with Jackie about. "Come inside." As Daisy invited Jackie in she realized this was their first time alone together in compromising circumstances, despite months of travel. She was ashamed to have such a conventional reaction to his presence. They were old friends. But a divorce changed things.

She took the bed as her seat again, defiantly. "There is something you're afraid to tell me."

Jackie laughed ruefully. "I only thought about it afterward."

"Sit down. Please." She indicated the stool.

He did. "It was easy getting that blight—getting Laurie to leave Lily with me, and he was practically silent when Ellen protested letting Rosalie stay behind, feeble enough protests anyway . . . He wanted George, though. His oldest, primogeniture, you know, a powerful idea even if it *is* a legacy of feudalism and tainted beyond— But never mind all that. Thing is, George very much wanted to stay in Africa. Fourteen, almost a man—why shouldn't he? And I knew you'd miss him. So I—" He covered his forehead with one large-palmed hand.

"So I lied. I claimed George as my own. My son."

Daisy took a moment to work out what he meant. Then she blushed, which made her furious. "You told Laurie we'd had intercourse."

"It was possible—theoretically."

"Yes." That conference fortnight at Jackie's estate, the right number of years ago. Laurie had insisted on a separate room. Daisy could have slept with Jackie one night or many; he was just a short walk down the passage's soft blue carpet.

"Don't be angry. Please."

"I'm not. But you think I ought to be?"

He hesitated. The hand came down from his face and he gazed at her, unblinking. "Adultery will make his claim of your unfitness as a wife—more difficult to dismiss."

Ah. Laurie's adultery had never mattered. Hers, however, was grounds for divorce. "But I don't wish to dismiss his claim." Let they two be put asunder. She had loved her husband, once. But now, Lisette . . .

"Don't you see? Such a character flaw as that? If George or Rosalie or even Lily is ever found within British jurisdiction again, their father will take them away from you instantly. They'll be his. No recourse.

"I *am* sorry."

"You're right." Appalled, she felt the numbing cold run off and drain away. "You're . . . right." Oh, her heart, hot and dry and hollow—but they were coming here, coming now, all but—"Laurie Junior? No hope they'll let me have him? If I fight?" Solicitors and pleadings, long, weary months of it, and that would mean leaving the three older children here, or taking them with her into jeopardy.

"Not a single judge on Earth will award him to you now." Which was only what Daisy knew already. Laurie's indiscretions meant nothing; hers, far too much.

"I'm sorry," Jackie repeated. "Truly. I only meant to help."

"Thank you." She tried to feel grateful. She would have George. And the girls. Unless she went back home.

No. Unless she went back to England. She opened eyes she hadn't known she'd shut and looked around in a circle at the sturdy walls, boards stitched tight over thick layers of banana leaves. Her charming cottage. Home would have to be here.

Bookerville, Everfair, December 1895

Jesus didn't mean for her to die here. Mrs. Martha Livia Hunter glared at the filthy white man before her, daring him to raise his gleaming gun. The wooden cross she wore on her bosom symbolized her protection: she was on a mission, doing the Savior's work. She lifted her chin, stiffened her shoulders, and felt a faint stirring in the hot, wet air at her back as her fellow toilers in the vineyards joined her on the infirmary's front steps.

"They're not here," she repeated.

"Bloody—beggin yer pardon, ma'am, but I ain't even told ye their names or nothin!"

He was a brave devil, she must admit, coming here all those miles, armed or not, with but one bearer. "You know the names of your escaped captives?"

"The two what ran away was Mkoi, an old nig—I mean, an old man, and a little wench he took with im, think he called her Fwendi—"

The roaring inside her drowned out what he said after that. She knew them, knew all their patients: Mkoi, half-starved, half-mad, had stumbled into Bookerville only a week ago, yet was on his way to recovery. Fwendi, his grand-niece—the nearest any translator had been able to render their relationship—Fwendi would never recover her amputated hand.

Oceans of rage surged in Martha's bosom—black, clashing billows towering up and crashing down—

"Peace; be still," she prayed. The words of the Savior calming the storm on the Sea of Galilee: "Peace; be still." And the waters subsided. And a dove rode down a sunbeam from Heaven and nestled in his hand, soft and angerless as her heart ought to be in his service.

Leopold's lieutenant seemed to have heard her, for his mouth hung open, silent, empty. She must have prayed aloud.

"You had better go back," she said to the man, as kindly as she could. "You had better go back and tell your friends: you will not find the prisoners whom you are seeking here."

"Why, that's rich! When they're standin right ahind ye!" The white man pointed.

Martha shook her head, unwilling to fall for this transparent ruse. Then she saw Chester coming down the muddy path at a run, with a smaller figure just after him—George, the eldest child of Mrs. Albin. She smiled. Menfolk to the rescue. As they came to a halt, the midday mist turned to drizzle.

"You had better go back," Martha repeated.

"Not without them I come for! Mkoi! I'll let you off light this first time if you—"

Martha risked a look over her shoulder. Yes, Mkoi was there indeed, dark face blank as some heathen mask. At his side tottered little Fwendi, right arm swathed in bandages once white, now yellow, brown, and grey; skin shining with sweat; eyes dull with pain and hopelessness. Old at seven.

She would not give the girl up. She whirled back to confront Leopold's man, who had seized the chance to creep closer to the entrance. But now—

"Hi! Let loose of that!" he shouted.

The Albin boy had both hands on the man's rifle, trying to wrest it from his grasp. A second's silent struggle and Chester joined in. A loud report—the gun had gone off! Chester gained control—of course. Martha looked to see if anyone had been struck. Not Chester—thank God! What would she have told his mother? Mkoi, Fwendi, her fellow missionaries, all safe. She turned again to demand that the intruder depart. Chester held the rifle uncontested—his height and build had served him well, as usual. The white man stood combatively in front of him, stubborn though alone. His bearer had disappeared—but where was little George? Flat on the ground—he had been hurt!

The boy levered his shoulders out of the clinging mud, sat up, and made a face. One sleeve, the right, and that whole section of his shirt were streaked with blood. A bullet wound. How serious? He coughed, spat. Gazed up with hate-filled eyes at the intruder. "How many times has the *lady* got to ask you to go?"

The rifle shifted in Chester's grip. Not even aiming it, keeping the muzzle pointed downward, he managed to threaten the rubber collector—without glancing in his direction. Without speaking to him. Instead, he said to the boy, "I'm willing to bet he knows by now he's not welcome." Her godson's soft tone and gentle words belied his strength.

Adam's apple bobbing in his throat, the white man edged away. "We—we'll be back!" he proclaimed, his voice cracking.

Martha watched him trudge off down the track and vanish into the jungle. She didn't laugh at his promise of vengeance. She had learned from experience that scared men were dangerous. This one would be no exception.

Nurses and helpers carried a feebly protesting George to a mat on the infirmary's dry floor. Martha returned to her "office": a corner furnished with a stool and a makeshift table piled with paper and barkcloth. A precious lantern lighted it, the gift of a refugee. She seated herself and arranged her skirts as tidily as she could, then set to work: writing a brief report on the incident for Mr. Owen and another, longer, for Everfair's Workers Council; reviewing three conflicting accounts of the church building's progress—optimistic, pessimistic, and incomprehensible; and approving a plan for planting an experimental field with the hidden stock of seeds they'd found. It certainly looked like millet, which was what the Zan-Dee woman claimed it to be. Wheat from the settlers' stores had gone in earlier, and seemed to be thriving well enough, but perhaps local produce would have an additional advantage.

Food stores were running low at an alarming rate, no doubt due to the influx of natives fleeing that papist tyrant. Dozens, hundreds—she and the reverend had not foreseen how many would seek sanctuary with them, nor how quickly. Of course they couldn't turn them away.

Done with office work for the moment, she made her rounds, visiting the infirmary's male and female wards. Martha had no medical training, but knew how to compel people to do what needed to be done. Firsthand supervision was required, though she issued her commands through the mulatto, Miss Toutournier.

Fwendi had slipped into the men's side yet again. The girl kept refusing to be separated from her old relative—perhaps the lone member of her family to survive? Martha hadn't the heart to send her back to the women's ward quite yet. "Let her stay till supper," she instructed Miss Toutournier, who followed a pace behind. "Mr. Mkoi will help persuade her to take nourishment." The nurse nodded, outwardly agreeable to whatever Martha wished. Inwardly, Martha felt sure, she rebelled.

Further down the row of mats George Albin slept like the little man he was, frowning, serious. He lay on his left side, right shoulder hunched high, arm folded away from the site of his wound. Miss Toutournier assured her that the injury was minor, a mere graze. Below the bandage the poor boy's pale skin was grooved with shadows that followed the curve of his ribs. "Has he been skimping himself of rations?" Martha whispered, hoping not to wake the patient. In vain.

Blue eyes opened, focusing on her. A smile sprang to his lips instantly, but it didn't last. The boy blanched, struggled to sit, turned his head all around as if searching for something.

Miss Toutournier handed him a shirt she took from a stub protruding from a post in the board-and-banana-leaf wall. She had been young George's governess, Martha recalled. Now she said a phrase in French that seemed to calm her former charge.

"You're all right, then?" he asked Martha, buttoning his stained shirt with scarcely a wince.

"What? Of course I am! That was never the question." Jesus had his eye on her at all times. "The Lord takes care of his servants." An expression she didn't care for crossed Miss Toutournier's bold face.

She knelt so her head was level with his. "That was courage on your part," she told the boy, "coming to Bookerville's defense the way you did."

Surprisingly, he blushed. "Wasn't for Bookerville."

She thought she understood. She nodded. "Any good Christian would have done the same."

Again that knowing smirk from the mulatto.

"But I thank you, nonetheless. I thank you from the bottom of my heart." She stroked his damp hair back from his brow. The red in his cheeks deepened. "You have done well. Now rest."

"No, ma'am!" The boy rose with her—such a beanpole! He reached nearly to her chin. "If it wasn't for that dose of laudanum, I'd be out of here already—the veriest scratch the rotter's bullet gave me. There's plenty here worse hurt than me, though I'm grateful for your visit."

Let him think she'd come to the men's ward expressly to see him. "Then may I walk you home?"

The hut the natives and settlers had insisted on building for Mrs. Albin lay on Bookerville's farther side. Martha and the young man stepped carefully, avoiding the largest puddles, but the rain soon fell so thick it soaked them through. Martha wished for her umbrella, as she had over and over again for the past month.

Her wet garments hampered her, and she feared the unseemliness of her appearance. Fortunately, they reached the Albins' without encountering anyone. The settlement's huts, tents, and hovels weren't good for much, but they did provide shelter from the elements, and few of Bookerville's inhabitants would be found out-of-doors just now. However, as they approached young George's home, the low notes of a man's speech issued from inside it.

No words could be deciphered, but Martha knew who spoke—not the lady's husband, who had decamped months ago. Improper for these two to meet alone. Her advent would solve that problem, yet she hesitated, hanging back, catching George's arm to prevent him going ahead of her. Mr. Owen was a single gentleman but he was, at least, a *man*.

Then came another voice, thin and piping. Children were not any sort of chaperone, but their presence did indicate Martha wouldn't be interrupting anything romantic in nature. She let loose her hold on the young man and knocked.

Mr. Owen spoke. "Ho! There's someone at the door; do you mind—"

"Yes! A moment—" The high, sweet voice grew louder, nearer. The door opened to reveal a child she'd never seen before. Which meant this must be another heathen refugee, another conversion to make, another trial she must undertake in service to Christ. Martha strove to dissect and classify the vision before her: bare feet, canvas trousers, naked torso—so, likely male—sharp-chinned, hair black and straight, eyes slanted. Slanted. Skin tanned. But the eyes.

Undoubtedly Chinese. In the middle of Africa. How could this be?

Suddenly she remembered the railway, the camp full of coolies they'd gone off the path to avoid. But apparently they hadn't gone off it far enough.

Bookerville, Everfair, April 1896

None of them were devils. Tink reminded himself often that calling them that was impolite. More important, it simply wasn't true. Even Leopold's drivers, the railroad gangs' cruel and grossly ugly overseers, had been human. Horrible, with their floggings and starvation, but human.

Everyone here was much better. And the elders had been right not to try for Macao. Home would have been too far, impossible to reach. The trip upriver from Matadi had been hard enough.

With a nod to Yoka, his English student and recipient of his first attempt at a prosthetic, Tink laid his blowing tube in the sandy mud beside the kiln's flat-topped mound. A thread of smoke curled out of the mound's interior through the hole where the tube had gone. Only a thread—the fuel had burnt off correctly. Yoka, too, set his tube aside. Together they heaved away the river stones blocking the pouring channel.

Molten metal, red and golden, flowed through the gap in the kiln's side and down to the molds they'd dug into the Sankuru's lower bank. They leapt eagerly after it, the steps too steep to take slowly.

Sweat beaded Tink's skin. Fierce heat shone up out of the greensand molds. Their new knives looked fine and wicked, glowing a blackish red now, like drying blood. Yoka spit on them the cud of the root he had insisted on chewing, "for blessing." *Crackle! Hisss!* Loud sounds issued from clouds of steam. Then the air cleared and Yoka grinned at him. "Scared?" he asked.

"Not at all," Tink claimed, though that was a lie. But he would act in a way that would make it good as true.

Yoka humphed. "Next time you can do it, then." Testing, always testing; Tink wondered when the Mon-Goh youth would finally trust him. Perhaps never. Perhaps when your family, your whole town was destroyed and everyone and everything you loved and knew was gone—

Someone approached—footsteps, boot steps, on the recently dry path. A few of the white men had shown interest in Tink and Yoka's project. But it was a woman who peered around the sapling tree marking the side trail to their workplace.

"Have you seen George? Hello!" Tink still hadn't learned the tree's name, but her he knew. She was the Day's Eye, Albin Daisy, a mighty poet according to the many tribes gathering here. He bowed, noticing that Yoka did the same, imitating how he clasped his hands.

"What are you doing here?"

"Miss Albin, we have not seen your son."

"Mrs." The Poet frowned.

"Mrs.," Tink agreed. He straightened and looked directly into her eyes, which whites here preferred. "We would be glad to help you, but—"

"He isn't here," Yoka interrupted, showing off his freshly acquired English. "But we can tell you where he was soon ago."

"You mean, 'not long ago,'" Tink corrected his pupil.

"Where?"

"Hospital," Yoka told her.

This appeared to displease the Poet. "Of all places," she said, again frowning. "Well, if I must go, I must." Still she failed to leave them. "Would you—one of you, at least—come with me? Tink? I know the reverend was hoping you'd answer a few questions for him."

So Yoka stayed to guard the cooling knives while Tink escorted the Eye of Day, Miss—*Mrs*. Albin, to the hospital buildings. On the way she asked him why none of the white workers were helping him. Several were familiar with metalwork already, she said, and would have nothing else to do with the harvest just in. He struggled for a diplomatic way to tell her how Mr. Owen seemed to discourage that. Perhaps discouragement wasn't even all that necessary: older whites likely would choose on their own not to believe in the abilities of those younger than themselves and "foreign." Though here the whites were no more at home than he was.

They passed among a cloud of tiny, clear-winged moths. Tink assured the Poet that he and Yoka had cast only agricultural implements, to supplement those brought with them. Knives were often used in farming.

After a brief silence Mrs. Albin went on. "Really, though, we're going to need a forge, soon, to repair things, and if you can manage to—to conciliate yourself with Jackie's followers"—A sharp-eyed glance reminded Tink of every poet's greatest gift: observation. She knew he was out of harmony with these men, and she knew, to some extent, why—"I, for one, would consider it a favor." Granting a favor upon this most revered poet would put him in a powerful position; Tink considered again how best to involve Mr. Owen's smiths and smelters and welders and such.

In silence they neared the hospital buildings. Tink slowed his pace to match that of the Poet's. Why did she wish to avoid this place? Only the Christians' temple, their "church," was newer, bigger, with better ventilation. Sometimes there were screams, yes, and the smell of flesh gone bad, or burnt to keep people's wounds from rotting. Also, however, there could be laughter, peace, strengthening.

In any event, George wasn't actually inside either building, but serving porridge out of the kitchen at their backs. Not the most interesting work, but he seemed happy. Beside him sat the reason. She was nicely shaped, but of course so oddly brown, as were all the women in this land who were not oddly white.

The Poet asked her son to come home and add to the letter she was writing to her husband, his father.

"Now?" He was plainly loath to leave Miss Hunter's vicinity.

"Jackie will be heading for the coast again quite early tomorrow morning, almost the middle of the night—"

"Very well." He pulled the apron he wore over his head and

began rolling down his sleeves, then stopped suddenly, desperately addressing the other woman: "Unless you need me to stay?"

Miss Hunter turned her graceful head. "No, it will be fine. We're almost finished for the evening. Miss Toutournier can see the cookpot is clean."

The Poet's face went through one of those swift color changes whites were prone to. "Tink, do you know where to find Reverend Wilson? Shall we show you to his office on our way?"

She was in a hurry, and made George hurry, too. They walked off without saying anything more. The church door was open. Tink said goodnight and went in. Then he had to wait while the reverend conducted another interview. But not long. This person had no French, no English. Tink had gradually come to realize that not everyone possessed his facility with languages; this unfortunate man could say his name and that of his home village, identifying them as such in Kiswahili. After that he counted over and over to ten until the reverend dismissed him, guiding him out of the church's entrance by the man's abruptly truncated left arm.

Three stools occupied the area screened off from the church's main space by patterned mats. The reverend sat on the lowest of these with a wooden box balanced on his knees, and pens and inkpots on top of that. He gestured to Tink to take either of the other seats. A brazier cast light and flickering shadows on the walls and floor. The high ceiling remained in darkness.

"You've been here the entire rainy season, haven't you? Arrived with the other Macao Chinese?"

Tink bobbed his head in the white motion for yes. Though this man was black he dressed and spoke much like the English tribe.

"As you are already familiar with our ways, I'll save some time by not going into those. Tell me, if you will, how you came to Everfair."

"We were treated so badly—"

"No, no, no! Start from the beginning. *Your* beginning. When you were born, with what name you were christened, and so forth."

As if he were the only one in the world. The only important one.

This was how these people thought. They *thought*. They were not devils, but human beings.

"I was born on the island the English call Macao. My family name is Ho. My given name is Lin-Huang, meaning 'bright woods,' or 'shining forest.' But because of the sound my hammer makes when I work, most people grow to call me Tink."

Ilebo, Everfair, August 1896

Once more in his beloved bush, Mwenda had heard many sweet musics, seen wonderful and restful sights: ceaseless songs from the beaks of invisible birds, dark leaves drifting down through soft rains to float on shining pools.

But also he had waged war—indirectly enough that he was still in alignment with his destiny, he hoped. Silent as hunting dogs, his fighters had circled a few of the whites' smaller stations and attacked without needing a word of command. Of course those dying had shouted, and their guns had banged loudly, cracking apart the night. Silence had not been the same thing as peace, and it had not remained whole. And while noble casualties have an appealing look as they lie fallen, opened bowels stank, always, without fail.

Worse, though, than the slaughter of barely wakened enemies were these smoldering ruins, these villages emptied by death. This was the third such he had encountered on his way south.

Mwenda stood on beaten earth, on vanished Ilebo's central plaza. A heap of vegetable-smelling ashes to his right must have been the remains of whatever sort of guardian plant his dead subjects had placed here. The charred sticks beside it told of the ancestor house once sited beside it. That was most likely what it had been, since at the time of its firing it had held no living inhabitants.

Not so most of the others.

Some had sought to escape the town's burning. Mwenda ordered their corpses gathered up and brought to him so that he might see to their final speech and burial. He summoned Old Kanna to his side, and asked for Josina as well.

"You will tell the dead ones' story," he commanded his counselor. He turned to his favorite. "What can we give them?"

Josina's round eyes slitted half-shut as she considered. "Flowers we pick," she said. "Not much else. The cloth is gone." Used in the two earlier funerals; she did not need to explain. He had seen.

"I've asked my women to fetch water from the river," she added. "And I have brought my fan."

Mwenda took his place upon his throne, waiting as the corpses were laid in quiet rows before him and washed. Most were children of various ages. One a baby.

Wives and other women emptied baskets of loose white blooms, stars falling over the wet, ruined skins of the dead. Josina fanned the air above them gently, blowing the flowers lightly back and forth like clouds. She took a long time. The fan had been presented to her by tribes far to the west, he recalled, just a month ago. Brass, like a knife or mirror, it proved her to be some sort of priestess in those people's eyes. How pleased she had seemed to receive it—not expecting, he was sure, that she would first bear it publicly while conducting death rites.

He heard the grind and clink of axes digging up the soil, felt through his feet their thudding as the grave opened in the high ground to Ilebo's east. Properly, burials should occur at the sites of new houses. The dead ought not to be left on their own. But no one would be building anything here for quite a while.

At last the digging stopped. Soon after, the fanning. In these lowlands dampness clung and clung to whatever, wherever. Josina might have fanned till the light was gone and not gotten the bodies fully dry. This would be enough. Mwenda nodded to Old Kanna and he cleared his throat and spat ceremonially into the ashes of the ancestor tree.

"These are named the Blessed of the King," the old man began. "Newly his subjects, the Blessed of the King were on their way to him. Newly his subjects, the Blessed of the King were coming.

To fulfill their lives, the Blessed were approaching. Fleeing murder, searching for their lives' fulfillment in the presence of their king. Fleeing murder, frightened for their lives' fulfillment, the Blessed of the King sought righteousness and peace.

"And now they have found it."

A good story Old Kanna was making, forging meaning out of this stupid destruction. Mwenda gazed at each dead face, committing it carefully to his memory. White stars had drifted over the sightless eyes and stuck to the unsightly wounds.

Someone was running toward him—quick breaths and shouted interruptions. A sentry knelt down in front of him and panted out: "King, King, we have discovered one alive, a man! Alive!"

"A white? A black traitor?"

"Neither! He says he was working for them and ran—and ran away—"

Screams of wordless horror. Mwenda stood and waved aside those whose job it was to protect him. Taking advantage of this traveling court's informality, he strode past the sentry to where a stranger had collapsed on the hard, burnt earth, wailing, groaning, rolling himself into a tight ball. A hand of additional sentries surrounded the unfortunate, and one of these held his nearest shoulder, looking foolish, unable to do more.

"Let him go."

The sentry edged away.

Gradually, the man's grief appeared to subside a little. "Get up," Mwenda told him, in the language of the people of the Kasai. "Get up and greet your king, Mwenda, and tell to me your troubles."

He was Loyiki. He knew the names and lives of all the dead. He believed his actions had killed them.

Loyiki had been taken away with many others of Ilebo's strong young men, those roughly the same age as Mwenda. They were supposed to harvest the tears of the vines-who-weep, of course, like all the rest of those whom the whites claimed to rule. Scared by threats of harm to the women, children, and old ones left behind in their village, Loyiki and his fellows had toiled painfully to satisfy the whites' demands, which only increased when met.

Finally, hearing of a refuge in the east, at the base of the Virunga Mountains, Loyiki had escaped. After much hardship he had found his refuge and been welcomed into it: a land called Everfair, of which Mwenda had heard in great detail since his "surrender." Yet he remained curious about it and let Loyiki tell him further, listening attentively to his accounts of a hospital, farms, and foundries.

After a time Loyiki had journeyed home again, intending to persuade his family to join him in Everfair. And now he had learned that this would never happen.

The sky stayed light, though in the forest around Ilebo's edges the shadows grew. Mwenda assigned Old Kanna to finish up the burial services with Loyiki's help and withdrew to a less conspicuous spot for the night. No fire, but he didn't need to consult the shine of his blade for his next move in this game of *sanza* his enemies were unaware they played. He knew what to do next and how, which weapon to deploy, and who would fetch to him that weapon: Josina.

Bolombo River, Everfair, August 1896

Rather than rush, then wait, Queen Josina planned to take her sweet time upon the king's mission. Whether those she had been sent after were to be regarded as weapons or as allies, the queen didn't like rising early to find them. She had better things to do than stay in a boat all day.

The river flowed against them, slowing them. Though her paddlers made steady progress toward the refugee-welcoming settlement at Mbuji-Mayi, she expected Loyiki to catch up easily.

As usual, she was right. On the fourth day of their journey a pair of small, swift-moving canoes came into sight, filled with strange, grey-skinned men. One hailed her: "Queen! Let us go before you, making sure the way is safe!"

They came closer. She had her paddlers hold the big boat still so she could look at them. She saw that, as she had thought, it was Loyiki who had hailed her. Loyiki's face was clean and dark, but some pale substance covered his chest, arms, legs, and back. The same with his companions, all men from his home, as he explained.

She motioned him to pass ahead. "But we're stopping soon to sleep," she told him. "When Sifa calls out for you to come back, you must do so at once."

"Aren't you worried shouting will attract the whites' attention?"

"They're nearby?" That was not what her scouts reported.

"We may have been followed. Also, in the collection camp there were rumors—a new outpost of Everfair is not much further up this river, and some people there are white. Though they haven't murdered anyone yet."

They decided that as their signal Sifa would imitate the call of a long-tailed mountain cuckoo, which anyone but the whites would know didn't live around here.

The Sankuru River grew suddenly narrower, then wider again and more turbulent. Another river emptied into it. Sifa said its name was Lubishi; she counseled that they go up this tributary a little ways and land for the evening. Josina accepted her advice and gave the signal.

The men of dead Ilebo roasted a large monkey for her and she ate as much as she could of the meat. Then she let Sifa and Lembe do her hair, arranging it simply in two smooth mounds on either side of her face. Fan in hand, she summoned Loyiki and the others to sit on the ground in front of her mat and thanked them for the meal.

The grey they wore was hardened tears. Loyiki explained that this was how they transported the material to the whites' collection camps. But now, escaping, they had instead chosen to give the fruits of their labor to the people of Everfair.

The tears were ugly. Without saying so, Josina doubted anyone but ill-bred whites would want such stuff, though even they showed signs of taste: gold was pretty, at least. But the next day she received a shock.

The presence of an Everfair outpost not much past the confluence of the Sankuru and Lubishi rivers having been confirmed overnight, Josina spent the morning preparing herself carefully for meeting these potential allies: bathing, chewing fragrant barks to freshen her breath, arranging her hair again—a more elaborate style for this occasion, with five combs inserted. On her upper arms she used a little paint she had been saving.

Josina was not naïve. She knew that fashions varied in different places, among different peoples; after all, she was a foreigner, from Angola. And though she'd never been to Europe, her mother's father had been born there. Those she met with might find her appearance as uncouth as she found theirs. But her king and husband had given her the goal of cultivating this connection, winning the invaders to their side. This she knew well how to do.

The breeze coming down from the village stank oddly. At first Josina worried it might be caused by some sickness, though there was a burning quality to it. Though not like wood . . .

The paddlers pulled their canoes ashore. Lembe assisted her in stepping over the side and supported her so she didn't slip badly in the mud. A little path led higher. At the top everything looked normal—except that a house to one side appeared to be on fire. So much smoke—far more than cooking would produce—pouring out of . . . a hole in its roof? A window? She couldn't quite tell, and no one acted like it mattered.

Walking calmly toward her were women, men, young ones, old ones, representatives of many nations, to judge by their features and accessories. As they neared, she heard them talking, and recognized several languages. Of course they grouped themselves together with those they could understand.

More than half of them had some visible injury from which they were recovering. Mostly they were missing hands. Usually only one. Some wore sparkling metal hooks and other devices as replacements.

Josina and her followers stood front-to-front with the refugees. Silence fell. No court musicians had come with her. No horns or harps or bells, only Sifa's voice ringing out suddenly: "Behold your queen! Josina, favorite of Great King Mwenda, visits you here! Bow with joy and pleasure before her beauty!"

Josina smiled. She lifted her fan and waved it playfully, flirting with her eyes. Sifa had made her announcement in Lingala. In Kikongo, and then again in Tshiluba, Josina echoed her: "I, your queen, am here, and you can lay your burdens down! Sorrow is banished!" Like a king, she danced. No musicians played. Her women sang and stamped their feet. Her paddlers slapped their broad chests.

Feeling for the land's rhythm, she held out graceful arms and spun slowly. Turning, turning—holding one foot high and finding where to set it down. Then the other. The pulse was there. The blood. It had not all run out, run dry.

She laughed and beckoned to a little girl who watched her

wistfully from the crowd's edge. She was shy. Josina took the child by her bright brass hand and dragged her forth. Surely such an embellishment showed she was beloved of the goddess.

An impromptu circle formed around the two of them. Bending to match her partner's height, Josina hunched her shoulders and dropped them, up and down, letting the movement travel to her fingertips, the feathers of her imaginary pinions. "Fly! Fly!" she told her tiny dancer. Soon all awkwardness was forgotten.

But despite the trance of movement Josina remembered the reason she had come here.

She mimicked a final glide downward and ended with a flourish of her figurative wings. She looked around to measure the effect of her dance and met wide eyes much like her own. A white woman—yet a sister? Possible . . .

Smiling, the white woman approached and held out her hand. Josina took it in hers, as she knew was generally these tribes' custom. The woman's palm was pink, her nails clean and trimmed. But no patterns decorated the pale skin, which smelled of sweat as well as sweetness. How to classify her? Josina assumed her longest, haughtiest, most direct gaze, testing her. The white woman didn't blink.

"Welcome to Bolombo." The woman spoke French. Josina thanked her in the same language, which didn't seem to startle her. They exchanged names and Mademoiselle Lisette offered beer, as was proper. They drank seated in the shade.

"How long is your stay? You will of course share my quarters."

"Not sure." Josina had Sifa fetch and stow her belongings.

They emptied the gourd quickly. Mademoiselle Lisette stood and shook the creases from her too-heavy skirt. "Would you like to see our—" She used a word Josina had never heard. Nodding, the queen allowed the white woman to precede her.

As Josina had reasoned, there was a fire in the house from which so much smoke poured. Contained, of course—in a stone and metal oven! Astonishing heat rolled out when the oven's door was opened, and she understood why three of the house's walls had been removed.

Just beyond a row of posts sat a pile of black, stinking clods, source of that peculiar odor that had hit her as she arrived. Two men picked up several handfuls each, threw them into the oven, and shut its door. One, dressed in clothes like a white, talked English a short time with Mademoiselle Lisette, for which rudeness she apologized as they left. "Winthrop is much too eager for my advice. Soon, he says, he'll be ready to show us how his machine can make possible—"

A man screamed. Josina looked around. Only women escorted her. The paddlers would be guarding the boats. Another scream. Shouts of anger. Mademoiselle Lisette was running toward the disturbance. She scrambled to follow.

They entered another house. Loyiki lay on a mat. Shreds of hardened tears hung from the hands of women kneeling at his sides.

"It hurts, my queen," he complained. "I had forgotten."

Others crowded the doorway, obscuring the light. She could barely see that Loyiki's arms and legs were dark again. The tears had been ripped away.

On other mats lay his companions, glowing like ghosts in the dimness.

"We so much appreciate this gift," said Mademoiselle Lisette. "It will help our machines to suck and hold the air—" Her sentence subsided into sobs. The poor woman, Josina suddenly understood, was feeling her people's pain. Again she took her hand. How to explain?

The connection always went both ways: people to sovereign, but sovereign to people, too. The solution was happiness.

There were no words. But there was another method of communicating what must be told. Tugging her new sister out to the central plaza, the queen set about teaching her to dance.

Bookerville, Everfair, October 1896

They were losing. No. They had lost. The church and hospital burned. The huts so painfully constructed—Thomas Jefferson Wilson batted at a large flaming leaf blown toward his face by the heat pouring out of the doorway he approached. Ducking under blots of smoke, he checked the interior. Empty, thank goodness. That was the last of the outlying structures. He turned to join the evacuation.

· The crusader in him, the reverend portion of the reverend lieutenant's soul, simply didn't want to believe what was happening, though as an experienced military man he knew quite well. Those Morel had warned him about seven years ago had caught up with him at last, and exacted their revenge.

He set out to walk a tight circle around the eastern edge of the settlement. All he heard now was the soft roaring of the fires that had been started in their buildings and the shouted commands of Leopold's men. The refugees' and colonists' shrieking had stopped, which he chose to look on as a positive sign. The quick dusk of the Equator had no doubt helped most to escape.

Finding his way through the thick, dark vegetation by touch and memory, he cursed his refusal to accept the inevitability of this assault. He had been warned, but had thought Everfair too remote, too obscure, for Leopold's dependents to seek for its destruction. He had thought that because this land had been legitimately purchased they were safe. He had trusted to his enemy's basic humanity to preserve them. This was the cost of that folly.

He almost collided with a man—a hand caught him, and something hard dug through his clothing and snagged itself in his trousers' waistband. Thomas struggled briefly before he recognized who it was: a boy, in truth, and not a man. The metal hook gave his identity away, the curve of it smooth against Thomas's skin. The flaring of a roof some distance off confirmed that this was the young African named Yoka. Not one of Leopold's cowardly bullies, but a refugee, and a useful one, despite his handicap.

Thomas silently assented to letting Yoka guide him along the path to the foundry, and past it, to the agreed-upon rendezvous. The smell of the boy's perspiration reminded him of working in the hospital, and he choked back unmanly tears at the thought of the colony's new casualties.

The ruffians' shouts grew fainter, and the fitful light cast by their fires faded. In the gloom ahead Thomas saw a dim, grey shape he took to be the white garment of one of Mrs. Hunter's nursing recruits. Rustling foliage informed him of others' progress. No one dared whisper.

They must have been traveling parallel to the path, for here was the low rise immediately beyond the foundry, and here the entrance to the shallow cave the hillock sheltered. Yoka's hand pressed down upon his shoulder; he stooped under the vine-hung arch of the entrance and pushed his way through concealing boughs. A lamp guttered inside, one of the crude clay versions employed hereabouts. Thin white roots snaked against the black rocks overhead.

The little cave could have been no more than forty feet across. Yet even in such a confined setting, even after their common enemy's attack, the survivors segregated themselves. Nearest to him were those he had trained, however haphazardly, to defend the colony. They guarded the way in, clubs, knives, and rifles to the ready. Beyond them he saw the newest refugees, members of a tribe calling themselves the Bah-Sangah, who appeared to be engaged in an argument. Further off, Mrs. Hunter and her godsons formed the nucleus of a group of a few—only a few—Americans mixed with the more assimilated refugees; on its outskirts the white workers who'd come at Owen's request stood hunch-shouldered and shamefaced. He could not discern that any of their number were missing.

With Everfair's co-founder off seeking support for the colony in Europe, Thomas had taken it upon himself to reach out to these English and Irish. But though many were Christians, or at least had been raised as such, race proved a barrier to his minis-try. Indeed, these men seemed to feel the majority of the Negroes blamed them, at least partially, for the crimes committed by Leo-pold's thugs. Perhaps because they shared the tyrant's papist—

Shouts interrupted his thoughts. Loud, unintelligible babbling from the Bah-Sangahs—it could bring the raiders down upon their hiding place! Shushed simultaneously by everyone else, they sub-sided to angry murmurs. Yoka, whom Thomas had lost track of in his woolgathering, came to join their talk, along with that inter-esting Chinese boy Tink—who before this would most likely have been huddling against the cave's lowest wall, over with the other runaways from the railroad. Who were also many fewer than he remembered.

Thomas, too, approached the Bah-Sangahs. "What is the diffi-culty?" he asked, though he knew he'd not be understood. Yoka attempted to translate.

"It is an issue of religion." As was everything, even war. "The elder believes we should seek the guidance of the spirits. Seek it now. The younger insists that since they don't have the proper tools, asking for divine help wouldn't work."

Thomas nodded. Primitive superstition often relied on quack-ery and showy trappings. "Please tell the old man I agree with him." Yoka's short remark elicited an obviously gratified response from the senior of the two principal conversants. The junior ap-peared to acquiesce, though softly grumbling.

And in his way, the old man was right. In a crisis such as this, there was no one else to turn to but the Lord. Thomas cleared his throat and folded his hands before his heart. "Let us pray."

"O mightiest of comforters," Thomas began. "Heavenly Father, protect your foolish children. Now, in our hour of need—" He broke off. Yoka spoke quietly under Thomas's voice, apparently rendering his words into the refugees' tongue. When the youth paused and looked at him meekly, he continued: "Show us plainly the path you would have us take to safety, that we may praise thy name and share the glory of thy wondrous light with all creation. Amen." Far too brief, but it would have to do; at least it had been sincerely felt. Yoka ended his incomprehensible translation soon afterward.

But the Bah-Sangahs wanted, it seemed, to say something more. With eyes first cast down toward the cave's uneven floor, then turned to his Chinese friend and tutor, Yoka formed hesitant sentences of explanation. "They say," the boy told him, "that your request of the sky—the sky king? That it is fine, but that we are under the earth. In the realm of another. The realm of theirs. No, of the one who is their owner. So that another pleading is necessary. To him. They want to add a petition to him."

And without further preamble a frightful noise burst forth from the old man's mouth. A growling roar far louder than the yells that had previously erupted from these savages. A gibbering, a yipping, a howling like a pack of wild dogs: "Waow! Waow! Yee yee yee!"

Astonished, Thomas raised his hands again in supplication, but the horrible din refused to stop. Would no one silence these madmen? He made to move but his feet were rooted. He couldn't lift them. Leopold's police would come—but as the cacophony continued, he understood that they would not. That no one would dare approach such unholy, *unnatural* sounds, sounds it was inconceivable had originated in a human throat.

Silence. At last. Contrary to Thomas's expectations, though, none of the settlers were staring in the direction of the source of those weird cries. Mrs. Hunter glanced up at him curiously from her small coterie of converts. Half-healed casualties, nurses, porters—and that white boy who followed her everywhere, George—all seemed unperturbed. The faces of the Chinese were harder to read, especially in the lamp's uneven light, but they, too, looked calm enough.

Of the men standing nearest to Thomas, only Tink's face held anything like an expression, the boy regarding him as though he had just uttered a particularly sagacious pronouncement. Even the Bah-Sangahs were bland of aspect, as if they had not, only seconds ago, emitted those awful, baying barks.

"You are right, without doubt," said Yoka.

Right about what? The crippled youth addressed the oldest of the Bah-Sangahs and received a reply accompanied by vigorous nods. He turned again to Thomas.

"They agree to your request. They will escort us to the mountains of their home and shelter us in their god's caves, since you have shown how he favors us."

What had he requested? What had he ostensibly shown these—Thomas looked around him at the other occupants of this dark hole. Had no one else heard what he'd heard? Had they instead heard him say something? Something of which he, himself, had no recollection? He touched his brow as if he might detect a fever there.

But, no. No disease provided him a convenient excuse. And there had been earlier incidents, lapses of memory he'd confided to no one. Hallucinations lasting less than a minute. They had not seemed serious. There had been no witnesses.

But this was worrisome.

Unsleeping, Thomas comforted his motley flock as best he could while the long hours passed. He told them they would build again, a better home than this, in a new, safer location. And when morning broke, and the scouts he sent out returned announcing that their attackers had fled like the black night, he did his best to act as though leading the remaining colonists' coming retreat eastward was a choice he had made.

Kamina, Everfair, December 1896

Daisy had been away in Kananga when the raid occurred. She would never forgive herself. True, she'd brought Lily and Rosalie with her, thus sparing them the brunt of the violence. But her quest for representation in the custody battle had proved fruitless. Neither of Kananga's two legal gentlemen had been prepared to travel to Britain and plead for Laurie Junior's return. When they heard it was Ellen who had given birth to him, they refused to consider Daisy his mother.

The caves were a little bit damp. Everywhere was, this time of year, in what would have been winter back home.

No, this *was* home.

She patted Rosalie's feet dry using what was once Lily's second-best frock. Both girls had grown out of their shoes earlier that year. Her fault for letting the two run unshod like wild things? No matter. Done was done. Soon enough Rosalie would fit into George's abandoned brogans.

Satisfied with her ten-year-old's cleanliness, Daisy pivoted to drop her from her lap onto the chamber's main mat. "Next time I'll let you wash yourself," she promised.

Rosalie nodded. "And Mama, will you let me work in the hospital like my brother, too? Et comme Mam'selle Toutournier?"

"Like your *older* brother," Daisy corrected her. She would not let the baby, Laurie Junior, be forgotten. "No; you're still too young."

"But Fwendi works in the—"

"Fwendi's mama and papa are dead." Perhaps that was too

harsh a statement. "We believe so, at any rate. But I am quite alive, and doing my best to keep you alive also. Now, go eat your porridge before it becomes lumpy and cold."

Lily had not yet risen. The chamber allotted to Daisy and her children was situated far from the caves' entrance, and correspondingly dark. How she missed her light, airy house in Mbuji-Mayi—or Bookerville, as the Americans had called it.

Standing, Daisy took the oil lamp from its niche and went to wake her oldest girl. The caves' darkness was no reason to sleep the day away.

Lily had claimed a high, deep shelf as her bed, then plaited a rope ladder to give access to it. Daisy's heart misgave her when she saw a pair of rough workmen's boots waiting next to the ladder's dangling end. Had some male sneaked in to lie with her fifteen-year-old? Daisy had heard no one, had not been wakened by any noise.

She lifted the lamp. "Lily? It's morning, dearest."

A round, tanned face topped by boyish brown curls leaned out into the light. "Really, maman?" Her child. "What hour?"

Daisy wore a repeater on a ribbon round her neck, a chiming watch Tink had repaired and improved so it told seconds as well as hours and minutes—though the lamplight made it unnecessary to set off its tiny bells. "It's just thirty-one-and-a-half past seven. Are you—" She hesitated. Did she betray her principles by asking questions rooted in bourgeois morality? "Are you alone up there?"

Innocent laughter was Lily's gratifying response. "Maman! How silly! Of course! Why wouldn't I be?" As she spoke, the girl swung her loosely trousered legs onto the ladder, turned to grasp its two sides, and began climbing down. A wayward air current caught George's shirt, making it billow on her slender frame.

"It's only—the boots—I thought they belonged to someone else—"

"They did. Tink gave them to me when he got better ones. I took care to scrape all the mud and ashes off—nothing objectionable on them, is there?" Picking up the boots, Lily looked them over quickly before sitting on the main mat's far edge to slip them on and tighten their laces. In a trice they were tied and Lily striding to their family chamber's exit.

"Wait! Your porridge!"

"Maman, there's no *time*. Tink has a demonstration!"

"Yes, and I am going to see it, too. And Rosie." On the mat, the younger girl looked up from her gourd and began to try to say something. Daisy cut her off. "There's plenty of time for us *all* to eat; they won't start for half an hour yet."

The cooked grains were thick and, she hoped, nourishing. Strange food, strange lodgings, strange weather—even the stars were different here, so near the Equator. And then there was the divorce. But that, she thought, was nothing she hadn't expected of her husband eventually. Ellen, whom he found so fascinating, was much too conventional to have put up with Laurie's romantic and sexual arrangements for long.

Daisy ate her own porridge swiftly and tucked her notebook and ruling pen into one of her smock's capacious pockets. The pen, also, had been a gift of Tink's. He was turning out to be a good friend to the family, though of course not enough of one to make up for Jackie's departure to attend to the Fabian Society's affairs. Or Lisette's.

No one could make up for Lisette's long absence, nursing in the field. Daisy would not even have had to pretend to like the cave— one of the things she'd done to satisfy Jackie—if Lisette had been here. With Lisette present, it would have been a paradise.

She had promised to return by Christmas. Sooner, if she could. Daisy would do her best to wait patiently.

She carried the lamp to their chamber's entrance. "Are we ready?" Lily, who had been in such a rush, suddenly realized she had left some vital piece of equipment in her sleeping niche. The repeater's wire gong struck the three-quarter hour while Daisy waited for her to retrieve it.

They walked toward the caves' largest chamber, cautiously at first. Shattered stalactites had left sharp rubble where they fell, which the colonists pushed to either side, but which kept accumulating. In the worst spots, Daisy made Lily help her barefoot sister along. Gradually, sunshine filtering in from the outside overcame the lamp's little brightness.

People filled the huge cave, their murmuring voices echoing off its lime walls, pale with indirect light from the nearby entrance. Smoke-holes pierced the ceiling and let in even more sunshine, though this was tinted green by sheltering vegetation, and supplemented with the faint illumination, in the shadows, of other colonists' lamps.

Tink knelt before the crowd, eyes focused on a glinting object about the size of a dog. If a dog were made of gold. Chester knelt beside him. Winthrop, Chester's brother, stepped carefully backward behind them as he uncoiled a length of something brown and black—rope? No, this was much wider—flatter, too—

Lily made a sudden movement, drawing Daisy's attention to her. She dug a large brass screw from her trousers' front pocket, then ran ahead to hand it to Tink. The youth smiled and took it, and Daisy had a sudden presentiment of trouble.

A romance between these two would never do.

She arrived as quickly as possible in Lily's wake. "What's this?" she asked, pointing at the device on the cave floor between Tink's knees.

"I call it—" He spoke a few Chinese words. "Or, to translate, 'Littlest Heater.' It will drive the balloon once we've got it lifted high enough."

"In here?" Daisy glanced up at the chamber's ceiling. It was perhaps fifty feet above their heads, on average. "I suppose there's room."

Lily rounded on her mother. "Of course there's room, if Tink says there is!"

Bad. Very bad. How had Daisy not noticed this problem developing?

The balloon bag was sewn together out of lengths of barkcloth lined with the rubber brought to Everfair—stolen—by refugees. Winthrop attached the canvas and rubber hose he'd been unrolling to a valve on the lid of a stone cask. He opened it. Gas hissed and the bag filled and rose. Daisy judged its length as about the height of two men: ten or twelve feet. When fully distended, it could have been encircled by four men holding each other's hands.

Now she saw the basket that was made to hang down below the bag. It, too, was undersized, and also of a curiously open design. Tink and Chester lifted the miniature engine—she was sure it was an engine; it had a chimney and a boiler box like the larger ones she was familiar with—as if it were much heavier than it appeared. They set it into the basket. A shaft protruded through a gap in one side. Chester and Winthrop held a propeller with five blades, which Tink attached to the engine's shaft using the screw Lily had brought him. Each time he gave it a twist he bowed ceremoniously to the individuals Daisy had determined were the Bah-Sangah's priests.

By this time, the ropes running between the bag and basket had grown taut.

"The 'Littlest Heater' is based on the deepest principles of Bah-Sangah cosmology," Daisy's daughter informed her officiously. "I can't tell you anything more than that. Tink had to swear not to reveal the secrets of its operation, but he says it is the most powerful—"

A gasp from the crowd of spectators interrupted Lily's speech. The basket surged suddenly upward, rocking waist-high in the air. Tink pulled something out of the engine's exposed side—a dark oblong shape—a damping device of some sort? Sputtering noises like the sneezing of a sick cat filled the momentary silence. Daisy thought it rather humorous. Then they blent together into a burbling, whistling whir and the whole contraption cleared their heads and went swooping triumphantly toward the caves' entrance.

It didn't make it. With a shout, Winthrop abandoned his cask and grabbed a rope still tied to the basket. Tink and Chester joined him, taking up other lines and coordinating their efforts, so that finally the balloon toured the cave's circumference in graceful—almost stately—revolutions.

London, England, December 1896

The man's gall infuriated him. With a curse, Jackie Owen snapped shut the hackney's door and bid the cabman go. Leopold—Jackie refused to call the tyrant a king—insisted that his bullies in the Congo acted against his orders, that he could not control them. A patent lie! Obviously they obeyed he who paid their wages.

Why wasn't all the world equally enraged by the greedy Belgian's blatantly noxious enterprises? He and Laurie and the other Fabians must make them so.

Nestled in his coat's breast pocket, Daisy's last letter to him detailed the fall of Bookerville. All the casualties seemed to have been blacks—which was to be expected, given their greater numbers. She, thank fortune, had been elsewhere during the attack. Since the first of their sexual liaisons following Laurie's desertion, Jackie had found himself harboring an oddly protective attitude toward her. Distance weakened this atavistic tendency, but not by much.

From a thousand leagues off he continued to worry. Though his dear—no, his colleague, dammit! Though Daisy had escaped injury in October, there might well have been subsequent attacks since. He couldn't know. That, too, infuriated him.

A feeling of helplessness, utter helplessness, threatened to overcome him. He lowered the cab's window to let in light and air, to let the cold, brisk wind clear away the stench of his despair. If only he could somehow select the colony's martyrs—those who'd raise the right sentiments in the right breasts. Excepting Daisy. But this broad attack on everyone did little to help the cause.

Particularly as many of the whites he'd brought with him had deserted it.

The Society could put an end to Everfair's harassment, even if only temporarily. Leopold had let this be known—indirectly, as was his cowardly, snakelike way. All it would take was money.

Jackie stuck his hand inside his coat and fingered the soft folds of Daisy's letter again. Then he found and pulled out the pasteboard square he had tucked behind it. "Matthew Jamison, Esq." Below the name was printed an address. It would not be far out of his road to make a call there. He thumped the cab's roof for the driver's attention and instructed him where to go. Time enough for the bank afterward; it would still be open another hour or two, and, anyway, the draft Jackie had obtained from his publisher was not nearly enough.

They slowed in front of a park green with holly and yews. Children trampled the muddy paths, shouting at one another and waving sticks. The driver pulled up to the stylish townhouse just past it, a dark red door at the top of its immaculate steps. He agreed to wait while Jackie transacted his business.

There was barely time to register the fresh scent of the Christmas wreath hung on the door before it was opened. Not, Jackie saw almost at once, by the establishment's butler, who hovered behind the gentleman welcoming him in. "I'm Matthew Jamison. Matty to my friends. You're not who I was expecting, but I recognize you from Thomson's description—John Owen? The author?"

"Yes, I'm he." Jamison was slight and golden haired—Jackie might have taken him for a boy if not for his moustache and rather too-dapper attire. "You've heard of me from—whom? Thomson? I'm afraid I don't know who you're referring to."

"Joseph Thomson? The explorer? He attended a talk you gave on Everfair."

"Ah. Yes." Jackie remembered him now. A Scot. He had pledged 150 sterling.

"But let us retire to my sitting room instead of standing about here in the entrance hall!" Jamison led him through a low arch and a doorway framed in dark wood. The room faced the park.

Large windows with drapes pushed to their sides gave a good view of it. A desk scattered with papers occupied the center of a sturdy-looking carpet.

A fire burned on the hearth opposite the windows. Jamison offered Jackie one of the two chairs drawn up before it and took the other.

"Sherry? I suppose it's too early for that. Tea? I can easily ring for something to be sent up."

"You said you were expecting another caller?" Jackie asked.

"Oh. Not exactly, but a professor at Oxford, come to town for the holidays, had promised to perhaps—that is, if he were to find the time to talk with me about his researches on the rights of the unenfranchised in ancient societies, this would be the afternoon he visited."

"You are interested in such things?" The woman who'd provided Jackie with Jamison's card hadn't mentioned that. Perhaps the man's reputation as a lightweight playwright was undeserved. Perhaps Jackie's mission was more likely than he estimated to meet with success.

"Of course! As an author it seems to me I must know all I can of the myriad ways mankind has chosen to regulate itself. Surely you think the same?"

He allowed himself the luxury of a small smile. "Indeed, and I do my best to ensure that my knowledge is more than academic. Not to disparage your professor—"

"No! But I'm intrigued; how do you mean, 'ensure'? And shall I ring? Biscuits? Fruit?"

"Nothing for me; if anyone else comes, I'll share in whatever they have."

For thirty minutes or so, judging by the shadows under the park's trees, Jackie regaled Jamison with stories of life among the Fabians, and more to the point, in Everfair. He ended when his host rose from his desk—where he had taken a seat midway through Jackie's monologue—and placed a cheque for fifty thousand pounds sterling in Jackie's hand. That got his attention.

But the cheque hadn't been signed.

"You haven't asked me for anything," Jamison said, smoothly resuming his chair by the fire. "But I've saved you the trouble of doing so, I believe, for I don't see why a man of your stature would have come to a man of my stature, if not in need of funds."

"Our relative statures—"

"Of course I don't mean the mere difference in our physical heights. You're a forward thinker, a philosopher, founder of an organization far ahead of its time, a genius whose opinions on serious matters will sway minds for centuries to come.

"I'm a popular entertainer, and nothing more. But I am also wealthy. Extremely wealthy. And I should like to do something of good with my wealth."

Jackie stared at the slip of paper he held. It trembled only a bit. So large an amount would help immeasurably. With it, the Society could buy outright the additional lands Leopold now offered. Which would afford time to prepare for the inevitable sacrifice.

If the information Jackie had gotten from the woman who'd provided him with Jamison's address was as sound as her posterior had turned out to be, the money was there. The cheque would be good. Once it had been signed.

"You note my omission," Jamison continued. "I will sign once you promise I'll be allowed to join your colony. I must be able to come and go, to enter and leave as I choose." Jamison moved to the red brocade bell-pull on the hearth's far side.

Was the man mad? Why not ask to be made an officer of the Society, a trustee? Had Thomson not painted a sufficiently somber portrait of the dangers to Everfair's settlers?

But what an opportunity!

The butler entered. "Clapham, I want to shut up the house somewhat earlier than expected. We're going to Africa."

Usually Jackie was the one who left others gasping in his wake. "To Africa? To Everfair?"

"As soon as you can arrange passage."

"But we can't! I mustn't go yet—not till I pay Leopold! We need to buy the land—more land—"

"Calm down! Be seated, sir!"

With a jolt, Jackie realized he stood, hands clutching the empty air. The butler, Clapham, met his eyes briefly, then turned back to Jamison.

"That's all for the moment," the little man said. "I'll let you know the exact schedule for our departure presently." He sat down at his desk once more.

Uneasily, Jackie allowed himself to reflect consciously on the Fabians' secret program, the deliberate loss of white lives in a black cause. The plan had been Laurie's at the outset, but Jackie had come to accept its necessity early on. How else to stir up support for the colony except through the deaths of innocent Europeans? And now he thought, who better to fill the role of martyr but a famed yet meritless author?

Still, he could barely admit to himself that violence would play a part in the accomplishment of their goal. He turned and walked abruptly out of the center of the room as if leaving what he knew to be true behind. Then he traced his way back into the middle. Good ends must justify unsatisfactory means.

At his desk, Jamison was waiting. "I accept your stipulation," Jackie told him. The playwright stretched out his hand and Jackie put the cheque into it.

He nodded and signed. "You'll make the arrangements, then?"

"Yes." A swift glance out the window: twilight fell more slowly here at home, but he needed to leave now if he were going to conduct any further business today. "Yes. I'll inquire as to sailing times, finish up negotiations with that ass—" He gathered his hat, gloves, and coat from the side table, and made as graceful an exit as possible.

The bank was very happy to receive his deposit, though Jackie explained clearly that these funds would be gone soon. He returned to his apartments and sent for his secretary to take care of the details of the journey back to Daisy, and Everfair.

He'd wait to deal with Leopold and the land purchase tomorrow. In anticipation of the grind that would entail, he penned a hasty note to the woman who'd helped find his new beneficiary, asking her to come to his rooms this evening and receive his thanks in person.

Lusambo, Everfair, April 1897

Lisette lay in the early morning darkness, once again alone. The return of Mr. Owen had hurt her. She was willing to admit that, though not to Daisy. Only to her fanciful memoir's imaginary readers, which was akin to saying: herself.

Of course, a dozen others slept in the same shelter as Lisette. She heard their even respiration, smelled it, a calming, natural scent in the humid air, like recently mown hay. But she was not in love with any of them. They weren't any of them the one she missed.

She shifted her cheek to a cooler spot on her thin sleeping mat. When Daisy was married, it had been easier to maintain the correct perspective. Laurie's tolerance of the two women's burgeoning romance provided nothing like the resistance Jackie's ignorant disapproval did. Coming up with the passion required to subvert that resistance upset Lisette's careful emotional economy.

She ought to have remained heart-whole.

Instead, she had gloried in the reward for her recklessness: the intimacy of her and Daisy's brief month together, the four warm, wet weeks of the holiday season between the time Lisette came to Kamina and Mr. Owen's arrival there. During the day, they had been the dearest of friends, and at night—

Lisette wrenched her thoughts away from where they could do no good. In the morning, she and the others of this expedition would open a new clinic. Here, they were much closer to Leopold's camps, the site of his filthy, murderous thievery. His victims would have shorter journeys to make, and fewer would die fleeing to Everfair for help. Consequently, they would be suffering from worse wounds. She should brace herself, prepare for nause-ating stenches, rotting flesh, stories of merciless, inhumane treatment. She should rest—

It was no good. She was awake. Awake and incomplete. She sat up.

Outside the shelter, the misting rain of the "dry" season no longer hissed against her bicycle's firebox. Had the embers died? Crawling in careful silence between her non-mechanical companions, Lisette emerged into the open.

Her solace had been left leaning against a tree a short distance away for safety. She found it in the dark by the warmth still radiating from the steel box hung on its rakish black frame. Gingerly nudging up the iron latch, she pushed wide the little door to the bicycle's sweetly compact furnace. Dim, but not yet cold, the coals shed a changeful, shimmering light.

Reassured, Lisette used the fire's fitful radiance to attend to her toilette. Her bodice had somehow twisted itself down through the neck of her chemise; her stockings had fallen to her ankles. Perhaps she should do as Josina advised and cease wearing them altogether. But that would affect how her shoes fit.

Clothes adjusted, Lisette felt more herself. She shut the door of the bicycle's miniature oven, having decided that the hour was still too early for her to stoke it up.

But then, a rustle behind her. Another was astir. Lisette reopened the firebox and blew the ashes off the top layer of coals. Peering over her shoulder, she saw, revealed by their fresh brightness, the face of the child Fwendi.

"'Soir," the orphan whispered. She had the rudiments of French. Lisette responded in that language. "You are in pain?"

"No. Are you?"

Lisette laughed briefly, bitterly. "No." Though she was, of course. But nothing she could complain about to this girl who had just one hand.

"No?" Fwendi wore only a wrap below her waist, a somewhat imaginary line imposed on her thin body by Mrs. Hunter and the other Christian settlers. "How makes you awake, then?"

"I am"—she searched for the best way to summarize her non-Daisy thoughts—"concerned. We're near where we used to live, where they tried to kill us."

Fwendi nodded knowingly. "Yes. The soldiers. The evil men."

Indeed. Doubtless the selfsame evil soldiers who had murdered Fwendi's parents and given the girl her disfigurement.

The child crouched down beside the steam bicycle, slowly, as if lost in reflection. "You act as our guard?"

What an idea! That she should stand guard against Leopold's depraved thugs! Lisette shook her head.

Fwendi leapt up. "Then who—"

Lisette clasped the girl's bare shoulder, urging her to reseat herself. "It's all right. Men from Mwenda's entourage see to it. No need for agitation on your part."

The girl subsided warily. Perhaps she wondered why, if all was well, Lisette sat vigil instead of sleeping. Yet she did not ask.

Silence. The bicycle gleamed softly where Lisette had burnished its clean, straight metal parts. White moths gathered, drawn by the firebox's dull red glow. Fwendi waved them away with her false hand.

Which whirred and spun entrancingly.

Almost against her will Lisette reached for the girl's glittering brass hand. Its many intricacies delighted her touch. "It is new?" she asked.

"Yes, and much better than the last Tink made to me. It moves—" Fwendi showed her the key for winding the mechanism contained in the prosthetic's long cuff, fat around the refugee's forearm.

Most of the motion the wind-up hand was capable of consisted of flapping up and down or rotating a full 360 degrees. Also, its four fingers and thumb could grasp an object with the flick of its wearer's wrist, and it maintained its grip when a locking slide was pressed into place. Showing off, Fwendi opened and closed her hand several times and swung it through the meager light, spooking more moths.

"What else can it do?"

Manipulate the hand into any desired position, set the lock and it became a tool—strong, hard-edged, impervious to pain—in fact, a weapon.

How had her mind come to think this way?

How many more of these things could Tink and his helpers make?

Kamina, Everfair, August 1897

Tink felt Lily's kiss on his dirty cheek as she handed him a basket full of ore. He kissed her back, aiming for a place on her forehead above a streak of reddish mud. No one else worked this seam. No one else would see what they were doing.

She grabbed him by his ears, lowered his lips to her own. Heat, tenderness—he felt himself open, like a leaf. So new, so green. . . . Tink had left Macao well before any uncle or older brother could be bothered to bring him to a teaching woman. Compared to even the prostitutes at home, Lily's face was ugly: nose prominent, eyes a peculiarly metallic blue. But her body radiated pure beauty. And her heart and mind—this feeling she brought over him was unlike anything he'd ever known.

He set the basket on the ground and stepped around it without looking. Hands free now, Tink stroked the back of Lily's head—the lightest of pressures, such as he had learned she liked. Feathering lower, his fingers caressed her soft neck, which no one but he was allowed to touch. Which he had not allowed himself to touch till the day after her sixteenth birthday.

Lily broke away from their embrace. "We have time?"

Reluctantly, Tink shook his head. "They'll check on us soon. The departure is scheduled—"

"Of course." She gave him another kiss, this one brisk and sisterly, then handed him the basket once again and picked up the lantern. When she squeezed past him, her bare arms brushing his, her thinly covered hips nudging against his thighs, he regretted his choice. Surely two more minutes, or one, would make no difference?

But he followed Lily out to where Chester and the rest waited.

The wide, high cavern was nearly full of people and equipment: casks being emptied of hydrogen, hoses curling away from them to converge on the caves' hastily built exterior platform, curving to pass the gondola, which was growing heavier by the moment as the loading finished up. And the bag, unrolled so most of it covered the platform and the stony sill between it and the caverns' entrance. Most of it outside, but sticking a short way in. The bag squirmed and rose as its individual cells received their quotas of gas. When fully inflated, it would measure forty feet high and five hundred long.

Albert, one of Mr. Owen's Englishmen, approached. "Do you want all those bags of ballast we was discussing earlier?" he asked. Gone was any vestige of the doubt the older man used to harbor about Tink's abilities.

"Half of them. Let's see how she lofts." The gasbag's rubber-coated barkcloth was heavier than the silk Albert and many of the other workmen knew. And the Littlest Heater weighed a lot. But the fuel for it was less bulky by far than for more conventional boilers.

Besides, there'd be other things to throw overboard.

Chester signaled the crew stationed at the gondola's bow to begin attaching the lines that would tie it to the quickly filling bag. Those secure, they hauled the gondola over a bed of rounded river pebbles and out through the caves' mouth. The narrow shelf between the mouth and the platform overflowed with workers. Tink took his post in the gondola alongside Yoka, Winthrop, and Lily. He had been unable to argue her into staying here.

Brown and green and crimson, the bag inflated till it tugged at its lines, bobbing in the misty rain. Tink nodded at Chester, standing now in the caves' entry. Beside him Winthrop nodded too. His brother gave the signal and they cast off.

The mountain fell away below them. Mists covered the crowd who had gathered to see the launch. This was not the first voyage of *Mbuza*—the name Yoka had selected for the vessel in memory of his country's best king. Three times previously they had flown some version of her, using half-built engines, temporary gondolas, larger cells within her bag.

But never before had she carried a cargo. Never before had she had a destination.

On the platform projecting from the stern, Lily slid away the barrier between the two earths powering *Mbuza*'s Littlest Heater, allowing them to interact. Soon the pressure grew high enough. She engaged the propeller and they darted forward. Winthrop held the wheel steady, steering them north and west while depressing with one foot the lever that angled the gasbag's tail and vanes.

The plan was for them to sail south after navigating northward to the lowlands. South, then west to the coast, to Luanda, a stronghold of the Portuguese, and the nearest friendly city where they might find outlets for the colony's produce. Sample stocks of nuts, oils, ores, roots, woods, and wild fruits formed part of their freight.

Even had he intended to follow this course, Tink would have passed so close to Mbuji-Mayi that he would have felt obligated to see how it fared. They had left midway through the morning, taking advantage of sun-warmed updrafts. Yoka and Lily consulted together on landmarks, but that first day *Mbuza* just stuck to the course of the Lomami River, making sure not to turn up one of its many tributaries. Around sunset they lowered the gondola to within a hundred feet of the ground, anchoring fore and aft in tall trees at a big bend in the river. Too anxious to sleep, too exposed in the open gondola to take advantage of the absence of Lily's overwatchful mother, Tink huddled with her and the others as far as possible from the Littlest Heater's platform. The Bah-Sangah priests advised against spending much time in its vicinity.

In the morning, after relieving themselves over the side, they gained additional height by tossing out a quarter of every sample the colonists had supplied. They turned west, Lily and Yoka counting the river valleys they crossed and naming them.

They reached the former town site at noon.

Everything had been flattened and burned. In the empty clearing Leopold's men had planted rubber vines. Not even smoke rose from the deadened earth—only too-even rows of curling green stems.

Lily went out to cut the Littlest Heater's fuel compartment in half with its fitted slab of rubber. The engine slowed and stopped. Winthrop maneuvered so that the barely noticeable west wind pushed them back over the empty spot where Mbuji-Mayi had been.

Yoka said something in the tongue of his faraway home, sounding sad. Tink remembered his first welcome sight of the settlement, the lights just starting to show through open doors as night descended, falling as swift as any time during the workers' journey there, but no longer so frightening. Because they had finally gotten where they'd wanted to. Safely.

In silence, Tink felt *Mbuza* drift further east. A sudden increase in the light to his left drew him to the gondola's side. It came from below. Looking down he saw the river again, the Sankuru, bright with the pale brass of the day's last glow. To the north, in the distance, a boat sailed smoothly, steadily away. It vanished around a bend before he could bring his binoculars to bear. But its movement—swift, even—was that of a large motor-driven craft rather than a small canoe. One of Leopold's vessels. Carrying what? Thieves? Murderers? Spies?

Lily moved beside him, her welcome heat bridging the cool, careful gap of air between them. "Can we catch up with it?" she asked.

If they did, they would have to destroy it and kill every passenger. "No. Let it go."

"But our weapons!" she protested.

"Oh yes. We'll be using those."

They rejoined Winthrop. "Rest," Tink told him. "I have skill enough to keep us over the water till dawn. Tomorrow, we'll need you piloting."

"You'll keep us over the water going which direction?"

"North."

"Toward the Kasai and the Kwango rivers?"

Tink nodded. As if there had ever been any doubt. Too many pacifists sat on the council to talk about it openly, but *Mbuza* had never been meant for anything else. "We take the back way to Kinshasa." If they made it home afterward, they'd be considerably lighter. By fifty bombs.

Bankana, Everfair, to Kinshasa, Congo, August 1897

The smoldering wood of fires in the nearby village scented the dark, quiet air around them. Mwenda fought against the feeling of comfort it brought. Here on this high, barren hill, he and his warriors were exposed. Shortly, when the sun rose, the others would also realize this. Sunrise would allow them to see their surroundings—and to be seen by anyone looking for them. Such as their enemies, the invaders.

Also, of course, their allies. He hoped and expected these would arrive first.

"King."

Mwenda had allowed his camp no lights, not wanting to give away their position while they waited. In the dim shine of the waning moon he couldn't make out the identity of the petitioner facedown before his throne, but he judged the voice as belonging to Loyiki, who now served as Josina's messenger. Loyiki, who had brought Mwenda word of this arrangement.

"You have news?" he asked. "You may rise."

Shifting to squat in the damp grass where he had prostrated himself, the man shook his head. "I apologize, but no, it is merely a rumor from"—he hesitated—"those in the town we go to."

Kinshasa lay over two days to the east, but Mwenda had heard the drums. Though he knew only the simplest of the codes they carried. "Relate it to me."

Skirting past vaguenesses obviously intended to disguise his sources, the burden of Loyiki's report was that Leopold's half-built railroad had at last been completely abandoned. Naturally the inhabitants of the town assumed that they, too, had been deserted by him.

They would probably fight weakly, then. He would be foolish not to take advantage of that. Mwenda thanked his spy.

Color crept into the sky, blue soaking through the black. Then the sun appeared to rise out of the east—at first silently, but soon accompanied by a faint, droning hum. Louder, louder. Blinded by the dawn, they couldn't see the aircanoe until it had come so near that many of its details were also suddenly visible: brown mottling the swelling red sides of what looked like a giant gourd; lines connecting that thing to an elongated nestlike construction below; faces above the nest's high sides—two as pale as Europeans'—attitudes showing clearly that they turned their gazes Mwenda's way; dangling vines or ropes hanging down, sweeping the hillside's stunted trees.

The growling of the aircanoe's engine had grown to a roar like a waterfall. It was matched by the astonished cries it pro-voked from his local subjects as they poured from their homes and out over the countryside. Above all that noise came shouting from the flying boat, indistinguishable words. Then the device's sound was somehow dampened. The shouts could now be under-stood: "Grab hold! Pull us to you and hold us still!" Quickly Mwenda commanded his people to do this. Other young men jumped high and caught the ropes and hauled the aircanoe to where he sat.

A wood and fiber ladder was lowered. As his warriors climbed, the aircanoe sank, so that by the time the king mounted it, several rungs lay on the ground. He had only five hands of steps, five steps per hand, to take upward before his fighters pulled him carefully over the boat's rim.

It truly did resemble a nest, he saw, looking around. Its thick walls were woven, though the shape overall was like an enormous dugout. Two of his soldiers stood in the far end next to a tall, pros-perous man clothed in shirt and trousers. The others gathered together around their king, on guard. A final follower reached the top of the ladder and threw a bundle over the nest's edge: Mwenda's collapsed throne. Then that one, too, took a protective position.

There were three other passengers already aboard. Motioning aside those who got in the way, he studied them. A man with a golden arm. Another man who looked like he was squinting—but Mwenda marked that the muscles around his eyes were too relaxed for that. So this was one of the Mah-Kow who had deprived the tyrant of his iron road to the interior.

The fourth passenger was a woman, a white. She smiled directly at him and spoke: "Greetings, Great King." It was she who had called to them earlier.

Mwenda was impressed despite himself. Though attired, like the others, in European-style clothing, she pronounced words properly. More, she responded to his questions about their mission in Kinshasa simply and clearly, without error or evasion. He noted that she consulted a few times with the Mah-Kow, whose name, he soon learned, was Tink. The woman, Lily, translated for Tink, for the large and prosperous Winthrop, and for golden-armed Yoka, who besides English knew only his native tongue, a form of Bah-Sangah.

The day passed. When he walked about the boat-shaped nest Mwenda could look down on forests, rivers, and the scablike spots where the invaders had planted their useless vines-that-weep. These last areas became more numerous as they progressed west.

Lily and Yoka offered them fruit; beer; and cold boiled grain rolled up in leaves. Yoka's arm turned out to be brass rather than gold. Special knives could be locked into place on its end, which excited the smiths. It rotated more freely than a hand, and had an unbreakable grip. Mwenda was glad Yoka would fight with rather than against them.

The sun caught up with them and then raced on ahead. Evening came, and Mwenda's eyes pained him as he stared into the west from the nest's prow, searching for his first sight of Kinshasa. A river of fiery brightness, the Congo shot back the setting sun's reflection. Finally the sun lowered itself out of view. Though still safely distant, their target was now easily visible.

Square stone houses absorbed the sky's last light. They lined a wide path climbing a steep slope to a high terrace. High, but not so high as he was: Sailing lower would mean the aircanoe would likely be spotted.

The arrogant invaders had erected only one fence, and that was situated inside their city, houses masking it so that no more than one small section showed. It confined prisoners: wives, children, mothers of men forced to harvest tears and kill themselves carrying the whites' heavy loads.

A sudden quiet filled Mwenda's ears; the aircanoe's engine had been stopped. The day was done, the journey accomplished.

Lily approached him. "You are ready, Great King? You are sure?"

The king didn't bother answering. They weren't stupid questions, merely pointless. Already he had listened to those counselors who wanted him to hide from his enemies rather than battle them. Already he had consulted his spirit father about the course of the war, and about this expedition in particular. He had accepted more prohibitions, including one against lingering in confined spots. There was danger, but Mwenda would continue as planned. He was fully a man. He would carry out his duty.

The woman seemed to understand. "Come, please." She beckoned Mwenda and his men to a place midway along one of the nest's bowed sides. The ladder was there, neatly piled next to a basket of knives. No guns. Nothing that would give away their movements.

Dropped into the surrounding forest, Mwenda and his fighters made their way stealthily, slowly, toward the town. Then waited. Insects bit them. They had drunk potions, endured rituals to avert sickness.

BOOM! BOOM! Bombs fell and set fire to thatch and wood. *BOOM!* Yellow flames, red flames, lit the underside of the aircanoe as it glided silently away, its work of destruction finished. Shouts and screams filled its wake. All were concentrated on Kinshasa's eastern side, far from the fenced-in prison yard.

Wordlessly, the king and his fighters swarmed forward, taking advantage of their enemy's distraction.

The burning houses cast deceptive shadows, their flaring light screened by those left intact. Mwenda and his warriors paid little attention to what they saw, more to smells, sounds, the evening flight's memories. Deserted paths opened before them as they slipped down the hill. A shallow pit sent the five in front stumbling, warning Mwenda and the five beside him to avoid it. Another five followed them, fanning wide or drawing in as the paths dictated. Behind them came two more hands.

The prisoners were of course guarded, and not every guard had deserted his post when the fires broke out. Sensing something wrong, one issued a challenge in nervous French. Before Mwenda could respond, he felt on his cheek the little breeze of another person's knife cast in the unfortunate guard's direction.

A half-choked cry must have alarmed the dead guard's comrades. A lantern beam split the night—a rifle shot rang out—and another—and the air around Mwenda filled with ill-aimed bullets.

Sheltering against the rough poles of the fence's gates, Mwenda slashed apart the chains securing them—cheap, badly made iron, no match for his spirit father's blade. He had already dealt with one when Yoka joined him.

The brass-armed man spoke a sentence in his unintelligible Bah-Sangah dialect. Mwenda let him take the two remaining chains. Impossible to see just what he did, but a pair of loud snaps sounded above the rifles. Then they were dragging the rattling chains away to fall loose on the ground. More men—the workers Yoka had freed from the camps on the other side of the rise on which Kinshasa stood—arrived to force open the gates against the guards' resistance.

So many men! No weapons except for bits of wood and stone—Mwenda caught flashes of raised fists, cocked arms, in the jittering light of the lantern. They spilled over the guards, ignoring their shots, bearing them down, grabbing away their guns, trampling the foe into the mud. The light died from sight and was reborn a moment later in the hand of Mwenda's spearman, Yambio.

The king sent four soldiers to the lands of their ancestors, killing them neatly and cleanly with his sword as soon as they came in reach, forgiving each traitor as he died.

A crowd of subjects swarmed around the king, liberated workers calling the names of family members Leopold's thugs had kept hostage here. An axeman, Kajeje, swung and split a huge post to which chains were fixed. Link rattled against link as the released prisoners pulled themselves free. Moans, cries, chattering in many tongues, most unknown to him, overwhelmed Mwenda's ears. Curses, prayers—he lifted an old woman fallen to her knees, thin as a snake and light as a palm leaf, set her on her feet, motioned for a younger woman to help her away.

A horrible smell hung over a long, low house on the enclosure's far side: an odor of clotted blood, rancid waste, rotting flesh, painsweat, fearsweat. Looking about, he found Yoka holding a second lantern—no, a torch—no, it was some extension of his metal arm that burned. Not that it mattered. Mwenda summoned him and they crossed to the house's thick door. Kajeje appeared at Mwenda's side before the king knew of his need, smashing the wood with his axe.

The smell poured over Mwenda's face, its full vileness released. Shielding his mouth and nose, the king shouldered past the door's remnants into the stinking dark.

His feet sank into a floor of muck. He took only a few steps before Yoka entered with his light. Then Mwenda could see.

Perhaps half the house's occupants were dead. With some it was hard to tell. Also, looking closer, he saw that several—parts—were not—did not—make whole people.

Mwenda raised his hand from his nose and mouth to cover his eyes—but stopped himself. Blocking out the ugly sight would not truly erase it. Kajeje dispatched the rest of the door and came through the opening. The king would need to set a good example. Not to behave as a boy. He lowered his hand. He looked directly ahead.

Many very ill people lay on the ground, which was soft with excrement. He met a girl's eyes. She lay naked, arms curled around a tiny corpse. She blinked at him. Alive. The thing she cradled was not. Nor the one on whom she rested her head.

Behind him Mwenda heard Kajeje stumble back through the ruined door. The noise of him vomiting reminded the king that outside there were others. He called for them.

Those in this house who still lived couldn't walk, even with help. Mwenda had his ablest followers lift and carry them off toward the rendezvous. If these most miserable of Leopold's captives died, it would be away from here. As far away as he could take them.

To make sure no one living got left behind, Mwenda stayed till the last safe moment. Or what he thought was the last safe moment. Of the fighters, only he and Yambio remained, and a hand of untrained, unarmed workers. No enemies. The prison yard was almost empty. Then it was full—of Leopold's police. The stupid fence prevented any exit. King Mwenda was trapped.

Mushie, Congo, to Lusambo and Bolombo, Everfair, September 1897

What did Josina have? Even the water underneath their canoes belonged to him, according to Leopold. Whose thieves held captive her king.

The queen hated giving up. But worse than that, she hated losing. The mission to which she had assigned herself had failed. Alonzo, her cousin, who had hidden himself among the thief's men, had warned her. "Leave," his message ran. "Or they will throw you in jail too."

So the lies she'd told Leopold's men about the colonists of Everfair paying fighters for the attack had done no good—the lies, and the promises to share secrets she didn't have. So the thieves would refuse to let King Mwenda go.

Josina knew exactly who lay where in the guesthouse's black interior. Lembe, as always, to one side of her, and Sifa to the other. Neither slept, for she had instructed them to be ready. She rose from her mat and they rose with her. Bypassing the chamber pot, a nasty thing she had spent the last six days pretending not to understand the use of, they exited the room silently. The three policemen on the front porch dozed, as expected. Josina and her women slipped past them. She had her excuse ready—a full bladder—but it wasn't necessary. The charm worked.

Chilled by the night, Josina wished she'd wrapped herself in her blanket before coming out. But no, best to leave everything, for now.

Sifa had the keenest sense of direction. She led them down to the moorage. Their canoes were tied up with many ropes, but un-damaged. While her women struggled to undo the knots by touch, Josina strained her eyes, watching for discovery.

Half the paddlers joined them. No time to wait; the others would have to make their own escapes.

Fewer paddlers, so fewer boats. Only two, in fact; Josina seated herself on Lembe's shoulders and let Lembe wade out to the first launched, raising small waves. These waves were unsafe—not only because of attracting the police but because the crocodiles, who hunted often at night—

A huge splash! Josina twisted, though she could see nothing behind her but water churning in the scattered light from a house's shuttered window. She heard shouts on the riverbanks, but not the screams of someone dying.

The paddlers worked hard, their grunts and deep-drawn breaths loud. They fought the current, which the Kasai River's many is-lands here divided yet did not weaken.

Nothing attacked them, or nothing further. Morning rose. They'd reached a large island. Assured by paddlers who knew this course that those who gardened here kept it free of dangerous animals, they camped briefly ashore.

Sifa explained that the commotion in the water as they left Mushie had been occasioned by bait, a distraction: on their way to the moorage a paddler had taken a pair of fowl and thrown them in. An appeasement. A sacrifice.

In the afternoon, rested, they left the island. Four more days, a market, and they turned again up the Sankuru. Another two days to confirm that Everfair had deserted its outpost in the disputed territory, Bolombo. It had retreated rather than advanced. Josina had known this when she lied about it to Leopold's representatives.

Almost a market longer it took to travel to Lusambo. Josina tried not to think of how her king must be suffering. Because that would do no good, and was against all her training.

But when she met with her white sister Lisette and recounted her failure to obtain the king's release, she wanted badly to cry.

Anger—it must be anger, not fear—choked her, blocked her throat. Politely, her host pretended it was the beer's fault.

"Apologies! Such a musty brew—it is too old!" The woman looked to the maiden at her side, also a white. "Lily, have we anything better to offer?"

"Mother sent tea"—Josina did not miss the girl's defiant glance—"that Uncle Jack brought us from England."

Lisette screwed her smooth mouth into a sour smile. "Yes. Let us use that."

"There isn't much," warned the girl. But she rose from the mat they shared to fetch a packet of paper—Josina had seen paper before—out of a basket on the far wallpost. "I'll get the hot water," she added, and left.

The two women sat in momentary silence. "Of course I must ask Council what we can do to help," Lisette said, and then Josina did cry. Tears only—no sobs, no moans or wailing. But it was more than she'd allowed herself in front of those she ruled.

The connection went both ways. She could not expose her subjects to this pain.

A softness touched one cheek. Blinking clear her eyes, she jerked away from a blur of yellow—cloth, she saw.

"You won't let me dry your face? Lily will return soon. Do you want her to—"

The girl walked in, holding the handles of a covered metal bowl. Too late, Josina understood that Lisette, also, wished to spare her subjects, of whom this Lily must be one. She turned to hide the signs of her distress.

"It's steeped almost long enough, I daresay, just during my walk from the boiler," said the maiden. "Shall I—oh. I'm so very sorry. Oh."

No good. Fresh tears pricked at her lids. She let them spill over.

"Don't! Oh, please, don't!" Small, rough hands on her arm. The maiden Lily knelt beside her. "Tink and I—we didn't mean him to get caught! We've been miserable, blaming ourselves—"

Brushing her eyes with the back of her hand, Josina looked in

Lily's face. "You were—sailing the aircanoe? You brought the king to the attack?"

"I did! Though Mama"—another of those glances at Lisette—"Mama insisted it was all Tink's fault."

"If you had stayed to the mission Council assigned you—"

"Then I would not be stuck here with you!"

"Ah! 'Stuck'! Your mother trusts me to look after you, and because of this you are 'stuck'!" Lisette shook her head. "Forgive us, Queen." Her peculiar eyes, color of a raincloud, didn't seem truly penitent. "We're grateful for King Mwenda's message. I'll convey it onward. You must need to rest now."

"No. I need to leave for the place of my father." Already she had wasted time, traveling the opposite direction from N'dalatando. Josina had come here only because Mwenda had made her promise in their one, tense meeting.

"At least take some tea," the maiden insisted. Not to be rude, Josina accepted their foreign drink. Going down the river would be quicker than going up, and there were still many hours of daylight left.

The bowl's cover was a pair of smaller bowls stacked inside each other. Clever, but undecorated. Lily set them out separately on the mat and poured a warm, golden liquid into them from a spout in the big bowl's side. Copying Lisette, Josina carried the little bowl to her lips, inhaled briefly, sipped, and swallowed.

"It's good!" she exclaimed, surprised. Lily giggled. "Tea" tasted somewhat acrid, like beer, but also a bit sweet. Dried leaves went into boiling water, Josina was informed; and left behind their virtues when removed. "This plant is grown where you come from? In Europe? England?"

The tea plants' sources were far countries much hotter than their homes. Josina rapidly consumed two more bowls, talking in greater detail than before about her negotiations for the king's release. Her heart rose. Her mind understood this rising as having to do, in some measure, with what she had been given. Tea was a drug, like dagga. A drug they could learn to cultivate here, also?

Dismissing this question as untimely, Josina parted with Lisette to return to her women and paddlers, sure to be waiting already by the canoes. She would have parted with Lily, too, but the maiden insisted on accompanying her to the riverbank.

The reason for this became obvious as Lembe jumped up to help her queen on board. Suddenly the maiden spoke—rapidly, again in French. "In two days you will be back in Bolombo."

"Yes. Or a little longer."

"When you get there, look up. Into the sky. Look up," the maiden urged again. In a blink she was running away, back along the path.

Some conflict, some trouble. Secrets being kept. Josina recalled how Lily had regarded Lisette. She didn't know enough to pick sides yet, so when they came, finally, to the open space near Bolombo where the Lubudi River flowed into the Sankuru, she did as invited.

Thus she was the first to see it. Though naturally not the only one: the aircanoe was too large to miss. Shortly it loomed above them, a huge shadow, its boat-form basket just barely above the tops of the trees marking the rivers' sides. Higher than that, bigger than that, loomed its other portion, which reminded her of the pods of cacao beans her father had shown her . . . the shape and even the colors, yes. But did it swell in size? No, it was coming closer, lower . . .

Lengths of rope appeared over the basket's rim, and a figure climbed down one of them like a monkey—Lily. "Shall we give you a lift?" she asked. "On our way to rescue the king?"

Kinshasa, Congo, October 1897

Tink argued stubbornly. Vainly. "No. You can't. Let Captain Renji—"

"The captain doesn't speak French. Or English. And besides that, you've no way to prevent me."

He was stronger than Lily, but only physically. "I won't let you land."

"Then you'll have to call the entire rescue off. If anyone goes, it's—"

"Me."

"I!"

"I, then, if you insist on correcting my speech. I—I will go," Tink said as calmly as he could. "And you will stay here on *Mbuza*. Safe."

"Oh! You're as bad as any white man!" Lily stuffed her hands in the front pockets of her trousers and turned away from him, staring off at the final moments of the red and purple sunset. Light lasted long up here on the aircanoe, high over the trees. But now, the third day of their trip north from N'dalatando, they descended toward their goal almost as fast as the sun sank.

No more time to argue. Darkness would arrive soon, bringing the shadows so necessary for hiding their rescue party.

"All right. Fine. We will both go, then." Tink regretted the words as soon as he said them.

"Of course we'll both go." Lily sounded matter-of-fact, but her eyes shone with delight as she turned back to embrace him. A mock-solemn kiss and she left to gather the others who'd take part.

Tink shuttered and extinguished lamps on his way to the steering apparatus. After nightfall the chance of them being spotted from the ground was low, of them being recognized even more negligible, but he would do everything in his power to make the danger less than nothing. Though Old Kanna had determined by divination that the date was not the most fortunate.

Once again Winthrop held the wheel. His brother Chester, in Kamina, worked to build a second aircanoe for Everfair. Others Tink had instructed made more weapon hands. They must maintain their advantage over Leopold.

Tink led their group to where the scoop in the gondola's woven sides made it easier to lower their ladder. Captain Renji, who had joined them at N'dalatando at Josina's insistence; Yoka; himself. And Lily, his fierce love, the skin of her face and hands and throat streaked with dark dye, smiling down at him like a constellation, like a stubborn, wayward divinity.

He could not have stopped her.

They leapt from the dangling ladder to a grassy hillside south of the main settlement. It was a different approach than that used by King Mwenda, in case Leopold's men watched for them. Neither did they rely on a fire nor any other distraction this time. Their party was small enough that they passed to the wall of the prison yard without notice. Yoka tossed the weighted rope the captain had provided over its top. The weight's hooks caught as they were designed to do. Tink's grip on Lily's soft upper arm was enough to keep her back till the two others had climbed the rope. He followed her up.

On the other side, on the ground, Tink smelled old death and new. The unnamed sense that always informed him where Lily was whispered that she knelt a little ways off. She rose to stand, small patches of her pallor winking at him furtively, stars in the blackness. At her feet slumped a corpse reeking of blood and offal.

As ever, she seemed unsurprised by Tink's movements. When

he came close enough she clasped his hand in hers—her left. The one that didn't hold a wet knife. Her mouth grazed his ear. "He was sneaking along behind Captain Renji," she breathed. "Not crying for help. They must already know we're here."

Josina had suspected a spy among her entourage. This was probably proof. They should leave. But how to convince the others?

Like a ghost, Yoka appeared noiselessly, a mere silhouette. He urged them further inward, away from the wall. The earth humped high and low beneath their bare feet, loose and uneven, stinking of incomplete burials.

More freshly dead men littered the dirt before the jail's open door. Tink saw them—parts of them—in the narrow slit of light spilling through. Slowly his eyes adjusted, and Captain Renji appeared, beckoning them inside.

The first room was wide as the whole building, and its ceiling as high as three tall men balanced on one another's shoulders. Deserted, and that felt wrong—so wrong—

Lily pulled a jangling ring of keys from the drawer of a desk in front of her and shared them around equally. The rescuers exited the room to a short passageway lined with four heavy doors. Tink tried both his keys in a lock Captain Renji had abandoned in frustration. The second worked, and here, at last, were people: captives staring at him, at first in silence. Then crying out—in fear? Tink understood their words poorly, but they huddled away into the cell's corner. He realized they must fear his axe. And his strange appearance—had they ever met a "Mah-Kow" before?

"He isn't here!" Lily had run to the end of the passage. Tink barely heard her above the loudening clamor of the prisoners calling to each other, the shouts of Yoka and Captain Renji telling them they were truly free in English, French, and other tongues. All the doors were open now, and the corridor getting crowded. Tink pushed his way to Lily.

"But Josina said she met with the king here, in this building." He reassured himself as much as her. "She had no cause to lie."

"No. But he may have been moved. There are other quarters,

worse ones. Someone heard the drums calling for mission volunteers and told them we were coming—they *knew*—"

Just-released prisoners surrounded them in ever-thickening
clots. Tink lifted his axe overhead to avoid accidentally wound-
ing any. That was when he first saw their way out.

The captain and Yoka led the men and women filling the passage through to the outer room. Lily and Tink went, too, checking
there for more doors to other cells. Behind one door, unlocked,
they found a long, thin storage space containing chains, hammers,
baskets, a pair of wooden ladders, whips. Behind another, a room
holding four low cots and a dry water bucket. Four cots; how
many dead men outside?

With the king or without him, it was time to go. Sure enough,
when Tink stuck his head outside to count how many Yoka and
Captain Renji had killed, a gunshot drove him back in. They bar-
ricaded the entrance and the one big window beside it. Four other
windows ran in a row near the wall's top, too small for coming
in and out of.

"Use a ladder. Get up to the window and signal through there,
yes?" said Captain Renji, gesturing. Yoka nodded and slung the
drum strapped to his back into playing position. "Then we must
bring these lanterns and fight our way out of the compound—"

"Wait!" The jail's interior and exterior slid together, clicked into
place, within Tink's mind. "There's a way! Ask them—" Most of
those freed looked ill and emaciated; after building the barricades
they had collapsed to the floor. Some, probably imprisoned a
shorter time, seemed stronger. He waved in their direction. "They
can carry the ladders. Both. I saw a—a hatch—" No, that was the
English for it when you were on a ship.

But Lily, as usual, knew what he meant. "I saw it, too!"

While Yoka drummed to *Mbuza* from atop one leaning ladder,
Tink climbed the second's rungs till his arms reached the ceiling.
The square door lifted easily. Darkness above it. But not night. The
stifling air hung still and sweaty, and then it moved without wind
and he heard breath—soldiers? More than one person. "Hullo?"
His voice struck dully against walls and ceiling. How large—

Metal sang. Tink ducked. *"Haaaghh!"* A blade chopped down where his head had been. The ladder rocked as a flashing sword sheared a chunk from the top of one of its legs. Tink fell, stunning himself. He heard the bang of a rifle. Several more shots. A lengthy quiet.

"They must be out of ammunition," Lily said.

What if they're bluffing, he thought, but he couldn't say it. His mouth wouldn't work. Nothing would. He lay helpless in the dirt as Lily went back up the broken ladder to the trap. The trap door. Why?

"Give us the king and we'll spare you!" he heard her demanding. So that was why. What made her think, though, that King Mwenda was in the jail's attic? She couldn't know that. Could she?

Beyond the passageway's far end, Yoka drummed on.

A rush of cool air flowed over Tink. The ceiling boards creaked above as whoever had been hiding up there crossed the room—which must have an additional hatch open now: the breeze! The drumming had ended. He made an effort and rolled onto his side. One more push and he was sitting, lolling against the wall. "Lily!"

He had called to her aloud. She came back to him. Her odd eyes gleamed. "I'm sure they've run out! But they won't escape," she informed Tink. "Captain Renji's asking Yoka to redirect *Mbuza*. Come along. You'll be fine. We may not even need to pull the ladder up with us if there are steps."

"Steps? Steps where?"

"In the attic. From there to the roof, of course." Of course.

Tink wanted to climb up on his own. His left hand refused to clamp onto the rungs, so he gave his axe to Yoka and used the right. The ladder's top was whole again—no, this must be the second one, the ladder Yoka had been using.

A lamp lit the rough boards of the roof's underside. A slanting square of black marked the hole in it. Lily and Captain Renji stood underneath, with two men who must be released prisoners. No one else was in the room. But quiet whispers and soft scuffling noises filtered in by way of that hole.

Yoka emerged into the attic after him. Lily mimed drawing the ladder up and they did as bid, dragging it over to her. The new men made to lift it and prop it into place, but Captain Renji blocked them. Tink knew why: it was long enough that setting it up so close would leave several feet sticking out in plain sight of the men waiting on the roof.

Yoka and the captain stared up at the empty heavens. Tink put his bad arm around Lily's shoulders and got his recalcitrant fingers to caress her short, curling hair. He could feel its slipperiness sliding against his skin. She leaned against his side, moved her sweet mouth next to his ear. "Stay still. After a while, they'll think we've given up. When *Mbuza* returns we'll act quickly: swarm up and take them by surprise. Capture the king and sail off safe."

He nodded. It sounded like a good plan. He turned her toward him and they kissed. For a very long time.

A far-off thrum he'd hardly noticed in his desire came nearer. Lily backed away from him a little. "It's here," she said, though he didn't hear her, only saw the words' shapes on her lips. By now the noise of *Mbuza*'s engines drowned out everything else.

No need for silence anymore. The ladder hit the hole's sides and up onto the roof went Captain Renji. Somehow Lily was right behind him. Tink shoved the new men out of his way and went next—but Yoka still had Tink's weapon! He ran forward anyway, over the roof's shallow peak. Shadows at the roof's opposite end rushed toward him. Leopold's police. He ran faster, past his love, yelling, waving his fists. Punching, kicking—then he broke through the thugs to where a man lay on his face on the tiles. Iron links bound his ankles and wrists. This must be the king.

Tink bent over him. Lily caught up and together they helped the king stand. He would need to be rid of these chains to ascend *Mbuza*'s ropes. The king attempted to say something, but shouts surrounded them: incomprehensible orders, a gunshot, confusion—then he and Lily were once more free of attackers, and somehow he'd got his axe from Yoka. Blood dripped down the handle. It was becoming slippery. He wiped it clean on his thigh and tightened his grip.

At this side of the roof, *Mbuza*'s wood and rope ladder swung low. He urged the king to lie flat and gestured for him to hold his arms over his head and wide as possible. Then Tink chopped down through the chain. His axe's blade bit deep into the roof, but several links broke—more than necessary. He wrestled the axe's handle around till it came up. Kicking the king's legs apart, he prepared him for the next blow. It took three. The third came down an inch from Lily's hand as she tugged on a damaged link. Tink stared, aghast at what he'd almost done, wasting precious moments.

A yank on his arm made his mind start to work again. Escape. *Mbuza*. Silhouettes were visible against the aircanoe's one light: the captain and Yoka, already on their way up. One freed prisoner had followed them; it was another who urged Tink toward the rope ladder, then grasped its dangling foot.

Tink looked around. Lily, unhurt, lagged behind, helping the staggering king. Tink turned back and propped the man's other side. The ladder's foot had dropped temporarily lower. The king pulled himself up along it, groaning but making progress. Lily let him get a few rungs ahead before she started. Tink waved at the man who'd brought him to his senses, indicating it was his turn. The man shook his head no. He wanted to stay. Tink couldn't argue with him. He didn't even know what language to use. The ladder's end rode up. Tink clung to it, then hoisted himself higher till his feet rested on a rung.

Only he, his love, and the king remained on the ladder. He heard the thud of ballast hitting the ground and *Mbuza* rose suddenly. One of them could fall! He cried out for the captain to be more careful, but of course no one heard.

Their ascent steadied. Tink glanced down at the bright square in the prison's roof, the attic's entrance. The light would blind him; averting his eyes, he caught a writhing movement and a white flash. A gun banged—a last shot by a wounded enemy. He only knew they'd scored a lucky hit when a hot liquid began to rain down upon him. Softly.

He prayed the blood was the king's. He saw when at last he tumbled into the basket behind Lily that it wasn't.

Sticking to the plan, *Mbuza* flew high above Kinshasa's perimeter, loosing bombs and baskets of burning pitch. Plenty of havoc. Plenty of chances for the rest of those freed to escape the town. Plenty of time for Lily to tell Tink how to construct a tourniquet for her ruined right leg.

Lily had worked with Mrs. Hunter and Mademoiselle Toutournier for years, so she was the closest the rescue expedition had brought to a doctor. By the light of the lamp the new man held, she examined her own wound, shivering. "S-some of the sh-sh-shot has prob-probably l-lodged in the-the t-t-t-tibia." She lay back panting, sweating through the dye.

"Where?" Tink's own sweat was drying fast in the high air. Which wasn't cool enough that his love should tremble like that.

"My sh-sh-shin."

"Why are you cold? What can I do?"

"Shock, I th-think. I n-n-need cov-covering."

His own chest was bare. He had tied his shirt below her red knee, sticking his axe's handle in the knot, trying as he twisted it not to look at the shattered mess above her ankle. The new man wore only rags. A woman carrying a cup came into the lamplight. Tink grabbed the piece of barkcloth hanging from her shoulders and tucked it around Lily.

"Drink this. You are thirsty." The woman with the cup was Nenzima, a fighter and elder. "Water." Tink raised Lily's head and she swallowed eagerly. He should have thought of doing this.

"Thank-thank you! But it t-t-tastes—s-something else?"

"A root," Nenzima confirmed, "to take away your pain."

"I am afr-fr-fraid it's w-wasted." Her eyes closed. "T-Tink."

"Yes, love?"

"You must loose—loose the tourniquet again s-soon. Every twenty m-m-minutes."

He did as he was bid. Seeping blood formed a long puddle on the mat beneath his love's terrible wound. It sank away swiftly as he reapplied pressure.

"It w-will probally still havva be amputatate," Lily mumbled. Tink looked at her face, its bare patches paperlike even in the lamp's golden glow. It had blurred, its tightness slackening. The root water. Would she sleep till they got her home, to help, to the clinic?

"I will fix you a new leg," Tink promised. "A better one." He told her all about it, how it would work, how fine it would be, how strong, how beautiful. For a while she answered his questions, asked him her own, laughed, even, as he described the envy others would feel at her mechanical limb's awesome powers. Then she stopped talking. Then she stopped breathing.

Then she died.

Lusambo, Everfair, November 1897

At least in the caves of Kamina they'd gotten a church started. Here Martha Hunter had no weapons with which to win souls but the field hospital and the tiny village supporting it. And the jungle felt nearer here in Lusambo, somehow, seeming to encroach more than it had at Bookerville. That might be due to this location's heathen name. They would have to come up with another, eventually.

She sighed and stood up from her precarious resting spot. Soon the rainy season would descend upon them, and she must organize the roofed spaces so that there would be room enough for any incoming patients. Since the raid freeing King Mwenda last month, refugees had inundated them. More shelters were being built. They would be finished before the rains if time allowed, but best not to rely on that.

Many natives slept under dugout canoes. She had come down to the river to inventory the vessels in the mission's possession, and to convince herself that others—she among them—could do the same. Again she sighed, remembering the state of the soil below the upturned boat from which she had just risen: damp. Whether due to the river's proximity or the precipitation occurring even during Everfair's "dry" season, it had, in fact, been muddy. Bearable, perhaps, with a thick mat for protection, but it would get worse in only a few weeks.

Perhaps it would be best to give up. Though Mr. Owen turned the colony's conditions to good account in his letters to subscribers, they were, in truth, sadly sordid. Add to a bed of muck the certainty of retaliation by Leopold's troops, the probable danger from crocodiles and other wild beasts—

A loud slap, like leaves against a tree trunk, caught her attention. Animals? An attack? There were sentries; there'd been no shots. Next came footsteps: fast, but walking, not running. Chester? She had told him they needed to talk about changing the traction engine's accommodations; was it entirely necessary to have it take up a whole shed on its own? Fwendi must have informed him where to find her.

But the figure coming out of the bushes flanking the path to the hospital was that of George Albin. Tall as her godson, but not as well muscled—though the shirtless native dress he affected showed developments along those lines . . . and white, of course. And half her age. And madly in love with her.

Martha had avoided him since his arrival from Kamina yesterday. As long as she could. "You find me malingering," she joked. "Really wasting time."

He shook his head, coming to sit on the boat bottom she'd vacated. He smiled up at her through his lashes—unforgivably long and beautiful. "I doubt you're ever really idle, Mrs. Hunter." His language was always respectful. She'd come to believe he wasn't simply expecting her to fall at his feet.

"Well, then, I was planning how we might better utilize the facilities. Miss Toutournier did the best she could before leaving us"— before abandoning her post and necessitating that Martha should come here in the hussy's place—"yet I'm sure I'll hit upon improvements to the current scheme." She went on in some detail, hoping to bore the young man away. He appeared to listen, but then, unexpectedly, her hand was captured and held—tightly—in both of his. From his seat on the boat, he'd gone to kneeling in the dirt.

"Look here, that's all fine, but—what I mean to say is, I want you to marry me." The haughty refusal she should give him caught in her throat. Such desperate eyes.

The boy rushed on. "In another ten days I'll be seventeen. Almost legally a man, in some countries. My father has nothing to say in the matter. As for Mother—"

At last she found her voice. "Your mother would be crushed."

"She would not! There's not a bone in her body that—"

"Crushed," she repeated firmly. "Let go of my hand."

With a start, he freed it. "I'm sorry—I didn't mean—"

"What you propose," she interrupted, "is utterly unsuitable."

"No, I want you to *marry* me! My intentions are hon—"

She continued mercilessly. "The difference in our ages, our races—impossible!"

He was trying so hard. He opened his mouth—Lord God Almighty, his mouth—and she had to speak again to stop him from saying something she wanted to hear. "After losing your sister, your poor mother couldn't bear to have you disappoint her in such a way."

He leapt up as if scalded. "Marrying you wouldn't be anything like that!"

Childless, Martha could only imagine how much Lily's death had hurt Mrs. Albin, who, despite her unnatural tendencies surely had a mother's heart. "Perhaps not quite so bad . . ." She felt herself weakening and fought her feelings down. They must come from the Devil. Mustn't they? She steeled herself: ". . . but bad enough. You will always be a good, Christian—"

"I see how it is." George laughed, a laugh dark and bitter as badly roasted coffee. "Tink's right. I have to *prove* myself."

"What?"

"You need a man, not a boy. I'm going to show you! I'm going to fight under King Mwenda!"

"No!" What could be worse than the death of a daughter? The death of a son.

"You'd dislike that? Dare I hope—"

How could the boy be so foolish? "Of course not! But Mrs. Albin—"

"Hang my mother! Hang her!" Color mounted his smoothly tanned throat, crested on his cheeks. "I mean—it's got nothing to do with her. I love you!" He stood.

Martha remained a little taller than him—though he'd been growing. "George. Are you sure? This is what you want?"

He nodded, started to say something, thought better of it and simply nodded again.

"You're young. In England you could meet—"

"I don't care! Since I saw you onboard the *White Bird,* Mrs. Hunter, I've known I was yours. *Yours.*"

Good. He hadn't presumed to think the converse: that she belonged to him. So many men would have. "I will consider it, then. Consider it seriously—seriously enough to pray." She knelt as he had, smirching her dress. Closing her eyes. The air beside her heated with his nearness as he joined her.

Sometimes God was eloquent. At those times, words came to Martha, songs, whole symphonies played in the quiet moments after she'd made her pleas.

This was not one of those times. Yet, once several long minutes passed, she understood what steps she had to take.

The Reverend Lieutenant Wilson was wrong. Mr. Owen, though a hopeless atheist, was right. What happened here didn't matter unless the story of it could be told to those who would profit by their example. Everfair must send forth a missionary. Since the reverend lieutenant refused to leave his "flock," it would have to be George. Her groom.

"We will become man and wife the day following your birthday," Martha said. And the day after that, they would part. Without consummation.

"Mrs. Hunter! May I—" He reached his long, bare arms toward her.

"Call me Martha," she said, "but refrain from embracing me for the moment." She gave her fiancé a rueful smile. "I have conditions for you, George, and if you can't accept them, there will be no wedding."

London, England, April 1899

◄ "Splendid to see you again, George." Jackie meant it. Since he couldn't be with Daisy for the moment, her son would do. Though of course not in all ways. Dismissing his unsuitable recollections from his mind, he pushed back from his overloaded desk. "You made good time from Bristol. I was this moment leaving to make sure my landlady had arranged every—"

"Shall I go with you?" The boy's voice was identical to his mother's; an octave lower, but otherwise hers.

"Are you sure? You may stay here if you like, and recover from your journey."

"Oh no, I've been cooped up in a railway carriage since morning."

"In that case, we must get you a walk."

The day outside was more like May than April, but Jackie, remembering his own adjustments to the climate, insisted on George wearing a cap and muffler a clerk had left in the offices last week. Surreptitious glances and reflections on windows they passed let him study his companion further: the same short, dark brown curls as his mother's; the same long, fine nose. His growth during almost a year's separation had sharpened the resemblance. Even the young man's gloveless hands, slender yet capable-looking, brought Daisy's to mind.

"Just a half-mile or so more," Jackie announced, upon unexpectedly meeting George's piercing gaze.

They passed a pastry-maker's establishment with tables and chairs on the pavement, in imitation of a Parisian café. The boy's pace slowed, and Jackie remembered how few chances he must have had to feed himself while traveling. "Mind if we make a stop here?" he asked. "I'd forgotten my dinner till now, and Mrs. Hoate generally doesn't serve anything in the way of refreshment before evening."

"No, I—"

"It shall be my treat. Come, now." He held open the shop door. After several seconds, the boy consented to enter.

They split a pork and apple pie accompanied by weak cider. Their server, a sturdy-boned woman of middle years, brought it out to them on a tray laden with china, glasses, and cutlery, and left as soon as she'd been paid.

Public though the spot was, Jackie judged it safe enough to talk. Though he kept himself to inconsequential topics while the boy dispatched his fair portion of the pie, and let him drink a third of his drink.

Then he got to the nub of things. "You did not see your sister die." Best to be blunt.

"No. No, sir. But I have no doubt—I saw—I did see her— remains." Beneath its tan the boy's face paled.

"But as to how she died—"

"No doubt," George repeated. "Murdered by Leopold's men. There were witnesses, reliable witnesses to that."

Sorrow and triumph mingled in Jackie's emotions. Communication with the region was not secure, and he'd been unable to stress the importance of clarity on this point. "You have no qualms about appearing as a speaker? About countering any claims that might be made by our opposition?"

The boy shook his head. "It's what she would have wanted, sir," he mumbled to his crumb-strewn plate.

Not, perhaps, as commanding a figure as Wilson. But a white, which would open certain important doors to him. And young. Teachable. Handsome, of course.

They began that night, in Mrs. Hoate's parlor, at the meeting of the Fabian Society he'd called when the wire warning of George's arrival came. His own rooms were too incommodious for a gathering of more than five people, and this was eight. Ellen Albin acted as secretary in her husband Laurie's absence, as she had for the eight months of his prolonged illness.

With a bit of prompting, Lily Albin's brother told the story of her death quite affectingly, placing the blame for it on the head of the tyrant, where it ultimately belonged. Jackie's proposed itinerary for him met with complete consent. He was also able to arrange for the Society to pay travel costs, as he'd expected when asking—no more than a formality, given his importance.

After the room emptied, Mrs. Hoate emerged from her sewing corner to survey her precious furnishings for damage and Jackie escorted his protégé to the second floor, where he would lodge. The serving girl, Polly—Mrs. Hoate's niece—had already been in and left the boy's one small piece of luggage.

"You'll be comfortable," he assured George, watching him pace between the bed and washstand. "Not much difference between this and your shipboard quarters, I believe."

The boy turned and traced a new path, window to wardrobe. "This is larger." A pause. "And it feels—much higher up."

Nothing to be done about that. "W.C. is the next door down, to your left." A moment of doubt; would he remember how to use a toilet? "Shall I show you?"

An enigmatic smile lit George's face. "Thank you, but that's not at all necessary."

"Is there anything I can get for you before retiring, then? I'm in the apartments right below you and fronting on the street. If you find you require something, never mind the hour: send the girl or come and knock yourself—"

"Have you paper for writing letters? Envelopes, and so forth?"

Astonished by the simplicity of the boy's request, Jackie strode off to comply. Returning, he saw through the partially open door how George had set a few books on the wardrobe's flat top. Creaking hinges betrayed Jackie as he stepped in. The boy started as if caught stealing, banging an arm against the wardrobe door. The books and an indistinctly seen, unframed photograph propped next to them—he got the impression of a seated female—fell over.

"Here you are." Jackie offered the boy a pile of stationery and a pen. "Anything more?"

George made no attempt to right the books or portrait, but took the supplies from him immediately. "Will I be able to buy postage to Africa? Or—how do you manage your correspondence with Everfair?"

Of course. The boy was writing to his mother. "Let me take care of it for you at the offices when we go in tomorrow morning."

At breakfast, George ate only oatmeal, seeming bemused by Mrs. Hoate's eggs and sausages. Jackie supposed they weren't the most African of foods.

They waited briefly on the street for the omnibus, time being too short for a repeat of yesterday's strolling walk. "I nearly forgot!" George exclaimed. He reached inside his worsted jacket for a thick, unsealed envelope and gave it to Jackie.

The envelope was not addressed to Daisy. An unused strip of the new adhesive gum coated its open flap, but Jackie didn't close it himself, merely tucking it into his own inner pocket.

The 'bus came. It was crowded; even the "garden seats" on top were taken. Jackie and George stood surrounded by men and women on their way to work, so no more was said till they arrived.

Upon his most recent return from the colony, Jackie had taken up residence at Mrs. Hoate's and acquired, at Matty Jamison's urging, the business offices housing the Society's campaign against Leopold. Matty opined that established offices gave the enterprise an air of credibility. The playwright was paying for them, so naturally, Jackie—and thus the Society's trustees—humoured him.

Climbing the stairs to their prime first-storey location, Jackie grinned and ushered the boy ahead of him. A brass plaque screwed to the outer door proclaimed the premises as those of the "Inter-Benevolent Anti-Dishumanitarian League," a new organization Jackie had created to orchestrate the actions of the many disparate groups—some in fact sponsored by churches—the Fabians had forged into a movement aimed at Leopold's defeat. His total and utter defeat.

Inside the door lay a warren of rooms meant to be divided up according to the importance of their occupants. Jackie had demolished this hierarchicalist notion, placing his desk in the first and smallest room. Filing cabinets and deep shelves lined most of the walls, with maps pinned above them. The back room, intended for the chiefest officer of whichever enterprise claimed these apartments, he'd filled with a broad-topped table and hard-backed chairs. Here he bestowed George, giving him materials with which to prepare a more formal speech than last night's.

For privacy's sake, Jackie then repaired to the floor's washroom.

The letter was addressed to "Mistress Martha Livia Hunter Albin, Lusambo, Everfair, Central Africa." But the opening salutation ran: "My darling Wife . . ."

Jackie held the pages aside, considering whether to continue. He'd had no scruples previously, but they emerged upon learning now that the letter was personal—had the woman actually *married* the boy? Surely Daisy must have had some say in the matter?

The door's knob rattled as someone tried unsuccessfully to enter. He thrust his guilt aside and began again.

My darling Wife,

I have arrived safely in England, thanks in great part to the Reverend Lieutenant's warnings. We took on threats, besides coal and more provisions at Freetown, in the person of a business agent for a concern dedicated to the manufactur of bicycles in Lyon. This smoky-sounding enterprise was called either "Brummages Freres" or "Clement et Compagnie"—the gentleman made diffrent answers to me and to the ship's purser on this head. Perfectly innocent if it was true, but no explanation for him entering my cabin late on our first night out. I don't believe his tale of thinking it was his own. He wasn't *that* drunk—probably wasn't drunk at all.

But don't worry, I was awake and waiting for him. Had my knife out, pretending as if to trim my nails—in the dark! That sent him off mighty speedy!

Well, I kept my wits about me, and I won't bore you with
what were most likely his other attempts, but will only say
that I got a rope to rig up my door so even if he had the key
it wouldn't open for him, and took care never to sit at his
table during mess. So you see I mean to return to you and
hold you to your promises. And then you'll finally realize I
really love you and am not just infatchuated.

As for Mr. Owen, he's friendly as before, so maybe he don't
know about you and me. So I've left this letter open so he'll
have no trouble reading it—

Here Jackie flushed with chagrin, but persevered grimly, since he
was near the letter's end.

—and will mark if he treats me worse afterwards. Though
he doesn't seem to turn up his nose at my mother despite her
affaire with Mlle. Toutournier, who as you say admits to
being mixed.

A deeper flush.

At any rate I suppose it's inevittable that a spymaster like
he is figures a way to find out everything, so better to expect
he will from the start and play along with him.

The last page after this is my copying down of the schedule
he has set up for me to go around speaking about Lily, and
the names of people I am to meet with. There does seem
some overlap with your list.

I have tried my best not to tire you with "romantickal
schoolboy effusions" like you asked. It is hard, but I am
grateful for what time we have had together and the hope for
more soon, and will close with,

> My deepest and most *patient* adoration,
> Your husband,
> George Albin

Loka, Everfair, to Yaoundé, Cameroon, August 1899

At his word, men flew.

King Mwenda wondered if his success since Kinshasa meant he had regained his spirit father's favored course. First in Bangui, now here, soldiers he had recruited floated down from hovering aircanoes to fight Leopold's fleeing invaders. Each wore a jumpsheet: one thin cloth-and-rubber wing tied to his back. Astride the steam bicycle his paddlers had moments ago unloaded and rolled up the Ubangi River's banks, the king stared searchingly at the patch of dark, dark blue visible above the looming trees. There! A black figure descended slowly, dangling below his wing, vulnerable—but no lights shone upward yet from the unsuspecting town.

Only three more men flew down before the shots and shouting started. Mwenda yearned to join the battle. But look at what had happened to him last time he gave in to so typical a young man's urge: capture and imprisonment, with the Poet Daisy's daughter dying during his rescue. And he had lost his right hand due to the tightness of his bonds. Yes, the new arm the Mah-Kow Tink provided served to impress those Mwenda talked to with his allies' prowess. There would have been other ways to do that, though, without so much suffering.

He had been warned. He had learned to listen.

Sighing, still reluctant, the king turned away. His path lay westward, in the opposite direction from besieged Mbandaka. He and his attendants could have gone by aircanoe, but Mwenda had rejected the suggestion: it wouldn't have allowed his subjects to feel his presence among them. Travel upon rivers would have been easier; however, those were watched. Captain Tombo had advised against them, and the king had listened, though according to Fih-rank, the white coming with them to take care of the bicycles, the machines' maker Winthrop wouldn't like that the machines stayed so wet for so long.

It took sixteen days—four full markets—till they reached Weh-Sso, on the swamp's far side. Men who lived in this land had led them through by the driest trails they knew, which meant a considerable time. The distance was nearly as far from Weh-Sso to the rendezvous at Souankay, but that part of the journey lasted only eleven days. They were able to ride the bicycles more frequently than they pushed them, for the earth was less mirey. The noise of their engines was the only worry, as they were nearer the Dja River's—now called the Ngoko—course than was truly safe. Any of Leopold's thieves sailing there might overhear them. The king worried about that only a little, trusting in his spirit father's protection. But he did worry.

At last one morning they arrived upon higher ground: cultivated fields rose in gentle ripples above the forest's lingering shade. Empty houses were dispersed among them. This was another magic the king's commands had worked: towns full of people had become invisible. Even those not sworn to be his subjects.

Potential recruits awaited them in a shallow valley near the highest hill's crown. Gratefully, Mwenda breathed in the cool air. Fih-rank assisted him to dismount, and another attendant set forth his throne. He assumed his seat, Captain Tombo standing to his side.

This was a small group: only two hands of hands. Men and women both. No young children; that was good.

"You are all prepared to kill and die?" asked Captain Tombo. "Or have you any questions?"

Of course they had many. Fih-rank demonstrated the power of the bicycle, riding it around the gathering in faster and faster circles. But most fighters wouldn't be using these, since so few of the machines were yet available. In answer to brave offers from prospects willing to try riding one, the captain unrolled instead a sample jumpsheet. Broad as half their meeting space, its thin fabric rattled softly in the morning's breeze. The hardened tears coating it made the barkcloth impenetrable to the air.

A round-bellied maiden fingered the material thoughtfully. "This is wonderfully beaten!" she said. "So thin—nice and even, too! But why haven't any women painted designs on it?"

"They have," Captain Tombo explained. "But Queen Josina conceived that the blessing decorations and their background could both be rendered in black. She caused gardenia juice to be added to all the vine tears used. You may sense what has been drawn by touch."

"Ah!" Amazement lit the girl's face as she discovered the truth of this.

Several would-be recruits were missing hands, left or right. They approached the king, but said nothing. It wouldn't be wise.

Mwenda spoke into their silence. "I wield a gift from our allies." He raised his arms, and, with his flesh hand, removed his other hand's sheath. Two blades gleamed in the sun. Murmurs of appreciation at their beauty rose from his subjects' mouths.

The heat of this mechanical hand's working was kept far from his body by a wooden extension—the Bah-Sangah had insisted on that, and even so countenanced its use for short periods only. Reaching past the arm's base he pulled out the globe-shaped engine's baffle and the power of the separated earths mingled and burned. Steam flowed inside its tiny tubes and soon overflowed out of vents pierced in its glittering sides. To pass the moments till it became fully pressured, he slashed at a broom an attendant held before him, clipping its thick, braided handle into pieces.

When that was gone, he polished the knives of his hand and looked about for a more impressive target. The leaves of a grove of young figs danced lightly in the wind near one edge of the valley. Close enough? He judged so, and had Captain Tombo clear people out of the way.

On his feet now, Mwenda cocked his arm back to position his weapon hand behind his head. His other hand he brought in front of his chest, palm up. Praying to his spirit father for good aim, he slapped the spring on the elbow joint and threw free his new shongo.

Thok! It had flown true and buried itself in the tree trunk he intended! Just as when he had announced how to answer their enemies eleven seasons ago. . . . He grinned, satisfied, and brandished the remaining stump, the end of the arm off of which the new knife had launched. This was fitted with short, sharp spikes: a wicked club for fighting face-to-face.

Of course none of the maimed among the new fighters would merit such a fine piece of work. They were happy enough, when *Mbuza* arrived, accompanied by the recently built aircanoes *Zi Ru* and *Fu Hao,* to receive the simple hooks and knives their crews distributed.

That day and the next were spent in training recruits how to drop out of the aircanoes. Early on the third morning, all but six of them boarded *Zi Ru,* bound south and east to take Matadi. A larger force would be needed soon for the conquest of Kinshasa. The king's party forged onward.

Rumor spread ahead of them, sped by the drums' voices. Twice as far they rode to the next rendezvous, their party growing to double its size. Twisting paths clung to the hillsides, barely sheltered by bananas and oil palms, their long, green leaves affording only spotty protection. When boat motors grumbled up and down the Dja, the travelers hid as best they could, flattening themselves sometimes in the dirt. Finally they deserted that river and all the others for the hills' highest crests. Soon after, they descended to Yaoundé.

A crowd of more people than the king could count awaited them there. He asked the white man how many. They had numbers as high as those of the sky-watching tribes to the north. The word the white man used was "thousands."

Accordingly, he gave orders for music to follow their demonstrations. Tonight, a dance of celebration! Mwenda would display his skill and stamina, would laugh and show his shining teeth. Would make himself believe in happiness, that others might share in his belief. So many wanting to fight for their most just cause— assuredly they would win! They must.

N'dalatando, Angola, to Luanda, Angola, Aboard Santa Librada, and Aboard Gloriana, May 1900

▌Gratefully, Josina turned her cheeks to receive the kiss of N'dalatando's light evening breeze. The high ground of this outpost of her father's people made it convenient for aircanoes to come and go. Also it rendered the environs of the sacred well located here invitingly cool—appropriate to Oxun's mysteries.

She'd stayed here sufficiently long, participating in the proper ceremonies. Stopping at this temple accorded well with her king and husband's desire that she voyage out of Everfair in search of allies against Leopold. Disguised it also. But now she must move on.

The Poet's malaria-stricken daughter Rosalie lay in the temple pavilion's shade. Satisfied that the ants had bitten her patients' arms and ankles enough times, Josina gathered them up again in her honey-lined basket. This she set inside the jar of earth to be carried back inside. Then she turned to her not-quite-white sister, who knelt next to her. Lisette had followed the queen here to N'dalatando after the queen's recent arrival. She had dared to bring the sick child in her care across the border dividing Angola and Everfair, seeking learning and healing. Would she go further?

"The maiden will sleep for five more days—a market, at least," Josina told her. "Recovery will be slow." She spoke in French.

"But she will be well now? You've cured her?"

"Yes." To Lisette it could be said; eventually she, too, would be a priest. "Yet you must give her only water at first—boiled water. Cover her in a fever, fan her in her chills."

"And when may we return her to her mother?"

Josina frowned. "Best to bring the mother here. A flight to Kamina would not be a wise undertaking during recovery—not for a good while." Aircanoes often flew so high now to avoid Leopold's forces that their occupants were exposed to a measure of cold much less beneficial than the mild coolness of this place.

"If you accompanied—"

"I don't plan on going in that direction. As you know. And I'm staying on here only a little longer. Send a message."

A moment of quiet. The maiden Rosalie breathed slowly, evenly, already. The small animals inside the ants had begun their work after just one application; the ritual called for five. This had been the fifth.

"I prefer not to have to see the mother," said Lisette.

"That's easily done. Come with me, as I've asked."

"Nor Mr. Owen, if you are to meet with him."

Josina peered up through her long, dark lashes. Her sister's face was calm; why did she bother to mask her jealousy? "When you see him, he will have to see you," Josina pointed out.

A sour laugh. "That's no disincentive. The man hardly knows he hates me. Or why."

"Those are things he may eventually figure out. Perhaps your absence will help? No, I don't plan to encounter him."

"You really wish me to continue with you? Really?"

Josina did. Respect and genuine affection were part of this; practicality, too, for Lisette's familiarity with Europeanisms would be a great help on this trip; also, the time could be used to tutor her in Oxun's mysteries. Most important, though, the cowrie oracle had specified that she should come.

The queen used words and more than words—charms, offerings—to persuade her, but not till she saw Lisette mounting her steam bicycle next to the track to Luanda was Josina sure of her sister's decision. The maiden Rosalie had been awake for a whole day by then; the Poet, her mother, had arrived just the previous evening. Apparently there was some scene. Perhaps the Poet demanded to hear from Lisette how her eldest daughter had fled from Lisette's care. Perhaps Lisette hadn't felt quite as firm as she wished about rejecting the chance to be with her love again, compensating for her wavering desire with the bruising brusqueness of manner Josina had frequently observed in her.

At any rate, there Lisette was that morning, smiling as if everything had been arranged for weeks. A cart attached behind the bicycle held her belongings, which Josina recognized from the house they'd shared here—though not last night.

The first day of their journey there was no need to engage their bicycles' engines. They rolled ever downward, the slightest of slopes leading them at last to the encampment at Itombe her father's people had prepared. That night, again, the queen and her sister stretched out their mats together. Sifa and Lembe, who had walked the miles Josina and Lisette rode, slumbered beside them, exhausted, seeming undisturbed by their whispers.

Since anyone could be listening, even those she supposed asleep, Josina didn't dare talk of secrets, but only of customs needful to know. "Do they truly wear more than one layer of garments? And cover their arms and feet as you do?" she asked.

"Yes."

"It must be colder in your country than on a mountain top. I will trade some of the jewelry my mother's father gave to me, and purchase proper clothing," the queen declared. "And you will help me choose what to buy."

Luanda's markets supplied the queen with strange, rich fabrics and matching thread, feathers, dyed palm fronds, beads, and tanned skins. Lisette was not much assistance there, but later, in the quarters provided by the Portuguese governor, she described to Sifa such European women's fashions as she recalled after fourteen seasons away. Sketching them out on their house's walls with the last of the body paint, Sifa grew quietly thoughtful. Then she and Josina consulted on what to change.

The results were elegant, though not, perhaps, what anyone would expect. Lisette tactfully alluded to this as they stood on the deck of their ship, *Santa Librada,* sailing south. Because of the freshness of the ocean air the queen had finally been able to don one of her new outfits: flaring panels of cotton gathered at her waist and sewn together down to just below the knee; a low, long-sleeved bodice formed of tightly wrapped silk; four pieces of barkcloth set end-to-end and worn as a shawl; sandals; netted gloves; and an open-weave hat adorned with beads and peacock plumes. In this it would still be possible to dance. And as her sister said, "The queen doesn't follow the style; she sets it."

They'd taken passage to Cape Town aboard an ancient coastal vessel sailing under the Portuguese flag. Lisette was much vexed that *Santa Librada* moved without use of her beloved steam, and heartened when they changed, after landing and negotiations there, to a newer ship. Though Lisette tried to disguise it, pretending interest she ought to have felt in the treaties Josina entered into for her husband, her father, and Lisette's own country, she was clearly more interested in the ships.

Patiently she explained how impressed with her pseudo-European dress and manners regional leaders had inadvertently revealed themselves to be at every meeting. Her sister nodded. "Yes, yes. You've made quite the splash. But you should have brought Daisy instead," she complained. "She cares more about politicking and so forth."

Spiritual lessons progressed more easily. Sifa and Lembe knew the earliest part of what Josina had to teach; on *Santa Librada* classes were held in their presence, anywhere, and at any time. Their British vessel, *Gloriana,* carried few passengers from the start, and by the time it reached Durban, it was virtually empty. Without seeking the purser's permission, the queen availed herself of an unoccupied cabin. She always left its door open, but spoke quietly enough that only Lisette heard.

"All Africans are with us," she said as they left their next-to-last port. "Khoi-Khoi to Haya—Cape of Good Hope to Dar-es-Salaam. And you have convinced the German tribe. Now the British, and then your French—"

"Don't call them mine!" Lisette twisted her mouth, blinked and shook her head as if to rid her wide eyes of an ugly sight. "I am an Everfairer, through and through."

"But they must be yours, the French!" the queen insisted. "They'll only laugh at *me,* like the Germans did." She removed her hat and bent to set it on the floor in front of her. This one was more closely wrought than the first Sifa had made, and broader, and higher, and decorated merely with a strip of barkcloth. "When we reach Mombasa—"

"The English won't laugh. You take yourself far too seriously for that."

"Which is why they most certainly will!"

Lisette splayed three fingers over her closed mouth, considering, then opened it. "You are probably right. So it is to be up to me again? No doubt most of them will still believe me wholly white, if Mrs. Hunter's silence is to be trusted." She didn't mention trusting her lover, who also knew of her black roots.

"I'm sure it is. That will make a difference in your treatment—"

"But which embassy shall I start with? English? French? *Belgian?*"

"Of course you must avoid Leopold and any of his agents, as you very well know how. You did so before—don't even joke! Begin with whichever of the others you like." Josina gestured dismissively. "The English will have the biggest presence, but that makes no importance—you'll take them in turns, in any order. Then, on each ambassador, you will perform our charm."

"The Five Yellow Scarves?"

"It is the simplest."

"And once I've done the charm, you'll ask them for support, which the spell will render them agreeable to give." Lisette frowned out of the cabin's little window.

"You do not believe? Yet you study diligently."

"Let us say I entertain multiple possibilities."

The question of which embassy to visit first was settled upon their steaming into port. A British emissary boarded *Gloriana* before they could disembark. A thin-limbed white, Mr. Twicket stood dry beneath the warm rain pouring from Mombasa's sky, protected by a red-clad servant holding an enormous umbrella. He offered them the use of more umbrellas, servants, and a carriage, and personal escort to his country's compound, where, he said, a letter awaited Mademoiselle Toutournier.

Kamina, Everfair, January 1901

"My dear Daisy," began Lisette's response to the letter Daisy had so unfortunately sent to Mombasa. Daisy had memorized its entire text, from blithe salutation to pointed close. She might as well have sewn its pages into her undergarments—she never parted with them. They were all of Lisette she had left.

In the cool darkness of her cavern chamber—shared now with but one child—Daisy pressed the letter paper to her and visualized the contents as if reading them by grace of the gift of psychometry:

> I'll do as you say. But don't write me. I feel sure you are correct, and I can best serve Everfair's interests by continuing abroad. However, and let me be blunt, your promise of a sustained correspondence would cause more pain than pleasure—especially via your proposed go-between.
>
> Of course, if you have some urgent reason, a matter of life and death, you may reach me through sending a message to Mr. Owen. As you suggest, I'll be in contact with him regularly, making him my reports.
>
> For the other matter, I quite understand. Nor do I blame you, or Mr. Owen, or Laurie, or anyone else concerned, though I hope you are mistaken. But I will do nothing to upset your scheme of provoking a possibly dangerous response from Leopold by your continued presence within his reach.

Only I don't like it. Especially not as a motive for our
continued separation.

Yours (as you well know),
Lisette Toutournier

Paper being precious, Daisy hadn't managed to keep a copy of
the letter that prompted these brief lines. However, it had taken
her so many drafts to get it right—well, it had not been right even in
its final version. But trying to shape it into some semblance of what
Jackie had said was needed, she'd come to know it well enough.

What she'd ended in sending—in addition to urging an appeal
to the Congressional Committee on African Affairs—perhaps said
too much of the idea of using Everfair's white settlers, and she
herself in particular, as bait. That strategy, as she reiterated multiple times, was why Daisy must remain in the colony while her
love lived indefinitely abroad as a spy.

There was very little danger involved in staying here, in Daisy's
own opinion. Too little to matter. In truth, nothing did much
matter, since Lily's death.

She'd thought that if she wrote as Jackie asked, that he, at least,
would remain in Kamina. After their last encounter, especially. He'd
said he loved and esteemed her. The latter word rather undercut the
former, but never mind. The needs of the Society overrode her own,
and no use pitying herself. She still had Rosalie, recovered now
from her illness, but at thirteen, endearingly dependent on Daisy,
and likely to continue so for years to come.

Tucking the grimy letter inside her skirt pocket—the last time
she'd looked at it in the light, it had had a distinctly grey cast—
Daisy emerged into her home's main chamber.

Here there was light. Sparse wood and metal furnishings threw
shadows on the cave walls: some bare, some covered with woven
grasses. Daisy picked up a brass lamp from the tin stand near the
exit. She believed the wick protruding from its spout was also
made at least partially of metal, though thin enough to burn. A
globular, pierced screen shielded it, casting moving points of light
on the stone walls of the passage as she walked.

Only a short distance up the uneven incline of the passage, she came to the high-ceilinged, cisternlike cave designated by them as the Mote Room. It was too inconveniently shaped to be of much use other than for these meetings: nets and baskets full of stored goods hung overhead, but the floor could hold no more than the mat Nenzima had created to cover it; the white cloth, on which rested the Lamp, a larger copy of the one she held; and the ten people seated around it on the oval mat's tight-sewn edges.

Daisy took the place they'd saved for her near the door. As usual, she was the last to arrive, though she lived the closest. All, however, stayed somewhere within the cavern complex, except during the dry season. Next to her knelt Nenzima, the Bah-Looba fighting woman, and just past her, Alonzo, Queen Josina's cousin. Beside him sat the little Scotch playwright, Mr. Matthew Jamison—or Matty, as he preferred to be called. He took Everfair's principles of equality seriously. Loyiki, back from another round of messages, hunched between him and Old Kanna, who memorized the Mote's monthly sessions for transcription into Everfair's many unofficial tongues—adopting English as their *official* language had been one of their first initiatives.

To Old Kanna's right sat Daisy's foe, Mrs. Hunter—now Mrs. Albin!—the smooth-faced Negro woman who had sent George away. She alone had contrived a chair for herself, a short stool. Her right flank was occupied by her allies: the reverend lieutenant and the youngest of her two inventor godsons, Winthrop. Naturally Mr. Ho Lin-Huang had chosen a seat near him, and Albert, one of the remaining white workers, who completed the circle.

The Mote's factions were made clear enough in its seating arrangements, though the separation between herself and Matty had long posed her a puzzle.

Daisy removed the guard from her lamp's wick and joined its flame momentarily to that of the Lamp, a ceremonial lighting each of the others would have done as they arrived. Then she set her lamp before her on the mat, as with both hands she upended a big pierced-metal bowl—the same design, but for its size, as the guard of the lamp she'd carried—and lowered it onto the lip flaring out around the Lamp's tall spout. This signaled the meeting's start.

Loyiki reported that the war went well on all the fronts he'd visited. Alonzo concurred: the drums told the same story. Tink and Albert had recently returned from the crash site of Leopold's vain attempt to match Everfair's prowess in the air, *La Belgique*. The silk with which he had fashioned his *ballon dirigeable*'s bags was superior to their best barkcloth, the two admitted, but both methods of propulsion he appeared to have tried had proved obviously inferior. His electrical batteries limited flights to round trips of roughly five miles each. They knew this for fact, having stolen and tested one, "and they can't be haulin around endless supplies of em for recharge," Albert explained. The tyrant's new internal combustion engines gave him an improved reach, but their fuel still weighed more and took up more storage space than the Bah-Sangah's special earths, and were quite susceptible to fiery explosions, as well. Such as the one that had destroyed this latest experiment.

Mr. Ho had made quick sketches of the scene, black ink brushed on pale brown bark, and of pieces of equipment too large or fragile to be transported to Kamina's workshops. He seemed glad to turn these over to Old Kanna, and listened quite intently afterward to Winthrop's exposition on their most recent advances in the creation of artificial limbs. His dedication to improving medical prosthetics verged on the tragic.

Daisy had long since forgiven Mr. Ho—Tink, as she'd called him when he was a boy—for Lily's death. He had not killed her. Though he had not saved her, either.

Lisette, who'd been looking after Lily right before she was killed, had gone far away, exactly as Daisy had asked her to do.

Mrs. Albin, on the other hand, she simply couldn't stomach, though if Daisy were to look at the thing rationally, George's exile from Everfair was only what she herself might have ordered to prevent those two from consummating their marriage. What of their probable offspring?

"What of their souls?" the missionary asked, her question a

warped echo of Daisy's thoughts. Dark face and hands speckled with the Lamp's golden glow, like the pelt of a reversed leopard, her eyes glinting in the shade of her straw hat, Mrs. Albin was no more satisfied with their potential victory than if it had been certain defeat. "Church membership has risen by a ridiculously small number: only sixty-two in the last year. The merest fraction—not even a tenth of the natives we've rescued and healed in that time!" She turned to address Wilson. "Can we not be fishers of men? Shepherds of lost sheep?"

Wilson blinked rapidly, his eyes directed across the mat but not meeting Daisy's—or anyone's, as far as she could tell. His lips began moving a moment before he spoke. "Are you sure? We were voted for, chosen to be representatives here . . . and so many attend Sunday services—"

"But do they understand what you're saying? Or is the attraction really your voice, your manner—"

"The sermons are translated."

Daisy interrupted. "Is this truly a matter for the Mote? Can't you discuss such issues elsewhere, another time?"

Matty agreed. "What we must consider today," he said, "is how far we've come in meeting the most common requirement asked of us by those we seek as allies: a national constitution. Do we all have our copies?"

They did. Daisy's comprised a sheaf of twenty crisply folded sheets, into which she'd inserted notes on any clear scraps she could find. She took it out of her skirt and unfolded it. Each of the Mote's other members consulted their own draft, even Loyiki and Nenzima, whom Daisy knew to be illiterate.

The document set up Everfair's political structure in the form of a highly decentralized representative democracy. It was very rough, only the bare bones of what they needed.

Mrs. Albin riffled through the pamphlet she'd sewn together of her copy and shook her head. "Nowhere in here is God mentioned. Obviously this document was drawn up by atheists."

That was probably a good assumption; the framework of it must have been devised back in England by Jackie and Laurie.

"Many of us *are* atheists, ma'am. Skeptics, at the very least," said Albert. "Seems in keepin' with that."

"Hmmph. So I've been complaining. Atheist savages and heathens." Mrs. Albin turned to look at Wilson. He stayed silent. "Winthrop?"

Even seated, the inventor bulked above the other Mote members like a bear. "Well, Godmama, I don't see why we should ask for such a change. Americans are a Christian enough nation without the country's constitution defining them that way."

Was the slaughter of declared Christians—disregarding the Negroes—more likely to gain their side the necessary supporters? Probably. Yet, Lily, their only white martyr so far—

"No! We will lose our strength in lies!" Wilson had risen to his feet, shouting. His hands were balled into trembling fists. "All blessings! All blessings! We call all blessings! They come! They come!"

Shock kept Daisy seated. The lieutenant raved on—was he mad? Nenzima crawled from her spot beside her to the far side of the Lamp and wrapped her arms around the poor man's legs. Oddly, this quieted him.

Mrs. Albin had also wrapped Wilson in her arms—though she stood to do so. Her body shook twice, visibly, containing the throes of his fit, then subsided, slumping with his dead weight.

"Help me. He must lie on his back." Mrs. Albin instructed her godson and Nenzima how to stretch her patient out in the crowded space. She slapped his cheeks in a businesslike way and called for water and more room. Feeling useless, Daisy retreated into the Mote chamber's entrance. If only Lisette had been here . . . or if Lily had been able to continue her studies . . .

"Shall we postpone the rest of this session till later in the day?" she heard Matty ask. "Or—when will he be recovered?"

George's erstwhile wife shook her head, fluttering the Lamp's shielded flame. "I can't say. I haven't the slightest clue."

Baltimore, United States of America, March 1902

A man gestured to Lisette to take his seat, fooled by her appearance. She declined, and gripped the thin pole next to her more securely as the streetcar started up again. She was done expecting to be treated as white consistently. Her clandestine mission seeking financial support from the congressional committee had come to a standstill; this showed the long-term futility of concealment.

In any event, she preferred to stand. The brisk spring breezes of these northern climes no longer chilled her so much, and from her position on the outer edge of the novel open-sided car she could see the tracks, the wires, and, leaning a little, the rounded prominence from which the car's driver controlled their speed—perhaps also their direction? If she could only watch carefully enough, she might learn.

This was her second trip of the day. The first had taken her outbound to Riverview Park, home of an enchanting miniature railway and a beautiful Ferris wheel—not as large as the Grande Roue of Paris, but nonetheless distinctive. It would feature as the setting for an amorous rendezvous in her current tale.

Now she was inbound. She had over an hour of daylight remaining in which to find her way back to the Marble Hill home of the family with whom she stayed. Like the majority of this city's inhabitants, they were Negroes, and they proudly called themselves such, though nearly as light of complexion as Lisette herself.

The car's comfortably regular rocking slowed, and it turned

onto a wider thoroughfare. Traffic thickened, and with it the noises of horses, poorly maintained engines, and independent vendors crying the virtues of newspapers and early farm produce: strawberries, peas, daffodils. Also present: the competing fragrances of many meals being prepared in the hotels and restaurants lining the street. The ripe tideland scents of the wharves, which she was fast learning to ignore, sank beneath these more appetizing aromas, but didn't entirely vanish.

She thought the stop at which she must change lines would come soon. Here was South Street, here Charles. Park Avenue's stop, confusingly labeled "Liberty," would be next. She reached for the cord past the shoulder of a short man in a bowler, but before she could touch it, the bell rang. Apparently another passenger wished the same stop. It was a busy one.

The car drew up to the platform and she was able to dismount quite quickly, thanks to its open sides. Hurrying forward, she caught a mere glimpse of shining levers and switches in the operator's compartment. Its occupant winked at her over a bushy white moustache as he pulled away.

She descended to the crosswalk. She had already rid herself of Mr. Owen's latest missive, taking advantage of a waste receptacle at Riverview. She saw now that, as she'd remembered, a letterbox waited patiently on the street's far side. It was painted a glowing green very different from the crimson used in Britain and on the Continent. She slipped her report on Washington into its slot. None of the committee's members had promised to push for allocating any official monies to their cause, even when approached separately and assured of secrecy.

Mr. Owen would not be pleased to have to inform the Fabians of such poor results. Well, let him form his own embassy, then. Or perhaps he'd rather send Daisy's son in her place? Both he and George were men, both indisputably Caucasian. Perhaps, because of that, they'd succeed where she had failed.

It was not the worst of her failures. Even now, almost six years later, Lisette couldn't fathom how she'd let Lily get away. *There was no use in wondering,* she told herself once more. No use in lamenting the impossibility of asking Daisy for forgiveness. She should not linger in the lost past.

The Park Avenue car was more conventionally designed than the one she'd ridden from Riverview, with fifteen wooden benches mounted perpendicularly to sleek walls. The windows were large, however, and the aisle free of crowding. This time, Lisette did take a seat without urging. A breeze played gently with the spray of artificial violets on the hat of the woman directly in front of her.

Women were frequently given the names of flowers. Lily, whom she refused to think of. Rose; Rosalie, whom she had taken to be cured. Daisy: the day's eye, sun of her existence. Allowing herself the foolish luxury of remembrance, Lisette rode past Madison. The next stop came not much beyond, but by the time she found the entrance to St. Mary's Park, *l'heure bleu* had fallen. Glancing back, she thought she noticed another former streetcar passenger walking in behind her: the man who had sat immediately ahead of the woman wearing the violet-trimmed hat. Another look as he cleared the shadowy trees planted near the park wall and she became sure.

She kept the same pace: fast, but not too fast, the sound of her bootsoles dulled by the bricks' dampness. Lisette was armed. As casually as she could, she pulled apart the looping handles of her carry-all and undid the buttons fastening its top.

It had been her intention to exit the park along its northwest boundary, following Tessier up to Orchard, site of the Lincolns' home. Instead, she took the path curving southward, toward the seminary. Lights shone from the dormitory windows—already the evening's darkness provided a contrast. But the grounds around the buildings were empty.

The curve sharpened. She could no longer see her pursuer, which would mean he could no longer see her. A short hedge set off a small, sweet-scented grove, ghostly flowers clinging to low branches. She hurried around the obstruction and crouched in the trees' midst, bringing her shongun free. Cool brass warmed in her hand.

Yes. This man *was* following her. The growing dusk concealed his features, but not his attitude and movements as he searched for his vanished quarry. Hesitantly he proceeded further down the path, his head turning left and right as he scanned his surroundings. Lisette blessed her sepia-toned leaf-print dress—valuable camouflage—and rose stealthily, drawing aim.

"Halt!" she commanded.

Her target became gratifyingly still.

"Tell me why I should not shoot you dead."

He attempted speech unsuccessfully, his throat seeming not to cooperate. A strangled cough and another try: "Mademoiselle? You might prefer to strike a bargain instead."

"How? A bargain of what sort?"

"Between our governments—an agreement—clandestine aid—"

Lisette refused to let herself relax. "'Our governments'? Which is yours? How come you to be sneaking about, *spying* on me"—easiest to accuse him of doing what she did—"hunting me as if I were a beast?"

"I—I'm a Pinkerton, Mademoiselle, a U.S. government operative, and I apologize—deeply apologize, profoundly! I never meant to approach you *here*."

"I'm certain you're very sorry!" She dropped one hand from the shongun, but tightened the other's grip. It was heavy with the weight of the five blades with which she had loaded it. "Lift your arms. High. Where I may see them." She hoisted her skirts and swung one leg, then the other, over the hedge.

"My identifying papers are in my breast pocket," he said as she came almost within arm's reach. He must have judged her distance by the sound of her steps.

"I'll satisfy myself on that point later, when we're in company." Circling around him, she confronted the man to his face. "Walk ahead of me."

"What an odd pistol!"

"That way." She waved the shongun to indicate their direction and he turned slowly, with what looked like reluctance.

"Is it indeed a weapon?"

"Watch," Lisette answered. She lifted its flat muzzle and pulled its trigger, slicing off a blossoming tree limb, which landed with a sigh at the man's feet.

"Noiseless? Impressive!"

No need to tell him the shongun would have to be rewound after its next shot. "Thank you. Now if you don't mind, let's go." She'd return later to retrieve the poisoned blade.

Should she assure herself that the man was defenseless? That would mean searching him, subjecting herself to the same risk she'd refused to take when invited to examine his papers. If she did so, he'd find a way, no doubt, to take advantage of her nearness— his physique was that of a prizefighter.

At the park's gate, Lisette kept walking but opened her carryall. She shoved the shongun back inside, still aiming it at the man's back. The streetlamp high overhead burned steadily.

Hands lowered to a more natural pose, though well away from his body, the Pinkerton turned his head—enough to see her with one eye. In profile, his forehead sloped outward from beneath his hat brim; his nose was broad, his lips full, his chin jutting. She couldn't tell how dark his skin was. "You're staying with the Lincolns, aren't you?" he asked with hateful assurance.

"Do you know how to go there?"

"Yes." Of course he did.

It was only two more blocks. The Pinkerton walked unerringly to a gently rounded bank of stone stairs leading up to the Lincolns' wooden porch.

"You'd like me to come in?"

"Please." She glanced suggestively at the bag inside of which her hand held the shongun. "We can talk. About making bargains." A servant ushered them through the house's entrance and into the yellow wallpapered room where Mrs. Lincoln and her eldest daughter waited for their guest. Both were scant of figure and sandy of complexion; the mother's face was scattered with brown freckles. Their hair was an impossibly silken black.

"You've met a friend while you were out?" Mrs. Lincoln asked. All the family's members, contacts of Mrs. Hunter's, were jealous of Lisette's time. They wanted her to devote it exclusively to making arrangements for trade between Everfair and those they represented: would-be hoteliers; merchants eager to exploit new markets for their gadgets, herbal formulas, and gambling systems; entrepreneurs looking to Lisette to promote their unnecessary services and help them establish trading bases. Today's excursion to Riverview had been her first escape from such expectations.

"No. Not a friend. He's an agent of some sort. He was following me." She took the shongun out. "Let's see those papers. Place them there, on the piecrust table."

If the documents were to be believed, the Pinkerton's name was Cassius Snopes. It seemed unlikely.

While Miss Lincoln stood ready to pull the bell rope and Mrs. Lincoln pointed the shongun at "Snopes's" heart from across the carpet, Lisette removed from his person three palm-sized guns; a folding knife; a small sack filled with lead pellets; a tiny, corked, blue glass bottle of what was probably acid; and a length of steel wire.

"There was no call to do that," the Pinkerton protested. "I wasn't going to use any of it on you."

"Good." Lisette signaled for Mrs. Lincoln to set the shongun down. Her daughter remained at her station. "To do so would have been an enormous error."

She shut the collection of weapons inside a convenient sewing stand. "Where is Mr. Lincoln?"

"At the Masons," said his wife. She glared like a tragedian at "Snopes." "We expect him *presently*."

"Well. If he interrupts my proposal to you it's all the same to me, if *you* don't mind, Mademoiselle. If you believe he can be trusted, which it seems you might."

"Is your proposal a long one? Perhaps I should be seated?"

"Not necessarily. I'm supposed to tell you that since U.S. citizens were victims in Leopold's attacks, you'll be getting the support you asked Washington for after all. But in secret. Unofficially. Because—" He shrugged and sighed. "You know."

Lisette did know.

Because none of the slain Americans had been white.

Alexandria, Egypt, September 1903

The caves at Kamina were the home Fwendi had known longest in her short life. But Grandmother's Brother Mkoi prophesied she would die—or worse, be captured—if she stayed there to fight. Therefore, he had petitioned the local Mote to find Fwendi a new home, a new life. Mrs. Albin, their representative in Kisangani, had brought the matter before the Grand Mote, and the Poet and even the queen had become interested.

So, heeding their guidance Fwendi had come here to rendezvous with Mademoiselle Toutournier, escorted from Everfair by Matty, who was quickly becoming her favorite friend. During the open-air meals they shared aboard *Fu Hao,* Matty had explained to her that though Grandmother's Brother was correct, there were always other ways to fight and win, and he was going to teach them to her while they waited for Mademoiselle's arrival. That would help Fwendi not to miss Everfair.

So much to learn. The light. The sea, the desert. Horses. She drove one now, down the near-empty boulevard into the public square, cool with dawn. Began circling the still, silent fountain. The sun rose over the Bourse and shadows flung themselves suddenly to her right. From the horse's feet—*hooves*—sprang a floating darkness like an even larger animal. It kept the same pace, rippling over cobbles and curbstones and—

Matty tapped the flesh of Fwendi's left arm. "That's good! Nice and steady! Now you want to tighten your grip—only a little—on this rein."

Easily done. Completing the turn, she noted how the horse's

shadow—and the shadow of their carriage following it—swung behind them and then was swallowed up in the shadow cast by the Bourse.

"Pull up here." Matty pointed past her.

"Here?" Fwendi angled toward the street's extreme edge and told the horse in rein-language that she wanted him to stop.

"Yes! And I'll play groom." Her friend hopped down out of the carriage and went to the horse's head. "Well done, Nash!" He stroked the animal's long brown face. Nash dipped his nose low, resting it on the little man's shoulder.

"If you were to take over fifteen minutes or so upon your errand—"

"But I *have* no errand," Fwendi protested.

"*If* we had come here on an errand and you were taking a long time," Matty said, "and the weather were cooler, Nash would need to be walked about so as not to catch a chill."

"Is he really so delicate? Wouldn't it be better for me to learn how to operate an automobile, then?"

"That, too," Matty agreed. "However, there are far more horses than automobiles at the British embassy." That was where they stayed, thanks to her friend's friends.

"Come down and pet him a bit; let him know you appreciate his hard work."

Tying the reins in a neat knot, Fwendi descended and joined Matty on the ground. The horse shied from her metal hand.

"Just let him get a sniff," Matty said.

"He did that before, back at the stables!" she objected. "Can't he remember?"

"They're not always the brightest creatures, horses."

Fwendi tucked her prosthetic under her left arm for a moment to warm it. When she raised it to Nash's nose again, he tilted his head and flared his black nostrils, then ran them up and down the length of the brass, over the leather cuff, and along the web of straps concealed beneath her dress's sleeve. "Shall I move it?"

"If you're ever going to get used to it— Let me hold the bridle, though."

This model of prosthetic was mostly for show. By flexing her muscles a certain way against the straps, she could bend the jointed fingers; if she crooked the thumb, they would squeeze shut on anything they held. A gear cocked the wrist and a spring released it. It was much less useful than some of her hands. But prettier.

With her flesh hand she caressed the horse's smooth-haired cheek. Done investigating her strangeness, he turned back to Matty, dropping his nose again onto his shoulder, which was not a lot higher than hers any more, Fwendi saw. She was still young, but catching up.

Later that day she selected a different hand to wear. In her opinion it was as beautiful as any. Its polished brass shone brilliantly in the sun streaming through the half-open shutters of the embassy room in which she lodged. But it bore much less resemblance to what most people had at the ends of their arms. Five knives, three of them detachable, stood in place of the fingers.

Matty raised his eyebrows at her choice when she met him on the embassy building's steps.

"I thought our host would like to look this one over," she explained. Really, she didn't know why she'd picked such an outright weapon to wear.

"Do you perceive Mr. Owen as so bloodthirsty?"

She smiled and nodded.

Their appointment was for afternoon tea. She had watched restlessly while the streets outside the embassy filled as the morning wore on, then emptied again in the heat of noon. Now there was once more enough traffic that Fwendi was happy they took a taxicab.

Its windows were lowered. As they bowled down the avenue toward the harbor, cool air blew against them—more than the wind of their passage, for Fwendi saw how the dust stirred ahead of them and to either side. No trees for shade.

Almost as soon as the dazzle of dancing waters became visible between buildings, they pulled up in front of the white-stoned entrance to Le Metropole Hotel. The cab's roof had given Matty shelter on their way here, of course, and during their brief time outside his hat would protect him. She was easier of mind once they had stepped inside the hotel's dim lobby; the sun was never kind to her friend.

As usual, there were stares. Europeans lived at the Metropole. Any non-Europeans in evidence were working, and did their best to efface themselves. They didn't wear fashionable dresses or elaborate, if odd, coiffures. And none of them had brass hands.

Matty had visited Mr. Owen previously here. He ignored the too-loud offers of help coming from the man stationed at the desk straight across the marble tiles, and made his way to the mechanical lift. It was tucked out of sight around the corner, as he had said it would be.

Mr. Owen occupied a room on the fourth story, the Metropole's top floor. They were the only ones going up. Upon arrival the operator opened the sliding doors for them wordlessly. Matty, though older, waited for her to precede him—a form of politeness she believed Europeans such as he would think due to her maidenhood.

Under the ring and rattle of the doors closing behind him Fwendi heard—something. A shout, then something softer. A groaning sigh? A muffled shriek? Then the clap of another closing door, but wooden—that one! At the passageway's end—she saw it shut! She ran toward it and snatched it open—darkness and the clatter of shoes on naked stairs. As her eyes got used to where she was, she found the railing. She clung to it with her left hand, the one that could feel, and started down. Her right she held ready to fire. A lamp flickered two landings below. It went out. Everything was invisible—like at home, in Kamina.

The sound of the footsteps had stopped. Fwendi froze in place. Grandmother's Brother Mkoi had hunted in his youth; he told how one's prey could hide and turn to show teeth and bite. And why was she running after this door-slammer anyway? What made her risk—what was she risking?

"Fwendi!" Faintly, she heard her friend calling her. She went back up to him. At first she thought not to make any noise, then thought again.

"I'm coming!" Fwendi yelled. She stepped as heavily as she could. The door showed bars of light along its edges. She pushed it wide, but the sky blue–walled passageway was empty.

"Fwendi?" The voice came out of an opening on her right. She entered a room hung in shimmering white cloth and trimmed in gold. On the patterned crimson carpet lay a man from whom seeped more crimson. Blood. He was on his back, his face turned away. He rolled his head and she saw it was Jackie—Mr. Owen. His eyes were shut but his mouth was moving. He must be attempting to speak. Matty knelt beside him. Her friend's skin was paler than she'd ever seen it.

"Where is he hurt?" Fwendi asked. She didn't believe the wound was bad; the patch of red wetness grew larger very slowly. Matty removed Mr. Owen's coat and fumbled at his shirt buttons. Blood soaked the collar and sent scarlet fingers up the white cloth covering the man's chest. He breathed quickly, irregularly. She pulled him over onto his side. What showed looked worse. She helped Matty peel away the gore-soaked shirt. She had experience, but the cut on Mr. Owen's scalp was low and hard to find, hidden by his hair, so flat and now so sticky. A long wound, but fairly shallow. Head wounds bled more than others.

Matty brought her a towel and a bowl of water, and she washed away the drying blood. She folded the towel and pressed its freshest surface against the sluggish flow.

"Might I trouble you for—a spot of—spot of brandy?" Mr. Owen's words, a bare whisper, made her look more carefully around the room. Brandy? On a table at its center she could see dishes, silver, glass bottles. Perhaps— Yes, Matty was pouring a clear brown liquid into a china cup. Fwendi supported her patient as he tipped it to his mouth and swallowed.

"What happened?" Matty asked.

"Opened the door. Thought it might be you two or . . . or her. Wasn't."

The wound began bleeding more profusely. "You shouldn't talk," said Fwendi, but Matty kept asking him things.

"'Her'? Who does that mean?"

"Toutournier."

Mademoiselle. Who would say to sew the wound up.

Hearing how she'd just the day before returned from the United States, Mr. Owen had invited Mademoiselle Toutournier to join them. That was who he'd expected. But according to him it was a man in women's clothing who shoved his way into the suite and fought to slit Mr. Owen's throat. The lift's arrival had frightened him off.

Fwendi could sew up the wound herself. Perhaps the hotel provided needle and thread? Matty hunted for them, leaving the room for others in the suite but calling questions over his shoulder: Should they tell the police? The hotel's staff?

A knock. No one answered it. She didn't remember having closed or locked the door. The knob turned. In came Mademoiselle, stopping after only a few steps. "Oh! Is—are you—"

"My apologies," said Mr. Owen, letting the cup fall. "Not dead yet." His eyes were slits.

Mademoiselle crouched down, set aside the cup. "No. Daisy wouldn't care for that. Not in the least." She cocked her chin at Fwendi. "You'd like some help tending to him? Shall I call for a doctor?"

"Don't." The eyes glittered like fish scales. "That's what they plan on."

"That's what who plans on? Fwendi, my emergency kit. It's in my bag, at the bottom."

"The ones who attacked me. The police will blame you. The man wore your sort of costume, you see. And if I'm forced into hospital . . . they'll come again for me there. I won't be able to get . . . get away."

Mademoiselle made a face. "Leopold?"

"His . . . supporters."

Fwendi located Mademoiselle's kit. It was wrapped in yellow-dyed leather. Untying it she found lint, tape, scissors, a curved needle, a reel of thickish black thread, a jar of honey, and three tiny flasks containing colorless liquids. She guessed correctly; the first one she opened was alcohol. She set her handkerchief on her left thigh to soak up what spilled, doused the threaded needle, and handed it to Mademoiselle.

"Thank you. Matty, more brandy?"

When Mr. Owen had drunk another near-full cup and Fwendi had swabbed the wound, Mademoiselle sewed its edges tight together. Fwendi smeared it with honey and helped her bandage it. Matty supported Mr. Owen's staggering steps to the sofa with both arms; he insisted on sitting upright but let them pile pillows around him to keep him that way.

"Let's have a looking glass," he said, once satisfied with his position. His breath had slowed and quieted. No more gasps or panting. "And you may as well eat those sandwiches and cakes and things as let them go to waste."

"Haven't the appetite," murmured her friend. "I doubt any of us do. Looking glass? Where shall I find you one—in the bath?"

"Dressing room table."

Fwendi took a seat with Mademoiselle at the useless tea table but stood almost immediately at a cry from the direction Matty had gone. She met him coming back between a pair of folding doors. In his hand he held a small blade like a miniature shongo: ammunition for the shonguns Winthrop had created. "What's this?" he asked in triumph. "Seems our would-be assassin dropped his weapon!"

Carefully she took it from him with her metal right. Blood coated the largest of its triple cutting edges. In one place this was still wet enough she could dab it off. Gently, gently. Her delicacy was rewarded: a grey gum revealed itself beneath the red.

"What?"

Fwendi carried the knife to Mademoiselle Toutournier. "Mr. Owen, is this what you were attacked with?" she asked. "Fwendi, let him see."

"Is it poisoned, Mademoiselle?"

"Yes, but—have a care!" Mademoiselle reached out, though it was only a momentary spasm, and then Fwendi had her arm back under control. "But if the poison were truly effective, Mr. Owen would by now be dead."

Alexandria, Egypt, September 1903

▰ The bandages looked like an old-fashioned cravat, Jackie assured himself, gazing into the glass above the twin armchairs. The poison had operated as a purgative, and had also weakened him considerably. After a couple of nights' rest, he was not much recovered, but impatience kept him from accepting his condition. He would do. He would have to do. He returned his attention to his visitors. This was the conversation he'd planned to take place the day of the attempt on his life.

"George has rejoined his wife in Everfair," he announced. "Who can blame him?" The boy was twenty-two, almost twenty-three years old, crammed full of all the randiness that age implied. Mrs. Hunter—Mrs. Albin—Mrs. *George* Albin, not dear Daisy—must be on the shady side of forty, and couldn't be getting any younger. Gather ye rosebuds—well, perhaps not buds. Be that as it may—

"Be that as it may, the Inter-Benevolent Anti-Dishumanitarian League needs a replacement. Another inspirational story to tell to prospective backers." He let his gaze rest on Fwendi's hand. "Yours, child."

"*Mine?*" She may have blushed. He couldn't tell with that black skin.

Jamison hastily gulped down the tea he held to his lips and grimaced—probably at the taste. "I've begun working on a new play. Loosely based on Fwendi's life—"

"Yes?"

"I should be able to finish it soon, and when it's produced—"

"It will raise plenty of money for us, yes. But what we *need*—"

"This one will be different—important—it's going to— This is the one people will remember me by. It's going to change the *world*."

A play. "My good man." Making stuff up changed nothing. Careful action such as he advocated by way of the Fabian Society was sure to do the trick. Although propaganda had its place in the big picture . . .

"It's for the children, and—"

Jackie cut him off. How much longer must he feign wellness? "I'm sure it's very fine. What we want, though, is for Fwendi to take over the speaking engagements George was to have filled for us."

"But—but how can you accompany her as you did him?"

"I can't. Europeans would judge it to be entirely unsuitable." He turned to meet the wide, grey eyes. "That will be the job of Mademoiselle Toutournier, who is already charged with her care."

"Fwendi is not of European descent. Not a white," Toutournier objected. Must she fight him at every opportunity? Why blame Jackie for Daisy's choice of him as a carnal partner? "Our backers won't care so very much how poorly she has been treated by Leopold."

"True," Jackie admitted. "But with the example of your sympathy—"

"Nor am I white. Not purely." The Frenchwoman looked as if she gloried in her mongrel status.

He made himself get up and go to the marble-topped side table, taking up the folded papers he'd set there in preparation for this meeting. "That no longer seems to be the case. There was an investigation. New evidence has come to light. Your lineage is no more adulterated than my own."

Quick as anger, fingers snatched the papers from his hand. "What is this? What *tromperie*—deceit—"

"A witness, a sworn statement! This is proof that you are not, after all, a descendant of the man you call '*le Gorille*.'"

Toutournier read rapidly in silence, flicking pages aside. "An outrage! My *grand-mère* was never unfaithful to him! Never!"

"Nonetheless. Here it says otherwise."

The Frenchwoman flung the document onto the newly replaced carpet. "You expect me to swallow this—*histoire*? This packet of lies? You think this—*this*—is more acceptable to our potential supporters than to have dealings with *une Négresse*? You—"

Help came from an unexpected quarter: the girl, Fwendi, grasped Toutournier's gesticulating arms and stilled them. "Mademoiselle, Mademoiselle, calm yourself, *calmez-vous!*" With unlooked-for strength, the young girl guided her to a seat on the sofa. While she poured cups of the fragrant cocoa Jackie had ordered to supplement Le Metropole's unfortunate tea, he withdrew to a strategic armchair and considered his next steps. He knew what they would have to be, though he didn't like taking them.

However, it was for the greater good.

Jamison pulled a matching seat up to the sofa, positioning it between them.

"Do you see why we must do as I suggest?" Jackie asked him, continuing to hope that he wouldn't have to force the necessary outcome.

The Scot nodded. "Surely, though, I'll be able to join the two of them in their travels from time to time?" He reached out to pat Fwendi on her metal arm. "My friend? Our paths will cross—there will be touring productions—missions to England—"

The girl smiled, though she kept her eyes on Toutournier's face. "That would make me happy."

Mademoiselle Toutournier smiled too. Jackie didn't like her smile. "I imagine, then," she said, "that you will be ecstatic to learn that there is no need to part from your friend in the first place. For I have no intention of helping you to take up Mr. Owen's offer. Matty may escort you home as he did here. I'll seek some other job with another employer."

"I wish you wouldn't. I'd hate to press charges."

A dead quiet.

"Charges?" asked Jamison, sounding bewildered. He glanced momentarily at Jackie, then turned his gaze to Toutournier.

"For trying to kill him." The Frenchwoman's voice was steady and cold. "Am I correct? You would perpetuate a falsehood?"

"Yes."

"But you—you couldn't have!" Jamison protested.

Jackie leaned forward to rest his elbows on his knees and clasped his hands together. "Fwendi, did you indeed see the attacker—the presumed attacker—you chased? Can you swear—can you say under oath it was not Mademoiselle Toutournier?"

A swift, unreadable look from the girl. "No, sir. I cannot. But—"

"But she treated your wound! She—"

"She was most providentially present only moments after the attempted assassination."

Jamison stood up out of his chair. "Because you had invited her!"

Toutournier made an inelegant sound, half-sniff, half-snort. "Do you really believe me innocent, Matty? I can assure you that your position on the matter will be a lonely one. What passes for justice here will easily find me guilty."

Apparently she was no longer giving vent to her mood. Or her most violent feelings had receded. She sipped her cocoa and delicately set her cup in its saucer. "So you'll call the tune to which I dance. *Bien*. Where first must we go?"

"You may begin coaching Fwendi in how to give her lectures here, in Alexandria. In a fortnight or so we will sail north and west, to Europe, before the worst of the winter storms."

Kamina, Everfair, January 1904

"Bury him." Thomas pressed his forehead with the heel of one hand, leaned back in the throne they had made him assume, and closed his eyes. A true Christian would not have pronounced that sentence so easily.

He couldn't close his ears, though. There was no escape from the prisoner's pleading as the pagan congregation's ushers dragged him to the pit they'd previously dug. Blessedly, Yoka refrained from further translation, but the captive's wailing cries were obvious in their meaning. As was the hiss and slap of gravel being poured over his legs, body, and arms.

He comforted himself with knowledge born of earlier trials: the prisoner's head would remain aboveground.

One of Thomas's new congregants helped him rise so the folding throne could be moved to a better vantage point. He had to open his eyes again to walk to the fast-filling pit. Shadows cloaked the cavern's walls. How had his noble-hearted intentions come to this? Currents of damp air bent the smallest lamp's naked flame, and made the tiny golden points cast by the larger, shielded lamps shiver.

Behind him, muffled clucking announced the arrival of a speckled hen. Its handler gave it to him to hold while priests—*other* priests—his *colleagues*—traced symbols in the packed earth now spread round about the prisoner's neck and head. Over this, the youngest of them, a mere boy, threw kernels of dried corn.

Thomas resumed his seat. Best for all to begin and end this as quickly as possible. Afterward he would pray for God's forgiveness. Again. Perhaps someday he would receive an answer.

Surely he was yet deserving of one, despite listening to the priests' entreaties over the last several years to commit himself to their heathenish cult. His fits, they asserted, marked him as fated for full initiation. The throne was one of many compromises he'd agreed to, hoping them harmless.

He returned the hen to its handler, rolled back the cuffs of his sleeves and removed a clinging feather from the red sash they had insisted he wear.

"What were you doing on the slopes above Mwilambwe?" he asked. Yoka rendered the question into Bah-Sangah and then Lin-Gah-La, then the prisoner's response into Bah-Sangah and English. The young man was good at his task.

The buried captive claimed he had been doing nothing, nothing, he had simply become lost and was wandering innocently when King Mwenda's men found him near their camp. With a nod Thomas signaled that the hen should be allowed to peck. The captive regarded it with dread, his words failing. It freely chose the corn nearest the character for "big lie."

The buried man began to shout, repeating the same phrase over and over.

"'Don't kill me! Don't kill me!' he is saying," Yoka told Thomas. "Some peoples do similar ceremonies to accuse a person of practicing magic. Then they execute him. Shall I tell the prisoner he's safe?"

"No." For, in fact, he was in danger. Perhaps even a Christian court would have treated him no better.

The handler picked the bird up. No witch could keep such an animal as a familiar—all history, all church tradition ran counter to the idea. Cats, dogs, toads, rats, lizards, yes. But not roosters. Not hens. They were too cleanly, too righteous, too irretrievably associated with the Lord.

"Who do you work for?"

Checking with Thomas, the handler set the bird back down. According to Yoka, the captive said he worked for no one, no one, unless they would hire him, of course, in which case—but Thomas stopped attending to the man's words, for the hen had resumed its feeding. With three precise movements of its head it indicated that the prisoner was in Leopold's employ.

As they had naturally suspected when he was found creeping through the army's perimeter guard. Validation, the first step, had taken place. The Urim and Thummim, so to speak.

Now for the difficult part. Thomas preferred a white cock for the latter portion of these interrogations. The handler took the hen away and relief filled the buried man's face.

"What services do you offer us? What will you do?"

A torrent of eager words poured out of him. "He will work hard for us in any way we require," Yoka told Thomas and the Bah-Sangah priests. "Digging in the mines, gathering rubber, paddling a boat, even cooking like a woman."

As the response, and Yoka's translations, continued, the handler returned with a rooster. It was the right color. The buried man talked faster, seeming eager to say everything at once. As the rooster was set down, it flapped its wings, disarranging the careful, even distribution of dried corn.

But not the symbols incised in the packed soil. Calming down, it pecked this area, that area, another, another, watched carefully by the Bah-Sangah priests. Two made notes on lengths of bark. Apparently finished with its meal, the cock left the corn to climb the little pile of stones left from the pit's excavation.

Thou shalt not suffer a witch to live, Thomas remembered. Exodus 22:18. But what of Endor? Hadn't she, though of course cursed, revealed Jehovah's will? What if his association with the Bah-Sangah religion was foreordained?

"What does the oracle teach us?"

The recording priests consulted with their apprentice, Yoka, who said, "The most likely outcome is for him to betray us to Leopold."

Executing the prisoner would be a mercy, then. Would save innocent lives. Yet Thomas couldn't bring himself to condone killing him in cold blood.

He thought a moment more. Doubtless Leopold had threatened the spy with a family member's death in order to get him to act in the tyrant's interests. To turn that monster's own tool against him—that was what would hurt him most; not to let him sacrifice his pawn.

"The final question." Which, according to the instructions he followed, was never directed at the prisoner. Thomas lifted his eyes and held out his hands, palm up, to receive the righteous knowledge of Heaven. Though he wasn't sure it would come.

All other eyes, he noticed, were lowered.

The handler retrieved the rooster and tucked it under one arm. A knife glinted in the opposite hand. Yoka faced him, holding a large gourd.

"How can we further the highest good of all involved?"

The cock died swiftly, silently. Only the knife's flash and the hiss of life pouring into the bowl told what had happened. A few kicks contained by the handler's hold and the bird was meat.

A different gourd, covered, was carried forward by a different young apprentice. Thomas had seen its contents before: rough and rounded stones, brass implements, figures of wood and glass and gems. Yoka spilled into it a measure of the hot liquid—the blood—within his own gourd. Then he approached Thomas.

Thomas had twice already drunk such offerings. On the first occasion, he had—much to his shame—done so out of fear of death at his congregants' hands. On the second he'd feared to offend them. A third instance would, he thought, impel him that much closer to his fate. If this trend continued, he'd soon be a full-blown heathen—worse, an apostate.

Wanting to rescue these brands from the burning, Thomas had caught fire himself.

He took the gourd from Yoka. Guiltily, he sipped. Salt ran over his tongue, down his throat, like a thin gravy. As he passed the bowl to the eldest of the Bah-Sangah priests the remembered vertigo assailed him.

He meant to stay seated, but the world whirled and he was on his feet, dancing. Glimpses of his surroundings penetrated the glowing fog of his ecstasy: swirling stars—or were those the myriad little lights the lamps cast through their shades? Wise faces—his friends, his brothers—went and came, bobbed up before him and twisted away. Out of an opening leading deeper into the caves poured music, waves of horns and harps and bells and drums. Stamping down! down! he gloried in the strength of metal, the knife and the hammer he'd been given spinning in his nimble grip. Round and round and round and round and then he reached the place just right.

The center. A vision. He could see . . .

See them sweeping over the forests like a scythe, blazing above the river surface, fire reflected in the waters' steel, going there! There! In chains, iron's perversion, children stooped to tend rubber plants, the vines-that-weep. Whipped and starved—they must not die. Attack! Attack!

Then he was back on the folding stool Yoka called his throne. No music. He couldn't remember when it had stopped. Now he heard only the soft murmurs of the priests discussing what he had told them in Bah-Sangah. What he had told them using a language he didn't in the least understand.

Sickness filled his stomach and threatened to overflow it. Yoka gave him a cup of water. Four women entered. They often arrived after such ceremonies, though how they knew the proper time he had no idea.

Two of the women squatted before him and patted his feet with a white powder like talcum. The first time this happened, he had balked. Then he'd remembered how, initially, Peter had refused to let the Lord perform a like service. Jesus had rebuked Simon Peter, and the disciple had come to accept the Christ's anointing.

It was obvious by now, though, that that was not what he, Thomas, had accepted.

He wished he could be alone and think about what he was doing. He wished he could lie down and sleep. But Yoka reminded him that there was no time. The Mote, he said, was scheduled for that very evening.

He let Yoka guide him to the Mote's tall-ceilinged cave, let the apprentice "light" the already-burning wick with their shared lamp's flame. As always, they were among the earliest arrivals.

Only Albert, Tink, and Winthrop preceded them, though Mrs. Albin's stool awaited her. Beyond it stood another, higher and more elaborate.

Lately Thomas had been leaving the space on Mrs. Albin's right for Old Kanna to take. And the space on her left—with the better stool—was filled these days by Queen Josina, who had replaced her cousin Alonzo as Yoka had replaced Loyiki. These substitutions were for the same reason: the work Alonzo and Loyiki did away from Everfair. The work of war, which he was to join in again on the morrow.

Yoka sank onto the central mat, out of the way of the entrance, and Thomas knelt beside him. His attempt to pray silently was interrupted by plump Mrs. Albin's bustling entrance. Her young husband accompanied her, and though Thomas tried to ignore the man's solicitous stare, he felt it even with his eyes reverently closed. Queen Josina came in next, with Old Kanna and Nenzima in her wake. The new chair was, of course, hers. As usual, the Poet, Daisy, was last.

Winthrop had lists of weapons they'd made, and in what quantities. Queen Josina had one list—a short one—of African allies' promises. Daisy was able to supplement that with news from Europe courtesy of Mademoiselle Toutournier. She also gave totals of funds available from white supporters to be spent on necessary supplies, "*not* squandered on useless religious paraphernalia—"

"Bibles? Hymnals? Those are hardly *useless*!" Mrs. Albin's indignation was plain in her raised voice, her narrowed eyes. Poor George Albin had no hope of reconciling his mother with his wife. Their quarreling drowned out his attempts.

Mrs. Albin turned to Thomas for his agreement, as he had expected she would. But despite her effectiveness in hushing up the scandal associated with his frequent episodes of—possession—by demons? gods? unchristian spirits of *some* sort—he didn't think he ought to side with her any longer. Eventually, she'd be contaminated by his reputation as a madman subject to fits.

"I defer my vote," Thomas said. "We haven't yet heard all the reports, have we?" Including his own.

Tink's only concern since the death of Daisy's eldest daughter Lily was the invention and refining of artificial limbs. As if one of his clockwork prosthetic legs could somehow retroactively replace the fatally wounded one. Thomas scarcely listened to him. Albert was marginally more interesting to a military mind: he discoursed first on improvements to the engines powering their aircanoes and the resultant higher speeds and carrying capacities, but then he switched to the much duller topic of making Kamina's caverns more habitable.

At last it was Nenzima's turn. Queen Josina had remained silent for all sixteen of the fortnightly Motes she'd attended—after all, she was not technically a citizen of Everfair, but the favorite spouse of its closest ally. But Thomas thought Nenzima said what the queen would have said if she were not quite so discreet.

"King Mwenda is within sight of victory. He has lured Leopold's soldiers high, high up the Lualaba River. Soon they will be trapped in the swamplands and ripe for defeat."

Thomas cast his mind back to Nenzima's last speech, during the last Mote. "In Kibombo?"

Nenzima nodded assent. "Our friends from Oo-Gandah are gathered in the mountains nearby, ready for transport."

"How many?"

"The fighters of a hundred villages. All they could spare."

Roughly three thousand "men"—many of the Oo-Gandah warriors were female—would be waiting for aircanoes to carry them into battle. Combined with King Mwenda's force, which at last report was double that number . . . "What is our latest and most reliable estimate of Leopold's army?"

"As many as the fighters of two hundred villages are left to them."

Seven thousand against nine thousand. Better than equal odds, then—though the tyrant's army would have more and more accurate rifles. "Their ammunition? Supply lines?" So much depended on the latter—food, medicine, and thus morale.

But the Poet assured the Mote once again that their secret U.S. and European supporters had let nothing get through since March two years ago. Spoiled and poisoned rations, diluted medicine and malaria, had greatly reduced Leopold's army.

Thomas had Yoka give his report for him. Mrs. Albin no doubt thought this a tactic to avoid disasters such as the barking fits that had overcome him so many times in the past.

The truth? Often enough he simply could not recall what it was he was supposed to say.

"The Reverend Wilson has learned of a camp of child slaves nearby to Lukolela. He will take an aircanoe there on a detour when we leave for the battlefield tomorrow."

Thomas understood that, while in the chicken blood–induced trance, he had said something of the sort. He, or the spirit temporarily inhabiting him. Lukolela. That would probably be found to be the holding place of the captive spy's hostage. The statements he'd made earlier under a similar influence had all proved helpful and correct.

Mrs. Albin was intrigued. "Is Lukolela a large camp? How many of these poor creatures can we rescue?"

"We're not sure," said Yoka. "Perhaps twenty-five. Perhaps more. But they will need food, bandages, replacement hands—you understand."

"But first, Bibles! Yes! I insist! We must procure more, one for each—and picture books, too, telling the story of creation—"

"They can share those belonging to others," Daisy said firmly.

The vote went predictably, except for his own choice. Not that that would have changed the outcome: only Mrs. Albin's godson and her husband sided with her. Thomas ought also to have favored buying religious texts over more grossly physical supplies. That he'd chosen otherwise would be viewed as treachery on his part. Mrs. Albin awarded him a sour look, but by morning he was able to forget it.

Albert and Chester and their construction crew had been busy. Four new craft were ready fly north to join *Mbuza*, the first vessel of Everfair's ever-expanding fleet. *Zi Ru* and *Fu Hao* were unavailable, attached to occupying garrisons at Mbandaka and Kikwit. But *Boadicea* and *Brigid* were even bigger, and the untested new aircanoes, *Kalala* and *aMileng,* were supposed to be much lighter, much faster. New materials, Albert explained. One more of similar design, *Phillis Wheatley,* was scheduled for production later this year. At the moment too many colonists lodged inside, but during the dry season the space of the largest cavern would be free for the necessary work.

Rain hazed the relatively cool air. Dawn had always been Thomas's favorite time of day. He walked out along the wooden dock to *Kalala* with no worry that he might slip and fall dozens of feet to the steep, rocky mountainside below. There were no handrails to hold, but the bark had been left on the logs out of which the docks were built. That kept them from becoming too slick.

The prisoner was already aboard. He'd spent the night beneath one of the aircanoe's storage shelves, safely sedated by juice extracted from the roots of an herb known to the Bah-Sangah. Yoka showed Thomas the supply he carried in a horn in case another dose was needed before they arrived.

Kalala's capacity was about eighty adults. Thomas had thirty fighters board, bringing their jumping sheets with them. Typically, slave camps were guarded by no more than six or seven soldiers. So it was when they arrived at Lukolela after a journey of a little over twelve hours.

Night was about to fall. Bare red dirt passed beneath *Kalala*'s gondola, darkened to the color of an old wound by the sun's absence. A hut hove into view—that would be the overseer's quarters. Just past it, a smoldering fire fought against the rain. By its fitful light, more than by that of the failing day, Thomas saw a huddled group of children. He counted thirty. Two guards with guns stood over them. There'd been two more by the hut. That left another two or three out of sight, most likely patrolling the clearing's perimeter.

Bombs could provide a distraction, but Leopold's thugs had become more wary as Everfair and King Mwenda's warriors increased their raids. At Bwasa, according to Loyiki, the soldiers had for the first time shot and killed their slaves before fleeing the attack. That was almost two years ago. Since then, he had been developing different tactics.

They circled back around and all but ten fighters jumped, their falls slowed by their rubberized barkcloth sheets. Of course the guards hit some with their rifles. Venting gas, *Kalala* came lower. The ten fighters remaining aboard had a harder time aiming than those thugs on the ground, but there were only four targets. No, five: the overseer had come out of his hut. He was armed too, but Yoka downed him neatly. The way he worked his shotgun's action with the fake hand, you'd never know the man ever had a real one.

Full night now. Gunfire came from the woods, but it was sporadic. Thomas ordered *Kalala* lower, but kept the bonfire in the distance. Fighters shepherded the pitifully thin children toward the aircanoe's rope and wood ladders. Still in partial shackles— the chains linking them had been struck off—no time for more— they had difficulty climbing up. Thomas leaned forward to help and felt a sudden heat under his arm.

He'd been hit. He knew the sensation; it had happened before. Always a surprise—he fell to the side, against the gondola's slanting bulwark. In the dark and with the confusion of the starving children coming aboard, Thomas managed to conceal what had happened. But once they'd cast off their ballast and set course for an overnight berth above the Lomami River, Yoka hunted him down. Thomas was staunching the bleeding as best he could with his coat balled up and held tight against his armpit. The lamp Yoka carried showed it soaked in red.

The apprentice touched Thomas's arm carefully, with his flesh hand. "Does it hurt?" he asked.

"No. Worse. It's numb. But I think the bullet's in there. Still."

Yoka replaced Thomas's coat with his own and made him lie flat. He used something—a belt?—to hold the pad in place. "There are healers on *Mbuza*."

Thomas knew that. "I will go to them when we reach Kibombo." If he didn't die before then.

"Perhaps." Yoka's face disappeared from Thomas's narrowing

field of vision for a moment. "I must prop you up to help you swallow."

"Swallow what?" It was a hollowed-out horn Yoka lifted to his lips—though he wasn't sure this was the same one containing the soporific drug they'd given the prisoner. The taste of what he drank from it was both bitter and sweet, like licorice and quinine.

"Now you will sleep. And dream. And very likely, you will live," Yoka seemed to be saying. His meaning floated free of the words. "If so, you should promise yourself."

Promise himself. Thomas wanted to open his mouth. He had questions. Or at least one. Promise himself. Promise himself what?

Then he was walking up an endless mountain. Or down? Sometimes he thought one, sometimes the other. Whichever, it was hard work. Why shouldn't he stop? But he smelled—something. The scent of fire. He wanted to find who it belonged to. It wasn't out of control, a forest burning up. How did he know that?

Rough stones gave way to soft soil, plants clinging to the ground, mounting up the walls of a rude shelter, an open-sided shed. Here was the fire. A forge. The smith working it wore a mask like a dog's head. He was making—Thomas couldn't see exactly what. Shining shapes stood upright in pails to the forge's right side. They resembled giant versions of the symbols used by Bah-Sangah priests. On the left loomed a pile too dark to discern more than vaguely. Hoping to see better, Thomas went just a little nearer, but not near enough to get caught.

The mask's muzzle turned sharply toward him. A powerful arm reached too far and a huge hand wrapped itself around his neck. It pulled him closer, choking him.

From behind the mask came a man's voice. "What are you doing here? Stealing secrets? Or are you dying and you come to me for your life?"

Of course he was dying. Loss of gravy. Loss of blood. He said nothing, but the smith seemed to hear his thoughts.

"If I give you your life back, you will owe it to me. Acceptable?"

The big hand loosened and Thomas nodded. Yes. Its grip tightened again and drew him in next to the fire. It draped him over the anvil. He shrank, or the anvil grew until it held all of him.

Turning his head, Thomas saw the smith take a shining symbol from one of the buckets and bring it toward the anvil. He rolled his eyes up to follow its progress, then lost sight of it. Then cried out as it burnt his scalp.

"Silence!" commanded the smith. Two hard blows on his skull stunned him into compliance. Another scalding hot symbol was slipped under his neck. The smith's hammer smashed into Thomas's throat, driving his tender skin down against the letter of fire. Scarcely had he recovered, breathing somehow, when a large new letter was laid on his chest, and hammered home with three mighty swings. Smaller symbols were burned and bashed into the palms of his hands. Radiating pain and heat, Thomas wondered if this was how Christ felt when he was being crucified. Then he scolded himself for his blasphemy—but without speaking, for the smith had bade him to make no noise.

If life was suffering, it belonged to him yet. Under the next letter, his left knee smoked. The dog mask spit on it. The hammer hit. It must surely have broken his bones, Thomas thought. But after the final symbol was affixed and the smith told him to stand up, he found that he could.

"Do you have a weapon?"

"I can get one," Thomas said.

"Remember whose you are now."

"But I don't know your—"

"Ask Yoka my name."

He awoke. He presumed he did; he must have been sleeping. Dawn again, and the aircanoe was moving, clouds and the pale curve of last night's moon passing behind *Kalala*'s red-and-purple envelope and coming swiftly back into sight. He could feel both arms. He clenched his fingers and released them. That hurt. Cautiously he sat up. His senses swam, but not unbearably. He shrugged his shoulders. Some pain, and an annoying restriction—Yoka's makeshift bandage. He eased off the sash and the pad it had held in place tumbled to the deck. It was stained and dry.

Dry.

It ought to have been wet. It ought to have *stuck to his skin*.

Slowly, Thomas lifted his arm and examined the wound. The healing wound. Where the bullet must have entered, his flesh had started to pucker into a raw, raised scar a little darker than the rest of his armpit. With the hand of his unhurt arm he probed his shoulder and as much of his back as he could reach.

Nothing marked an exit.

Yoka approached, carrying a clean shirt, seeming unsurprised by Thomas's convalescence.

Thomas took the shirt. "What happened?" he asked, then almost gagged coughing; his throat was tight, rough, swollen.

"That's not to be talked about. Not here. Besides, the drums say we'll soon be busy. You won't have time to wonder about all that."

Thomas was stiff; he needed Yoka's help putting on the shirt. Its warmth was good. His head ached. His arms and legs throbbed and trembled. He leaned against the nearest woven panel and forced himself to his feet.

They'd brought few provisions. Thomas's chief want was water, but he knew he'd need more than that to get through the coming battle. As they passed over Malela en route to Lutshi, he was eating his second plantain. The thirty fighters had been deposited at Ombwe an hour earlier, as planned. King Mwenda had split his troops, leading and chasing Leopold's men into the swamp. The majority of the king's fighters were to the north of the invader's army; in order to reinforce the southern contingent, *Mbuza, Boadicea, Brigid,* and *aMileng* had been ferrying Oo-Gandahns all morning. *Kalala* was to join them for this final trip of four.

The small aircanoes could only transport eighty adult fighters. The rescued children had proved reluctant to leave *Kalala* with the fighters from Kamina. The countryside was strange to them. They had endured enough. Strategically speaking, Thomas admitted to himself, it had probably been a poor choice to add their rescue to the day's mission. But the spy had cried with joy when reunited with his newly freed son.

In the end, only space for thirty-three fighters was needed. Most Oo-Gandahns had already been taken to their battle positions, and many of those left seemed to prefer flying in the other aircanoes. Perhaps it was the dispirited attitude of *Kalala*'s passengers, which was of course due to the children's exhaustion, malnourishment, and sores.

It was nearly an hour after *Brigid*'s departure that they, the last to leave, finally took to the air. Ignoring his own weakness, Thomas did his best to help tend to the unfortunates. He'd learned a little Kee-Swa-Hee-Lee, but only a few of them understood it; he had a hard time remembering which and telling them apart.

The bonds restraining Leopold's spy had been removed. He still wept with his son in his arms, saying something to the boy Thomas wasn't quite sure he fully comprehended—that death was better than what the child had been saved from? Then the spy rose and ran for the lit lamp hanging by the prow. He opened its top and dashed palm oil liberally over the aircanoe's wood decking and bulwarks and touched the wick to them. They blazed up like torches.

Shrieks filled the bright air. Panicked, stampeding fighters ran to *Kalala*'s stern, tilting the deck. The stability vane pedals must no longer be working. Or else they'd been abandoned.

Thomas clung to the bulwark's head-high gunwale, hauling himself forward, hand over hand. He encountered a living obstacle: Yoka, who apparently had the same thought. His metal hand took more effort to operate, but gave him a surer hold.

Side by side they inched upward. The fires grew unstoppably, unreachably. It was hopeless.

Yoka glanced overhead at the envelope of rubber-coated bark-cloth. Filled with balloons holding explosive hydrogen gas. "We must cut the lines."

"We'll die," Thomas objected.

"No." He reached one of the ropes tethering gondola to envelope and began to climb. "I'll open a vent first and lower us."

The way to the deck-level vent controls was blocked by the fire. "But how will you—"

A penetrating scream rose above the general wailing, then fell further and further away. Thomas pulled himself up to sit astride the gunwale and caught sight of a man pinwheeling to earth sans jumpsheet. The trees below looked no taller than lettuces.

"That was the prisoner," said Yoka. "The others pushed him out."

"We'll never know why he did this, then." He commenced shinnying along the gunwale like a child sliding up a bannister.

"I believe he had more than the one boy held hostage," Yoka shouted.

"What?" It was becoming hard to hear Yoka as the distance between them widened. A logistical concern sprang suddenly to mind: he'd have to walk across the burning deck to cut the lines connecting it to the airbag. They were as far from reach as the vent release.

"Just before the spy set us on fire, I overheard his boy ask him where was his twin. Another boy or girl."

A second hostage. Death was better. It seemed obvious now. "Do you have a shongun?"

"Here. Catch!" The polished brass of the knife-throwing gun slipped through Thomas's fingers. Fortunately, it landed on the deck instead of following the arsonist to earth. He retrieved it, then scrambled onto the gunwale again with the shongun clenched between his teeth. He heard Yoka yelling something but couldn't understand what he said.

Sixteen-blade magazines for Winthrop's latest model, if Thomas remembered rightly. Enough, if he didn't miss a single shot. If the shongun were fully loaded. Madness.

The heat stopped him. He leaned out to his left. A cool wind blew upward from rapidly enlarging trees and pools.

It must be time.

Thomas was an excellent shot under normal conditions. Which did not usually include wracking pain and exhaustion, but always, always, the threat of death. He aimed carefully. The first line parted. The second, third, fourth. They'd been damaged by the flames. The fifth seemed at first only to fray. Would he have to waste another blade? Seconds passed till it gave way.

The gondola lurched, and Thomas held desperately to the slick gunwale. It looked almost level now. He nodded. Naturally. The loft that had been lost because the fore end no longer hung from the airbag had been counteracted by the uneven distribution of terrified passengers and the abandoned stabilizer pedals.

He was amazed he could consider the matter so calmly.

The sixth line, exactly opposite his present seat, was obscured low down by the frontmost of the advancing flames. Thomas aimed above them. This time he did need two shots. No help for that.

He retreated to the deck and shot away the seventh line. Half done. Almost. He'd never finish soon enough. They were going to crash burning into the swamp. His ship, his crew, his command.

He took aim at the eighth line, but an Oo-Gandah fighter got in the way, smiling and brandishing a spear. Stupid woman! "Go! *Mwanamke!* Go!" He flourished the shongun, indicating she should move aft, but she only grinned and began sawing away at the line with her weapon.

New shouts died on his lips. She understood! Turning to the line directly behind him, he shot it. Three times, but he had ammunition to spare now. The Oo-Gandahn finished and went on to the next starboard line. This one took her longer. Evidently her spear's point was dulling. She called out something and took a long machete from the man who answered her. He didn't seem to favor the idea. Thomas lost sight of the disagreement as he dashed to his next target. One shot only this time.

But now he was in among the crowd of passengers. None of them spoke English. Why should they? Confused and angry babbling greeted him on all sides. What had happened to his men? He caught a brief glimpse of a couple of them stationed roughly where *Kalala*'s steering wheel ought to be. The twelfth line—thirteenth if his assistant had succeeded—was right there. A clear shot. He raised the shongun. A blow to his back threw off his aim—he barely maintained his hold on the gun. He pushed his way to the bulwark and braced himself, tried again. Bingo!

Shoving hard, he got through to the last of the port lines. Here were the slave children, huddled together, so tightly packed there was no path between. The only road was up. Thomas climbed the line with cramping arms and legs. He craned his neck to look for Yoka. No luck.

Kalala's gondola dropped precipitously. The deck lay at a sharp slant. All lines to the envelope but this one and the stern's were loose. Cries of horror, wordless screeching—bodies tumbled down into the relentless fire or over the gunwales into the green and black swamp.

Thomas pointed and shot anyway. The knife hit. The gondola jerked again and more passengers fell.

Two knives left. Thomas aimed down and pulled the trigger. Its last tie to the gondola severed, *Kalala*'s envelope rushed skyward, whipping him around furiously at the end of the cut line. From below came an enormous hissing splash. Thomas dared to look down. The gondola was in a single half-charred piece. People moved on it, swam and waded around it. They sank further and further away. Or rather, he and the envelope rose—and Yoka also, spidered across the ropes of the envelope's net.

The higher one went, the colder and thinner the air. Without the gondola's weight he'd—they'd—fly too high to breathe. Thomas attempted for a few moments to slow his twisting and spinning, to steady himself by wrapping the line's slack around his wrist. He gave up. The envelope was big; how could he miss? Praying not to hit Yoka, he shot his last blade.

Falling, falling—yet the envelope acted like a giant jumpsheet. What went up must come down, but at least at a survivable speed. Dizzy, ill, aghast at the deaths he knew were his responsibility, Thomas still clung to the hope something would go right. Something had to.

Something did.

Leopold lost. He had been doing so for more than a season. Thomas and Yoka, drifting eastward on prevailing winds, witnessed much of the final rout. From the net around the punctured envelope, Yoka tossed Thomas a makeshift sling. Gliding lower and lower, they saw soldiers and policemen running in every direction. They saw massive disorder and piles of surrendered rifles. They saw King Mwenda's fighters herding captive overseers back the way they'd come, uphill, toward the rendezvous at Lutshi. And they saw many dying, many dead. Most wore the Belgian tyrant's uniform.

At last they landed gently on a hillside on the swamp's far side. Against all likelihood, they were alive.

So, too, was almost everyone else who'd been aboard *Kalala*.

When Yoka told Thomas this, he refused to believe it. He sat, at the Bah-Sangah priests' insistence, underneath a length of undyed cotton. Apparently his dream of the dog-headed blacksmith— which he had related to Yoka—decreed the immediate completion of Thomas's initiation. So far these culminating steps had involved bathing and fasting. And isolation. He wasn't even sure where the two of them were, since he'd been blindfolded before being led there and could see nothing now but the white cloth over his head.

The air around Thomas was cool and musty and still. Yoka's impossible words echoed very slightly as he relayed the news he'd gathered while others laved Thomas in chalk-whitened water.

The crew and passengers of the *Kalala* had suffered no casualties.

"But they fell!" Thomas objected.

"Not far," Yoka responded.

"Into the *fire*!"

"And out again."

"And the waters of the swamp—"

"All shallow."

"No one was bitten by poisonous serpents? Eaten by crocodiles?"

"No. We were protected."

"Protected by whom?" asked Thomas.

A moment of silence. Under the white cloth it seemed long to him.

"Protected by him to whom you have promised yourself. The god Loango."

"I didn't—"

"You did. Or else you would be dead. Others, too."

"But I—" Thomas remembered. *If I give you your life back you will owe it to me.* "I have dedicated my life to my lord, Jesus Christ."

"Yes? When was this?"

"What? What does it matter when?"

"If it was before you met your new lord, you must take it back."

Take it back. Be forsworn. He couldn't do that.

Could he?

"You will remain here overnight. Alone. Considering. In the morning I will come for you, for your final decision."

"I can say no?" His voice sounded weak, even to his own ears.

"You can. So think well. Think what that will mean.

"When I am gone, remove the cloth. You will see you have been provided with water, food, a candle, a pot into which you may relieve yourself, and one more thing: an object to help you make your choice."

The sound of footsteps leaving.

Thomas lifted the cloth and looked around at a small cave. The food, water, candle, and chamber pot were all present as described.

The only other thing there was a mirror.

Thomas removed his clothing. He looked at himself as long as the candle's light lasted, using the reflective surface to examine sides he would normally be unable to see. He stared at the healed bullet wound hard and often.

He had faced death. Now he must face the choice he had made to live. Must decide whether to pledge explicitly the new allegiance he had earlier and implicitly given.

The candle burnt out. He couldn't use the mirror anymore, so he used his mind.

All he had was his life. It was all that was wanted.

The sound of footsteps coming back.

Part Two

Kalima, Everfair, May 1914

Hissing gently as if to attract the sky's attention, *Okondo* turned in the evening air with loverlike deliberation. Lisette watched from the new warehouse's loading dock as it left her. Up there the sun still shone, flashing brightly on the gondola's rear window, gilding the balloon's purple sides. A gigantic cacao pod, rubber-backed barkcloth molded over aluminum girders and rings: when first she came to live in Everfair, way back in the nineteenth century, the existence of such an apparatus was not much more than a dream. But now it was a matter of course to ride one.

Away down the Ulindi River's long, lush valley the aircanoe floated, freshly loaded with tin and tea, cocoa and hemp, the region's produce. Belgium's guns posed it only the slightest danger; officially, they were out of commission. The flight to Angola's ports would likely be as uneventful as her voyage here. This was 1914. The tyrant Leopold had been vanquished for almost ten years.

Lisette need have no concern. Yet she yearned after the departing aircanoe till it became indistinguishable from the periwinkle dusk. Or did she yearn for another?

A cool wind fell upon her, descending out of the Mitumba Mountains. Someone wrapped a soft shawl over her shoulders. It was Fwendi—her brass hand glinting in the lamplight spilling from the warehouse door. With the faintest of ratcheting whirs, Fwendi's hand released the woven cashmere to settle against Lisette's still-smooth neck. "Merci, mon ami."

"Pas du tout," Fwendi replied. Though they'd traveled extensively—Europe, Middle Asia, and the United States—French remained their shared tongue, serving as their secret language. As it had served with Daisy in Lisette's vanished youth.

"You ought to come inside," Fwendi scolded, continuing in French. "Come to the hotel." Lisette wanted to rebel against this bullying nursemaidery, but in truth there was nothing left to see, the sky darkening so swiftly here, mere kilometers from the Equator.

Nonetheless, she affected an injured air. "As you desire, Maman," she replied—a jest, since she had fifteen years more than Fwendi, according to the best reckoning the refugee had been able to provide. She bowed her head and stalked inside.

Fwendi ignored Lisette's playacting with the practice of years. Unfussed, she contrived to be first to reach the lamp and remove it from the long chain dangling off the high rafter. Her own cloak she looped over one arm—the one of flesh.

Neither had ever before come to Kalima, not even when they'd last lived in Everfair: fourteen years ago for Lisette, eleven for Fwendi. The younger woman assumed the lead, taking them down the bluff and into town, past the homes of farmers and mechanics, by workshops that on the women's way to the warehouse had been loud with the clang of hammers on hot metals or heavy with the reek of rubber, vertiginous with the incense of volatile chemicals. Now all these establishments sat silent, doors shut but windows open, airing out in preparation for the morning.

The "hotel" could be distinguished from Kalima's other houses by its three stories and its condescending facade, like that of an American plantation house. The Lincolns, Negro immigrants from Maryland, owned the place and occupied its ground floor. They rented rooms to travelers who visited Kalima without alliances of kin or trade among the locals.

They climbed the stairs to the top story. Lisette occupied her own room; Fwendi followed her in and used the candle to light the small lamp beside her bed. A pleasant warmth lingered from the day. Lisette's trunk, repository of her next-to-be-revised manuscript, brooded in one corner, upright, like a wardrobe. A valise, open on a wicker chair, offered gloves, scarves, handkerchiefs, and stockings to wear on the morrow, when she would have to decide . . . what she would not now think of.

Lisette removed her hat and suspended it from a peg beside a looking glass. A blue-glazed water pitcher stood on a washstand near one white-curtained window. Shades of barkcloth curled behind the curtains, ready to unroll. Altogether, it was as comfortable a home as she had occupied in years.

"'Soir," she said carelessly as Fwendi retired to her own room, which she shared with Rima. Those two did not harmonize. In moments, as Lisette had expected, she heard a sharp rapping on her door.

"Enter," she said. Not in French. This newest member of her makeshift, itinerant household spoke only English.

Rima—Serenissima Bailey—blew through the opening door like a storm. Her namesake, the tragic, forest-dwelling white heroine of William Hudson's popular novel *Green Mansions,* had been described as fragile, small, demure—but that was not this tall nineteen-year-old, strong and swift as a cyclone. Rima's long brown shins thrust impatiently free of her dress's slit panels. Her half-bare arms reached for Lisette, crossed behind her back and pulled her close to murmur mock-angry reproaches for her late return to the hotel: had she planned to stay out all the night?

Lisette sighed and avoided the offered kiss. "No. But—"

"But you wasn't meanin to spend time with me, was you? Naw, I thought not." Rima dropped to sit on the bed in an attitude that ought to have been graceless: face jammed in cupped hands, elbows dug into her knees, feet planted wide.

"Of course I was. But not in my room. Not alone." Not in Everfair, with its memories. Its possibilities.

A shy smile played over Rima's berry-dark lips. "It was good, though, wasn't it? What we done?" Her enchantingly slanted eyes peeked upward. "Don't make neither one of us no bull dagger." The last in a worried tone—the girl still feared social consequences due to their encounters; these would have been harsh, indeed, in the Florida village where Lisette had first found her. Even in cosmopolitan New York, where Lisette had introduced her charmingly brash protégée to the emerging literary crowd, the code was strict. One had to be careful . . .

"You'd best go to your room."

"Yes'm." Rima rose to leave and turned her back, posture suddenly elegant as a hussar's. Perversely, Lisette wished her to stay. In that instant Rima whirled around and crossed the room in two strides, bending to embrace her. "Promise! Promise!" she demanded, pressing her brow against Lisette's as if seeking to force her way into her mind.

What should I promise? Lisette wondered, but she knew what was needed: a vow of love. A vow she could not, despite Rima's captivating energy, bring herself to make.

Morning. Breakfast was included in her arrangement with the Lincolns, but they provided it between the uncivilized hours of five and nine. Lisette girded herself for the day alone: she had dismissed Rima well before midnight.

Matty awaited her on the net-veiled verandah, pouring chocolate into a large, ugly cup. The smell of it had lured her to this table spread with a clean enough cloth and set with fresh bread, jam, curls of butter in ice, and a revolting pyramid of small, dead fish.

In blessed silence, Matty filled her cup too, and pulled forward a chair for her. As Lisette sipped and composed herself, she noted that he placed three of the fish on his plate before assuming his own seat. Well, he was a Scotchman.

"'Jour."

"The Grand Mote is next Market Day, and you'll be there in plenty of time," he told her needlessly. He must mean to soothe her. "Enjoy your holiday."

Matty's hatred of Leopold was legendary. Someday soon the king would die. What would Matty do once his old enemy was no more?

She should tell him her official reason for stopping here—which was almost the real one. Yet his loyalty to the Triple Entente formed between Great Britain, Russia, and France gave her pause.

Did it outweigh his concern for Everfair? Would he favor the Entente over the Central Powers—Germany and Austro-Hungary—regardless of Everfair's benefit?

Instead of trying to assess the persistence of Matty's patriotic feelings, Lisette asked whether he thought her understudy capable of performing her part. In many ways Rima was ideal. Her darker complexion needed little or no makeup compared to the cosmetics with which Lisette disguised the European portion of her heritage.

"She brings to the stage a certain"—Matty hesitated diplomatically—"a definite *verve*."

Lisette glanced up suspiciously from a critical examination of her cuticles. Did he not care for her protégée? Perhaps the Scotchman thought her unschooled? "I have been coaching her voice."

"No, she'll be fine—brilliant, quite—quite active; I've watched—"

Ah! It was *Lisette's* self-regard he was wary of damaging. She relaxed. Writing, rather than acting, was where her self-regard resided. To tease him, she responded, "Fwendi is pleased also."

At this, Matty blushed. Fwendi was approximately twenty-six, and he was all of fifty-four. One year younger than Daisy. Though the gap between those two was nearly double that between Daisy and Lisette.

Aircanoes could fly by night, given a sufficiently bright moon. The newer models traveled sometimes as many as 120 kilometers in an hour. If Daisy had received Lisette's message immediately upon *Okondo* mooring in Kisangani, she could well have boarded the vessel for its return trip. Allowing four hours to unload, Lisette had calculated the aircanoe's arrival here to be at ten this morning. Then she had laughed at these calculations, so obviously her own desires disguising themselves as reliable estimates.

With Fwendi at her side and Rima trailing sulkily behind them, Lisette proceeded back through Kalima to the warehouse, considering how unlikely it was for Daisy even to have been awake at such an hour—two a.m., assuredly, by the time the aircanoe tied up to the Kisangani tower.

It was 10:45. In daylight the town's streets were filled with people. A cluster of toddlers stared straightforwardly at Fwendi's hand—such prostheses were uncommon now the atrocities necessitating them had ceased. The attention in no way discomfited Fwendi: she obliged her impromptu audience with a little show, rolling her sleeve high and spinning her hand like a weathercock at the end of her beautiful, glittering arm. This latest version included flint and steel: she struck sparks with thumb and ring finger, and one chubby boy tried to imitate her, squealing with frustration.

A shadow passed. Lisette looked up: *Okondo!* Her heart sped, and she slipped eagerly through the ring of children. Some seconds later, her entourage was back beside her. The dust their boots kicked up hurried before them, whipped by a little wind. Worried, Lisette scanned the clouds, the mountainsides, but saw no sign of turbulence in the sky's upper reaches.

Ten wooden stairs, then a gravel track. Then a few more stairs, but these were mere indentations in the bluff's earth, buttressed with sections chopped from some poor tree's trunk. She fell behind Fwendi—age had its advantages, but physical alacrity was not one of them. On the flat area above she regained her lead. Rima continued to trail them both.

Again the glad shade. Dark against the dazzling sky, the aircanoe hovered, now merely seven meters above her head, lassoed to the mooring post.

Freight comprised the line's primary business; though the gondola was of the new enclosed sort, it wasn't equipped for passengers. She recalled the process by which she had disembarked yesterday. Perhaps she shouldn't watch Daisy subjected to such indignities? A makeshift sling had lowered Lisette to the ground, or fairly close—only a bit over a meter she'd had to jump as the sling swayed and shifted with the balloon's small but constant movements.

Too late, though. A black square opened in the gondola's tight-woven bottom. Leaf-wrapped bundles cascaded out, followed by crew swarming down ropes and leaping to stack them neatly at the dock's far end, nearest the warehouse. They were all clad in colorless loose shirts and wide trousers, shod in sandals. It took Lisette more time than she would have expected to recognize that one of these gymnasts was Daisy.

But at fifty-five years, what was the dear woman thinking of, to be so active? On her feet without recollection of rising, Lisette ran over the stones of the loading dock to her, to the one she had no right to ask anything of, who had joined her here anyhow at the first invitation—the first direct communication between them in a decade.

Daisy had seen her, of course. She said something unintelligible to her companions and approached Lisette with the free-limbed gait of an adolescent boy. Her hair, still dark, remained shockingly short, mere inches below her lovely jawline, restrained at her neck with a ribbon the greenish-blue of a redwing's eggs; a matching length circled her throat. Only faint lines creased her well-tanned brow and bracketed her thin, smiling mouth. That was all Lisette had time to note before being crushed in an embrace so tight it threatened suffocation.

Released quickly, she would have staggered, but Daisy kept a hand on one shoulder, kneading it with a kitten's loving fierceness.

Lisette blinked and saw that tears filled Daisy's eyes also. "You came," she pronounced, rather stupidly.

"Naturally." Daisy attempted to give Lisette a look of severe reproach down her long nose, which served merely to lower the spillways of her lashes. Then both wept openly a little while, laughing as well.

They wiped their cheeks. Lisette made the introductions and they walked to the hotel. Rima displayed an awful, forced cheerfulness, pacing backward along the uneven roads, chatting amiably with her rival. Who seemed as youthful as ever she had been. Her work on the aircanoe aided her, she claimed, in writing her poems.

Rima answered Daisy's questions about the Continent when Lisette couldn't bring herself to speak. This occurred frequently.

Fwendi had a parasol, which she clamped in her brass hand

and held to shade herself and Lisette. By the time they reached the hotel the sun was noon-high and broilingly hot, even so near the mountains. Rima's determined gaiety had mercifully subsided and the party mounted the hotel's exterior steps in silence. In the dim entryway the eldest Lincoln girl offered them luncheon, then, when that was turned down, iced tea, which they gratefully accepted.

Once more to the verandah. Lisette was tempted to stretch out upon the wood and raffia divan, but knew better. The straight-backed chairs kept her head up, her chin becomingly high. Matty had intercepted the tray and bore it out to them. The drinks' chill revived her somewhat. Ice also had been formerly unknown in Everfair.

"Ah, Fwendi, I need your opinion of a change in the script I'm contemplating making." Pathetic, the lengths to which the man went. At some recent point the encounters he'd contrived with the two of them had become trysts—platonic, evidently, yet affording him obvious pleasure. Really, despite his help with the British in Cairo, there was no need for him to have joined them for this trip at all—but Lisette could not grudge him whatever happiness he found in the young woman's company.

"Yes? A change in the play? You'd like to read a passage to me, perhaps?" Fwendi rose from her seat on the divan. "In your room?"

Matty followed her within as if mesmerized.

Rima remained. "Well. I imagine y'all have plenty things you wanna talk about." But she made no move to depart. Uneasiness thrummed in the silence like a hidden insect.

From above came an interruption to the awkwardness: Fwendi's voice. "Rima! Rima, come up here—to our room—please?" With apologies for giving them what they wanted, the actress at last left Daisy and Lisette alone with one another.

Perhaps . . . perhaps only a couple of meters separated them now. Jackie had died last August, in Ireland. Did Daisy still mourn him?

Of course she did. But how deeply? For how long?

"I was told you've been entrusted with—"

Lisette shook her head, a warning that they could too easily be overheard, and crooked her finger. Daisy comprehended. She closed her mouth and crossed the verandah's wide planks to Lisette's side.

"Make believe you love me," Lisette instructed her. Muffled laughter in Lisette's hair. "What is the joke in that, Mrs. Albin?" she drew back to ask, pretending offended dignity.

"Oh, chérie—"

Lisette found herself on her feet, drawn up into Daisy's arms. Balancing on her tiptoes, she put her lips to one of Daisy's ears. "Now we whisper." She shut her eyes.

"Yes. Chérie—"

Lisette wanted only to listen—to the fast beat of Daisy's heart, to her soft, uneven breathing—but she must speak, and quickly. "Others may intrude at any moment." Their hosts. Or Rima, who'd left them so reluctantly. "I have received secret offers for the Mote from both Central Powers and Entente. Let us pledge an assignation to discuss them in detail."

"Yes." The Poet bent over Lisette's other ear. "Where can we meet? Chérie—how soon?"

Cool and blue, the night fell swiftly. A smudge of a moon hung low over the Ulindi River. Lisette set the lamp carefully atop her trunk and turned it low.

Europeans told their secrets inside locked rooms. Lisette had learned other ways, here and in her journeying. She saw their merits: if one had a clear view of the surroundings and an evident absence of spies, it would seem one might say anything.

But the lips could be read. Lisette was content to meet Daisy inside, in her own quarters, privately. As of old. As she had often dreamt of doing again.

A steady, even knock on her door. "Enter," she called.

Daisy had changed out of her work costume into a slightly more conventional garment: a gown like a loose duster that covered her knees but ended well above her ankles. Which were still trim and neat.

The room's one chair was empty. Daisy took it, and Lisette sat on her bed. The windows were opened, but their shades down, their curtains closed.

In the lamp's honeyed light Daisy regarded her expectantly.

How to start? Not, Lisette felt sure, with personal matters: not the too-insistent memories evoked by Everfair's sights and sounds and scents; not the reasons Daisy had stipulated originally for keeping Lisette away from the country they had helped to found—which of course the Poet would immediately have regretted stipulating, but never mind that now . . . In letters shared with her, one hoped, by Jackie, Lisette had chronicled the labors her travels as actress and author had disguised: the training at the hands of anonymous operatives around the globe; the clandestine calls on Russian and Italian diplomats; the cipher she and Fwendi had devised, based on the girl's half-forgotten native tongue.

Now she described how she'd been able to continue gleaning intelligence since Jackie's death last year, thanks to the practice afforded by his many illnesses. He had never been really well after the assassination attempt in Alexandria, though they'd only guessed as to the cause of those illnesses, that death.

"So. He often mentioned having seen you when we were together. He would always say you were well." Daisy's keen eyes were turned away. Lisette couldn't tell whether they sorrowed. Would that have helped, though? She'd only want to know who they sorrowed for.

The rest of her obligations, she reminded herself. Take care of those, and she would be at liberty . . . "The French, British, and Russians offer us the lands between Kigoma, Kakonko, and Uvira, an approximate triangle."

"German territory, isn't it? Urundi?" As Lisette had expected, Daisy took her position as the Mote's Poet seriously. In that capacity, she must hold in her awareness all Everfair's concerns, then present the Mote with her peculiar view of them.

"It is German," Lisette affirmed. "And they would establish embassies, accord us more complete diplomatic recognition."

Daisy nodded. "But what do they ask for all that?"

Lisette heaved a sigh. "Much." She enumerated each item on her fingers. "They would like access to our minerals, and especially the Bah-Sangah earths, which they correctly believe are the pitch-blends needed for their manufacture of luminescent paints. They want to call upon our expertise with aircanoes, and the manufacture of shonguns. They ask also for our rubber."

"But we have no rubber! Or hardly any we can spare. All right. What else?"

"A staging area for the campaign against the Cameroons. A blind eye turned toward breaching the neutrality principles of the Berlin Conference in any and all African colonies." She switched hands. "Our medicines—"

A snort of disbelief. "They'll have difficulty abiding by the proper administration protocols." Daisy assumed an expression of annoyed superiority like that to be found on the faces of most Europeans confronted by traditional African practices. "'A load of superstitious nonsense!' they will call our instructions. I know the attitude they'll take; I doubt they'll get any good out of *that* proviso. You haven't mentioned—"

"Soldiers. Yes. And mechanics. And bearers."

Daisy gasped. "No! We *could* not."

"As you say."

"The blacks—these politicians want to make slaves of them, to repeat Leopold's cruelties anew, to— No."

Slaves of "them," thought Lisette. *Not of "us." Yet, not of "you," either. "Them."* But she said nothing.

Daisy was silent too, though only for a bit. Then: "You met also with the Germans?"

Lisette nodded. "Yes. They also would like Everfair to commit to fight upon their side. We could declare ourselves neutral, outwardly, and in return for supplies and aid in transportation we would receive"—she breathed a soft huff of laughter—"the same territory as we would from the Entente."

Daisy laughed too. "Well, neither has a legitimate claim, though I suppose theirs is more generally accepted."

"And in exchange the Germans require the same materials and expertise as do the French and their Entente."

Lisette leaned forward to impart the information Daisy would desire most. "Interestingly, the governor of Zanzibar is for real peace. At least upon this continent—he has no influence on European events. What his Fatherland proposes he agrees to, for his domain and ours as well. Sans treaty violations and soldiers."

Daisy rose to her feet. "Well, then, do we truly need to discuss how I ought to present these offers? Peace or war? Freedom or bondage? Promises broken or promises kept? Our answer is obvious." She lifted a hand to rake her curls; catching her fingers on the ribbon restraining them, she tugged at it impatiently.

Almost against her will Lisette rose also and reached to help her. The knot persisted. "Sit," she told Daisy, as if the other woman were a child or a dog, and found herself dragged back down onto the bed in arms irresistible, smelling as before of lime and sweet herbs.

"Chérie, chérie, do you want me again—still—"

Why else had she come so far? With her teeth Lisette renewed her attack upon the stupid ribbon and at last it loosened and dropped to the counterpane. The sandals were off in a trice, and Daisy's gown was just as easy to remove. Underneath it, time had treated Daisy's body kindly—kindlier even than the drying sun and wind had treated her tender face.

Lisette's turn. All her faults would be visible—how well she knew them, and how professionally she took them into account. But what use caution here and now? She stripped—tossed her blouse at the abandoned chair, snaked out of her skirt where she lay, shoving it aside to the floor. Lifting her chemise—

"No. Stop. Let me—please?"

She felt her arms drift to her sides. With a mother's solicitude Daisy divested Lisette of the last of her defenses: stockings and slippers, silk and leather and lace. And then skin touched skin: no hindrance. Only unsparing pleasure and unremitting happiness.

Rattling metal woke her. The bed was crowded—ah, but with Daisy, not Rima. Lisette settled closer to Daisy's back—but that noise—again! Louder—she turned her head toward the source.

The door of her room's handle shook. "Lisette?" Rima's urgent voice. "Lisette! You oughta open this—"

Behind her the bed dipped and rustled as Daisy shifted. Rolling to lie flat, she met Lisette's eyes with a frown barely discernible in the room's dimness.

Bam! The door shook in its frame. "Lisette! Lemme in! Fwendi ain't been to our room at all last night and I—"

Furious, Lisette jumped to the floor, but Daisy sat up, reaching to restrain her. "Wait—" She donned her gown and Lisette saw her wisdom. She called to Rima, who was still haranguing her from outside, and assumed her own peignoir before turning the suddenly subdued door's handle.

"Awww . . ." Rima hovered in the entranceway. "I apologize—I didn't know y'all was sleepin together."

Of course she had. "Nonsense. But what's this about Fwendi? What time is it?" Lisette spared a glance for the shades, which showed light around their edges. Morning.

"It's around six-thirty, seven."

Up again so early. Mother of god. "And you saw her when? Have you informed the Lincolns?" She gestured for Rima to come in. The passageway was empty. She closed the door and once more locked it.

They had all supped together—Lisette could not recall on what, but that made no difference. At the appointed hour she had excused herself from the verandah and gone to her room, to be joined by Daisy after a suitable interval.

"It was my night for a bath," said Rima. "So I left em together down here and didn't think nothin of havin a couple hours to myself up there, since she woulda waited for me to be finished fore she went to wash herself. And then I come over all relaxed and I lain down on the blankets and next you know, here I am."

Blessedly, the Lincolns had not yet been told. There was a simple answer to the mystery.

But at Matty's door Lisette's discreet scratching elicited no response. She opened it. The room was empty, the bed undisturbed.

She entered, and Rima followed her unsolicited. "So they's finally together?"

Ignoring her, Lisette looked for a note of explanation. The wash-stand bore only toiletry items. On a spindly-legged table was a stack of three books. Pegs supported a nightshirt and dressing gown, and a coat she couldn't remember Matty wearing. Not his favorite. A Gladstone bag sat behind the bed's head. Lisette didn't examine its contents; its presence alone argued that Matty had not departed. The other belongings supported the bag's assertion.

The top book purported to be sermons on the virtues of national pride. The second related to chivalrous legends of the British Isles. The third had seemingly been bound blank. Draw-ings and sketches filled its pages.

"You would have appeared rather fetching in that little num-ber," said Daisy, peering over Lisette's shoulder. She had entered the room also. The "little number" in question was an abbreviated grass skirt wisping away mid-thigh, worn in this fanciful repre-sentation with a brief bodice—really, no more than a brassiere—made of orchids.

"It needed modification to render it practical for the stage," she replied, shutting the covers. Matty's head was ever in the clouds . . . "What do you look at so intently, Rima?"

"Nothin but another a them aircanoes comin here every day." The actress turned from the window, letting go of the curtain. Could Matty, that dreamer, could he possibly have schemed to depart undetected? Thus the display of a brush set, a razor—

Lisette paused only to clothe herself presentably before dash-ing across town once again to the mooring platform, Rima and Daisy in her train. To think that she had half-suspected Rima, the Lincolns even, of spying upon her—and not Matty.

Scrambling up the steps, she groaned at her idiocy. Matty need not even travel far to collapse the negotiations' secrecy. There was a wireless in Bukavu, only a hundred kilometers east. Though why hadn't he sent a message when they passed through on their way here?

The platform was deserted. All activity concentrated itself in the field's far end, on the warehouse's loading dock. Lisette hesitated, unsure what next to do. Daisy continued toward the workers— comrades of hers, perhaps.

The newly arrived aircanoe loomed overhead, a dark eminence. Not *Okondo,* but its sister vessel, she believed: the older and bulkier *Mbuza.* It hadn't yet been fitted with one of the new closed gondolas, but could still carry passengers and provide the possibility of escape.

"You wanna tell me what you think is goin on?" asked Rima.

Lisette had treated the girl unfairly—though was this sufficient reason to trust her now? "I'm sorry, but to do that is impossible. Affairs of state."

She scanned the people carrying parcels into the warehouse and saw no sign of Matty from where she stood. She walked closer. Daisy spoke Zan-Dee with a man of lesser height than the others. Both gestured to several points around the warehouse, after which Daisy brought him to her, introducing him as Ekibondo. When Lisette questioned the man concerning the likelihood that the Scotchman had booked a flight with them, he kept smiling while managing to look worried. "We don't expect passengers, no," he said, seeming to misunderstand her. "But it wouldn't be too much trouble to accommodate them—if they are ready immediately?"

"Thank you. We'll see—it may not be necessary." Could this man be a foreign agent also? Would Lisette need an excuse to search the gondola for herself? But that would mean the whole crew was in on the deception.

The warehouse was built of bricks, tall to retain coolness, and painted in intricate designs. Lisette passed its open iron gates and entered a dark interior three times her height. Five-meter arches pierced its walls, admitting the morning's every breeze.

"Look for Matty here. And Fwendi," she added, remembering Rima's original concern. Could he have made the girl his hostage? She sent Daisy to search above the loose-planked ceiling and split the ground floor with the American.

Grey bundles rested in numbered racks, redolent of chocolate. She passed baskets pungent with the odors of spices, of dagga and other herbs clamoring at one another over thinner, subtler aromas: tea and milled ores. She gazed up and down the branching aisles and saw no one, till she returned to where the women and men of *Mbuza* were unloading their cargo. They paused momentarily in their work, but she waved off their help.

In the opposite corner, she found Rima peering doubtfully into a cask of palm oil. "If either of them is in there, they are dead," said Lisette, settling the cask's lid firmly in place.

"So you figure they alive?"

Fwendi knew well how to take care of herself, and Matty was much the shorter of the two—

"Lisette!" Daisy walked toward them quickly, almost running. "I— Come. Please—quietly? Please. Ekibondo was right; I'd have missed this if he hadn't told me where to look." She whispered the words, leading them away from where a ladder clung to the west wall, away from all the walls, to the building's center. Here, bricks had been set in the tamped-earth floor to form a rectangle filled with irregular diamond shapes. At its center gaped a large golden hole.

Lisette knelt and peered down into a room brimming with light. Slowly, as her eyes adjusted, the glow resolved into bales of glittering hay interspersed with splintered glimpses of something else, a shining substance—glass?

"They bring it down from the Ruwenzori Mountains and store it underneath, here—there's a larger entrance outside—"

"Bring *what* down from the Ruwenzoris? Store *what* underneath—" asked Lisette, struggling to comprehend the scene before her—below her—

"Ice," said Rima. "They keepin it frozen in the ground and then ship it over to Kisangani and where people need it. You an me seen the same thing up North in America, ice cut in winter for usin in the summer."

Lisette wondered what any of this had to do with Matty and Fwendi's absence. Then she saw them off to the room's left, stretched out on a bank of yellow hay, wrapped in a single blanket. They were sleeping. Fwendi's brass arm reflected the light of the lamp

hanging on a post at their heads—no sleeve covered the join between her brown skin and the metal levers, screws, pumps, and
pistons. As Lisette looked down, enthralled, the blanket slid further
off to reveal Fwendi's shoulder, ribs, and strong, scarred back. With
half-conscious fingers she stroked Matty's smooth-shaven cheek,
then reached for the blanket, which eluded her several times. To
make sure she caught it, she opened her eyes—and saw them
watching.

Lisette blushed. "'Jour," she said, managing to sound casual,
as if encountering Fwendi on her way to breakfast. In response
she received the most extraordinarily joyous grin.

The covering for this revealing hole must be nearby. Lisette
lifted her dazzled eyes to search for it in the dark there above.

"You are awake, my dearest?" With feelings of extreme awkwardness Lisette heard Matty address Fwendi in quite intimate
terms. Evidently he had no idea of his audience. Daisy held one
edge of a large wooden square in her hands. She tilted it forward.
Rima leapt to help. The two of them lowered it over the hole and
scraped it into place.

"Who—" asked Matty, cut off mid-question.

"I agree we ought to keep this affair quiet," whispered Daisy,
as though Lisette had said as much. "Of course I wouldn't dream
of speaking of it, or showing anyone else. Only you—I wanted
you to see proof of what I've found out. Now how can we prevent a scandal?" She rose from her knees with enviable ease.
"We'll discuss it between us, privately."

Rima assisted Lisette to stand, squeezing her hand tightly a second before she let it loose. "Without them? Ain't you think they
got somethin to say?"

"No, you're right. The way down— According to Ekibondo,
the real door's outside. That trapdoor's only so one may lift out a
block or two at a time."

To the building's north they found the ice cellar's entrance, disguised by a low hill. As Rima put her hand on the latch of the
double doors set in its side, they were already opening. Out stepped
Matty, shirt collar slightly askew, one telltale end of a grass stem

caught in his tousled hair. "Good—you received my message." He looked pointedly at Rima.

"I did?"

"About moving the rehearsal." The Scotchman's face reddened. He was surprisingly bad at lying, considering his career. "Didn't realize the dock would be so busy," he lied again, and turned to Daisy. "Glad to see you, too." Another lie. "This way."

The dirt ramp was short and shallow, ending in a stone-floored room that didn't look like the one into which Lisette had inadvertently spied. It was wide, yet not deep, and would not have reached the warehouse's center. It ended in a wall bristling with palm fronds, their points stabbing outward.

Fwendi greeted them as she slipped between two posts that framed a gloom in which Lisette could distinguish nothing—not with the lamp Fwendi carried glaring at her. She was more neatly clothed than Matty, having had, Lisette supposed, more time to arrange herself.

Matty opened his jacket—to which a few yellow strands still clung—and removed a sheaf of papers. Flipping hurriedly through them, he divided them into three groups. "Fwendi will read the lines of The Elephant Queen, and I will do the other animal ambassadors."

"They's more animal ambassadors? From other realms, like the elephants?"

"The action takes place after what was the play's last scene. Wendi-La and the other children are celebrating their victory over the monsters; their parents miraculously restored, you know, the elephants joyfully dancing. Then representatives of these other magical lands approach—the Realms of the Giraffes, the Lions, the Crocodiles—and ask for help against the monsters now invading *their* homelands."

Lisette thought she saw what Matty attempted. Listening to the stirringly martial tone of Wendi-La's new speech, she was sure. If this coda in which their national heroine pledged war against others' enemies influenced the Mote more deeply than the pleas

Daisy would make on the behalf of true neutrality, Matty's Entente friends could well triumph.

"Now you climb up on the gaol roof—will one of you bring out some hay bales for her to stand on?" Matty had forgotten where he was, who was with him, all but the world of make-believe. Lisette left, but not to fetch him his precious hay. Let Fwendi handle the properties—she loved the man. Evidently.

Aboveground, warmth stroked her face lightly, a promise of overpowering heat later in the day. She paused at the ramp's top to wait for Daisy, who seemed to have also chosen to abandon Matty to this ruse of a rehearsal.

One glance at her lover's face and Lisette knew the day's troubles had only begun. That smile, so slight, so distant. She must be worried . . . Could Lisette in some way help?

As it transpired, Daisy wasn't all that concerned about Matty's influence on the Mote. "My approach is direct. I will say exactly how I believe we ought to act. They'll hear and understand me clearly, no mistake. And I have a vote." Only one vote, but one more than Matty possessed.

They arrived at the loading dock just as *Mbuza* untied. Its giant shadow shrank, second by second. They watched it climb the softly straying winds. This ship's outsized airbag was a mottled green.

"So, then, what is the matter?" Lisette would not let silence divide them. Not any longer. Nor distance—Lisette would retire, cease touring. The better to compose her novels. She and her lover would be always together. Not parted by time. Not by that man's ghost. "Come, sit." She led Daisy to the bench beside the mooring pole, deserted now that the aircanoe had gone.

"It's the prospect of their marriage," said Daisy, looking back at the warehouse. "If the scandal their connection brings about can't be quashed. Neither you nor Rima seems to take that seriously."

"But my dear, I grant you've lived in Everfair longer, more continuously, so you no doubt have a better idea of what is and is not acceptable. But surely their ages don't signify so very much—"

"No! Not that! Only think—Fwendi will want to have a baby— several!"

Lisette didn't want to understand. But she did. "Their races."

"Oh—not that alone. For themselves it would be fine. In God's eyes we are all equal. But think of the consequences, the miscegenation. The children."

Lisette could say nothing. She wanted to rise up, to walk away. By the numbness radiating out of this moment, she knew the pain, when it came, would be bad.

For a while she was unable even to move. Her face must have shown something of what she was realizing.

Daisy took her limp hand. "Why should any of this matter to us? It shouldn't. We're not— There's no way we could have children with one another, chérie. We can't cause those sorts of problems."

She should forgive Daisy her preoccupation with an issue that could be said to have forced itself upon her notice. More than once. Lily's death was all that had prevented the green shoots of her attachment to Tink from growing to the point of bearing fruit. Because the girl was murdered by Leopold's men, the mother's prejudices had not been put to the test in that instance. "But George and his wife, they might have caused them." Though there'd been no issue out of his marriage to the Negro missionary.

"Yes. You remember how upset I was, ready to disown him? Who'd wish such a burden on anyone, especially a poor innocent: to be part of neither world, not black, not white, an orphan even though both parents live—"

Le Gorille, Grand-père, had wished such a burden on Lisette's mother. This miscegenation of which her love spoke so contemptuously? Of that, of *those sorts of problems,* Lisette herself had been born.

She glanced skyward. *Mbuza* was yet visible, its gondola a swaying trinket attached to the balloon by silvery chains. She had memorized the schedules. It would return at midnight to depart for Kisangani again at dawn.

Daisy would have to be on board in order to attend the Grand

Mote. So would Matty. And so would Fwendi and Rima and Lisette.

She would have to go. But not as Daisy's lover. Not yet. Perhaps—perhaps not ever.

Fortunately, she had other options. Rima was young and inexperienced, unskilled, but had so far avoided giving her this particular injury.

Gently, Lisette removed her hand from Daisy's grasp. Slowly, she stood up. Daisy was asking questions she couldn't answer. Without another word, Lisette returned to the hotel. Locked in her room, she drew down the barkcloth shades, suffusing the walls with a rosy twilight, and did her best to rest. When that proved impossible, she got up again and packed.

Kisangani, Everfair, June 1914

King Mwenda's capital Kisangani was now also the capital of Everfair, as the whites called this country. And it was a city: Kisangani had become home to many, many people, a hand of thousands. He could remember it holding fewer than a hand of hundreds.

During his time in Alexandria he had learned the European mode of counting. It was one of many pieces of knowledge he had brought back with him from Egypt. Another was the whites' calendar. According to this, the war against Leopold had ended in 1904, though weak resistance remained for a while in some areas. He'd dealt with the last of that in 1906. Soon after he'd gone to Alexandria's Fouad University to study for eleven seasons. From 1907 to 1912: six years of self-exile, of trying to master the whites' ways and prove himself their rightful ruler.

Six years without good connection to his spirit father. No, longer: almost eight. He hadn't made a serious attempt since his return. He had never seemed to find the right place, the right time.

Despite having lived almost eighty seasons, thirty-nine "ah-nays," he questioned his own fitness to serve as king. Despite having won.

The war's end had changed many things, but one thing was the same: King Mwenda had no peace, even here, at home. The steady, soothing roar of the river's cataracts had been drowned out by the hiss of pumps, the chugging of bicycle motors, the rumble of traction engines, the noisy steamboats coming and going and endlessly singing through shrill pipes. The beats of drummers' messages and shouts in many tongues surrounded him as he walked now at the head of his retinue. The shouts came from the Mah-Kow laborers erecting steel frames for Kisangani's high new houses; from the Zanzibari traders crowding the city's wide streets and increasingly rare open lots. Also he heard the chatter of returning whites—not as loud, but unavoidable, since they'd decided their lives were no longer in danger. From allies they and the Americans had somehow become something more.

Rain still dripped off of the overhanging beams of unfinished buildings and the leaves of trees. It had ended late that morning, as it often did this time of year. Nevertheless, king and courtiers walked the relatively drier paths heaped up in the streets' centers, raised beds of shells and pebbles rearing out of the mud. With Mwenda came Old Kanna, Alonzo, and his favorite queen's favorite ladies, Sifa and Lembe. Josina had spent several days outside the royal compound, staying with the Poet and her remaining daughter, Rosalie. He missed her.

Just past a freshly painted corner shrine to the Bah-Sangah's sacred earths, they came to their destination. Of course the Poet's home was in Kisangani's modern style, compounded of foreign and traditional influences. A short stairway of river stones led from a three-sided work yard to a porch running around its sides.

He climbed upward. Oiled bars of metal stood in place of wooden supports; the mats attached to them were much the same, however. The same sort of space was left open between the roof and the strangely flat walls, too. And the roofs and walls of the buildings resting on top of it.

The stairs paused at a door set in the house's narrow end. The king nodded, and Old Kanna came forward to knock on it.

The door was of fig wood, with iron cross-braces. A brass hook set toward one side of it turned and it opened, swinging outward—a mistake if this home ever needed defending. It was Rosalie rather than the Poet herself who had answered Old Kanna's summons.

"Here you are," she said. "We worried you might come late." She showed them where they could leave shoes, shawls, umbrellas, or whatever they'd carried here but no longer needed, then took them through an opening in a wall as flat as those outside. The floor creaked beneath his feet: wood lined with undecorated mats.

Josina sat beside the Poet, each on a backless chair. Three more, unoccupied, formed a circle with those, and cushions had been set behind. That was polite: Mwenda took one of the empty seats and gestured for Old Kanna to take another. Alonzo refused the third, lowering himself to a cushion as Sifa and Lembe had already done.

Rosalie had gone deeper into the house. A moment later she emerged from behind a bead curtain holding a lidded metal pot. Steam curled up out of its curving spout, and also the enticing scent of tea.

All was civilized. A low-legged table waited at the circle's center, its top a wide golden tray incised with tasteful triangles and representations of tall dancers. Polished horn cups had been placed in front of hosts and guests. Also on the table stood a lamp—probably the one the Poet had used back in Kamina. Unnecessary here except as a symbol of their unity.

The hot tea caused Mwenda to sweat pleasantly. But it was not the work of a king simply to sit and enjoy himself.

"Now that Leopold is gone we must reconsider our alliance," he said abruptly, interrupting the Poet's discourse on the Mote's most recent debate. He put down his tea. "How shall we divide our spoils? How shall we rearrange the region's government?"

A look passed between the Poet and Josina. "Why does there need to be any change?" the white woman asked. "After a decade—"

"Because I say so, and I am the country's ruler."

"But the Mote—"

"The Mote is not in charge! I am! This is my home, my land!"

"But Everfair is for all! We took you in, refugees, rescued you, fought beside you—"

"You bought our land from someone who didn't own it—a thief!"

There was nothing even the Poet could say in answer to this assertion. It was true. Mwenda had studied. He knew the laws.

Josina spoke into the silence. "You have talked of this with your spirit father?"

That was not the sort of thing one discussed. "I know what is right, what is my duty. I am king." He maintained his dignity, bending down a little in his mind, as if he addressed a child.

Infuriatingly, Josina responded using the same manner. "Yes, you are king. No one has disputed that in the twenty seasons since Leopold was defeated. So what has happened to make it necessary to question the presence of our allies *now*? Why today? Why during *this* market?"

Alonzo answered for him. "We don't ask why the king makes his decisions." He bowed his head quickly in Mwenda's direction. "But if your mind seeks quieting, think how before, the Mote made decisions only about what was best for us here. How it accepted on our behalf the help we needed from whites first to fight Leopold, then to recover from that fighting.

"Now. War is coming back. It will pit against each other powers beyond our country, beyond all Africa. Is it to be left to the Mote to choose our side in this contest?"

Very well put. Mwenda nodded, and took a sip of tea to show he wasn't angry.

Rosalie had sat next to him. According to the whites' customs, they were equals. "Well, why not?" she said. "Since you've agreed with everything it has decided so far, will you turn dictator over this? Like another Leopold. If we held a vote—"

He rose from the table as slowly as he could. "Good bye." He turned to go. After all he had given—his own hand!—to be compared to that devil! He refused to hear it. The woman—girl—was saying something more, but he would not listen. He walked calmly out of the house. The rain had begun again. His followers would gather the umbrellas and other belongings. He waited on the steps for them, but it was the Poet who joined him.

"Forgive my daughter, please." The Poet frowned. "Today is her brother's birthday—a difficult time for her. She misses him, and that reminds her of missing Lily—"

Who had died rescuing *him*. His head cleared. "It is forgotten." But didn't the Poet's son live close enough for visiting?

"Not George," the Poet said, as if she sensed his misunderstanding. "She misses Laurie. The baby"—she grinned ruefully—"who is now a fully grown man. In England. Looking after his father's affairs."

Alonzo and Nenzima slipped past him to the lower stairs. So did Old Kanna. Josina appeared in the open door, her women behind her.

"You must go back to your palace," said the Poet. "But I beg you to decide nothing rash."

Kisangani, Everfair, June 1914

Josina's room overlooked the garden. Before the war the palace had been a hotel for white criminals. Its painted stone walls were already fading, but the flowering bushes planted at its center still scented the rain.

Mwenda was right. Everyone was right. That was the problem.

The settlers of Everfair had come here naïvely at best, arrogantly at worst. Due to the orders of the king they had found the country seemingly empty. In the fight against Leopold, their assistance had been most valuable, and they had also brought to the cause the help of Europeans and Americans who would never otherwise have cared for any African's plight.

But by their very presence they poisoned what they sought to save. How could they not? Assuming they knew the best about so many things—not even realizing they had made such assumptions—they acted without considering other viewpoints and remained in ignorance in spite of the broadest hints.

It was to try to penetrate this cloud of ignorance that the queen had spent several days as the Poet Daisy's guest. With at least partial success. Now it was understood that other viewpoints existed; that the king's unhappiness could lead to actions against the colonists from which their "constitution" could not protect them.

A flash of crimson showed in the gathering twilight: the beak and tail of a bird flying to shelter in the branches of a tree on the courtyard's far side. Its feathers were mostly a pale brown, but a bright red streak surrounded each black and shining eye. Though cocks and hens of this sort of bird would raise their chicks together, and they foraged in large groups—sometimes their flocks numbered more than twenty hands—they had separate nests. Good. So it was with her and the king. This vision validated their way of life.

Tomorrow Josina would go to see her sister, the Frenchwoman, Mademoiselle Lisette. Quickly, before she left again.

Tonight Josina would seduce the king and pluck away his doubts.

Leaving the balcony to reenter her apartments, Josina signaled Lembe to close the folding door behind her.

Mwenda liked the bush. To make him more comfortable here, she instructed her women to put away her hangings and richly colored cloths—except for those on her luxurious bed. Sifa filled bowls and vases with water and arranged leaves and blossoms in them. Lembe procured honey, mangoes, seedcakes, and palm wine, and lit lamps to sit on the table and windowsill and hang from the walls. Sifa bathed Josina in cool water from the river, the second time that day, and gave the queen her mirror so she might check the arrangement of her hair and jewels. They were impeccable, naturally, because Josina never settled for less. She removed the necklace that had been given to her by the Poet. It would be stored with her other ornaments. She allowed Sifa to repaint the gardenia markings on her breasts. Then she sent both women to supplicate the king for his presence.

She calmed herself, slowed and regulated her breath. The door opened. King Mwenda strode in alone. A happy omen, though Josina could see a guard standing just outside the door before it shut. Also of note was the arm Mwenda wore: wrapped in soft leather from the wrist up, and likewise soft-palmed, with four fingers, though only two were in the strictest sense necessary.

So Josina knew to ignore his scowl. She patted the bed beside her.

The king shook his head. "You ought never to have mentioned he who guides me."

"Really? But I said nothing that isn't common knowledge

among your subjects." Since he wouldn't sit, she stood. He was still much taller. Let him be. "And if you would be advised by me—"

"Advised by you? Why should I care what a low and stinking *spy* thinks?"

Ah. "But you should! You should care very much! You are a ruler, but I am a politician—an intelligencer, not a spy, and I can help you! As I did when you sent me to win us allies against Leopold. And again when acting as your regent while you went abroad to Alexandria. I *want* to help you! Let me—let me help you. Please."

He frowned but was silent. She dared to take both his hands. He had not worn a weapon. "You have used me, yes? Used me to preserve your realm for our son. Used me to send messages to my father, oh, yes, and you can use me now, again, more!"

"Not if you tell the Poet every mystery of our people. These whites—they're good enough, I'm sure, in their homes, where they belong, but will they never leave? Will we never be rid of them?"

No, she thought, *we never will.* But instead of saying so, she asked a question: "What does your spirit father say?"

The king groaned and collapsed. Josina pulled him toward her so that he landed on the bed. That was progress.

"I haven't heard him. He hasn't spoken. I may have angered him . . ."

"Are you sure?"

"No! Of course I'm not sure!"

"When was the last time you—"

"Stop! I shouldn't have said—I should have lied to you, *spy.*"

"Since you journeyed to Egypt to go there to their school?" No answer. He'd visited the bush by himself two times since his return. She had assumed it was for prayer. "Have you tried since the war ended?"

"Promise you'll tell no one."

"I swear."

"No. I have not."

Josina swallowed the salty spit of her dismay. Tears pricked at the edges of her eyes, sharp and hot. She wished she could swallow them, too, but did her best to keep from blinking so they wouldn't fall.

She couldn't cry. She had to talk. "Do it now."

"What? No!"

"Now!"

"I need to make preparations—a pilgrimage—"

"You require only what—metal? Quiet surroundings? You have your new shongo. No one will disturb us here till dawn. My king—" She grasped both his hands tighter. Both. Time to reveal how much she'd learned. More than was wise. "You ought not to fear to find out you are abandoned. The whites in Alexandria who say your injury unfits you to be king are wrong! Vomit up the sickness of such notions!"

"How do you know—"

She began again over his interruption. "Your spirit father is the chief of machines, so why would he slight you for taking on an attribute of his own? Because of this new part of you, aren't you more sacred? More holy?"

The harsh sobs of stifled grief filled the room. But only for a short moment. King Mwenda turned to face her. "Woman, you're as brave as anyone I know. You make me act as brave as I want to be." Their clasped hands trembled—because of his shaking or hers? That was one thing she didn't need to know.

She got up and extinguished all but two lamps. Damp and darkness slipped in under the doors to the balcony.

"Do you have anything for a libation?" he asked.

"Only palm wine." It should have been something stronger. Gin. But what they had would have to do.

He poured the palm wine on the wooden floor. He whispered, asking blessings. He drew his shongo, the blade replacing the one that he had hurled upon declaring that *sanza* "truce." He sat on a cushion and gave her one last beseeching look. Then, to keep his communion with his spirit father solitary, Josina covered the king in a cloak printed like leaves, green and black and gold. And waited hours. Long, silent hours. The lamps burned on.

But the morning light had not yet begun to peep around the

sides of the balcony doors when the printed fabric slid down off of King Mwenda's big shoulders. His expression was too soft to be a smile.

"Come here," he said to his favorite queen, "and let me tell you what I have discovered: that my spirit father loves me even now." He held out both his arms.

Kisangani, Everfair, July 1914

Rima Bailey should have been happy. She knew it. She had everything: good work, a woman who loved her, money. Soon they'd be gone out of here, hit the coast, head north, away from the heat and back toward civilization. Soon.

She turned over on the mattress and saw that Lisette had already gotten up. Too hot and stuffy to sleep, anyway. Especially alone. Rima swung her long legs around and sat on the bed's edge. She checked her shoes to make sure no bug had crawled inside and put them on, found some clothes she hoped were clean.

Florida was hot, too, and the air always feeling wet like this. She hadn't liked the weather there, either. What if her lover had never discovered her, never come and taken Rima far, far away?

The noon whistle blew. Their last tech rehearsal was at two. She used the toilet Sir Jamison's guests shared, down a hallway lit by windows at either end. Enough light to see the door to Fwendi's room was open. Rima slowed as she passed it and peeked in. Nobody home. *Why'd they even bother acting like they didn't sleep together,* she wondered.

She took care of her business quick as always. Coming out she heard Lisette's voice drifting from the stairwell, that cute little lilt that turned up the end of every sentence like it was curling. She followed the sound down.

Sir Jamison—she'd never feel like she knew him well enough to call him Matty—had bought a house here even though he spent half the year traveling. He owned houses almost everywhere in Everfair: Bookerville, Bolombo, Kananga, Kamina . . . some places outside, too, like in Cape Town and Dar-es-Salaam. Must be nice having all that money, and the play was making him even richer.

Everyone in the cast sat in the kitchen, drinking tea. Rima missed coffee. They had that in the coast cities; up the Nile, too.

"Are you ready to replace me?" Her lover gestured invitingly at the bench where she sat.

"Naw, but you could slide over an make room."

Lisette must be at least thirty-five from the hints she let slip. She seemed years younger: no sagging at her neckline—none anywhere! Rima could attest to that. Still, perhaps the Frenchwoman wasn't that well suited for ingénue roles any more.

Lisette scooted to the bench's far end and Rima took the vacated spot. Swathed in an unconventional tunic and trousers of the lightest of Egyptian cottons, Lisette looked charming. Like always. And she smelled wonderful—only the slightest bit of sweat under the complex scent she wore. Rima was reminded of lotuses, of golden fruits, of the juices of dark, hidden vines and sun-soaked leaves. Her mouth watered.

So maybe she was a bull dagger. In Everfair that didn't seem to bother folks much, except the missionary people.

The Elephant Queen put a plate down in front of her: fried eggs and kwanga sticks. Rima hated kwanga, but she was a trouper. She unwrapped and ate both her sticks even though they tasted like hardened library paste. Somebody had sweltered over a pot cooking them for her.

Everyone else but Lisette was African and used to this kind of food. Sir Jamison had recruited The Butterfly and The Bushbaby in Bukavu; The Bird and The Elephant Queen and King were originally from Chibanda, and had joined the cast via Josina's father's court. Mola, The Elephant Doctor, had come on foot all the way from Boma; officially, the Belgian government caretaking Leopold's legacy allowed their Congolese citizens the right of immigration to Everfair, but unofficially it was discouraged so strongly it was almost impossible. Blockades on the river, sharpshooters posted over the best air routes—the invader was dead and the war was over, but hostilities continued.

Thank goodness the show's remaining speaking parts were small. Except for Mo-La and Bo-La, her character's younger brother and sister. They were played by Josina's son and daughter, thirteen-year-old Ilunga and eleven-year-old Mwadi. No political intrigue there.

Rima had barely finished her meal when Sir Jamison came in, followed at a trying-to-be-discreet interval by Fwendi. He pointed out it was time to leave for the theater. It was only a short walk away, but an irritating one: the rain didn't look like it knew how to stop.

The Grand Ideal Cultural Circus Building was where Leopold's thieves used to keep their rubber, and the prisoners who harvested it too: an old jail and warehouse combined. It was pretty obvious what those creeps had cared about: the airy offices on the Circus's upper floor carried a whiff of the grey sap balls once stored there. By contrast, the muddy pit below the stage Sir Jamison's crew had erected had needed a deep and thorough excavation before the crap and blood and piss and puke left there stopped stinking everything up. That's what the Lead Parents said; they were local and they knew the construction workers.

At least the building's brick walls and tin roof kept the worst of the rain out. The dressing rooms—only two, one for women and one for men—were crowded and windowless, lighted by hanging lamps shaded with pierced metal globes. Since tricks involving her fake mechanical arm were part of the run-through, Rima got into her whole costume. Not that there was much to it.

Flash-bangs went off on cue and smoke spouted out of her brass glove more or less when it was supposed to. The stage rotated so the right scenery showed for every act, and the steam-cranked scroll ran smoothly behind her, depicting her journey to the underground realm of Everland. The musicians didn't have the score memorized in the right order, though. They worked on that awhile. Then there was a short break before showtime. Not long enough to leave the theater. She met Lisette on the steam porch off the building's back.

"Are you hungry?" her lover asked, leaning her bicycle against the rail surrounding the engine. She gestured at a gourd fastened above her machine's smaller boiler. "I brought you sugar-baked plantains."

"Naw, I don't wanna be all logy when it come time to perform. Thanks anyways."

Rima stood under the far edge of the roof's overhang, wishing the coming night would make things cooler. Except where it butted up against the Circus, the steam porch didn't have walls. Just thick poles holding up the thatch. It was wide enough that even when the wind blew the equipment and the precious coal imported from Angola stayed dry.

They were alone. Soon, though, someone would come to shovel more fuel into the boiler's furnace. Rima took advantage of the moment, turning suddenly and rushing over to pull Lisette's belly against her scantily skirted hips. Bless the night that she got taught how to make love with other women. She bent and nuzzled the soft blond hair of her first and only's head, milk and honey. Lisette's lips were pliable enough, her polished teeth parted willingly enough—but the kisses she gave back seemed distracted. Rima opened her eyes and saw Lisette's eyes were open, too. She was staring past Rima's shoulder at the steam engine.

Ah. Rima had figured out about that quirk of Lisette's months ago. She let her loose a moment, then rearranged things so Lisette held the rail and faced the big machine. Rima pressed herself against those fat thighs and darling buttocks, that dimpled, curving back. She ran her nose down from Lisette's kitchen along her neck to where her spine sunk into a dip between mounds of flesh firm as living bread. Lifted the cloth of her lover's shirt and licked the salt gathering there.

A gasp of breath was her reward. She dragged her body free of contact so she could use her hands. Tracing upward with the tips of her fingers, she caressed the backs of Lisette's knees and legs through the filmy fabric, cupped the plump swell of her ass. Then, scraping her nails oh-so-lightly along its underside to the warm—

Bang! Wood on wood—a door slamming shut—or open? Rima dropped her arms, raised her head, and opened her eyes again. It had gotten dark. Light spilled onto the steam porch from the Circus's rear entrance. A woman's silhouette blocked it.

"Lisette? Chérie?" It was the Poet.

They would be invisible to someone dazzled by lamps. Rima held still and kept her mouth shut. So did her lover. The Poet took a few steps in their direction before retreating. The door closed much more quietly than it had opened.

"You think she smell us?" Rima asked. She meant it as a joke, but Lisette didn't laugh. When Rima tried to hug her some more and to at least position their legs together for a nice ride, Lisette wouldn't cooperate. Her arms stiffened, and her back, too, and they wouldn't loosen up under Rima's kneading. So, despite the tight ache like a cramp in her pussy, she gave up.

Anyway, it had to be time to go in. Time to check her makeup—it was sure to be a mess—and to re-glove and take care of the thousand and one details that would help the show go all right. Which it better, because this was her debut as lead.

All wound up the way she was, Rima danced and sang like a devil high on lightning. She didn't just speak her lines, she set them off like fireworks. She whizzed and banged and popped, and when the house lamps came on over the audience, the cast took their final bow to applause loud as the town's famous cataracts. She was a star. Rima, Rima, burning bright, in the jungle of the night.

Here, in the darkness, she shone. She could hardly wait to shine in the light.

Kisangani, Everfair, July 1914

Matty surged to his feet with the rest of the audience. He started to clap and thought better of it: His own play. He shouldn't. But, beside him, Fwendi snapped her flesh fingers together and shot sparks from her brass hand, smiling an enormous smile that more than made up for his abstention.

Of course, this was far from the first time she'd seen the play she'd inspired. But it was the first time she'd seen his new final scene performed in a theater. Apparently she liked it.

She nodded and hissed at him, "Bow! Accept their thanks, and graciously!"

He felt his face flush. She was right. He complied but made a jest of himself, flourishing his arms in silly, overly complicated patterns and nearly touching his nose to his knees. Still the applause continued. He leaned as if to address the Mote member beside her and whispered in Fwendi's ear, "You ought to acknowledge them, too, you know; a curtsey perhaps?"

She frowned. She had always rejected his desire to publicize the real-life origins of *Wendi-La,* though to him they seemed obvious. Was this of a piece with her reluctance to admit their relationship, to set her face against the disapproval attending the disparity in their ages?

The actors had come out for a third curtain call and remained onstage. The applause refused to die down.

Then, behind him, Matty heard a high voice singing. It wavered a bit, but the tune was clear, and everyone here knew the words. They'd all joined in the chorus by the time the anonymous singer reached its second line. The embarrassingly long ovation gave way to the national anthem's first verse:

> *"From many countries we journeyed afar*
> *To find the place where our dreams could come true;*
> *With eyes wide open, we dared to plan a paradise:*
> *A home for all and any, our home in you."*

So moving, the combination of the colony's many timbres and accents. The song seemed to satisfy an unrecognized need, to supply whatever it was the applause had been holding out for. Matty craned his head to snatch a glimpse of the singer who'd started the song, but the crowd defeated him. Afterward, as they filed out, he thought he saw Daisy slipping away between people standing in obstinate groups or walking too slowly. He couldn't get past them. He didn't want to abandon Fwendi or drag her with him, either, and the others in their party would wonder at his haste. And what did it matter?

Outside, darkness and dampness ruled. Rain dropped ceaselessly on the Circus's thatch awning, tiny patterings like the dance steps of the clouds' children. Matty positioned himself and Fwendi under a lamp so the others would see them—despite his care, he'd gotten ahead of his guests. But there came Albert and Winthrop, shoulder to shoulder, so deep in conversation they bumped and jostled unheedingly against the other theater patrons. And there were two of the African members of the Grand Mote he'd invited, Loyiki and Nenzima. King and Queen Josina had declined. But in the month since his return to Kisangani all had shown signs of favoring the British side in the upcoming conflict.

If this were a more cosmopolitan city, he'd treat everyone to supper at some hotel or restaurant now. Instead, he had invited them to his home.

They walked to the rail for a rope swing meant to carry pairs of pedestrians from the theater steps to the walkway along the center of Fina Avenue. A perfect hostess, Fwendi caught up a swing and offered it to Albert and Winthrop with a murmur of concern:

"You won't mind waiting for us in the wet? It's only a short ways—"

In answer, Albert produced a couple of fan hats, the pleated, folding, circular headgear invented by settlers fed up with Everfair's endless precipitation. He and Winthrop jovially donned them, then stepped onto opposite sides of the swing's wooden footrest and gripped its rope, Winthrop's hands well above Albert's due to his greater height. The fan hats proved awkwardly wide, their edges bumping together; the two got around that problem by each leaning slightly to their right. Matty pushed them off and they sailed easily over the sunken road, which was busy with the after-theater rush: dog- and goat-carts, and steam bicycles pulling passenger compartments instead of their more usual freight wagons.

To Nenzima and Loyiki, the girl offered a dignified, covered four-seater suspended by chains. He and Fwendi joined them in it. This heavier swing operated by a spring-wound pulley set. Loyiki did the honors and they landed and deployed their umbrellas mere minutes behind the two engineers.

He took Fwendi's arm and led the way. Loyiki and Nenzima fell in after them, and Albert and Winthrop brought up the rear. Soon the throng generated by the play's end dissipated. Fwendi lit her hand to show the path, keeping it well away from the oiled paper of the umbrella sheltering them. He gazed up surreptitiously into her lovely, serious face. He should marry her. He told himself the only difficulty was his age, and not the bad dreams brought on by the mere idea of a wedding. Though he understood from his inquiries into the natives' mores that the disapproval she feared would evaporate if their bonds were formalized.

At the corner of Vuba Street, he helped Fwendi descend the stairs in the side of the walkway. Now there was nothing for it but to wade straight through the brownish water. It looked to be about ankle high. Their feet would be soaked, but they were almost there. He turned to point out the lamps beside his front door and encountered Nenzima's swiftly veiled look of—what? Pity? Could that be right? What reason had she to pity him? She was probably older than he was.

Winthrop gallantly offered to transport Nenzima on his back to the house's raised entrance. She accepted with just a hint of coquettishness. If Matty were a bigger man, he could carry Fwendi across. Unless to do so would remind him of one of his marriage dreams, of falling under an impossible weight and drowning in mud.

Laughing voices came to them as they removed their shoes and put on the sandals Matty had thoughtfully had his servants provide. The cast party was, of necessity, being held here, but Matty had insisted it be confined to the courtyard. They would look in on it later.

Clapham opened the dining room door. As a concession to this continent's customs, the table was built low, the seats surrounding it more like footstools with backs than chairs, to Matty's eyes. In addition to plates carved from native woods, cutlery forged from local ores, a central runner of barkcloth, and a lamp with the requisite ball-shaped shade, Matty had ordered carafes of four different palm wine varieties to be placed in readiness for his party's return. All was as he had directed.

They had an even number of guests, but there were, unfortunately, far fewer women than men. Fwendi, of course, sat at the table's far end. To her left was Winthrop; opposite him, to her right, Albert. He depended on the restraints of polite usage to keep them from conversing with one another across the board, though it would be a hardship for the two engineers. Matty hadn't invited either so they could indulge in talk of technical matters.

Next to Albert, and thus on Matty's left, sat Nenzima. Perhaps it was as good to have gotten the queen's advisor to attend as receiving Josina herself. On Matty's right, beside Winthrop, was Loyiki. He had less confidence in either of the Africans' adherence to the etiquette of table conversation, but hoped the engineers would support him in his efforts to maintain standards.

Clapham served the wines, asking each guest which he preferred. Nenzima requested the sourest, and pronounced herself delighted to taste the herbs Fwendi's great-uncle Mkoi had earlier insisted on sprinkling into it.

During the first course—fried tilapia and boiled plantain balls—

Matty accepted compliments on his authorship of *Wendi-La*. He turned them as skillfully as possible, effusing over Rima's debut. The second course, a stew whose oily red sauce made it nearly inedible, was served and eaten to more general remarks.

Finally, they came to the sweet—not a traditional pudding but a mélange of fruits made ready to eat. Clapham was dismissed.

Without waiting for the women to withdraw—that would deprive him of Fwendi's much-needed support—Matty plunged into the business to be taken care of. "The play's last scene, you know, was written just a few weeks ago, with an eye to the looming shadows of world events," he said, trying for a casual tone.

"It fits so well with the rest," said Loyiki. "One wouldn't know it had been added on just lately."

That wasn't the line.

"Events? What events?" Winthrop's question was more like it.

"War. War is coming." A momentary cessation in the noise of the cast party toward the back of the house made his pronouncement more dramatic than he'd intended.

"Hah. There's always a war, somewhere," said Albert, the first to recover. "The masters take care that'll be the case."

"But this time, they say, there's no avoiding it," said Fwendi. "The next war will be fought everywhere. Even here."

Trust Fwendi. He thanked her with his eyes, meeting her steady gaze over the length of the table and the intervening lamp.

"But we've just finished up beating Leopold," objected Nenzima. "They ought to leave us alone so we can recover."

"I'm afraid it doesn't work like that," said Matty. He tried to avoid a sarcastic tone, but without much success, judging from the Africans' expressions.

Again, Fwendi rescued him. "The Europeans think us too small to concern themselves with our well-being." She chose a mangosteen from the fruit dish at her end of the table and pulled apart its scored shell. "Except as their allies. Or as the allies of their enemies."

Winthrop cleared his throat. "Not even those who assisted us before? The Americans? The French?"

"The Brits?" asked Albert.

"We're regarded as an investment, mostly, especially by the Yankees—"

"And all of their governments, you see, are expecting to fight on the side of the Belgians." These unwelcome words came from the mouth of Mademoiselle Toutournier, stationed at the silently opened door. She entered and walked toward Fwendi with her smooth actress's tread. Albert and Winthrop stood at once, reminding Matty he couldn't remain seated either. She ignored their offered chairs. "Their rulers are all such good friends."

Nenzima made a face at the black plum she'd bitten into, as though it contained half a worm.

"But Leopold has been deposed in favor of his son," Matty hastened to add.

"True." The Frenchwoman smiled coolly. "And yet . . ." She left her sentence unfinished, her implications unchallengeable. Since Kalima, she'd changed toward him. If not for the influence she held over Fwendi, he'd have found a way, by now, to switch Lisette's accommodations to the palace or, better, to Daisy's— why wasn't she at her lover's apartments tonight?

"Some other African countries have declared they would desire to uphold the neutrality agreed on at the Berlin Conference: Urundi, and so forth." It sounded like a statement. It was actually a challenge.

"German colonies," said Matty.

"The Germans will wage war against Leopold?" Loyiki asked.

"No! Against the Belgian government!" Frustrated, Matty clenched his dessert fork. "Leopold's gone! Over! Done with!"

La Toutournier seemed to ignore him. "The Germans will go to war, yes. But no one else will do so if they can help it. Nor should we."

"The Mote has discussed this matter," said Nenzima, lifting her eyes from her wine cup. "We're undecided."

"It must be decided soon," said Matty.

Mademoiselle didn't even turn to face him. "It must be decided correctly. With the head and the heart both.

"Everyone knows Portugal hasn't picked a side yet," she added. "Their colonies, too, are uncommitted. They may remain so, despite efforts by members of the Entente to drag them into such a mess." And then she *did* look at him, long and pointedly.

He managed to lead the conversation onto safer ground. They moved out to the courtyard, where, under the shelter of mats stretched between the branches of the baobab, crew and cast sang and drank and praised and embraced each other. "Hey, Author-La!" one cried, their pet name for Matty. "Success! We'll go on tour to Cape Town, won't we?" He endured their congratulations and produced his own. He applauded The Lion Ambassador's dance, even gave in to the urging and joined her in a dignified measure or two. It was much like a strathspey.

Somehow, the evening ended. The Elephant Doctor and The Giraffe Ambassador escorted Albert and Winthrop to their quarters; Loyiki, Nenzima, and Josina's offspring Ilunga and Mwadi returned to the palace in the company of the Elephant Queen and King, who also lodged there.

It was late before he could creep down the finally deserted passageway to Fwendi's room. They had agreed to trade visits; tonight was his turn.

She was already abed. But not asleep. As he pulled aside the sheet covering her, she blinked in the light of the little lamp he'd carried. Her many tiny braids, freed from the chignon in which she normally confined them, formed a dark mass on the white pillowcase like a night-blooming flower's rough shadow.

They shared intercourse. Gently, as if there would always be time. As if he were not twice her age. As if he'd never die.

Afterward he helped her remove her hand and kissed the naked stump goodnight. Then he lay by her side, their shoulders pressing close together.

"Is it truly inevitable it will come to us, this war?" she asked.

Drowsing, he told the truth: "As inevitable as our love."

Kisangani, Everfair, August 1914

Now that they no longer hid in caves, now that they'd adopted Kisangani as their capital, Everfair's Grand Mote met in a proper building. Daisy wished they'd been able to build something of their own; instead, they used the abandoned billiards room in the former hotel King Mwenda now designated his palace. The implications of this location were not lost on anyone.

The game tables had been taken out and chairs from the lobby brought in. An unused chandelier dangled over the room's center; below it Daisy had placed a plant stand to hold their Lamp.

For once she was the first to arrive. She lifted the Lamp's globe-shaped shade and struck a light with the tinder box set out beside it, touched the flame to the wick. Then she took her usual seat and waited.

She didn't have long. The king and Queen Josina entered together, their bearing formal. Yet, in some indescribable way, the air around them seemed filled with their affection for one another. That had been a trend for the last few Motes.

Next came her oldest son and his wife. His wife. At least they hadn't had any children to date, and that became less likely with every passing month. Daisy nodded and smiled, held out her hands for George to take or ignore. With a glance at Martha Albin, he gathered his mother's hands in his own and gave them each a brief kiss.

Old Kanna came in the door leaning on Nenzima's arm, with Loyiki bustling in before them, carrying the elder's beloved chocolate in a covered gourd. The fragrance of it leaked out and filled the room. Winthrop and Albert, closely followed by Mr. Ho, were the last to arrive, each with an arm draped on the other's shoulder. They were apparently engrossed in reading a piece of paper, each clutching it by a corner. Just as well that she had no new poem to offer this time.

"Please be seated, gentlemen," Daisy suggested.

But they remained standing. Albert said, "Oh! This is—this changes everything! We can't put it off now!"

"Put what off? What changes every—"

Mr. Ho interrupted her. "Great Britain has declared war on Germany. It's not just the French angry over Belgium. It's Russia and Turkey and soon—soon—it's going to be everyone."

"Everyone but us." But even as she said it, Daisy knew.

Her lyrics and lamentations had had no effect.

They voted. Finally. During previous Motes it seemed discussion on the matter would never end. Now it had.

The votes were officially tallied. They were not remaining neutral. Only she and Albert had wanted that—and Lisette, who wasn't a Mote member. Lisette, who had grown strangely distant from Daisy at Kalima, and after. Who hadn't responded to Daisy's offers of private recitations of her poems and speeches. Who, by watching her practice, might have helped Daisy frame the Mote's choices in such a way that their policy could have prevailed. Or at least not been quite so badly defeated.

The count was nine to two.

So, Everfair, also, would enter the all-engulfing war, and of course on the side opposite Belgium and France. And England, her England.

So be it.

Albert shook her hand as he and the others filed out. First to arrive, last to leave. Almost last. George had stayed behind. He must want to speak with her—surely not to gloat?

They were alone. The Mote had ended. Daisy raised the Lamp's brass shade and pinched out the burning wick. Twilight spilled in through the door to the wraparound balcony.

"Are you finished?"

Daisy looked up. He was standing, his face in shadow. "Finished? With what—the Mote? Everfair?"

"Yes. Finished here. Now that you've been defeated and we're going to fight Britain. You could go back. Father's dead. You could try to see Laurie."

Daisy shook her head and returned her gaze to the floor. "Ellen wouldn't like—"

"*Bloody Ellen!*"

Shocked, Daisy half-rose from her seat. "George—"

"Who cares what Ellen 'likes'! Doesn't Laurie get—doesn't he deserve you at least making some sort of effort to be with him? Doesn't—"

"He's twenty-five, George. He's a young man now. He doesn't need—"

"Listen to me!" George turned to go. For a second she saw the flash of tears on his face. "*I'm* a young man." He strode out. "Young men feel things!" he shouted into the passageway's dimness. "Think things! Young men are—are *people*!"

"At that age, one's loyalties are so easily confused," Daisy said, remembering. But it was too late. He'd left.

Walking home in the rain and the deepening darkness, Daisy turned the question over in her mind. To give up now didn't seem cricket. It smacked of temper, as if she were a spoiled child sulking.

Rosalie opened the flat's door for her. The one child left. Though not, at twenty-seven, such a child. But she'd been the baby so long, ever since Laurie Junior's abduction. Perhaps that was why Daisy'd cherished her so. Or it might be because of that ancient bout of malaria . . . But despite that close bond, oughtn't Rosalie to have formed an attachment to one of the other colonists and married by now? Had Daisy sheltered her too stringently? Well, when she journeyed to England to stay with Laurie Junior there'd be an end to close parental supervision. Soon enough.

"How was it, Mama?" Rosalie shut the door and went back to the middle room. Drills and materials for her current project covered the table's tray top; she was making beads from bits of bone and glass.

"Rotten." Daisy crossed the entry and middle rooms. In the bath she continued talking. "We're going to war."

"Again?"

"Again. And fighting on the wrong side." She stripped off her tunic and threw it over the rope zigzagging along the inner wall. "Only because Belgium's on the other."

Daisy had kicked off her sandals in the entry room. Now barefoot, she stepped carefully onto the smooth planks of the drain surface. Palm oil–coated leaves, loosely stitched into a privacy screen, protected her from view from the shoulders down. The boiler in the yard furnished pressure and hot water. She turned that tap to only a dribble, opening wide the sluice for cool rainwater.

Black soap lathered up brown. The soap had been Josina's gift; she had explained it as having sacred properties. It rinsed off, leaving no more trace on Daisy's skin than, apparently, her arguments had left on the queen's mind.

She dried herself and donned a fresh tunic, shorter, for sleeping. When she emerged from the bath, Rosalie had stored away her work, collapsed and moved aside the table, and strung up their beds in their customary locations. The lamp, too, was suspended.

"There's fruit if you're hungry, Mama. Melon and papaya."

"No thank you, dearest. Save it for breakfast." Daisy sat on the edge of her hammock and waited for Rosalie to clamber into her own before extinguishing the light. She dreamt, as she often did, of Lisette, who these days lodged only a quarter of a mile off, in a tiny cottage on the second block of Bafwaboli Street. With her American protégée.

She woke early. An effect of age. It was still dark. Last night she'd hung her repeater by a ribbon from the hammock's headbar. She refrained from setting it off immediately. Instead she tied it in place around her neck and slipped silently to the floor, deftly avoiding brushing against Rosalie on her way to the bath. Sheltering the watch in between her hands and chest, she made it ring. Two minutes past five. There remained almost an hour till sunrise. She changed back into the tunic and trousers she'd worn yesterday. Attending the

Mote hadn't soiled them much, and today she would toil heavily, loading and unloading freight.

The melon was a bit overripe, but the papaya seemed fine. Daisy cradled it in her arms, shifting it back and forth as she tried to unlock the door and depart without rousing Rosalie, as she normally did on her way out.

She failed. "Mama? Are you going? What about me?" Obviously not completely awake, her daughter blinked at the pale sliver of morning light showing where Daisy had cracked the door open. "Wait up—I'll only be a moment."

"I'll be outside."

Resisting the temptation to walk off on her own—that was no way to treat Rosalie—Daisy sat down on the cool grey stairs. Anyway, her ultimate destination, the airfield, wasn't a secret.

Her neighbors were mostly musicians and sailors of the rivers and the air. One man, Mola, had also been given a role in *Wendi-La,* though he played not the boy with his name, but The Elephant Doctor. The apartments across the yard where he and his wife and brothers-in-law stayed were dark-windowed; naturally, they'd have gone to bed late after the show. But life stirred in the residence above his—silhouettes passing to and fro, then little Za coming down to loose and feed the chickens.

She thought she shouldn't have gone to the show. But it had been a chance to see Lisette again. And Rima Bailey, naturally. Both women had looked annoyingly well, and their hands had stayed joined like lovers' after the new ingénue pulled her mentor out onto the stage. It had seemed they'd be up there together always, that the wild acclamation would never stop.

Everfair's anthem had risen in Daisy's throat unbidden, but she'd known from the first line that it was the only way to make that endless moment end. Even then, though, Rima had known all the words. The song hadn't separated them in the least. Daisy left the Circus as quickly as possible.

A speckled hen half-flew, half-leapt up the steps below. Did she expect Daisy to feed her? But Rosalie opened their door, emerging at last, scaring off the bird, and they set on their way. Without the detour to Bafwaboli Street she'd originally intended.

An airfield had been established on acres formerly given over to the cultivation of maize and cassava. This lay west of town; Bafwaboli was in the opposite direction. Daisy and Rosalie walked wordlessly. By the time they reached the field, the sun was just topping the surrounding verdant jungle. It peeped between clouds for a moment, gilding the rain-wet gas bags and gondolas. Tethered aircanoes cast huge shadows on thatch-roofed warehouses, open-sided or mat-walled according to the needs and resources of the various goods distributors. Suddenly the sun retired, probably for the day.

Daisy, accompanied by Rosalie, reported to the chief coordinator in his roundhouse at the field's center. She used his knife to slice and score the papaya, sharing it with him.

"I thank you." Mr. Beamond was Welsh, but since moving to Everfair, Daisy had learned to ignore these little differences. He wiped his face with a spotted bandana. "It's a shame I can't return your kind attentions with a little extra in the way of work assignments. But I can't—at least, not now. Perhaps a bit later?"

Daisy didn't understand. No aircanoes were due till next market, but— "There are watercanoes at the landing, waiting for their loads. Aren't there? Yesterday—"

"Those? They're all seized."

Every visiting French and Belgian vessel had been commandeered by order of King Mwenda. That was nearly all of them. Those Daisy had seen before the Mote were empty, then, and would stay empty for the time being, till the newly reconstituted army decided their disposition. So Mr. Beamond said.

And so it proved. Carefully descending the muddy slope to the riverside, Daisy and Rosalie found the paddlers gathered morosely about their beached canoes. Their white passengers and captains were nowhere in sight; overnight, the men said, they'd disappeared. Gaol was the best guess.

"And will you fight for their release?" Daisy's Kee-Swa-Hee-Lee was sharp with practice, but despite that, her question was misunderstood. It gradually became obvious that the paddlers wondered why they should wish their tormentors free.

Things had not improved so much as she had hoped in Leopold's other colonies since the end of his reign. These men didn't complain of conditions, but their manner made that evident.

"Will you return without them, then?" Daisy asked. Rosalie displayed signs of impatience, shaking the umbrella she'd brought to keep the warm rain off them, mouthing silent words to her mother that Daisy couldn't quite make out: a snail hunter? A meeting? But the paddlers discussed the issue heatedly, breaking into smaller groups. Should they throw their lots in with King Mwenda? They wouldn't have to attack their own people: *Okondo* would carry them to Lake Tanganyika to wage war on another naval front.

Against the British.

Bookerville, Everfair, September 1914

Martha Livia Hunter Albin refused to weep. Not even with joy. She clutched her Bible in one hand, her wooden pendant in the other, and walked downhill to the flats by the river as steadily as her fifty-six years allowed. No rushing, though the welcome sight of *Phillis Wheatley* coming round to anchor made her heart leap like it would burst up out of her throat. Either George was on board the aircanoe as the heathen drums had claimed, or he wasn't. Running and crying and losing her dignity wouldn't change the situation.

She arrived at the landing field just in time. A ladder was lowered from the gondola and her dear climbed nimbly down, the first to disembark. Surely that meant he was eager to be with her? She moved toward him, slowly beginning to smile. He grinned like the boy he'd been when they met and gathered her, Bible and all, in his arms.

"Did you miss me, darling?" he asked between kisses. "I came back soon as I could manage."

Had *she* missed *him*? Martha laughed, throwing her head back to avoid showing too many chins. Vanity was the devil's snare, but— No. She wouldn't give in to it. She looked back down.

"More than you missed me," she replied, "with all the distractions of the capital. Are you quite sure you needed to be present for every one of those Motes?"

"Don't tell me you didn't have your hands full here, rebuilding from the ground up! But look who's come with me to help!"

Peering up over her husband's shoulder, Martha saw two more

descending passengers: a man and a woman. The man she recognized as Mr. Ho, dressed as usual in the loose, short-legged trousers most laborers preferred. Not a Christian, but decently behaved. The woman she recognized too, less happily: it was Miss Toutournier, the mulatto.

"I thought the new military hospital was to be in Lusambo."

"The facilities for landing aircanoes are better here."

Of course. The terrain around Bookerville was much gentler, and they'd set up three pairs of tethering masts here.

Martha let George release her. Together they turned to welcome the others and invite them to stay in their home. There was really no choice, though Toutournier pretended she'd rather camp on the clinic's—now hospital's—foundations.

George vetoed that idea. "I have no idea what Martha has devised for our home, but I'm sure it has at least a roof. You'll sleep with us—won't she?"

"Not *with* us, dear. There are two separate rooms." Though the entrance to the back room was through the one in front . . . "You're very welcome, and Mr. Ho as well."

They dined out-of-doors. Six degrees south of the Equator, it was a little cooler and a bit drier than Kisangani. Rain was not actually falling from the sky.

George said the blessing: "Lord, we pray this food makes us strong to smite our enemies. Let them be stricken with fear at the rumor of our coming; let them scatter before us in battle like ants before the lion." Did ants even notice animals as large as lions? "We ask you to watch over us and keep us ever on the path to righteousness and victory."

Neither guest said "amen," Martha noticed, though Mr. Ho, at least, had bowed his head.

Afterward Mr. Ho insisted on helping Martha put away the used utensils and bury the dirty banana leaves that had served as bowls and plates. The traction engine was the first machine they'd resurrected. Drawing hot water off its boiler via its newly installed tap, Martha filled a rubber-coated gourd. She added the leaves and stems of a local sudsing plant. They would need to keep gathering it in sufficient quantities to wash patients before treatment.

George and Miss Toutournier went to the site of the clinic—hospital—to discuss its expansion. She must remember that the Frenchwoman had been like a mother to him. She must curb her jealousy, though Toutournier was exactly old enough to be of interest to her husband and exactly young enough that no one could truly blame Martha for her feelings.

"How does your family do, Mr. Ho?" she inquired politely. The man gave her a startled look. "You saw them on your most recent trip to Macao, I believe?"

"Yes." He laid the last fork he'd dried in the compartmented basket. "My grandmother and grandfather are well. They have selected my little brother's wife. I met her. And my second-eldest sister has married a good man who works as a doctor. My eldest sister and her husband share a home and place of business with them, a shop selling medicines."

"Oh! Have you brought any back with you?"

He nodded and shook out the damp cloth in the damp breeze. "I gave samples of their stock to Mademoiselle."

"How nice."

"I expect she'll show them to you tomorrow." He followed her inside. Light coming through the doorway gilded the lower portion of the house's dividing wall. "I used to wish my family would join us and become citizens. Now that we're back at war again I'm glad they've decided to stay clear."

What she'd gathered about the situation from George's letters was that no one would be able to stay clear of it, no matter where they were. Should she try to explain that? But Mr. Ho had been in the capital. He'd attended Motes himself. Certainly he knew at least as much as she did. Maybe more. How unkind to deprive him of what had to be an illusion he'd chosen—that anyone in the world was safe.

Embarrassed at being so unprepared for visitors, Martha showed Mr. Ho the narrow folding bed where he would sleep.

His silence remained as impassive as his face until she nervously pointed out George's pallet against the far wall.

"It's only meant for one? Then where are you going to sleep?" he asked.

"I thought that Miss Toutournier and I would reserve the more private inner room for ourselves."

"Don't you want to go to bed with your husband after three months?"

"Of course! But that can wait—"

"Why? Mademoiselle and I will be fine out here—"

The entrance of George and Miss Toutournier saved Martha from having to respond.

The mulatto had a duffle slung over her shoulder by a plaited strap. She hovered just inside the doorway, her wide grey eyes glinting brightly.

"Come see where we're resting for the night," Martha said, her gaiety feeling forced and probably sounding that way as well.

"'Where *we're* resting'? No, Mrs. Albin. Many thanks for the offer, but I'm convinced you and your husband would make the more harmonious pair."

"You don't intend to go off and lie out in the open, do you?"

"Why, no! But as we've discovered, your traction engine's shed has a roof. I'll be protected well enough from the weather, and since it's next to your house, I should be safe from animals."

Nothing Martha could say would change the stubborn woman's mind.

She hated to feel herself beholden to such a hussy. But after prayers, she and George retired to the back together to enjoy the pleasures with which the Lord God had provided them. Awake, at first, and later, dreaming, she was grateful.

Manono, Everfair, December 1914

Beauty had to exist somewhere. But Tink knew there was none here. Just raw mud. Stoically, he splashed along the path between the town's open-sided worksheds. December was the wettest month in Manono. Normally any rainfall drained quickly away into the Lukushi River. Or so he had been told. He'd been here since October and the rain had only gotten worse.

Why had he come? Why had he done anything since Lily died? Ten years ago.

Tink shut the lid on that old basket, the basket containing his sadness. Through the downpour, he spotted what he was looking for: the long, narrow building jutting out over the dammed river, and the spinning turbines that gave the manufacturing town its electricity. The Bah-Looba called it "waterfire." And so it was. Fire from water, flowing in currents like the Lukushi, streaming through copper wires.

Under the building's thick thatch, Tink was able to wipe and blink his eyes enough to see the huddled banks of charged batteries as more than shadows. A bigger space than usual had been left between the walls' tops and the roof's overhang. The lamp toward the middle of the single room also helped. By its speckled light, he even made out the smile splitting the face of his acquaintance from the hospital in the first Bookerville, Mkoi.

"We've done better than you expected, haven't we?" Mkoi was supremely pleased with himself. "Look. That corner where we stored the empty batteries is bare. All those we've made are full; no new ones will be ready for at least two markets. Maybe three?"

Tink hated to lessen the man's happiness, but he had been telling him the same thing since arriving. "These are good. But just good for boats. They're too heavy for the aircanoes."

Mkoi's smile shrank. "Then why do you say you'll use aircanoes to carry them?"

Patience. "As freight, they're fine. For one shipment. But as a method of propulsion, over time . . ." He shrugged and turned away, exasperated. "I'm sorry. The Bah-Sangah earths are much better." Why wouldn't Mkoi believe him?

Tink turned back to him. "I've reported to King Mwenda and the rest of the Mote. They've instructed Manono to return to making the earth engines. Of course no one can force you to do that, but this is a *war*."

The smile was entirely gone. "Another war."

That was why there was no more beauty in the world anymore. War had killed it.

Tink returned to the place where he slept, a small house on a little rise. The channel around it was flooded and the floor inside damp, but he'd put his belongings safe in his hammock for the day.

He unrolled the blank scroll of barkcloth Queen Josina had provided and stretched it out as best he could on the sagging hammock. In Macao he'd have a desk, ink sticks, brushes . . . He sighed and uncorked a jar of gardenia juice, dipping into it a reed he'd picked from its bed in a slow curve of the Lukushi.

"Your father will have as many batteries as he needs," Tink wrote. "Maybe even more than that." He used the English script the Poet had taught him. "It's hard getting Mkoi to go back to doing different tasks. The other dopkwes"—as the work parties were called—"proceed as normal, though. By the time the rains here lessen in January, they will have constructed and assembled a new aircanoe. By the time the storms cease in May, there will be a second, and before they begin again next August, a third."

That covered one side. He considered the reverse while the black dye set. The workshops for the automatic shonguns were well under way. He didn't have any important information to add other than that. Questions, yes—about Rosalie in particular. Lily's little sister, the Poet's solace; he shouldn't want such questions read or answered. He rolled the scroll back up and slid it into its rubber-lined sleeve.

The men whose house Tink shared came in from their labors. Tam Gan and Tam Deshi were two of several Chinese who'd stayed in Everfair after Leopold's defeat.

They drank tea still warm from the refectory. Tink and Gan occupied the house's only two chairs, because Tink had found out he couldn't politely refuse the offer of a seat from the younger brother. Deshi insisted he preferred to stand after spending the day painting rubber onto inside-out gas bags.

When they were finished with their evening refreshment, Tink gave the package containing the scroll to Gan, who was traveling on the next barge up to Kisangani. This had already been arranged. But: "Are you sure you wouldn't rather take it yourself?" asked Gan.

"No, brother! You know he means to wait here till our sisters come so he can choose one as his bride!" Deshi said.

Tink tried not to show how much this gentle teasing troubled him. He had meant to marry suitably on his last two journeys to Macao.

Lily would not have been suitable. Rosalie even less so.

"I wait—but not for your respected sisters," he told the Tams. "I will be flying with the reverend lieutenant to Nyanza Victoria."

Where there would be no beauty.

Usumbura, Urundi, to Mwanza, East German Africa, January 1915

They had tethered overnight at Usumbura. Now they left. Thomas watched the growing dawn dim away the town's receding lights. He'd allowed the crews of both aircanoes under his command to disembark, but gave orders to return by four. Now it was shortly past six. In tandem with Everfair's newest craft, *Amazing Grace,* he turned *Fu Hao* northward, flying above the waters of the Rusizi River to Lake Kivu.

The wind was cool. Thomas buttoned his goat-hair sweater and tucked it into the waistband of his canvas skirt.

At first he'd rebelled against Loango's directive to him to wear women's clothing. In the last hours of his initiation the pronouncement had appeared to issue from Thomas's own lips, according to those who watched him dance. Hearing their report as he rested afterward, he refused to believe the notoriety that would ensue was necessary. He hunted down his trousers where the Bah-Sangah and Bah-Holo-Holo hid them and put them on despite their worried looks and cryptic remarks about keeping the god's balance.

But soon he experienced a terrible, itching, oozing rash on his legs. Then came the dreams. He persisted stubbornly in thinking of them as dreams. Nightmares, to tell the truth, of blind worms creeping relentlessly over the Earth.

Since he'd given in to the inexplicable dictates of his god, his hideous nightmares had ceased to trouble him. His wounds had healed.

Full daylight. There was really nothing more to be seen from the stern, but his . . . flock, he had to call them . . . kept a chair for Thomas here, and a table stocked with his needs: pipe and tobacco, a miniature lamp, oil to soothe his chronically chapped hands, a pencil, and a prayer book whose wide margins he'd filled with notes. He settled himself in his seat. A woman served him chocolate tea warm with pepper and left so he could drink.

He was beginning his second cup when the first petitioner appeared. A young man. He and his fellow fighters wanted to be dropped—using jumpsheets, of course—into the valley between Lake Kivu and Lake Edward. But that would no doubt lead to discovery. Thomas persuaded him to wait until dark, when, according to schedule, they'd be over the riskier terrain of the swamps west of Masaka. This would be more dangerous for the jumpers, but safer for the two aircanoes.

Later, petitioners asked for his intercession with Loango on matters of personal injustice. He granted this routinely.

Amazing Grace gradually fell behind them. Tink, her pilot, had claimed that this new midsized class could move as swiftly as larger vessels like *Fu Hao*. Thomas gazed back measuringly at the second aircanoe's green and scarlet gasbag. The difference in their airspeeds wasn't much; perhaps *Fu Hao*'s advantage would vanish when she was retrofitted with bullet shields similar to those built into her younger sister.

They reached the steep lands of the Rusizi's headwaters and dumped ballast. The two aircanoes' drummers traded messages: food and drinking supplies on both ships were holding up well, as was steam; bomb preparation and distribution proceeded according to plan; five women and men stationed aboard *Amazing Grace* would join the six jumping from *Fu Hao*. Thomas paced the deck, ate, relieved himself, resumed his chair.

The sun started to set as they sailed high over Lake Edward. Halfway up its length they veered due east, and Thomas had a good view of the brilliant pinks, corals, and reds painting the slopes of the far Mitumbas. As the last glow faded, the volunteers jumped. They'd find Everfair's friends among the Oo-Gandahs and fight the British behind the lines.

Now all was dark below. Above, the sky shone, full of gentle starlight. Thomas ordered the two aircanoes to anchor to treetops at the edge of the marshy shore. A short wait and the moon rose into sight. It was only a sliver—too much light and they'd be easily spotted. With nervous anticipation tensing his voice, Thomas gave the order for the aircanoes to set out upon their prearranged surveillance flights.

About this he and Tink had argued. *Fu Hao* was larger and could carry more bombs, so Thomas wanted her to take the longest route, going first north and east along Lake Victoria's coast, then south, then west to Mwanza. But larger meant more visible, as Tink pointed out. Also, if troops stationed in Kampala got enough warning they'd shoot, and *Amazing Grace* was armored. *Fu Hao* was not, so she turned southward to examine the nearby Ssese Islands.

All lights aboard save Thomas's little lamp were extinguished. No sign of their companion aircanoe could be seen because of similar safeguards. Thomas knew she must be gliding quietly up one of the inlets cutting into the coast on the way to the British colonial government's capital.

Disappointingly, the islands sheltered only innocent-looking fishing boats. Hard to make them out, but there was nothing large enough to justify action. Then came unmistakable signs that they were passing the last Kenyan ports they'd marked on their maps. Far too soon, *Fu Hao* flew over friendly German waters.

Still vigilant, they were at last rewarded. The grey of the barely born morning thinned to reveal a thicker grey: a plume of smoke. Tracing it to just below Bumbire Island, they found a target. A steam launch that had been converted to use as a gunboat hid in the shallow straits dividing Bumbire from another, nameless, lump of land. They hovered high and to the west for a moment while Thomas reviewed his notes on Great Lakes ships. The vessel, either *Severn* or *Mersey,* definitely belonged to the enemy, the Entente. He gave the signal to spill lift. The boxlike gunboat swelled below till he could see its sailors' faces.

They were attempting to swing its six-inchers to bear on

Fu Hao. "Impossible," Thomas muttered to himself. But he told the bomb dopkwe to quickly arm and loose four bombs.

Two hit: one near the ship's stern, most likely upon the quarter-deck, though flames obscured details. Perhaps the bridge? The other seemed to have penetrated to a hold filled with coal or some other highly combustible substance; as *Fu Hao* rose, freed of the bombs' weight and an additional fifty pounds of ballast, another fire spread swiftly back from the ship's prow. It burned persistently. Sailors the size of grasshoppers ran to and fro, carrying tools and weapons resembling toys. Several shot futilely at the rapidly departing airca-noe. Others of a more selfish bent jumped into the water, intending to swim for the high, rocky sides of Bumbire.

These weren't the sorts of surroundings crocodiles typically favored, but they must infest this area of the lake anyway, judging by the screams.

If not for the risk of a bullet actually striking her, *Fu Hao* should lower a ladder to rescue prisoners, but it was simply too dangerous. Thomas refrained from giving the order. They flew onward.

Broad daylight meant that their mission was no longer a secret. He hoped Tink had been able to find a safe anchorage for the day, for, by both their estimates, he would still be in hostile territory.

His instructions to the new watch were the same as they'd been to the retiring one: diligent care and unceasing scrutiny.

He himself didn't retire. Older people, he'd heard, needed much less rest than young ones. Perhaps his venerable age was why he no longer needed sleep so often. Or perhaps there was some other factor. He didn't care to know. He imbibed another cup of chocolate.

They reached Mwanza without further incident. The Germans were comparatively enlightened; unlike the traders of long-ago Boma—had it truly been twenty-five years ago he'd gone there?—they consented to dine with blacks. But the rest of his extremely mixed crew needed more accommodations than could comfortably be afforded them in Mwanza. They would stay on board and he would stay with them, granting leave in shifts till *Amazing Grace* made rendezvous and the entire party could go home to Everfair. It shouldn't be much more than a day till then. Two at most.

Four sets of tether poles stood in a field some ways south of the town's center. By the time *Fu Hao* tied off, the sun shone almost directly overhead.

For some reason, midday aroused feelings of sadness in Thomas. The sun had reached its height and would from there only decline. Suddenly weary, he forced himself to vacate his chair. Everfair's superiority in the air was undisputed; their German colleagues wasted no opportunity to glean what information they could firsthand. A delegation would arrive to welcome him. It must be prepared for and received. The Bah-Sangah priests insisted on keeping the power of their sacred earths secret. Perhaps that was why they kept the Littlest Heaters so isolated. With power supplies for the main and auxiliary engines safely shrouded, and tarpaulins spread over several crates and baskets stacked up near them as decoys, Thomas felt ready for visitors. It was just as well. Schnee, the colony's governor, called upon *Fu Hao* in the unexpected company of his antipathetic military counterpart, Oberstleutnant Lettow-Vorbeck. Schnee was a philosopher, but Lettow-Vorbeck's sharp eyes missed nothing.

"You have no coal," he stated bluntly over gourds of honeyed tea.

"Have we not?"

"No. I should have learned of large shipments such as you would need. There should be dust—foot tracks—some marks . . . Maybe . . ." A shrewd expression flitted momentarily over his moustached face. Nothing showed in its aftermath.

"Maybe . . . ?" Thomas prompted his guest.

"It's not *petroleum,* Oberstleutnant! You surmised as much earlier, but we'd smell that!" Schnee's stupidity glared forth even in the gasbag's purple shade.

A polite change of subject brought them to the bombs. Thomas had ordered them displayed in twin rows near the aircanoe's bow. He watched Lettow-Vorbeck count them. There were twenty-four.

"You have used sixteen?" the Oberstleutnant asked.

"Ten are carried by *Amazing Grace*. Two were destroyed in tests. We deployed four when sinking the *Mersey* yesterday." He had decided to claim the slightly larger of the British ships as his casualty.

Lettow-Vorbeck inspected each bomb separately, with an almost proprietary air. That was understandable; he'd been largely responsible for procuring them.

At last the Germans left. Not one word had been exchanged about Thomas's unconventional clothing. Maybe they thought it was some sort of priestly garb. Which, in a way, it was.

Twilight gathered starboard, to the east. Thomas sought his hammock, hung for him in his private enclosure. Worryingly, the drummer going off watch had received no message from *Amazing Grace*. But anxiety didn't stop Thomas from falling asleep; it merely seemed to darken the colors of his dreams.

The slopes he climbed were cloaked in grey mist. They always had been since that first time. When he became aware of himself, he was walking. He kept going in the same direction he found himself headed. This had proved the easiest course over time. It was always best to go somewhat voluntarily wherever he'd been sent.

Noises of fighting grew loud enough to hear, then louder. Gunshots. Screams of fright and agony. Then the smell of death: blood and explosions and emptied bowels and bladders. The mist cleared and he looked down on a shallow, bowl-shaped depression in the ground, filled with struggling bodies.

Some of them shone. Some lay still. He recognized faces: men and women of Everfair formed a cluster on the side of the bowl nearest him. They were greatly outnumbered. They shot their weapons steadily, in rotation, on command, rifles and shonguns keeping the British soldiers at bay—Thomas couldn't see their enemies that plainly, but who else would it be? Leopold's men were vanquished.

He had learned over the course of many such expeditions what to do. Reaching up without looking, he filled his hands with fire. Since his branding, nothing burned him, though he was thankful, when awake, for the oil. When the bolt's weight felt right, he hurled it at the soldiers below. *Boom!* Thunder followed in the wake of Thomas's lightning. *Boom! Boom!* Again and again he struck. Wailing, the white men died.

Now Everfair's fighters rallied. He saw them looking up between bursts. Many could tell where he was. *Boom!* The odds evened. *Boom! Boom!* Over the ozone came the stink of seared meat.

He met Tink's eyes. The engineer asked, "You are dead? A ghost?"

He shook his head no and opened his mouth to explain—but what could he say? This wasn't the time, anyway. Ammunition had run out. The fighters dropped their useless guns and drew shongos, clubs—whatever they'd brought.

Where was the ship? "West of here, on the water," Tink answered him, though Thomas was sure he'd done no more than think the question. "We mean to win through to the lake. It's not far now—" A break in the line of soldiers caught his attention. In quick succession, Thomas threw six more lightning bolts in the opposite direction. The distraction worked: Tink and his fighters slipped away into the scrubby palms surrounding them.

Thomas moved in parallel to them. Downhill. He wouldn't be able to summon fire so effectively from lower elevations. Too bad. But then came a ridge, and at its top a family of giants huddled together—no, they were only big stones; boulders, in fact, stacked and leaning upon one another in mimicry of human forms. And, past them, Lake Victoria.

Thomas looked upward. There was no sign of *Amazing Grace* in the dull heavens. Tink and the crew seemed unconcerned. They pressed onward to the shore, rousing a huge flock of pale, long-legged birds. Hundreds, then thousands flew off into the dusk as he followed the fighters down to the high-grassed shore.

A steamer sat at anchor perhaps eighty feet out. A pair of British soldiers guarded three beached canoes. A woman and boy ran in front of the group from Everfair and tackled the soldiers before they could take aim. The next wave of fighters drowned them in kicks and punches. Leaving them lying unconscious or dead, the fighters launched the canoes in seconds. One they towed, since only two were needed for the twelve fighters. But *Amazing Grace*'s crew had been much larger—twice that many. Where were the rest of them? Where was the aircanoe itself? Had it crashed? Was the secret of the Littlest Heater safe?

Thomas wanted to stay with Tink and find out these things and more. Instead, he felt himself pulled irresistibly back to the family of boulders on the high ridge he'd just left. Taking steps forward brought him backward against his will. Sounds faded. Colors washed away. Thomas stared at the boulders as hard as he could. The smallest *twitched*, and startled him awake.

He *was* awake. But still staring at the stones. He lay in his hammock. The tops of the boulders from the ridge were visible over the mat walls surrounding him. The new day's sun would soon rise behind them.

Thomas got out of bed and dressed. He walked the short distance to the aircanoe's stern. The oddly anthropomorphic boulders were definitely the same as those he'd seen in his dreams. And yesterday they had not been anywhere near this place. The boundary between Thomas's nocturnal expeditions and the real world continued to erode. The heat of his lightning chapped his hands; those he slew in his sleep truly died. Now these stones from the field of battle had been transported here to meet his waking eyes.

He swore at what he saw, taking, from habit, his former god's name in vain. How had these huge, distinctive rocks arrived so impossibly this morning to Mwanza?

Mombasa, Kenya, September 1915

Should she tell Matty? Fwendi had never explained to anyone how she rode the cats. Grandmother's Brother Mkoi
knew—he'd protected her secret. But he'd always known; her
parents must have told him. Her parents, or at least one of them,
must have been the same as she was.

She sighed and rolled gently to the hotel bed's edge. Matty
barely stirred—he'd grown used to her leaving him in the middle
of the night like this. Her shift and robe lay where she'd left them,
carefully folded and stacked on the chest at the bed's foot. She
dressed in the dark and felt her way to the window.

This was her room as much as his; they'd given up pretenses
months ago. Fwendi was sure the hotel staff and others thought
her no more than a glorified prostitute. She wanted not to care, but
sometimes their mutterings and sideways glances overwhelmed her
indifference.

She pushed open the shutters. For a moment the only light she
saw came through the few high windows of the Colonial Administration Building across Kisumu Road, indicating rooms where
an official worked late hours—for Everfair's downfall, perhaps?
Then clouds parted and the white moon shone invitingly. She
stepped onto the room's balcony as a soft wind swept her cheeks,
drying tears she hadn't known she shed.

Closing the shutters behind her, she began softly to sing. The
carved stone railing felt cool against her arms as she leaned forward. Crooning, calling—soon the first cat came out onto the

pavement below. Then three more. Then another three. That should be enough.

Fwendi changed her song, her voice lowering, deepening. Up the vine clinging to the hotel's walls they climbed. She sank back into the rattan chair she kept waiting there as the gathering cats perched one by one on the balustrade. The lamplight spilling from the far building helped her see their coloring: two ginger and two grey tabbies, a black, a black-and-white, and one poor, thin animal darkly mottled like Lisette's treasured tortoiseshell powder compact.

Her singing dropped to a whisper. To hear her better, it seemed, the cats came forward and nestled around her feet, on the chair's back, even on her lap. Stroking their dirty fur she saw fleas leap before her fingers. She would have to bathe in the morning, as always.

The song stilled, became nothing but breath. The cats' breathing matched Fwendi's. She let her eyelids flutter shut. The pleasant drowsiness filled her.

As tempting as the idea of resting in this place all night was, her work beckoned. She entered the cats' heads.

When Fwendi was little she'd only ridden a single cat at a time. Partly this was because wildcats lived more solitary lives than their domesticated counterparts. By the time they reached Alexandria she'd graduated to prides of up to eleven. Lisette smiled indulgently and helped feed her "strays," noting almost casually that all limped slightly and most seemed to be queens rather than toms.

Her mounts lowered themselves back down the creeping vine. With practice Fwendi had become proficient in maintaining multiple viewpoints, though this was easier when dipping only lightly into the senses of all but a very few. So the spinning panorama of leaves and stucco and shadows, the dew-slick cobbles and sweet-smelling sewers underpaw passed almost unnoted by Fwendi as she herded her pride toward her goal: the British Administration's offices on the other side of the road.

She was her country's best spy. It was she who'd stolen that patent application for an automatically firing weapon.

All the building's doors were locked and guarded. That didn't matter in the least. Fwendi sent her mounts to the building's back. She let them take turns licking oily puddles and tipping over lidded baskets filled with tasty refuse while she surveyed the scene.

Of course, to anyone ignorant of her abilities Fwendi would appear to be asleep on the hotel balcony, and Matty could testify innocently to that effect if the question arose. She'd left this nearest target till late in their visit here, though, just in case.

No plants had been allowed to gain purchase on the pale, smooth walls, naturally—the royal governor was not that sort of fool. And neighboring trees had been trimmed back so not even a boy could use them to gain access. But she could see a branch that would bear a lesser weight.

She left the black-and-white to act as sentry, reinforcing its appetite and playing up the attractions of the feast of scraps. The others she took up the tree. The flexing limb-end deposited each in turn on the deep sill of a third-floor window, which soon became crowded. The room was dark behind the ill-fitting shutters. Fwendi had the tortoiseshell pry these apart far enough to slip in. With its nose she searched for and found the latch: a hook, which she had it lift away.

Cats and moonlight poured into the abandoned office. Through wide irises Fwendi saw a desk piled with stacks of paper. She leapt the youngest tabbies up to where she could have them read any document of interest. Ah! Orders for the touring company's detention, and the arrest of herself, Lisette, Rima—Matty, a citizen of the Crown, to be simply interviewed . . . Dated for tomorrow—no, today! She could wake the others to pack and escape on her return, but it would be best to offer them proof of what would seem unfounded fears. With claws and teeth she made the orders into a neat scroll and sent them off to her human body in the mouth of the young grey.

Five cats left to explore with. None of the other documents that had been left unsecured were of interest. She had to make the most of this sole excursion; she hurried her mounts to the door and successfully coordinated their efforts to turn its knob.

The lighted and no doubt occupied room she'd noticed earlier lay down the corridor to the left and around a corner—she remembered where it should be, and heard the low, steady murmur of men in discussion. Three of them? Too many. Heading to the right inside the tortoiseshell and remaining tabbies, she bade the black stay behind to watch over their path of retreat. But she returned within minutes, having drawn a blank in that direction: in every room the desks were bare, the cabinets locked or more difficult to open than her mounts could handle in the time Fwendi felt remained to her.

She released the tabbies with an urging to join the black-and-white below. They left. The rest of the building was silent. Empty, she was sure. Riding only the tortoiseshell and the black, she crept toward the conversing men. The cats' ears heard what was said long before there was any danger of being seen.

"—don't take our efforts seriously. That experimental gun that brought down a dirigible over Lake Victoria? Not being replaced. They as much as admit Europe is all the bloody government cares about!"

"If Portugal would declare for the Entente—"

"Or America! That would finish things off."

Fwendi recognized only one of the speakers: "Lord" Delamere, the lion killer. Before she could stop herself, she hissed with hatred.

"What was that?"

"What do you mean—"

"That sound!" Footsteps, a door opening, louder now—Fwendi ran the cats back toward the room they'd entered through. Too late—gunfire! Her ears! A second shot—she reached the empty room, but in only one body. She'd lost control of the tortoiseshell. It must be dead.

The shutters hung invitingly open, but Fwendi cowered safely beneath the desk. The door slammed back and the men rushed in with a lamp. Her irises turned to slits.

"Did you miss?" This was said in a high, boyish voice.

"Not I!" That was Delamere. "But I thought there was another. Black. Bad luck buggers. Search the room."

"What d'you want to kill cats for? Mightn't they be someone's pets?" the third man asked.

"Didn't mean to do more than frighten either one. But when I saw them, it gave me a funny feeling."

"Superstitious?" asked the boyish-voiced man.

"Superstition's nothing to laugh at in Africa," asserted the third man.

Fwendi had to decide how to distract them from searching the room. They'd find out the arrest orders were missing. There was only one horrible solution.

Maybe it wouldn't work out so badly. It was only a few feet from her hiding place to the window.

She dashed for freedom, pausing only an instant at the windowsill to calculate her jump onto the thin, thin branch. Taken by surprise, Delamere had no time to aim well. He missed.

Unfortunately, so did Fwendi. The branches she encountered on her way to the ground broke not her fall, but her bones.

Dar-es-Salaam, East German Africa, October 1915

"Don't say you're doing this to be helpful." Lisette hated lies. Though her own weeping was almost as regrettable as Rima's dishonesty. She wiped her eyes angrily with her last linen handkerchief. Why was she crying? Nothing was any use. Rima's luggage was packed. It had never been fully unpacked. Which truthfully had been part of the girl's attraction.

"But I *can* help. They gonna listen to me. I gotta go." Whirling suddenly to face her, a wild hope in her eyes, Rima begged again. "Ain't you wanna go too? Aww, honey, you know you do! We be livin the *high* life in New York . . ." The words trailed off.

Lisette shook her head. "You will be living the high life without me." Fwendi needed her—she had been ill for a month. Lisette looked anxiously up at the house as if she'd see her patient emerging from it into the courtyard.

This was certainly not the "high life." Though they'd fled Mombasa hurriedly to avoid arrest, Matty could have bought a mansion on their arrival here, in the well-to-do neighborhood of Oyster Bay. Instead, he'd purchased a merely adequate new construction in this concrete subdivision, one of the few places Africans could live. Had he done so because of Fwendi? Probably. Though he couldn't have anticipated her sudden incapacity. A more modern dwelling would have hygienic conveniences to make her care easier.

The only running water available was cold, and it arrived in the courtyard, not the house proper, via an unsightly pipe. Walking deliberately around Rima, Lisette filled her basin and set it on the worktable, determined to accomplish something with her time other than an argument. A pointless argument. She took up the paring knife and began peeling and deveining prawns. The rich reek of their iodine filled the warm, still air. Lately, all Fwendi ate was seafood. Fortunate that here it was cheap and abundant. But what of Matty's plan to return to the interior?

"Lookit you! Ain't you tired a workin so hard?" Accusation underlaid Rima's solicitous words. "I'll hire servants to do all that shit! Secretary for your book writin. Dresses made special for you by Paris designers—you know that's what you deserve steada this!"

"If I wanted those things, be assured they would be mine!" Really, the child assumed too much.

"But I'm gonna be rich!"

As if that were guaranteed. As if it would make any sort of difference.

Then someone did come out from the house. Not Fwendi, of course—she spent most of the day abed. It was Matty. In his arms he held one of Lisette's other patients, whom she had named Bijou. Her crown creased by a long, shallow wound—a glancing encounter with a bullet, Lisette believed—the tortoiseshell cat had been unconscious when they'd found her dumped on the refuse behind the building housing Mombasa's government offices. Along with the third patient, Minuit, also a cat.

Matty transferred Bijou into Lisette's arms. "Will you sit with her for a while?" No need to specify whom he meant by "her." Not either cat. "After you've said your goodbyes to Miss Bailey, of course."

The high, impatient horn of a taxi sounded from the house's front. Holding the cat gave Lisette an excuse to refrain from embracing Rima. "Goodbye." As coldly as possible, she kissed her lover's cheek. Her ex-lover. But she couldn't help crying one or two more tears. How Lisette would miss this gallant child whose usual sturdy forthrightness contrasted so well to her involved complications.

"You sure?" The girl stood unusually still.

"Of course I am sure!"

The horn blared again. And again. "Yeah. Okay. I'll write you plenty letters."

"Their contents should be such as to interest Queen Josina when I send them on to her."

Matty, three quarters Rima's height, offered to help carry out her trunks and cases. She loitered behind him on the steps and looked back over her shoulder at Lisette, eyes bright with sadness, but chin held high. "Lemme know when you change your mind."

The taxi engine's appealingly deep growl dwindled away. Lisette waited some minutes to be sure the girl had finally gone. She offered Bijou an empty prawn shell. Predictably, the animal refused it.

Lisette ascended into the house. Fwendi occupied the larger of two rooms shaded by the palms on the house's north side. It was dark and cool and quiet here. The bed filled most of the floor. On its yellow covering, Fwendi lay face up, Minuit stretched at her feet. The black cat's splints and bandages had come off last market day. She, in contrast to Fwendi, was healing well.

Lisette sat on the edge of the bed nearest the door. Bijou stirred against her chest and she set her free. With great dignity, the queen stalked to the bed's head, as far as possible from its fellow cat. Fwendi followed its progress with her eyes.

"How strange that this one limps too," Lisette said, as if continuing a conversation instead of starting one. "You would think she had suffered a broken leg as well as her sister. But all your pet strays have been just the same, have they not?"

Silence. Not even a look.

She didn't believe in lies. Only honesty made things right.

"Rima's gone back to America—without me. She wanted me to go with her, but I wouldn't—I couldn't! Yes, in part because there remains in me some hope of redeeming my love of Daisy. But there is also you, your so-mysterious illness, which I believe I understand."

No reply. A wrinkling of the forehead, though.

"Why won't you talk? Are you keeping a secret? Do you think I don't know?" The wrinkles deepened. The eyes turned toward her, full of worry. "After living with you all those years?" She forced herself to use a soft tone to continue.

"Fwendi. My dear. You don't need to tell me anything. I'm your friend, as always. I believe you are sure of that much?"

On the bed, the invalid opened her mouth. Lisette waited. Nothing came out. Then Minuit rose and Bijou returned to Lisette's side. Together they put their forefeet in her lap. They blinked in tandem: Once. Twice.

Delicately, Lisette stroked the cut velvet of their supple throats. With time, perhaps, she could hope for some more definite form of communication. This was enough for now.

Through the room's entrance she heard the back door open and close as Matty came in. "Thank you for the reasonable excuse to cut short my adieux," she said. She had always disliked dragging out the inevitable.

His moustache twitched in a quick smile. "I was glad to be of service to you." It seemed likely that he really was glad; Fwendi's poor health had eased their enmity. His face grew grave as he approached the bed. "She's getting better, isn't she?"

"Of course."

Matty nodded, satisfied, and leaned over to address Fwendi. "Do you need anything?" In reply, the patient raised one hand half the way to his rolled sleeve. He reached for it and took it in a hesitant grasp.

Frowning with embarrassment, Lisette stood up from the bed. "I must visit the market before it closes." Work made a sovereign remedy for the inconvenient aching of a newly deprived heart.

Matty took her seat without appearing to notice what he did. "Yes. The Sekhons will be expecting you, won't they?" he said, his tone absent. How far he'd come in accepting that Lisette's skills were being used against his former home.

Armed with a parasol and a shopping bag of woven straw, Lisette walked the five blocks to the market, wishing for her dear steam bicycle. When returning home, she would indulge in a taxi, though the air would be cooler by then.

Under the dark green awnings of the vegetable sellers she found peppers; ground nuts; okra pods like short, fat cigars; and the leaves of mustard plants, which she knew from experience tasted very much like cress. The top of her bag she filled with a bouquet of cheap flowers. Then she was ready for business.

The Sekhons kept a spicery in a modest building tucked between a newsagent's and a purveyor of "fine textiles." The disguise seemed flimsy. Lisette shut the shop's door behind her and set its brass bells ringing, summoning Madam Sekhon from the establishment's depths.

Inhaling the dry, astringently sweet air, Lisette moved forward to the counter separating them. Should she buy something? This was her second visit to Sekhon and Sons. Previously, she'd requested a blend to use in cooking curries. It had taken Madam Sekhon quite fifteen minutes to prepare, and in consultation with her husband, at that. Really, anyone knowing anything about India—Bharati, as Everfair's allies called their country—would see even without the display of such failings that the spicery was no more than a sham. With complexions as light as Lisette's own, the Sekhons were obviously of the wrong caste to be engaged in such an enterprise.

"May I help you?"

Lisette gazed at the tall, stout woman in astonishment. Did she not recognize her? They'd exchanged identifying phrases at their first meeting. Lisette had made her request for intelligence on the British Army's movements with not the slightest ambiguity.

The moment's passing must have brought clarity. "Are you back for more of that curry mixture? Or is there something else you'd like to try?"

"No—nothing else." All she needed was information on troop assignments for the upcoming campaign. Why would the woman not speak plainly?

"Then I'll go fetch it for you." She disappeared back into the building's inmost recesses.

A sudden feeling of being watched came over Lisette. Swiveling around, she saw the reason for Madam's reticence: on a stool by the door, which had hidden him as it opened, sat a small blond man. He had dressed far too formally for the climate, in a pale grey suit complete with vest.

"Splendid place, isn't it? Glad to meet another Englishman."

"But I am not—"

"Hah! English*woman*, should have said."

"No—I mean that I am French." By birth, at least, so that was in a way true.

The man grinned and nodded in a show of appreciation. "Should have guessed, you looking so elegant and all. Allow me to introduce myself: Christopher Thornhill. And you are—"

"Mademoiselle Toutournier. But is not your country at war with these German barbarians?"

Thornhill cocked an eyebrow. "Was about to ask you the same, Mam'zelle."

Madam Sekhon's reappearance saved Lisette from having to formulate a reply. The soi-disant shopkeeper carried in both hands a wide, flat, paper-wrapped bundle. It looked much too large to hold what it was supposed to. Lisette accepted the parcel without questioning its contents and left as swiftly as possible. Thornhill bowed and held the door for her. He followed her out, making an attempt at conversation, but fortunately the taxi parked at the next corner proved unoccupied.

Firmly closing the vehicle's weighty, well-hung door between them, she sank against the hide-covered seat back and gave the driver Matty's address. There was the tiniest of contretemps; the man—also Bharatese, but nothing like either of the Sekhons—didn't care to venture into that neighborhood. A handful of rupees settled the matter.

Surreptitiously, Lisette removed the "spices" from her bag and slipped her fingers underneath the parcel's wrappings. What she felt could be a stack of documents. But perhaps the pages were blank? Drawing forth a single sheet, she saw dark markings. Satisfactory. She would examine and copy them. One more trip to return to her source what she'd been given, and there'd be no bar to going home to Everfair. Where Fwendi would heal faster, Lisette was sure, nursed by her great-uncle Mr. Mkoi. And where Daisy waited, to hurt her again. But only if she let her.

Kisangani, Everfair, November 1915

Matty grimaced up at the rapidly clearing sky. He hated so to leave Fwendi's side. She might start talking again at any moment; there should always be someone present to hear her. That was why he'd first tolerated, then come to rely upon, Mademoiselle Toutournier. During that short but excruciating voyage south from Mombasa, the Frenchwoman had proven indispensable. In Dar-es-Salaam, while they waited for his dear to recover enough that they could continue traveling, she'd sat with Fwendi on her own, and often with him as well; her arguments had finally convinced him to accept somewhat the necessity of spying against Britain for Everfair. On the long train ride to Kigoma, and on *Okondo,* which still flew in civilian service, she'd spelled him as often as necessary.

Now it was necessary again. Though he supposed he could have asked Mademoiselle or another to meet Great-Uncle Mkoi and escort him from the airfield, Matty was schooling himself these days to show proper respect for blacks. Fwendi had never said as much, but he knew she'd found him lacking in some way he had yet to understand.

There must be nothing to divide them. They must be united. He would be brave and ignore the nightmares; he would ask her to marry him as soon as she could answer. Before then, even.

And of course he would have to find the courage to ask Great-Uncle Mkoi also. Constant proximity might help. Another reason for Matty's presence on the airfield.

At least the rain had stopped. Kisangani's annual December

respite seemed to have begun early. Banks of clouds stained purple by the sun's descent were dissolving like dreams. A deep, calm blue showed behind them. A few drops of water wetted Matty's face, falling from the oil palms under which he and Clapham stood.

He shook his head at the butler's silent offer. He didn't want Clapham to open his umbrella; he defied the weather. Surely the drums had spoken the truth and the aircanoe would arrive soon?

At long last, like a bright wisp of misplaced sunset, *Okondo* appeared in the east. Nearer and lower she came, her engine's distant hum becoming a bass rumble. Ground crew atop the designated tethers secured her. Altogether a much smoother operation than the pioneering efforts of eighteen years ago. There were even stairs being rolled out for use by her passengers.

Great-Uncle Mkoi had changed very little since their last meeting: spare of body, broad of face, piercing of eye. Matty relieved him of his cloak, handing it over to Clapham.

"I hope your journey was all good," he said in halting Lin-Gah-La.

"There was nothing to remark upon." Not how such a journey would once have been described. "It went quickly. You have a cart to bring me to my girl?"

Matty had hired a roofed carriage pulled by a steam bicycle. Great-Uncle Mkoi's few baskets of belongings fit beside them easily. Darkness fell as they rode, but lamps lit the stairs to Matty's home.

They went directly to Fwendi's room. Early as it was, she slept. He explained that these light, erratic slumbers happened frequently enough for them to have formed the habit of awaiting her natural waking. Mademoiselle Toutournier offered Great-Uncle Mkoi her chair, which he refused. He walked about the bedchamber muttering to himself, pulling aside the blinds at the open window and lifting the lid of the chest beneath it.

A stirring came from among the blankets. In an instant, Matty was beside his dear's bed. "Great-Uncle Mkoi is here," he told her. And there the man stood, suddenly, in a spot on the bed's other side.

"Fwendi," Great-Uncle Mkoi began, but Matty found the rest

of his speech incomprehensible. Fwendi seemed to understand, though—at one point tears appeared on her cheeks and she sobbed—crying! What was he saying to her? She nodded wildly—

"Where are the cats?" It took Matty a moment to realize what Great-Uncle Mkoi was asking—in *English*.

"Which cats?" he said, stupidly.

"You know. Those she goes on rides."

"I—I don't—"

"Yes, yes, of course," interrupted Mademoiselle. "Bijou. Minuit. They're outside somewhere—they'll be back to eat. We don't try to keep them in."

Those were the names she'd given the poor injured, flea-bitten strays they'd picked up in Mombasa.

"That's fine. You treat them well?"

"Of course," repeated Mademoiselle. "Why not?"

But Great-Uncle Mkoi was too busy talking to his niece, it seemed, to respond. More nods. More tears and sobs. And laughter! He had thought never to hear his dearest laugh again.

With that, Great-Uncle Mkoi patted the flesh hand he'd held, and lowered it to the covers. "I'll rest now," he told Matty. "Thank you for taking such care of her."

A low-burning shame withered Matty's insides. Why should he be praised for doing his duty as a man?

Great-Uncle Mkoi turned to Mademoiselle. "When the cats come back, you'll fetch me?"

"I, or whoever's here." She looked at Matty. "Do you mind me staying again tonight?"

He assented, as always.

Great-Uncle Mkoi's luggage had been left, as Matty ordered, in the room immediately to the right. Matty showed it to him. He also personally pointed out the toilet at the passage's end. Then, remembering the African manners his cast had attempted to teach him, he asked his guest if he had eaten.

"Fruit juice and bean cakes were served aboard *Okondo*."

Judging that this hadn't been enough, Matty went to the kitchen to order a tray sent to Great-Uncle Mkoi's room.

There were the cats, being fed scraps on the floor just inside the back entrance. Clapham rose from an undignified crouch. "Sir, it was at the request of Mam'zelle—"

Matty cut him off. "Never mind all that. Give them to me." In the end, the butler carried one cat and he the other—first into Great-Uncle Mkoi's room and next, accompanied by him, into Fwendi's. Mademoiselle relieved Clapham of his rather unwilling burden, and Matty dismissed the servant to his duties.

They gathered around the bed. Great-Uncle Mkoi threw several glances over the premises, as if wishing to continue his earlier inspection. "Is there a fire?" he asked.

"No! You're not going to—to *set fire* to the animals as an offering, are you?" Matty knew he'd said something stupid as soon as the words left his lips. Great-Uncle Mkoi's quickly veiled glare confirmed this.

"Perhaps you'll be so kind as to tell us exactly what you *are* doing?" Mademoiselle Toutournier's question must have been meant to deflect Great-Uncle Mkoi's annoyance. It worked.

"It is a family matter, which is how I am involved, and yet immune. Both Fwendi's parents were shape-changers, and she is too."

"Like the *loups-garou*? I think not."

"Werewolves, she means," Matty translated.

"It's not that way. She changes in and out, goes to different bodies. Her one remains the same, but she leaves it for another."

"Understood," said Mademoiselle. "What you say makes excellent sense."

Did it? Matty did not want to think too deeply think about what was being said. He noticed he was staring at Fwendi and looked away.

"So my niece has her—I know no English word for these things. Parts of her being—she can separate them off. Her seeing, balance, smelling, hearing—she puts them inside an animal. In our family, we're most comfortable with cats."

And now Matty was staring at the black cat—Minuit. Was there nowhere safe to simply rest his eyes?

"What has happened is she had to leave her animals so fast one of these parts got stuck behind. The part from where she can talk. She has to go back in and get it out."

Matty struggled to come up with the right remark, some way to counteract his previous display of ignorance. "How can we help?"

Fwendi clasped his arm in her metal hand and hauled herself into a more upright position. She smiled as she shook her head.

"I can't see much for you to do at this point. Already you've saved at least some of the cats." Great-Uncle Mkoi indicated them with his head. "That was *very* fortunate. I will sing. Without the music, she can't go into any animal. That's why this has gone on so long.

"A fire would be good, though, especially if it could be larger than the flame in a lamp. Not to burn things"—with a dark look at Matty—"but to gaze into and let go of our thoughts."

Clapham was sent for and procured a brazier from a neighborhood mechanic. Matty directed him to set it alight. Mademoiselle held the cats in thrall with a bit of string she set dancing before their noses.

When all was ready, Great-Uncle Mkoi broke forth in song. At first it was a melodious enough tune, though loud. Gradually it thinned and rose to a high keening. Then the cats joined in, screeching and yowling.

Then, all at once, the eerie noise ceased.

And after another moment, Fwendi spoke again, at last.

Kisangani, Everfair, to Bookerville, Everfair, to Luanda, Angola, January 1916

Queen Josina smiled, then frowned. Then she smoothed all expression from her face. Here, with her ladies and her king beside her, she could show what she felt. But in Luanda, anyone's eyes might be on her. It would be well to get into the habit of caution now, at the beginning of her journey. She glanced all around: the plants of the palace garden grew rich with leaves—which cast shadows—and flowers, with scents that could mask those of anyone who might hide among them. She rolled the barkcloth message up and placed it below her breasts. Even if found and read, it contained only a fraction of the information she was carrying.

Lembe handed the queen her mirror. The brass reflection showed her the crownlike arrangement of reeds woven over with her hair, an elaborate construction of basketry and coiffeurage with glittering metal set shining in its dark splendor. Satisfactory. The Portuguese would be impressed.

Sifa appeared at the head of the stairs outside the royal suite of rooms, holding a bundle in her arms: warm wrappings Josina would need in the cool, high air. The lady waited for King Mwenda to precede her down to the garden. His four followers hung back with Sifa as the king approached Josina's seat.

"I'll miss you," he said, simply.

They'd made their private farewells earlier that morning, in bed. This was for show. She rose properly from her throne. "My rivals will fill your arms in my stead."

"Yes. I've sent for them. My arms will be full, but otherwise I'll be empty."

The words should have been more formal. The courtiers were crowding too close—they would hear. She gestured Sifa and Lembe back and the others went as well.

"I have something you should see." She unrolled the message. In addition to describing their enemy's defeat in words, her sister priest had drawn a picture: bees swarming, attacking with their stings, Rhodesian soldiers dropping guns and running away into the Bangweulu Swamp.

King Mwenda laughed. "Ah, that's good! And this has happened four times already? Won't the English become suspicious?"

"We prayed. There are going to be five incidents altogether. After that we must ask for other kinds of help."

"My spirit father will provide what we need."

"Yes."

"And your body father, too, of course." So certain. The king's arm fell upon her shoulders like a warm, heavy length of cloth. She didn't want to leave. Never before had relations between the two of them felt so effortless, her attachment to him so natural.

But the whistle blew. Its three-note chord called workers to drink their midmorning tea. When done, they'd finish loading *Wheatley* for the flight to Luanda; she should depart to board the aircanoe now. Soon.

This was what needed to be done. The mission had originally been her idea. Then her husband had added the force of his agreement, a force that kept her moving in the right direction.

"When you're with me again, we'll have peace," said the king, in the cadence of received revelation. Did that mean they'd be separated for the rest of the war? That it would be short? That she would succeed?

He escorted her down the steps to their special carriage. It wouldn't be seemly for King Mwenda to accompany her all the way to the airfield. Lembe and Sifa took their seats. The partition against which they rested their backs divided them from the driver. The carriage's engine was a new sort, puffing black smoke instead of white steam. Reaching through one of the big windows in its sides, Josina gripped the king's hand hard. She let it go. They pulled away.

She gazed out of the carriage for a long while before she saw anything. By that point, they were on the city's edges, among the groves of oil and wine palms. Some of the more timid of the returning whites had built houses here with wooden walls too thick to replace easily, but too thin to keep things as cool inside as stone did.

They broke from the trees. The sun beat on the carriage's tin roof and she began to get hot. But, almost immediately, they came under the shelter of *Wheatley*'s bulky shade.

Bulkier than before: like *Okondo,* though dedicated to civilian service, *Wheatley* now wore the lightweight, bullet-stopping "armor" devised by Winthrop. Viewed from underneath, it resembled a tangled thicket of leafless vines and branches. Josina remembered the Motes at which its adoption had been urged. She was glad to see the brown mass split by scales of shining bronze that had been fixed to a shield along the aircanoe's keel. The king had insisted on metal armor as well, and Tink had obliged.

Also new were the stairs being trundled out and carefully positioned: much easier to climb than rope ladders. The queen and her ladies mounted the stairs to the aircanoe and entered the woven shelter near its prow. Josina accepted Sifa's help putting on the lady's latest cool-air styles: a skirt reaching to her ankles, formed from dozens of alternating strips of fur and unpainted, feather-sewn barkcloth; a fitted palm-fiber bodice also embellished outside with feathers and lined with very soft fur; cork-soled sandals tied on with crisscrossing ribbons of thick yellow silk that rose to her knees; more silk, cut to resemble banana leaves and gathered in bunches to hang upon her shoulders as a beautiful green shawl. Soon she was comfortably settled among the little shelter's pillows and headrests, with a quilted coverlet—the gift of Mrs. Albin—at hand for when she required more warmth. It was most welcome that night.

By the middle of the next day they'd reached Mbuji-Mayi, the

Everfair settlement Mrs. Albin's adherents persisted in calling Bookerville. Josina peered over the boarding scoop in *Wheatley*'s side and saw many thatch roofs, most set in long, hollow, broken-walled rectangles.

Sifa had created and brought another kind of clothing: cotton pieces draped over a woven form so it appeared that an enormous saffron blossom fell from the queen's shoulders, baring her face, arms, and feet. It wouldn't keep her warm, but would ward off the jealous disapproval from Mrs. Albin and those like her of her beautiful bare breasts.

No stairs here to descend to the muddy field. Mrs. Albin waited for her at the ladder's foot and escorted the queen to her home.

A pair of pink-scarred men with their eyes sooted shut walked past them, guided by children. Tattered skin and rags covered the adults' arms and legs. The children led them inside a metal-roofed building that stank faintly of old meat.

Josina tried not to hear the screams coming from the second building they passed. If she heard them, she would want to stop and help. She must rest in Mrs. Albin's house and go on to Luanda. She must do her best to end the war, and then there would be less pain.

"You have enough medicines?"

"What we can't get from China and America we are learning to make for ourselves. The Lord gives us strength and tells us what we're meant to do, leads us where we're meant to go."

So had Mrs. Albin's Lord led her people here to take over King Mwenda's land? Queen Josina didn't ask that question. She found out other things: how the hammocks at the ends of the "cranes"— the long poles—could be loaded with wounded fighters and gently lowered to the earth; how few of those hurt at the frontier lived long enough to arrive here and be treated; how deeply Mrs. Albin disliked Mademoiselle Toutournier.

"Really, it was a relief when she asked to go back to the capital. I hear she has left the country."

"For a while, she did go," Josina said. "But she has returned." And had given valuable reports.

Mrs. Albin screwed her eyes shut as if she'd rather not see something ugly. "I pray for her. God grant her peace."

That would be something good for everyone to have.

They ate dinner and went to bed. Sifa removed Josina's pretty outfit and they slept. They rose before the sun did so that *Wheatley* might rise into the sky with it.

Once over the Kasai River they turned south. North would have been easier and more direct, but that was enemy territory. *Wheatley* anchored for two nights in river valleys as far from any village as they could get, though Angola, a colony of Portugal, was supposedly neutral.

Lying between Sifa and Lembe, Queen Josina silently rehearsed the speeches she would make. Over and over she imagined conversations, interviews, approaches. The Five Yellow Silk Scarves would ensure favorable responses, if she could correctly target the charm. Some officials she knew of through Alonzo; some had been introduced to her by her father. Yet there would always be new faces.

At last they came to the city. Luanda was a long-established seaport, and the equipment necessary to service the transporting of goods stayed concentrated near its waterfront. By the great blue sea, aircanoe tethers beckoned to them like slender fingers. Both cranes for *Wheatley*'s freight of metals and hemp and wheeled stairs for the passengers were provided. Her father's servants greeted her with parasols and a white burro. Lembe and Sifa had to walk behind her in a cloud of the animal's dust and stink.

Away from the seaside the heat grew. Her father's servants led the burro up a slight hill and under an arched gateway through a good, thick wall. On its other side, a fountain's song came to her between blooming shrubs. Assisted down from the burro's back, Josina stood a moment on the grey flagstones, orienting herself. Then she walked forward. The softly splashing water was only a few steps further on.

Hamad bin Muḥammad bin Jumah bin Rajab bin Muḥammad, king of the Niassa, sat in quiet contemplation on the fountain's lip. His silk headdress shimmered with reflected light. His white beard was as full as ever, but below his smiling eyes, black smudges marred his dark brown skin.

"My daughter. Be welcome to my home."

"Is this truly your home now, father? So far from Pemba and the Madagascar trade routes?"

"It's where I do my work lately. Some of it. Having a home here is convenient." He looked past her. "Tell your people to ask my steward which rooms will be yours to use. While they arrange your things, we'll talk."

Her father was shrewd. The fountain's noise masked their exchange. Josina shared what her spies had learned about the Entente's lack of commitment to prolonged African campaigns. Nothing she said would weaken her in the coming negotiations. Portugal risked little by turning a blind eye to its colonies' military activity.

"But Macao? The Chinese won't want to be part of this," King Hamad objected.

"They don't," she agreed. "And it's not necessary, because, like Africa, China is of less concern to whites than Europe. Whites want Macao's wealth just as they want ours, but they want to take it home with them. The Portuguese would rather not have to stay there. Or here.

"If the Niassa and Angola are persuaded to join our side, that will be enough."

"Enough? No, my child, no. Nothing will ever be enough." Though king, her father had always acted as if he ruled his people for someone else.

To convince him they could win, she had to tell him about the machine-gun factory at Manono. "We are making twenty-five of them from market day to market day. And building a new place where we can make them faster and make more." And better. Tink had improved the stolen plans.

"Ah." One short word her father said. As he said it, though, she saw the fear flow off of him like water pouring off a leaf.

That was how she knew he would help.

Bookerville to Manono, Everfair,
May 1916

Martha didn't want to believe it. But it was true. She stared at the mercury of their only decent clinical thermometer. George's fever had pushed it up to 101.1. That must be due to more than the heat of the day. She was justified in making him quit his work early. She'd been right to bring him here.

"Lie down," she told him. He grinned but obeyed her. She drew the back of her hand across his forehead. It was damp. And under his tan, did she discern a flush?

He grabbed for her hand, missed, and closed his eyes tight, wincing. "How are you feeling, dear?" she asked.

"Rotten." Again, he grinned. More of a grimace. "I don't mind lying down in the middle of the day. Alla work for you . . ." He trailed off into stertorous breathing. Worsening so quickly.

She must drink this cup.

All the pallets in this wing were full, now. Young men—she refused to house the women in the same facilities, even if they *were* soldiers—groaned and sweated and muttered and yelled all around her. Not quite the same symptoms as typhus—there was very little vomiting, and no diarrhea to speak of once the intestinal tract had been voided. George had admitted to aching pains, but, when questioned, said these were general and not situated in his joints.

This was a new affliction.

Resolutely ignoring the hand her aide offered, Martha stood with as much grace as a fifty-seven-year-old woman could expect to muster. She shook out her skirts as a cover for the time it took to regain her composure. George's eyes were shut. "I'll be back in time for tea, dearest," she said, hoping he'd hear her, and walked calmly away.

It was best to maintain an air of imperturbability in front of the patients. Also in front of staff. Her one-walled office afforded no refuge. Sitting on the stool George had carved for her, at the desk he had built, she sorted papers into stacks as if they mattered. As if anything mattered.

She'd better get a grip on herself. Make another mark on the sheet tallying those who suffered from the new disease. George was number thirty-six. Move that page to the side. Try to finish her latest letter urging more churches to add their voices to hers in the matter of America's participation in the war. That *did* matter. Faith could move mountains. With the aid of the American government, Everfair would triumph over her latest enemies in practically no time. Surely the Lord would lift the scales from the eyes of congressmen blind to the sacredness and manifest inevitability of Everfair's mission. Though no other member of the Grand Mote agreed, Martha knew that making this request was the country's best and shortest path to victory.

But after staring sightlessly at her earlier words for what must have been five minutes—possibly more—she threw down the half-written epistle in disgust. Nothing would do but to find a cure for George's illness. It was a pity that she couldn't fool herself out of the conviction that she knew whose assistance to seek. When Queen Josina had shared her people's unchristian treatment for malaria—which, alas, had proved effective—she'd named other healers to consult on other matters. Pagans, all of them. Currently, one of them worked here in Bookerville.

In a last, vain effort, Martha took up her Bible and held it above the cross on her breast: her shields against the constant barrage of heathenism this land hurled against her. That did no good. Through the dappled light of the early afternoon, she saw Yoka approaching.

He climbed the three steps to the office's raised wooden floor.

He knocked on the doorpost and waited for her to invite him "in." She found herself nodding; God must mean for Martha to abandon her pride, or he would not have made this so easy. God was using the pagan priest for his own ends. As he used everyone. With a silent plea to her Lord that she be allowed to understand and implement his will, she told the man their problem.

"Yes. Of course we have been hearing about this infection. We trace its origin to contact with birds and beasts of the air." He turned down her offer of her stool and stood, clasping his flesh and prosthetic hands behind his back. "There are a number of treatments to prevent our patients from getting worse—especially in their lungs. But the main idea is just to let each sick person get well on their own. Most will recover."

Most. "Why? Why won't you even attempt to heal him—them?"

Yoka's shoulders rose. "We don't know how. We asked—prayed—for God to tell us. He said a surrender to this illness would protect us from something much worse, and—"

"God will never speak to you! Devil-worshippers! Filthy, lying, blaspheming savages—get out! Get out!" Martha collapsed to her knees and hid her face in her hands. She sobbed with tearless rage. How dare they pretend to have God's ear? How dare they?

How had she become so scared and weak?

Lowering her hands, she saw no one in the immediate vicinity. Yoka had gone. Her aides were all absent on their rounds—or, perhaps, taking meals at the canteen. She used the desk's edge to pull herself erect.

Discipline. The Lord would help her as long as she helped herself. In an hour, she would take George his tea. No one would wonder at that or think she feared unduly for her husband. Till then, she would work.

She returned to her unfinished letter. "Sisters and Brothers," she read, "our most Blessed nation must move to end this terrible, tragic War! It is a Scourge which threatens to engulf every continent of the Globe in wicked, pointless conflict. Let the brave example set by the missionaries of Everfair lead—" There the text broke off abruptly.

A horn of ink lay on the desk's broad surface, and a brass-nibbed pen in the open basket beside it. She took them up like they were blade and shongun, but thought furiously as she filled the rest of the page with yet another urgent call to arms. This was her sixth such in half as many years. If only she could go herself—but in America, her marriage was a crime. If only Winthrop could act as her ambassador—or Chester—

Yes. She would fly to Manono and ask her godson there to travel to America on her behalf—on behalf of all the colony's Christians.

At the canteen, she obtained a gourd of tea and four sweet plantain balls. Though George seemed asleep when she sat on the floor mat beside him, she saved the tea for him. Soon after her arrival, she was rewarded. First his slow breaths—already more regular than when she'd put him to bed—quickened. Then his long lashes lifted to reveal his brilliant eyes, like blue gemstones. His hectic flush had receded. In fact, at the sight of the food, his color ebbed further. That was all right; she folded the leaf back around the remains. A temporary loss of appetite was normal, judging by his fellow sufferers.

The tea, he accepted gratefully. The news of her plan to depart for Manono next market day didn't please him in the least. He thought she should leave in the morning.

Martha objected. "But you're ill!"

"But I'm improving, aren't I? Fast as all the others?" So far, the lengthiest instances of this sort of indisposition had lasted two markets. One market was more typical, as she had, to her regret, said to him while he lay in bed with her last night.

Couldn't she unsay it now? "As far as we know, though its symptoms are severe, the disease is of short duration. *As far as we know.* That doesn't mean your case will follow the same course . . ."

It was no use. No complications developed overnight, and at dawn she mounted to *Okondo*'s gondola. Two uncomfortable days en route. One day of pointless argument with Chester, who refused to see reason. "Why can't you go to America yourself?" he asked. "Or, barring that, send someone who truly *wants* to go?

Like Miss Bailey—she's already headed there, I'm told. Handy, don't you think?" What Martha thought was that Rima Bailey was a shameless tribade.

One more day waiting for *Okondo*'s return from Kisangani. Two more in transit back to Bookerville. One and a half markets, six days, wasted. Absolutely wasted. "Lost: Two golden hours, each set with sixty diamond minutes. No reward is offered, for they are gone forever."

At last, at last, she descended to stand on the same ground as her beloved. As he gathered her into his young arms she swore never to leave him again.

Ponce, Puerto Rico, to Harlem, United States of America, May 1916

Maybe Rima should have flown out of Cuba, but that was too damn close to Florida, which she wanted to forget forever. And the U.S. government claimed Porto Rico was part of America, which meant its routes were better: more dirigibles more times a week.

Shame the Germans had shot at that English boat with all them American passengers. At least they'd missed. Cut back on the sailing schedules, though.

Since the next dirigible north didn't leave out till morning, she decided to take in a show at the Pearl. From her hotel it was a short walk—a couple minutes if she'd gone direct, but she cruised around the square first for the glitter of its fountains, the cool rise of the evening shadows up its soft-colored walls, the noise of its birds cackling and scolding each other as they settled into the treetops for the night. She thought she could almost understand what they said.

Turning her back on all that, she marched along Cristina Street. It was a straight shot. Then she climbed six marble steps, slipped into the crowd threading through six tall columns and into three doors in walls painted a delicate yellow. Once inside, she squeezed between round-bottomed women in tight skirts; portly gentlemen in linen suits; thin, spinsterish-looking white ladies fanning themselves; smooth-haired youths and wrinkle-necked ticket-takers. An usher handed her a printed program and showed her to the third-row seat she'd purchased, maybe a little too close to the pit.

She put her back to the curtained stage and stared boldly up at the rest of the theater. Lavish appointments—sumptuous, even: velvet hangings, sparkling chandeliers, gilded fronts to the boxes lining the upper half of the horseshoe-shaped hall. The seating capacity she estimated as around a thousand. She would recommend it to Matty.

Her neighbors took their places: both of them men. Come to notice there weren't that many women, at least not down here on the floor. One man pressed his knee against her leg. She hit him with her bag. After that, he didn't try anything more. The lights went down and the violins struck a high, excited note, then plunged into a slow, tense dance. The red curtains parted on the scene of a café, with bareheaded boys and feather-crowned girls seated at its tables. In glided a man wearing a silk top hat, cravat, long tails, and diamond-studded spats. He stopped center stage, twirled his cane, opened his mouth and sang—and it was a woman! By Marie Laveau! The woman tripped and tapped and span about while trilling away like a black-clad canary.

Rima knew a little Spanish. The words were simple, all about love. The dance—*I could do that,* she thought. *I could do that!* The boys bore the girls to front of the stage, still seated on their chairs, and left them there to tread intricate measures with the woman—well, who wouldn't! Just lightly touching fingertips, they twisted this way and that, humming in harmony while the girls tilted their shoulders back and forth and sang along on the chorus. The finish found them at their tables again, the woman in the man's suit standing on two chairs at once, triumphantly straddling the space between them. The curtains swished together and parted again almost immediately on a bicycle built for so many riders it was silly. Scenery moved unevenly behind the "riders." It must have been a hand-cranked roll. Very soon, the woman reappeared, this time in shirtsleeves and a straw boater and a false mustache! And riding a unicycle as she sang!

The whole show went like that, one musical number following on the heels of another. As far as Rima could tell, there was no attempt to tie things together with a story or any kind of excuse for the songs. When an intermission suddenly cropped up, she stayed right where she was, examining her program. "The Blue Fox Revue"—a "revue" was a French concept borrowed by its star Carmen Delicias, probably *not* her real name—was booked to play here till next Friday.

Rima beat away the too-friendly hands of the second man seated next to her, then gave up for the night and left. It was rude. But, in the vestibule, she roused the ticket office and reserved a box for the rest of the Blue Fox Revue's engagement. At the hotel, she announced she'd be staying a while longer and asked the concierge to cancel her passage on *Compadre*. She got the address of a flower shop.

As soon as siesta ended the following afternoon, she went and bought everything: all the roses, all the orchids, lilies, iris, jasmine. A lot of money gone, but Rima called it an investment. She sent the delivery to the Pearl's best dressing room. That would have to be the right one.

It was. Two hours before curtain, Rima gained entrance to the backstage area. She knew immediately which door to knock on. Her tribute, in makeshift vases, had overflowed Delicias's room with scent and color, spilling into the corridor. Inside, barred from the tabletop, which was covered with makeup containers, they commandeered the floor's corners, the high windowsill, the sink.

Delicias wore women's clothing. If you could call a pink negligee clothes. Her skin was half as dark as Rima's; her hair was slick and short, like a dog's coat just swimming out of a swamp.

She spoke some English. They understood each other well enough. When the show ended, they had supper in Rima's hotel room. A short while later they went to bed, and a long while later they slept.

Rima wished Carmen would talk more. She didn't volunteer her offstage name. Rima booked passage to New York for her, too, and they left right away once the revue closed.

Two markets it took to go fifteen hundred miles—eight days. Twice as long as it would have taken in Everfair. No wonder cruise ships and aeroplanes could compete. By the time *Clementine* moored in Constable Hook, Rima and Carmen were through with each other.

They stayed on good terms. Carmen helped Rima find her first apartment; half the people in Harlem were Porto Ricans, and they all knew the woman's mama, or were related somehow. Almost as bad as Eatonville. Except not as prejudiced—nobody said too much about Carmen's choice of company.

Before Rima signed her contracts with Matty's Broadway producer, she made sure that he planned to offer parts to her friend. That's all Carmen was anymore; in fact, she introduced Rima to the lover who replaced her, and a few more later on—even some men. Rima was picky but open-minded; and besides, none of them meant anything really, compared to Lisette. She knew she'd eventually go back to her, to Everfair. Someday. Some distant day.

Kisangani, Everfair, December 1916

Daisy put the letter back in Lisette's waiting hand without trying to touch her again. It was no use.

She reached out with words instead. "You think this means we'll be defeated within a year?"

"Yes." Lisette folded the letter and tucked it into the bodice of her pleated shift. Her bare arms looked as plump and tanned as ever. "The Americans have everything in their favor: numbers, money . . . we should never have been drawn into this war."

"True. But now that we *are* in—"

"We should get out."

Daisy greeted the interruption with silence.

"But I suppose the Entente wouldn't let us," Lisette admitted. "Or the Central Powers, for that matter?"

"Probably not. I'll do my best to argue we should, though." She looked down at the wooden floor. Despite this amenity, Lisette's cottage reminded Daisy overwhelmingly of her primitive first home in Bookerville, where they had so briefly shared their love. Nostalgia filled every aching breath.

"The Grand Mote is coming soon. I suppose the representatives will need to be courted to our cause . . . Is there anything I can do?"

Kiss me. Daisy's thought remained unspoken. "Meet me again tomorrow." At least Daisy could ask for that much. "I'll have a new poem."

"Of course." Lisette stood. So Daisy had to as well. They went the short distance to the front door. Lisette opened it and waited expectantly.

"One other thing." Daisy did her best not to sound desperate. "If this course doesn't prove fruitful—can you help me decide what to do next?" It was a reasonable request, though she'd come up with it rather at the last moment. Of course Lisette agreed.

Walking home through the lightest rain—mere drizzle—Daisy wrenched her mind aside from the insoluble mystery of how she'd offended her love. Over and over she'd asked herself what she'd said, what she'd done. Useless. As for asking Lisette, that was like interrogating one's aged and partially deaf aunt. One was uncertain one had been heard, yet it seemed impolite to press the point.

Rather than pick over the past, she steered her thoughts back to the present. The political situation was deteriorating rapidly. In Europe, stalemate was ending as the United States sent over its troops. Portugal might finally abandon its precious neutrality and do more than turn a blind eye to the military activities of Angola and Moçambique. But its support wouldn't be enough.

She reached her flat and climbed the stairs. Za waved hello from the porch high across their shared court, the child's rain-wet brown cheeks fat and shining in the sudden noonday sun. Rosalie was out planting a new palm orchard and would be back for supper. Daisy dined alone on a gourd of leftover fufu and oil sauce, washed down with coco water. Then she set out again for the airfield, the dinner-done whistle clamoring up from the riverfront.

Mr. Beamond had assigned her to operate the mechanical mast. Daisy preferred to load and unload; brute labor gave her mind the necessary freedom to versify, but coordinating the three mooring lines and running the winch for them required too much thought. No doubt this was considered a safer assignment for a woman in her late fifties.

The drummers on the smallest, lowest platform had already started the winch engine before she left the field's roundhouse. It powered a lift. She'd looked forward to getting her exercise on the 150-foot-high spiral staircase. But Nenzima had booked a passage on the incoming aircanoe and was riding up in the lift, so Daisy decided to accompany her. She would try if she could to persuade this first Mote member with prose before composing a poem.

She shut the gate in the lift cage's low wooden parapet. Making sure the other woman had steadied herself, Daisy moved the lever that linked them to the power of the engine. Once she judged they were high enough above it that it was sufficiently quiet for her to be heard, she started talking, though she had no idea what to say. Something about the safety of the jungle, the crushing might of America, and how to escape its awful regard. Turn upon turn of the stairs encircling them opened overhead as they rose. Nenzima's dark face remained undisturbed despite the pessimistic picture Daisy tried to draw. "And if they do find us fighting them they'll mow us down, gas us in the trenches—we're only animals as far as they're concerned; to their minds we're no better than gorillas."

Finally, an eyebrow rose. "*All* of us?" Nenzima asked. "Whites, too?" The lift stopped. Without waiting for an answer, the African woman unlatched the gate and stepped out.

The passenger platform was only twenty feet in diameter. The mooring controls were right beside the lift at its center, but after sending the cage back to the tower's bottom, Daisy followed Nenzima to the platform's railing. The throb of the engine far below communicated itself through its wood, causing her hands to tingle as she clasped it. Lisette would have found this arousing—Daisy cut that thought off.

Nenzima maintained her silence. Daisy couldn't think how to pierce it. Ordinary words never seemed to work for her.

Straining her ears, Daisy caught the distant drone of *Okondo*'s powerful Littlest Heater over the soft rumble of the winch. Clouds filled the sky, but soon the aircanoe's roofed gondola appeared close by, dangling from the mist-greyed bulk of the airbag. Lower, lower—lines were tossed to the ground crew so they could tug the aircanoe into alignment, and Daisy went to her post.

Guiding the telescopic arm in the tower's turret was a tricky enterprise. Drums conveyed to Daisy the disposition of the workers managing the aircanoe's side lines and their pulleys. The wind was negligible, so after only three attempts she threaded the eye on *Okondo*'s bow with her hook. Then she retracted the arm till she heard and felt the gimbaled cup click into place over the bow. Next came the rasp and slap of the gangplank being pushed out of a port in the gondola's side and dropped onto the rail. Barrels of ammunition began rumbling sedately along its slight incline into the arms of the field's loaders. Daisy wished she could help.

Why couldn't she? The wind hardly blew, and the mooring cup would turn if necessary—but who else would translate the drummers' signals into shorter or longer side lines?

Impatiently, Daisy awaited the completion of the unloading. As soon as the noise stopped, Nenzima called a formal-sounding farewell. She would need help to mount the rail, but the aircanoe's sailors would manage that. There was no further excuse for Daisy to approach her. No further opportunity to change her mind.

A few dozen skins of palm wine had come up with them in the lift; these formed the bulk of Kisangani's freight to Kamina. In exchange, the mines at Kamina would furnish ores for Manono's manufactories.

Everything boiled down to alcohol and guns, Daisy thought. This wasn't how she'd imagined matters proceeding when they first came here, twenty years ago—longer than that. And the situation was probably worse than she allowed herself to believe. Rumor said children worked in Manono's forges and Kamina's pits.

Tears of frustration welled up. She blinked rapidly to clear her eyes. She could travel and see for herself. Then what? Talking. Writing poetry. More talk. Wasn't there anything else to be done? If only Jackie had lived, whatever the state of their personal relations. If only the war would end.

The drums' steady rhythm proclaimed the status quo until a loud thump, followed by regular footsteps, cut through it. Chester Hunter crossed the platform to lean his folded arms on the benchtop where Daisy worked. His round face took on a confidential cast. "You're worried about the Americans?"

Word got around quickly. "They're in the war now, and they're going to win." Not to put too fine a point on it. "We had better get out before we lose to them."

"Good idea, if we could bring it off." Another on her side! Chester had replaced his brother on the Grand Mote in last year's elections, the same that put Lisette in Mrs. Albin's seat. With Albert, that made four of eleven . . . not by any means a majority. But there was hope. As they talked, she obtained Chester's promise to have a discussion with Tink when *Okondo* reached Manono again. And George must, must see reason . . .

Of course if King Mwenda ignored the Mote, as Lisette had many times hinted he wished to do, and as he had indeed seemed often on the verge of doing, then there was no way of enforcing its decisions. The fighters were all loyal to him. Most were born Africans, besides.

Called back to *Okondo*'s care, Chester disappeared for the remainder of the aircanoe's hour at dock. Daisy thought she saw his hand waving in reassurance from one of the receding gondola's portholes. But it could have been any black's.

No other aircanoes were due during Daisy's shift. Performing maintenance with the crew filled her afternoon. Her relief showed at sunset.

Walking was almost the equal of labor as a breeding medium for poetry. Reaching home, she hurried to her basket of blank paper and her always-full fountain pen, her sole luxuries. A chorus had presented itself to her, complete with six variations. She had only one stanza as she sat to write, but trusted more would come. And soon they did.

Rosalie returned sometime during the composition of the second verse. Daisy heard Rosalie, saw her in a sense when she raised her head from the page. Most likely she greeted her daughter too, at some point—certainly when Rosalie brought her a gourd of fragrant steamed fish and vegetables, she spoke as if continuing a conversation Daisy couldn't recall starting.

"Of course I'll stay awake till you're ready to read it aloud. You always ask me, and I always do." Speedily forming and dipping her balls of fufu, Rosalie seemed suddenly African. Which just proved how false was the dichotomy Nenzima, Josina, and the rest professed to sense in Everfair's people. Race should not, could not, *did* not divide them. The next stanza was the perfect one in which to express the sentiment—

By the speckled lamplight, Daisy laid out the poem's final draft to let the ink dry. Glancing up, she saw that Rosalie had strung their beds without her noticing. Her daughter's sagged. "Rosalie?" Daisy whispered, and was rewarded with a frowsy face staring down over the hammock's headbar. She checked her repeater. Five minutes to midnight. "Go back to sleep. It's no matter."

But Rosalie shook her tousled curls. "Read it," she insisted. "I'm listening. As ever. Let me be the first."

Kisangani, Everfair, January 1917

Mwenda had come so far. Josina had helped him renew contact with his spirit father, and because of this he would go further. Princess Mwadi had retrieved the original shongo for him. Later it would be given to her brother, his heir. He fondled the wooden haft and considered the past, the future.

The poem was ending. The Poet's voice increased in volume and she once again repeated a long stream of words:

> *"Then let us put the War away,*
> *This wicked game we shall not play;*
> *We'll sport no more as wanton boys,*
> *Abandoning such murderous toys,*
> *And we'll live as God intended,*
> *We whom Heaven has befriended."*

Mwenda had learned English at the prompting of the Mote, when they'd made it his country's official language—a problem, but one put off to be dealt with after the tyrant's overthrow. And still unconfronted. For the moment, he merely listened, his favorite queen beside him.

Of the others present, only Old Kanna had formed part of the king's original court. With Nenzima and Loyiki, he had counseled Mwenda and Josina separately, in advance of the current Grand Mote. Though Mwenda alone bore responsibility for deciding his realm's destiny.

Politely, King Mwenda applauded the Poet in the whites'

accepted style, hand on hand. Flesh on metal. It served to spot-
light one of the most important differences between him and many
of his subjects.

As planned, it was Loyiki who brought up the first question:
"How can we offer a surrender no one has asked us for?"

"But they *will* ask for it," Mademoiselle Toutournier replied.
"The motion we consider is merely for us to prepare ourselves—"

"How can you *know*?" Unexpectedly, his hand's inventor,
Tink, stood from his chair. Mwenda listened and watched him as
he had learned to do so well from Josina. "Nothing has happened
yet. America entered the war only just last November; have you
found out a method of predicting the future?" Strands of his
straight black hair escaped its bindings and fell across his shoulders as he walked rapidly back and forth along the room's edge.
Evidently his passion was too much to conceal. But in which direction did it run? "There may be a truce! A cease fire! Anything—
you can't be sure—"

"Or is this another instance of your spying?" asked George
Albin. His lips were pressed thin. He meant the word as an insult.

"You don't approve?" Mademoiselle smiled as he flushed. She
would take it for granted that her sister Josina did approve of an
activity she herself engaged in. And therefore King Mwenda
also. "All I am saying is that if, in the eventuality—the very
likely eventuality—that the war in Europe—which is the only
theater in which Europeans are interested—should be decided in
favor of the Entente, we must expect to acknowledge to them
our defeat."

Then it was time for Nenzima to placate everyone, as she so
often did. She called on them to continue discussing the point and
to delay the vote till the next Grand Mote, eight markets off. This
was, of course, agreed to.

There should have been nothing more after that, but before he
could signal Old Kanna to make the request to close proceedings,
the Poet said she wished to bring up another matter.

"A happier matter," she went on, frowning, "and one we ought
to be able to decide more quickly: today, in fact.

"I want us to proclaim a national holiday. We—we have never had one."

"Ah." Tink sat again. "Yes. That's a very good idea. Our martyrs should be remembered."

"Thank you. That is more or less the idea. A nonreligious celebration, it goes without saying." So why had she said it? "The date of August 13 seems best." *Why was the Poet choosing that specific date,* the king wondered, *and using the white calendar?* These were answers of the sort his queen had been teaching him to seek out. Answers he had learned to care for more as his seasons increased.

"Even if we do continue fighting, we will have to halt temporarily then, with the rains at their worst. Before that, we'll have time enough to make our inaugural Founders' Day—"

"Our—what did you call it?" Queen Josina leaned forward with apparently detached interest.

"Founders' Day?" The Poet hesitated. "We could certainly use another name for it, if you think that would be better. Something with a more traditional or local association?"

"A traditional association with our founding?" Josina looked and sounded genuinely puzzled. "The king's line began several generations ago, but we celebrate that under no particular name and on no particular day. What is the significance of August 13—for you?"

The Poet's face drew in like a flower done with the day. "It's when Jackie died—Mr. Owen, the father of our country."

Silence. It was not for Mwenda to speak. But Old Kanna hissed.

"I beg your pardon?" The flower of the Poet's face stirred in its drooping.

"I believe," Mademoiselle Toutournier said, "that many of our citizens might rather give that title to the king."

"Yes," affirmed the queen.

Mwenda rose. "You may go now."

"But the Mote—the holiday—"

Mademoiselle took the Poet's arm and steered her toward the door. "It's over, Daisy."

Usumbura, Urundi, September 1917

Thomas brought only five of his brides with him. They shared their own house, at the end of a short path connecting to the house where he slept. For none of the four days and nights they'd stayed here so far had he escaped seeing a Sapeur as he slipped from one side to the other. Thomas's admirers were subtle. It almost could have been owing to chance that some emulator of his style was always standing nearby, waiting for a glimpse of the smartly be-skirted general visiting or leaving his harem. Thomas returned the salute of one, a white-shirted dandy in a charcoal-colored kilt leaning against the wall of the emptied building at the compound's entrance. Not a guard, but beneath the man's grey derby shone watchful eyes. Perhaps the Sapeurs' presence was for the best.

Shutting the door on the glaringly bright sunset, he took a moment to let his eyes adjust to the dimness of the women's house. Fatoumata, a devotee out of Mali, had insisted on covering the windows with chalk-smeared sheets to keep out malign influences. Perhaps she was right to do so—no assassins had attacked him yet. But tomorrow he would have to appear in public to play his part in Everfair's surrender to the British rulers of this colony.

He had attempted uselessly to refuse King Mwenda's commission. It hadn't helped his arguments against coming that he'd flown missions over Urundi and beyond. But being here on the ground was different. It made him much more vulnerable, despite the many men gathering to admire him. Well, if he died at the age of sixty-eight, that wouldn't be such a tragedy, would it?

Fatoumata's sleek, smooth back aroused him. While Nenzima, more of an age with Thomas, massaged and oiled his hands, he reveled in the roll of the younger woman's muscles as she bent to rub his feet. Then a third of his consorts—Uwimana, meaning "daughter of God"—but which god?—soothed his temples with soft fingers, circling, circling, slower, wider, brushing upward over Thomas's shorn head.

His eyes closed. A powerful yet languorous thrill surged through him, like warm wind through an opened door. His clothing slipped away, and the women's ministrations became defter and more direct. His manhood received caresses from multiple hands and mouths—too many for him to distinguish among them without an effort he no longer cared to make. Wet, supple delight surrounded him, skin to skin, breath to breath. No hurry, no pressure save that building within, which would crest and spill over in the fullness of its own sweet time.

When all activity ceased.

Rousing himself from his repletion, Thomas found Nenzima ready, as usual, to dress him in a clean shirt and skirt. The shirt's long sleeves—suitable to Usumbura's high elevation—were pressed into neat creases, the canvas skirt printed with the star-and-river pattern frequently painted on barkcloth. Having escorted him back to his bed, she once again removed the garments to hang handy on pegs till he would want them in the morning.

Three pegs. Since their arrival, the top peg had been empty. Now it held the most extraordinary object. "Nenzima?"

"Yes, husband?"

"What is—this?"

"It is for you to wear to the surrendering."

Gingerly, Thomas removed the thing from where it was suspended, finding at the center of its fountaining, two-and-a-half-foot-long, blue-black feathers an everyday square hat. "Loango wishes this?" Yoka had remained in Everfair to minister to the thousands of faithful there, but in his stead others such as Nenzima offered Thomas much-needed spiritual advice.

"It would make for good alignment."

Then yes. Mindful of past punishments, Thomas resolved to accept this obliquely given divine instruction immediately and unconditionally.

Usumbura was too small for a dedicated British consulate. The formal surrender was to take place in the mayor's offices. Thomas and his entourage arrived first and waited for the governor in the gardens for some minutes. A growing crowd of dandies in kilts and ascots and tailored morning coats, wearing ruffled cuffs and spats and glossily polished shoes, swarmed around him, staring in awe at his enormous hat. The stork-faced mayor joined them and made pointless conversation about the statuary he was going to install along the graveled walkways bordering future plantings.

An appreciable time after the mayor's clock had struck noon, a thrumming drone floated down from the eastern hills. Its loudness increased as its source came nearer: a motor truck colored a drab, brownish green. Eventually this drew to a squealing halt before the steps to the mayor's offices. Out of the passenger compartment climbed a white man with yellow hair who looked about a little confusedly, then appeared to recognize Usumbura's mayor.

"Apologies if I'm late. Bally lions in the road—pardon my language. Oh, but since there aren't any ladies . . . since you're not—" A fit of coughing and a bit of play with a large handkerchief saved him from having to finish either sentence. Folding the handkerchief away, he held out his right hand. "Major Christopher J. Thornhill. You're Lieutenant Wilson, I take it?"

Thomas made no effort to shake the offered hand. The hat prevented a close approach. "I was promoted two years ago," he explained. "My new rank is that of general." Thornhill must know that. He must also be aware of Thomas's sartorial eccentricity, which made his remarks about "ladies" a deliberate attempt at insult.

Fortunately, Thomas had no intention of being insulted. He had died and been reborn. Other experiences paled to nothingness in comparison. Without further comment, he turned to enter the building, waving major and mayor ahead of him. The feathers just barely cleared the frame of the double doors from the outside. The narrower interior door simply wasn't wide enough, but remembering Nenzima's strict enjoinders that morning, he left the hat on, merely pushing the feathers into temporarily vertical positions so he could pass through.

A large, rectangular, European-style table occupied most of the room. Thomas feigned interest in the portrait of a bearded white man hanging on the free wall, watching from the corner of his eye as Thornhill chose his seat. Not at the table's head, as would have been the least remarkable choice, but along the side nearest the door. Interesting.

Sitting with his back to the plaster wall, Thomas was happy to have the table's broad expanse between them. He had no reason for his instant dislike of the major, other than Thornhill's clumsy attempts at deriding his costume and pretending ignorance of his rank. These and the major's boasts of his extensive "African studies" were standard tactics, and ought not carry any weight with him. Yet when, at the proper moment, he laid his written surrender before the man, Thomas found himself turning his head so that the hat's widest extensions brushed against the major's face.

"I say!" Forced to lean back rather than forward, Thornhill pulled the roll of barkcloth toward him by one curled end. "Hadn't you better remove that rather—obtrusive—headgear?"

"As you yourself pointed out, there are no ladies present." By white reckoning, Nenzima and Uwimana didn't count.

Thornhill grimaced and unrolled the surrender. "It's in gibberish! I can't read this! Aren't you a Yank? You speak English. What do you mean by trying to pass off these . . . this chicken scratching as real writing?"

Evidently the major's studies hadn't encompassed learning the Lin-Gah-Lah alphabet. "I have provided a translation," said Thomas, laying a second scroll on the table and withdrawing his hand swiftly—but almost not swiftly enough, as Thornhill's hand shot out immediately to take it.

"Hmmph. This seems in good order. Conditions all as agreed

upon." The major pored over the surrender in silence for several more moments. At last he set it down, grinning triumphantly.

"And here's our treaty. You'll have to sign it."

That was why he had journeyed here. His signature was a matter of form; nonetheless, Thomas made a show of examining the document for unapproved clauses and other tricks. He caught none. Accordingly, he signed and pushed the paper back across.

"Shall we shake on it, then?"

"That's rather difficult—" Thomas began.

"—and not our custom," Nenzima finished for him.

This was a lie. Everfairers of all backgrounds had adopted American and European habit in this regard. But Thomas, relieved at the prospect of not having to touch Major Thornhill, nodded as if it were the truth.

He stood. Thornhill remained seated. Thomas had to leave, to get away from this repulsive individual. Soon. Now. If necessary, he would use the table to shove the man out of his way. He grasped its edge. He would explain the incident somehow.

Uwimana bowed low enough to duck under the feathers and plucked at Thomas's sleeve. "You're not forgetting our gift to the *bwana*?" she asked.

The "bwana"? He knew the Kee-Swa-Hee-Lee word; it meant "master." In Everfair he'd never heard it applied to anyone, but their gift of a barkcloth mantle was meant for Major Thornhill— and Thomas *had* nearly forgotten it. Not Nenzima, though. She brought the banana leaf–wrapped fabric forth from the sash at her waist and moved around the table to offer it to the major.

"Please accept this token of our respect," Thomas said, edging sideways into the space freed up by Nenzima.

"What? No—no, really, I—"

Nenzima snapped the bundle's bindings and unfurled the barkcloth within.

"This *bushti* symbolizes your sovereignty over our people's heads and hearts," Thomas improvised. "We hope you will wear it always in recognition of our faith in your protection."

"—not really necessary—" Joined by Uwimana, Nenzima set

the mantle on the protesting major's shoulders. She knelt to adjust its drape and managed to compel Thornhill to rise out of his chair and step away. Thomas's path was clear. He walked out of the room—careful to lift his feathers at the doorway—and into the sweet, cool air.

Not until he was safely returned to his house within the compound did Nenzima bring him the four poisoned slivers of wood she had removed from the cuffs of the major's tunic. A pair of these spikes had been hidden on each side of Thornhill's hands, ready to be jabbed under Thomas's skin.

Manono, Everfair, November 1917

Delicately, Fwendi prodded the gummed end of the splinter with her brass fingertip. She picked it up, tested its flexibility and springiness and set it back in the tin box lying open on the workbench. "Yes. I believe you're right. This wood belongs to a fig. Perhaps one of those we would find growing in the last woods before the savannah."

"But it could have come from somewhere else?" Nenzima flipped the box's lid shut.

"Of course." She shrugged off the wet rain cloak she'd worn to the workshop and spread it along the short rafter overhead to dry. "I don't know every tree and shrub in Everfair personally."

"And the poison?"

"Common *kan* milk, the same substance used on most ammunition. Why ask? You knew that when you saw it."

"Because of where I found it. And when." The older woman tucked the box in her sash.

"You found it a month ago."

"No—I wasn't entirely honest with you about that . . . it was a little earlier, at the surrender. In the possession of the British commander, along with three others like it. He seemed to mean to use them against General Wilson."

Fwendi paused on her way to the workshop's entrance, where already a few girls waited to attend the meeting she'd called. Though surprised, she thought through it swiftly. "But—but the British meant to kill him? Even though we had agreed to every term?"

"To kill him after they got his signature. Yes. And in such a way—"

"—as to make it look like one of us had done the deed," Fwendi finished for her. A memory fought to surface through her sudden comprehension. Hadn't this happened before? It *had*. This or something similar. The attempt on Mr. Jackie Owen's life.

"And the death of such a popular man at Everfairer hands would bring about turmoil. It might even contribute to splitting the country apart, might start a—" Fwendi didn't want to say it. A war. Yet another war. Inside Everfair. It wouldn't matter who won.

"You haven't told anyone else on the Mote." It was barely a question.

"Queen Josina knows." Not an answer. The queen knew everything. "I thought that because of this example of their trickery you might want to change what you're planning to teach the children about such dangerous deceivers."

Fwendi wrinkled her forehead, puzzled. "What should I change?"

"You may want to place less blame on the Europeans for their plight."

Fwendi shook her head impatiently. "But who else caused that stupidness? We were tired. We were done! Leopold was beaten, dying—then these people decided they must fight one another, and all the rest of the world must choose sides. Yes, it was all their fault! I swear it was, and I refuse to pretend anything else."

"Not even to prevent more fighting?"

Fwendi ignored that. She walked away toward the door once more. How could lies help anything?

Five girls stood patiently waiting in the dark, warm drizzle. Their skins glowed beneath the light of the lamps as Fwendi welcomed them in through the workshop's doorless entrance. None were old enough to bear babies—the Bah-Sangah priests insisted on that limitation for anyone working for more than a market with their sacred earths.

Nenzima retreated to the workshop's furthest, shadow-filled corner. As Fwendi entertained the meeting's early arrivals with her hand—tonight she wore a model that chimed like a repeater when she made particular gestures, and also on the hour—she considered what the older woman had said. Could her words be bent to make her listeners drive the whites out? Her goal was rather to make her followers turn themselves into exiles. Professional ones. Far-flung spies.

When her hand rang eight o'clock, only thirty girls had shown up, some with the younger brothers and sisters they were taking care of in tow. She let a while longer pass and a few more trailed in, but the meeting's attendance was far short of her dreams. Two hundred children had labored here at the height of the war, making shonguns and their blades, batteries, and Littlest Heaters. Now, many of the girls' places had been taken by adults; others had simply been rendered redundant as Manono's famous manufacturing force dropped from three to two shifts per day. Soon there'd be only one.

Fwendi rang her hand loudly for attention and launched into her speech. Would any of these girls throw in their lot with her? She watched their faces. Their gleaming eyes, unblinking, watched her back.

"If you decide you want to go to the school I'm opening," she finished, "be ready in two markets. You'll be picked up at the airfield by *aMileng*."

There were the usual worries: Would students' food and uniforms really be provided to them for free? Would there be anywhere for families to stay nearby?

Yes. Yes. Then came the inevitable, thinly veiled inquiry: How many of them would actually learn to *ride*?

Not many. Perhaps one child in eight had the necessary makeup. Fwendi refrained from saying so. Instead, she focused her response on the other methods of spying to be taught, and the skills she *could* impart, which would ensure her graduates were welcome anywhere on the continent—indeed, anywhere in the world.

But a tiny voice from the right of the audience asked if those who served abroad could ever come home.

Fwendi wanted to shout with sadness. What was home? Her

parents, her entire family and village were dead and destroyed. Home was the past. Home was gone. There was no returning.

But then she spotted Grandmother's Brother Mkoi. He must have come in the furthest doorway, the one beside Nenzima. He stood quietly behind the seated girls. At Fwendi's silence he looked up at her and nodded, smiling encouragingly.

Grandmother's Brother Mkoi was her home.

Matty, as she'd recently learned, never had been. Nor had he meant to become her home. Not seriously. If he had, he would have proposed marriage by now. He would have overcome his fear, or pride, or whatever foolishness kept him from speaking. When Fwendi tired of waiting for his question, he would have followed her here to pose it.

When the girls were gone, she walked with Nenzima and Grandmother's Brother Mkoi to the house where they were staying, once the quarters of a crew of canteen workers. Inside, she set her mind to sleeping and did tolerably well.

Early in the dark morning, after saying prayers, they made their way through occasional rain to the airfield. *Brigid* was due in from Kamina en route to Mombasa at eight a.m. While breaking their fast beneath the shelter there, Grandmother's Brother Mkoi told her again that he had given Matty permission to ask her to marry him.

As she'd thought.

She told herself it was just as well Matty hadn't done so. He might have wanted a child. So might she—but pregnancy could make riding more difficult for a while, according to Grandmother's Brother Mkoi.

An inconvenience—but not as bad, something told her, as watching the candle of love smoke and die.

Kisangani, Everfair, November 1917

Since Fwendi was gone, Matty thought he might as well go too. He had many mansions. He could travel to any of them at any time. Though that would involve making arrangements.

For now he sat stoically in his inglenook, staring at the egg on his tray. Eventually Clapham would remove it. Then he would be alone again.

If only he'd ignored the dreams; if only he'd asked her to marry him. He was an utter failure.

He raised his hands and buried his face in them. The opening door and the discreet footsteps of his servant came as expected. He didn't need to see what was happening to know it.

But Clapham didn't leave immediately with the egg. Instead, his footsteps stopped. He cleared his throat. "A visitor," he announced. "A Mr. Thornhill of Mombasa. I've asked him to wait in the dining room."

This house had no library or parlor. Matty sighed and lowered his hands. "Send him in."

The man who entered was white, which Matty had anticipated. Unusually, he didn't tower over Matty as almost everyone else did. Only a little taller than his host, Thornhill had the sense to seat himself immediately.

Looking down at the arm of his bench, Matty perceived that Clapham had left a pasteboard rectangle there. His caller's card, of course. He picked it up and read it. Nothing more was revealed by this exercise than the man's first name and middle initial: Christopher J.

"Will you have some tea—or chocolate?" Matty offered.

"Thank you, no." Turning his canvas hat in his hands—Clapham really ought to have taken it—Matty's guest made a few remarks about the rains, which were beginning to abate, as they always did as Christmas approached. At last he seemed to feel enough time had been spent on inconsequentialities.

"I represent a consortium of traders, merchants who have long been interested in this area's potential. But lately circumstances— war—have made it difficult for us to properly invest. Now, however, we're ready to take advantage of the situation here, which is actually more favorable than Europe's, where talks, as you know, are lagging—"

Would the man never leave? Solitude would be a blessing. With an effort, Matty dragged himself out of his lethargy. "What do you want from me?"

The words were perhaps blunter than Thornhill had looked for. He paused several seconds before answering. "You could benefit greatly by—" He held up his palm to forestall Matty's interruption. "Your contacts? You could provide us with crucial access to raw materials, even cheap manufactured goods, which we would then sell to our customers at a healthy enough profit to allow you a commission."

"Raw materials?"

"Rubber. Metals. Surely more could be mined, your country's productivity increased."

"But why have you chosen me? I have no influence—"

"You are a Briton, of course. Better than one of that Belgian lot we had to deal with a few years back, and your native hoor—"

"My *what*?"

"Your hoor. The black—the Negress with whom you—er— have congress? I understand she receives some sort of intelli—"

"Clapham!" Red rage lifted Matty to his feet, filled all five foot two inches of his frame. "Clapham!" he shouted over the man's stuttering apologies. With commendable alacrity, his servant appeared. "This—'gentleman'—is just leaving. Escort him."

"I assure you—a mistake—slip of the tongue—won't happen again—"

"Of that I'm certain. Had I been more fortunate, the lady—the *lady*—would have become my wife."

Short-lived satisfaction kept him standing in the inglenook for a while after Thornhill left. Nervous anger drove him back to his bedroom. There it deserted him. He collapsed upon the wide bed, one half of which was so tragically unmussed.

Had he been "more fortunate"? No. Had he been less of a coward. Had he gathered his courage and asked Fwendi to marry him.

In his way, he was as bad as Thornhill; perhaps worse. He need not have behaved so self-righteously downstairs; he ought to have listened to the man's request, at the very least. Was what he had asked so very bad after all? He couldn't know that Matty stood in need not of money but of something incalculably more valuable.

He found he was stroking a sash she had left behind on the bedside table, petting it over and over like some sleeping cat.

He made himself sit upright. Fwendi wasn't dead. She lived, and while there was life, there was hope. He picked up the sash and laid it in the tall basket packed with belongings waiting to be sent to the schoolhouse in Kalemie.

From what Matty understood, Fwendi would not have gone any enormous distance with the school's debut in the offing. Mademoiselle Toutournier had mentioned journeys to Dar-es-Salaam and Mombasa, even a projected trip to Alexandria. But none to other continents.

He should consult the Frenchwoman. Outside the bedroom window, the sky shone a tentative silver. No precipitation. Perhaps he could walk to Bafwaboli Street? One could never tell how the weather would behave at this season, though; he had Clapham drum for a cab.

Mademoiselle Toutournier's "cottage" was a brick-walled house half the size of Matty's. She met him under the awning shielding her large-windowed front door. The rain had, of course, started up as soon as he left the cab to climb the steps at the intersection with Post Way. Moderately heavy, it would have soaked him thoroughly had he not brought his fan hat; as it was, he was forced to hand over to Toutournier his jacket, the ends of its sleeves having grown decidedly damp. She seemed unperturbed by his disheveled appearance. He said as much—perhaps a bit waspishly.

"Naturally. I've been expecting you. Please to come in." Slinging his coat over one arm, she pushed in the double doors with the other. Without passing along a formal entryway, he found himself in a parlourlike room with round timber pillars rising in a row along its center.

The raucous cry of a jungle bird made him jump. Had it really come from the house's upper storey? He recalled mention of a pet parrot; looking nervously about, he saw no sign of the other denizens of the rumored menagerie. This was Matty's first excursion here, though he'd entertained Mademoiselle on numerous occasions at home with Fwendi. "Why 'naturally'?"

"*Brigid* has returned; I thought you'd desire to share your letter from Fwendi with me, as I will share mine with you."

"But I have no letter," Matty confessed. The years had taught him it was best to deal with his rival for Fwendi's affections honestly. He watched curiously as his hostess hung his wet coat on a pair of wooden pegs projecting from one of the pillars. Perches for parrots? Or for the lizards he'd heard of?

"Ah." Mademoiselle gestured to a low, padded stool beside a stand holding a primitive lute with its neck shaped like a woman. She took another such stool for herself, and Matty sat. "Then that explains why she wrote that I should show you what she had sent to me." The wide grey eyes met his. "You have quarreled with each other, have you not?"

Who didn't know that? Matty nodded.

"Over politics?"

Startled, he shook his head. "No! We hardly ever talked of—of those sorts of affairs."

"Then you hardly ever talked of anything. All is politics; all is power." She covered her chin with one sunburnt hand, paused, and continued.

"You've never married. Because she didn't wish it? Or perhaps you never asked her? Never mind. Unless it is about that you've come to consult me?"

Again he shook his head, his thoughts confused. Would Fwendi have refused his proposal? The idea had never occurred to him before.

"Then what?"

Matty told her of Thornhill's morning call.

"I have heard of him, this man," Mademoiselle said. "From Fwendi. Wait here." She rose gracefully from the low stool and walked with a swish of pale blue linen to a doorway on the room's far side. Disobeying her, Matty followed stealthily to where he could see her profile silhouetted against a bright window as she leaned over a table or desk. An oddly shaped shadow dominated it, something like a stack of books getting gradually smaller and surmounted by a ball or cylinder—a typing machine! As he came to understand what he saw, Mademoiselle reached across the surface and plucked a black square—a book?—from an unseen location. Before she could possibly see him, he returned to his seat.

Mademoiselle carried no book with her when she came back into the room, only a letter, which she presented to him with a brief smile. A letter written in Fwendi's hand, but all in French.

"Naturally, I will translate." Perforce, he gave it back to her.

"She is well. No ill effects have ensued from the—plants she used to avoid impregnation."

Matty blushed. Such intimate details—well, he supposed the two women had always discussed those sorts of things, as Mademoiselle stood in some sense in place of Fwendi's dead mother.

He had not known there was really a chance of the herbs doing any harm. Fwendi had insisted on them, had claimed Great-Uncle Mkoi had told her riding often became more difficult for women bearing young.

"In Manono, she learned from Nenzima how this Thornhill attempted to kill General Wilson."

"*What?*"

"He is an assassin. Or at any rate, an attempted one."

Matty reminded himself that Mademoiselle had already read the letter and assimilated its contents. Still, he found her unruffled calm vaguely insulting.

"I should not imagine you were in the least danger. He appears to have other plans for you." She turned back to the letter. "There's nothing more here about him. Supplies for the new school, logistical details of its preparation—"

"No particular messages for me?" he asked, as casually as he could manage.

"None—save her love, of course, at the end." A pitying look. "Perhaps she'll write more later.

"Now as to this Thornhill . . ." She refolded Fwendi's letter and waved it in front of her face like a fan. "If you'll take my advice, you'll change your mind. Do business with him. Excite no notion in him that you're aware of his ill intentions."

"But—with a murderer? He must be a—a complete swine!"

"Yes." Mademoiselle Toutournier stood, and so must he. Her manner became brisk. She walked to the cottage's double door. "I believe him to be both a murderer *and* a pig . . . but better you should turn in this matter to someone else, someone you trust. Why did you come to me? We're no longer close, since Fwendi's recovery, and I opposed you on the question of the war."

"Everyone did. Everyone on the Mote. You were honest about it."

"Is that why you're here now? If only Jackie were yet alive . . . You are amazed? Yes, we hated one another—but we both loved Everfair. And you, you love our country also? Then keep this man Thornhill close, for he means us no good!"

Kisangani to Kalemie, Everfair, February 1918

◤Lisette held her fingers high over the machine's circular white keys. Another paragraph and she would be finished. Was there enough humor in the article? Yes. Enough of the sensual? The playful? More would not be amiss. But what was most obviously lacking was impudence.

The missing elements could be combined, so:

When will you, my faithful ones, hear from me again? To be sure, when those in power least expect it. For just as soon as those dull minds lull themselves to sleep between the silken sheets of their arrogance, the sharp claws of our wit shall prick them! Shall swat aside the dreams clouding their sad and drooping eyes! Shall wake them to our furry, purring sleekness! Our rough-tongued beauty! Our pouncing doom! Our destiny! Till then, I remain, in hidden seclusion,

La Chatte Grise

A knock sounded on the door. No doubt this would be Daisy. Easing up on the pressure she was applying to the machine's foot pedal, Lisette shut off its switch and listened regretfully as the hum of its engine whined lower and lower, then stopped.

"I'm coming!" she shouted, tying the wrapper she wore over her pyjamas shut. She slipped the final page of her column below the other four. No time for proofreading—into the already-addressed envelope it went. She sealed it quickly, firmly. It and the story manuscripts written for profit must be sent with the morning's mail. *Amazing Grace* flew today to Angola, first leg on the shortest route to Rima and the paper, and Lisette's book publishers in New York.

Daisy stepped into the parlor. She would never look—or act—her age. Disdaining even the spartan comforts of Lisette's few furnishings, she sat down on the mat-covered floor with her legs curled to one side. She accepted the tea Lisette offered, sliding closer to the tray and reaching up for the ceramic cup.

"This is good." Daisy sipped appreciatively. "Better, I think, than we had in England. Fresher."

"Yes."

"Though I'm not positive I remember correctly." Another sip. "Do you think it's safe for me to go—to go back?"

Lisette knew Daisy had barely stopped herself from calling England home. Even after all these years. "You would probably not be one of this group's targets."

"It seems so . . . You're sure?"

Sure of what? The list of victims? Her omission from it? "Queen Josina is sure. Alonzo has just reported evidence of Thornhill's presence in Alexandria in the days before and after Jackie's shooting. The poison was weak, and took a long time to take effect, but though I did my best, it was the ultimate cause."

"You had your reasons for hating him."

So many reasons. "But that doesn't mean—"

"Of course not! No, I only . . ."

"I didn't kill him."

"Of course not!" Daisy repeated. "I merely wish, now and then, that you'd show yourself more supportive of my suggestion."

"The holiday? To honor our 'Founder'?"

"To *unify* us."

She shut her eyes and bit her lower lip. Mr. Owen had insulted Grand-père, Grand-mère—but he was dead. "I haven't opposed it."

"And yet—"

"Pay attention! I'm not the only person—not even the most important—whom you need to convince. The king, the queen, many members of the Grand Mote, have expressed their dislike for your idea."

"Yes, but they don't understand it! Their arguments make no sense to me!"

Lisette refrained from suggesting that it was Daisy who, evidently, didn't understand. Such astonishing naïveté! It was all of a piece, all calculated to make Lisette sob inwardly with the fear that there would never be anything more between them than these meetings fraught with the sight and scent of love but not its touch. Maintaining, as always, a calm visage, managing to keep their physical contact to a rational minimum, at last she was able to get her much-regretted darling to leave.

Her darling. Perhaps Rima was right, and Lisette should abandon Daisy and, with her, Everfair. Beliefs like the ones that had had hurt Lisette must be unpicked with utmost care from the weave of Daisy's mind to keep them from causing more harm. She didn't want to undertake such an onerous task of finding and pulling out the myriad noxious threads of assumed superiority that twisted through her love's disdain of the mixing of races. But who else could? Who else had a good grasp of the problem? And if no one took it on? Who else besides Daisy would want her, by now an old woman of forty-five?

Lisette wasn't stupid enough to believe that in a large, modern city such as New York Rima led the chaste life of a nun. Lisette had not asked for faithfulness. She had not, without asking, expected it. Nor would she travel to America again as Rima kept suggesting, and put their attachment to each other to the test.

However, to stay here constantly was unfeasible. Ever within sight of the one she loved. Ever outside her reach. She would make the occasional journey, a break in the pain.

She recalled the schedule as she packed. Two hours after *Grace* flew west to Angola, *aMileng* would halt on its way to Kalemie. There, Lisette would find the distraction of work.

And as for her little animal friends, her pets?

From her front steps, Lisette signaled the neighborhood's drummer to order two taxis. One she loaded with her manuscripts and luggage and sent off to the airfield. The other carried her to the palace, to her appointment with Queen Josina.

They sat in the courtyard's shady garden. Sifa squeezed juice for them from a bowl of mangosteens. After receiving Lisette's report, the queen pondered her imminent departure.

"Yes. Well enough. I see why you wish to go and come. I will grant your request. Only, in exchange for this, and the loan of Lembe to watch over your home and enterprises in your absences, you owe me a service, my sister. It begins now."

Lisette accepted. How could she not?

That was why she found herself escorting Mwadi, a royal princess, to the airfield, then aboard *aMileng*'s open gondola, and, the next evening, through the just-hung doors of Fwendi's fledgling school for spies.

Her mother's tutelage told. After only a month, the girl received her first field assignment.

Bookerville, Everfair, March 1918

The long misery of the rainy season must simply be endured. Martha fantasized sometimes of cropping off her hair. It would save so much effort, besides feeling so much cooler—but what would George say? And how odd she would look.

Heat and grease would have to suffice to keep her crowning glory in order. In so many ways it was a blessing that the war's torrent of wounded had run dry. Most trivially she could stay inside, out of the frizzing damp, and feed the fire. The brazier blazed beneath her ministrations. The iron comb balanced on its edge had now, she knew from past experience, reached the correct temperature. She picked it up by its ceramic handle.

Glancing down doubtfully at the royal head between her knees, Martha took a deep breath. She'd had nineteen years of practice. She was good enough at this to style her own hair. But what if she accidentally burned the princess? There would surely be some horrible punishment.

Mwadi twisted to look back and up. "Ready!"

Martha had divided the princess's hair into eight sections. Beginning with the easiest, the one on the forward right, she stroked the hot straightening comb out from Mwadi's thick roots, along the wooly shafts, to their kinking ends. The smell was nice, like pressed clothes. As soon as she'd finished with one parted-off area Martha braided it up.

While her hair gradually became glossy as satin, the princess talked nonstop. Did Martha know that Mwadi had her own shongun? And that she had already been given lessons in aiming and shooting it—though not as many lessons as her brother—but maybe that only meant that Ilunga was stupider? Even if he was four seasons older—but men often matured more slowly than women, did they not?

Reflecting on her husband's relative youth, Martha was glad the girl's onward rushing words allowed no opportunity for a response. She focused on folding aside the delicate ears, on reheating the comb exactly enough to continue the miraculous transformation. By the time she was finished with Mwadi's kitchen, the monologue had turned to analyzing the differences between her royal parents on one side, the white settlers on another, and the Negro settlers on yet a third. And so it continued as Martha pressed the rest of the princess's head.

"I want to change the world. But my father will never pick me as his heir over slow-as-mud Ilunga, so I've decided to seek other avenues. Maybe a career abroad like Mademoiselle Toutournier advocates—what do *you* think, Mrs. Albin?"

Choking down her antipathy, Martha turned the question. "I think your hair is long enough that I may fashion it into a very becoming coiffure. Hold still—"

But Mwadi must spin around and throw her arms about Martha's neck. "Oh! Oh! Would you? You would? I will love you always and forever!"

This seemed to be the case, for in the following days the princess spent nearly every waking hour in Martha's presence. Having put away that masculine throwing knife and adopted civilized dress on her arrival, she'd become nearly indistinguishable from Bookerville's most proper young ladies. Martha herself saw to her hair, and Mwadi's manner of speaking had already shown the benefits of her education abroad.

Unfortunately, the princess was not a Christian. Assuming it as her personal responsibility to remedy this sad state of affairs, Martha devoted several rain-clouded afternoons to witnessing, praying, and reading aloud from the Bible.

She had never had a daughter of her own. The work was a labor of love.

At last the rains lessened somewhat, and George set forth on a much-delayed expedition. Though Martha still didn't feel safe putting the hot comb in Mwadi's hands, she found it soothing to let the girl oil her scalp and brush her hair. They sat on stools on the far side of the ditch surrounding the house. The sun, weak and watery, felt wonderful on the skin of Martha's throat as she laid her head back on the princess's lap. Relaxing under its spell, she neglected to lead the conversation as she should have. The princess filled the silence inappropriately:

"So tell me how it is to be married to a white man."

The heat of Martha's shame was warmer the sun. It burned her face from the inside and drew the spit from her mouth like a sponge. "I—we—we are all God's children," she stammered.

"Yes, but can he . . . you know . . . does he have a good—"

"I'm not going to tell you anything an unmarried girl shouldn't hear!" Though of course poor Mwadi's upbringing had been much different than most Christians' . . . She relented somewhat. "We have normal marital relations."

"Then you wouldn't welcome a change?"

"A change? What sort of a—" Martha's voice cracked. It was too loud. "What sort of change?" The words came out in a whisper that was equally wrong.

Mwadi leaned forward. "My mother and my father, they grow tired of being told how to rule their own country. The government is going to have to take on a new form. The whites could be sent home to Europe. Perhaps there may be fighting? Unless the Mote retires itself."

"But—but the king and queen are themselves on the Mote!"

"Each with only one vote."

Martha's earlier warmth deserted her and she sat erect. What time was it? The bright but sunless sky above kept the day's passage a secret from her. It wasn't only darkness that hid things.

She checked the pocket watch Chester had given her for her last birthday. Six-thirty. According to the drummers, George would return from his journey to close the last field clinic in Lusambo before eight. River travel was fast, but he would be tired, wanting to eat and rest. Rocking twice on her stool for momentum, she rose to go inside and prepare her husband's supper. Mwadi protested that she hadn't finished with Mrs. Albin's hair; Martha assured the girl she had, and efficiently wound her loose locks into a homely bun. She didn't want to have to listen to any further insinuations as to the nature of her marriage.

George had promised to love her eternally, and he had been absent for just three nights; even so, she'd missed him terribly. For his part, he'd probably had his fill of smoked fish and grilled breadfruit by now.

She and the princess cut apart the pair of chickens she had scalded and plucked that morning, rubbed them in precious spices and a few local herbs, and set them in a clay dish in the house engine's steam chamber to cook.

It was just as well she had help making the cornmeal porridge, what the Bah-Looba hereabouts called ugali—it took both hands to stir as it thickened. Mwadi held the pot firmly in place over the engine's geyser. Then that was transferred into its serving dish, which went into the lower, larger steam chamber as they cleaned the greens, which it was now time to add to the chicken.

To bleed off the steam filling the chamber holding the chicken stew, Martha blew the engine's whistle. Over its dying note she heard a welcome shout: "All right! All right! I've come fast as I could."

"George!" Dropping the whistle's string, she plunged out of the steam shed and directly into her laughing husband's arms. "George! Supper's almost ready—"

"Supper! Is that all you can think about?" He kissed her heartily. "And here I believed it was always me on your mind." He escorted her inside. Princess Mwadi had set up the small collapsible table by herself and was busy sorting out napkins, spoons, and individual shallow bowls. George liked native foods, but he preferred not to eat with his hands, and Martha thought it best to avoid spreading contagion by sharing a common plate.

Of course her husband did the supper justice. During second helpings he asked after news of the Mote, which had met without him while he was in Lusambo. Martha didn't know quite what to say, though she could see her silence puzzled him.

"The drumming was a bit vague," she said as an excuse. "But surely if you were to write to Albert or your mother, they'd give you news of what passed."

"Or you could ask Nenzima or Old Kanna for the real story," said Mwadi.

"The real story? As opposed to the false account my mother would provide? A notorious liar . . ."

"Princess!" Martha reprimanded her charge. To the girl's credit, she looked uneasy at having spoken so.

Still, she defended herself. "The Poet may not know the truth. If she doesn't know it, she can't tell it."

George's face became grave. He set down his spoon and pushed aside his cup. "What is the truth our nation's Poet doesn't know?"

Martha stood and began gathering up the dirty dishes.

"No, no, sit again, my dear. Our guest has something important to relate." He put his hand on her arm to restrain her and she sat back down.

"Well, *my* mother—" Mwadi paused, then continued. "*My* mother, our *queen,* says that there is discontent. With the whites. And perhaps with all the colonists," she added, with a sideways look at Martha.

"What sort of discontent? What is the trouble?"

Then it came out. Everfair's constitution had been imposed on the country. As had its Mote. Even the name had been given to the country by foreigners, taken from a foreign tongue.

"But English is our official language!" George protested.

That was another of the royal grievances.

"But what should it be—French? No, I suppose an African language—which one? Kee-Swa-Hee-Lee? Lin-Gah-Lah? And which dialect? English unites rather than divides us, does it not?"

The girl avoided answering that, and finished her litany of repeated complaints with what she said was called the most recent insult: the Poet's drive to have the date of Mr. Owen's death declared a holiday.

To Martha's surprise, her husband listened wordlessly for the most part—except for his short outburst about English. Judging from his remarks, he finally seemed inclined to take the princess's report seriously. Eyeing her protégée's rolling hips as she helped clear the table, her smooth brow and velvety smile, her sprightly step as she set off to take their food scraps to the village goats, Martha couldn't help but wonder: Was the virtue of Mwadi's arguments simply her youth? Had George tired of his wife's embrace—the embrace of, to put it plainly, an old woman?

She sat alone in the room they'd decided would be hers, staring at her reflection in her seldom-used hand mirror. Its surface was spotted, marred with age. Her face, also.

Vanity. She scraped her hair tight into two unbecoming braids.

But when she had lain in bed for only a few moments, her husband entered and lay with her, eager as on the night of his return from England, the night he'd shown how sincerely he'd pledged to her his heart. As always, he made her laugh and cry. In the calm afterward, Martha told him of her fears and jealousies. And then he made her laugh again.

Mogadishu, Somalia, to Mombasa, Kenya, May 1918

Tink had missed four Grand Motes. That was as many as during his last visit to Macao, two years ago, and this time he'd been unable to deputize one of the Tams to take his place. But he could not have missed his little brother's marriage; the journey had had to be made. At least with the world at peace, it had gone a little more quickly. But only a little. Long stops in Bangkok and Kolkata, in Mumbai—most trying to his patience—and just now in Mogadishu, had made manifest to him the small differences between delays caused by war and by trade.

Mombasa and Dar-es-Salaam were the last remaining cities before they crossed into Everfair. *Okondo* made excellent time. Soon he would be home. A matter of days; not much longer than a market, if he was lucky.

The last visible spires of the centuries-old port sank below the Earth's curve. Ancient Mogadishu was newly free in the wake of a postwar rebellion against Italy; Everfair had supported its liberation, and Tink had happily left the aircanoe for a few hours to verify the rebels' continued success. But he was even happier to see the city fall behind them. The curve of the coast filled the rearward vista.

He shut the wooden blinds on the stern-facing window of his enclosed cabin and felt suddenly cramped for space. The new gondolas allowed faster speeds, and thus longer voyages. Also, higher altitudes. And yet he missed the old ways, the cold winds blowing on him as he flew the open vessels—though on such a one had his Lily died.

Perhaps now he would never be married. Little Min-Cheng could be responsible for the family's line of descent. Rosalie had turned Tink down when he proposed on what he thought would be an auspicious day. The Tam brothers' half-joking attempts to make a match between him and either—or both—of their sisters had been likewise ill-fated. The awkwardness of that situation had made it necessary first for him to find other lodgings and then, he sighed to think, for the Tams to return to China. Of course, the downturn in arms orders had provided a convenient excuse, but they had ignored other opportunities.

Opportunities like the one that had led to his sister Bee-Lung sharing this dark, crowded cabin with him.

Carefully edging around the hammock in which they took turns sleeping, Tink got nearly to the door before kicking over a basket of glass jars. They rolled back and forth on the floor, clashing noisily against one another at *Okondo*'s least tip and sway, evading his searching hands as if intelligently guided. By the minimal light the blinds let in, he could see his sister sitting upright.

"Apologies," said Tink. "I didn't mean to wake you."

"No, it was time to get up," Bee-Lung said. That was a lie. They'd left Wadajir airfield not much more than one and a half hours ago. His sister would have just had time for a nap.

"Is anything damaged?"

Tink knew that these jars were being kept in their tiny room because they contained healing compounds more precious than the supplies his sister allowed the crew to stow with *Okondo*'s freight. "As far as I can tell, everything is intact. You may wish to inspect things yourself," he said, catching hold of the last fugitive container. "Here." He presented Bee-Lung with the refilled basket and slipped back to open the blinds again.

"Thank you." The jars glittered in the late morning sun. All were unbroken. Seeing his sister's shoulders lower and relax, Tink turned with relief to gaze out once more at the blue and white sky.

They had risen significantly in only the last few minutes, though he could still distinguish the crests of the ocean's waves below.

Bee-Lung came to stand beside him. "How beautiful!"

"Wait until you see the Lakes! There is nothing like them in the whole world!"

But before he could show her Everfair, they must go into and out of Mombasa. As the British still in power there had been enemies till very recently, *Okondo*'s stay was short. Bee-Lung remained on board, poring over her inventory.

Tink returned from his brief visit to the town both worried and gladdened. Glad because, here as in Mumbai, the Bharati-born soldiers who'd found ways not to fight Everfair during the war continued to rebel against their European rulers. It became less and less likely the whites would hold their empires together, and they'd certainly be unable to expand them.

Everfair was safe.

Also, though . . . those with whom he and other Everfairers came in contact here in 1916 had suffered something very like the illness with which he'd been afflicted soon after setting out: a fever marked by heavy sweating, coughing, nausea, and loosened bowels. An illness from which he'd finally recovered in Macao, under the care of his other sister's husband.

Tink had not died. Nor had any of those who contracted that first fever, which had apparently affected every town on the aircanoes' routes to Macao as much as a month after each went through. But as he'd been learning, a second, more lethal version of the disease had appeared last year. It killed those the first one hadn't touched. It killed the young, the fit, those in the prime of their life. It killed Bee-Lung's husband.

Bee-Lung's husband had been away in the country for most of Tink's previous visit. He had not sickened then—not even slightly. Next year he was dead.

Bee-Lung looked up as Tink opened their cabin's door. "Ah! You're back. I suppose I had better pack these up, then?"

"Yes, Captain Ekibondo will be giving the order to cast off any moment." He stooped to retrieve a circular plug of spongy wood, its sides grooved with threads like a screw. His sister smiled gratefully as he handed it to her, then fitted it into the narrow mouth of a grey stone bottle. A smell like fragrant plums mixed with cave chalk and salts from an ancient sea filled the close air. Mustiness, too, rising from cured skins pinned to the cabin walls, and the bitter perfume of evaporated venoms.

Tink and Bee-Lung had discussed several locations where she might establish her business. He'd diplomatically brought up the hospital at Bookerville, and tried to be as positive in his description of the Albins' headquarters as he was when it came to Manono, which he thought of as his own home. Both sites were shrinking in size, though, and he didn't hide that. Nor did he disguise from his sister what he'd heard about Kamina's growth, though he hadn't gone there since Lily.

Their first stop inside Everfair was Kalemie. Shrill, long-winged birds soared in circles between the aircanoe mast and the scows tied to the wharf on Lake Tanganyika. Because of loads to be picked up and dropped off at the railway head, they'd be here several hours. Though dubious, Bee-Lung consented to descend to the ground with Tink in the loading crane's sling.

Fwendi met them on the field as arranged, four students in tow. Tink knew none of them. The white girl reminded him of his lost love, as white girls usually did. A tour of the new school and potential sites made no noticeable impression on Bee-Lung. Over hurried bowls of chocolate, Fwendi gave Tink disturbing news gathered by her pupils: a third war was brewing.

Politely declining to state a decision about coming back, Bee-Lung continued on with Tink to the capital. He fretted all the rest of the day. He stared unseeing at the blackness of the cabin's ceiling when it was his turn for the hammock. After midnight he gave up and called Bee-Lung in from the common room early. This didn't make *Okondo* travel any faster. Nor did pacing the gondola's guard-railed roof under the freezing stars.

Another seemingly interminable day passed. At last, at last, he heard the drummer signal their arrival at Kisangani's airfield. He opened the blinds. A sunless purple dusk set off the lights of fishers coming home along the river. And more lights, the distinctive lamps of his home, outlined the city's streets. Fewer and fewer the lower they flew, the closer they came to the field.

A taxi took them into town. At first all looked normal. Then Tink saw that more fighters had been stationed outside the palace—perhaps many more? Perhaps double their usual number? As they passed the homes of Sir Jamison and the Poet, he noticed fighters there, too. And others elsewhere, possibly guarding the homes of more whites. Protecting them? Imprisoning them? Impossible to tell. Without Fwendi's warning, he might not have spotted anything amiss.

After all, he and Bee-Lung hadn't been escorted from the airfield. Nor, when they arrived at the flat where he always stayed, were there any fighters waiting for them.

But then, according to Fwendi, Everfair's latest troubles were only just getting under way.

Kisangani, Everfair, June 1918

Daisy did her best to convince herself she felt the difference in temperature. Traditionally this month was held to be very slightly cooler than May, and quite a bit less rainy than July or August. Nonetheless, she continued to take her walks early in the morning or long after dark. And she always carried an umbrella.

She wished she could persuade her guards to do the same. But as they stepped out of the shelter of her building's eaves to join her, they held only their shonguns. And though the clouds overhead glowered down threateningly, for the moment, at least, the air was clear.

Bafwaboli was to her left.

Loyiki had explained to Daisy that her "escorts," as he called them, were meant to keep her out of gaol. They stopped her from doing risky things such as talking to other whites and members of the Mote. Though some would argue against counting Lisette in the first category, she belonged indisputably to the second. Further, rumour claimed Lisette was capable of travel within Everfair, performing in a special capacity for Josina. As a spy, probably. Better for Lisette not to have her standing compromised by a call from Daisy.

Going in the opposite direction would take her to the airfield. But Daisy was prevented by her guards from working there. For the first time in her adult life, circumstances forced idleness upon her.

She turned neither way.

At the intersection with Source Boulevard she hesitated again. The floods that filled the roads during the rains had receded, but they'd left in their wake a soft, ill-smelling mud. Many swings had been set up on this corner, though none bigger than a double; she shared the crossing with a tall woman fighter named Nadi.

They followed the boulevard down to its end: a pier extending a few dozen feet into the Lualaba River. As the heavy overcast lightened and the heat climbed, she watched the day's sailors come and go.

Her arrest—for so she thought of it—had started almost eleven markets ago, in late April. Surprisingly, it was apolitical Rosalie who'd told Daisy what was coming. Rosalie, who'd steadfastly refused to stand for the Mote, had known what she, Daisy, had not: that non-natives were on the verge of being declared personae non gratae in the nation they'd helped to create.

During the course of the girl's preparations for her long-postponed journey to England, some unspecified occurrence had enlightened her as to the prevailing mood among Everfair's black majority. As they sat in the mooring tower waiting for *Boadicea* to arrive, she urged her mother to leave with her.

"What, with no luggage? Why didn't you mention you wanted me to come earlier?" The lack of luggage, it seemed, was an important element of what Rosalie dubbed her mother's "escape." Daisy hadn't taken the idea seriously, even when Rosalie showed her where she'd secreted both their passports. Naturally enough, she wished now she'd given her more credence.

Well, at least one of them had gotten away to England safely. Rosalie would rendezvous with Laurie Junior in London, and perhaps meet someone nice to marry there.

Daisy's repeater began chiming and she pulled it out to silence it. Only 8:30, and already the sweat gathered on her back and arms and neck. She led her entourage back to her flat and took a cool shower.

There was nothing to do. Nothing to write. Passion fueled poetry, and what she cared about was quite indifferent to the king and queen. By what they claimed, the same indifference applied to most of Everfair. Daisy wanted not to believe that.

Not long after she'd emerged from the bathroom she heard someone scratching at the door. She opened it, expecting a guard with questions about what further expeditions she might go on that day. Instead it was little Za, who, after a short, civil preamble, declared she'd been sent on business by the block's drummer. With full consciousness of her importance, the child recited a memorized message:

"King Mwenda commands the Poet's attendance upon him at midday."

Daisy shivered. Not from the coldness of the room, which was more than warm enough, but from the summons's chilly tone. No embellishments or inquiries as to her health. Nothing but a bare order.

She offered Za a boiled sweet in thanks for her services, one of a treasured hoard sent by Matty many long years ago. Za accepted her reward with a pretty bow, unwrapping it before she was outside. Gesturing through the still-gaping door, Daisy invited Nadi and her two fellows inside. So far, no one had entered without her express permission.

The fighters had their own system of communication. Doubtless they'd known since dawn that she'd be sent for. "Will you drink tea with me before we leave?" Daisy asked.

Nadi's acceptance comforted her as much as the ritual of brewing, as much as the faintly bitter taste of the familiar beverage. She gathered her three guests around the tray like a screen against fear. You couldn't kill anyone you'd shared a meal with, could you?

Not that death was the real threat. She'd never truly thought so, and King Mwenda made his actual aims abundantly clear when at last he saw her, which was after making her wait in a passageway for over an hour. At least she'd been given a chair.

The audience chamber, on another floor entirely than the passageway, was the former hotel's old dining room. Its tables had been removed, and a long carpet stretched from the entrance to the throne. Over Daisy's head hung unused crystal chandeliers. French windows along one wall provided most of the light—and, her heart leapt to see, a lamp shaded by the pierced globe she had popularized.

The king sat on his throne. The stool next to it was empty—no Queen Josina. Old Kanna stood beside Mwenda, and against the pale pink wall ranged well over a dozen armed fighters. *They must be for show,* Daisy assured herself. Who expected her to attack the king?

"You should prostrate yourself before me," said Mwenda, indicating the carpet.

"I beg to be excused."

"Because of your age? Old Kanna has no difficulties."

She merely nodded.

The king decided, evidently, against pressing the issue. "The Mote has been dissolved. You and all the other foreigners will return to your homes before the next dry season."

Daisy's mouth opened, but for a moment no words came out. She tried harder. "Our—our homes?"

"Where you came from. England, America, and so on."

"Our homes are here!"

"I say they are not."

She took another tack. "Besides that, you can't dissolve the Mote. Only a vote of the Mote itself—"

"I say I can." He glanced significantly at the fighters surrounding him. "My people say so, too."

"We are *all* your people—all of us, all colours, all—"

"Then you will not argue with me!" Mwenda's voice crashed over Daisy like a loud wave, drowning her quite reasonable protestations. "No! Do what I tell you to! Obey your king!"

Trembling with anger, she refused to give an inch. "And what is to happen to General Wilson? And your builders, inventors, engineers? What of—"

The king slashed the air with his metal hand, cutting her off. He spoke more quietly now. "I see no need to explain any of this. My wishes are known to you. You may leave as you came."

Which should have been enough, more than enough, to satisfy her. Daisy would not die, only be exiled. Yet her mind whirled with questions, doubts, worries, as she followed her escort along the hotel's damp-walled passages. What of her son, George, whose marriage no other country would recognize . . . but perhaps that was for the best. But what of poor dead Lily? How dare the king exile his rescuer's mother? How could she ever bear to leave her Lily's grave behind?

And where would Lisette go? Somewhere Daisy could go too?

Light flared in a doorway: An unshielded lamp suddenly brightened steps ascending behind the beckoning figures of Josina's favorite attendants. Daisy's escort halted with her at the sight.

"Come," the farther off of the two women said in English. "The queen also wishes to speak with you."

Daisy climbed the stone staircase, the repeating grit and thud of her boots echoing loudly in the silence of the others' naked footsteps. Passing the first-story landing without stopping, they came to a second landing with an open doorway in its far side. Warmth and silvery cloudlight spilled through. And a smell, somehow familiar . . . questioning her memory about it brought no answers, so she followed it forward.

Outside, on the palace's roof, a brazier smoked. Tobacco! She placed the scent now: a European gentleman's vice, totally unexpected here. Other herbs appeared in the mix to lesser extent—she identified basil, lemon verbena, and what the Bah-Loobah called dagga.

Gathered in a rough semicircle around the bowl of burning plants, six hollow logs stood on legs like sawhorses, draped in veils of soft-humming bees. Josina glided toward her around their backs, her dreaming smile gradually melting from her face as she met Daisy's eyes.

"Yes," said the queen. "You are the problem."

"I?" Daisy looked around. Her guards had retreated to the door to the steps. Several bees detached themselves from their clumps and flew lazily toward her.

"You. Sit with me and we'll figure out how to solve you."

A small, round, thatched pavilion rose at the roof's other end. Its wooden floor came to Daisy's knees. Sifa jumped up there, passing pillows to Lembe, who tucked them around the queen as she perched on the platform's edge, well under the thatch's over-hang.

The queen patted the spot beside her. "Poet, I invite you twice." Daisy joined her and let herself be similarly becushioned. The bees accompanying her settled nearby.

"They won't sting you," Josina assured her. "Unless I command it. Which I will not."

"Thank you."

The queen bade her attendants withdraw to the roof's parapet. "You are my sister's lover."

Daisy didn't know quite how to respond to that statement. Most of Everfair's African peoples were as accepting of sexual inversion as the Fabians tried to be. She ought not to feel shame or worry. Assuming by "sister," Josina meant Lisette, she ventured to say, "We—we love each other, it's true, yes. But—"

The queen interrupted. "But you are estranged. Living apart." She shook her head. "This won't do. My sister suffers. Importantly, so does the work she performs for me."

Something—probably the brazier's trailing smoke—had got caught in Daisy's throat. She cleared it. "I want to be with her. In some mysterious way, though, I've failed her expectations. I've asked her what I did. She won't tell me."

"Then you must tell yourself."

Daisy opened her mouth to object that this was impossible, but no words emerged. A bee flew in between her lips and flew out again before she shut them.

In an odd way, what the queen said made sense. If love lived in Daisy's heart, she could let its sense rise to her brain and perme-ate it like heavily scented smoke. She need only open her nose and inhale. She need only suppress her fear of choking on hard-to-swallow knowledge.

Bees swooped over and around Daisy's head. Her hair stirred gently. So gently. As if touched by Lisette's long-fingered hand.

The insects landed on her cropped curls, forming a crown of wings. Their buzzing shimmered in her bones.

Josina nodded. "The bees accept you. They'll help. Retire with them to reflect, and you'll reach an understanding of the imbalance you've caused in my sister Lisette's life. Then do what must be done to right it."

The city's walkways carried Daisy home—or so she believed. She never saw them. Before her was the past: what she'd thought. What she'd said. How very stupidly she had behaved.

How she had insulted Lisette—her love!—with careless and ignorant remarks on the ostensible crime of miscegenation. No crime, but the sweetest of gifts, the blending of life's songs.

Within her apartment she found paper and pen, but all her ink had run dry. So long since she'd composed even a single verse . . .

As bees crawled questingly along her shoulders, she took a horn of crimson dye from Rosalie's stored supplies and thinned it to suitable viscosity, making it look all the more like blood. Well, she would be drawing the words of her apology directly from her veins.

Kisangani, Everfair, July 1918

Queen Josina trusted her sister Lisette almost completely. She had not just accepted her invitation, she had dismissed Lisette's guards once they arrived at the river's wharf. As additional proof of her trust, she had left Sifa and Lembe behind there, along with her own group of well-trained, well-armed fighters.

Josina had also entrusted her daughter, Princess Mwadi, to her sister's care over a year ago, with no serious ill consequences. Perhaps a slight loosening of the girl's allegiances, but that was to be expected of someone so headstrong and inexperienced. Time would provide the remedy.

But time now conspired to discomfit the queen. It took her further and further from those she'd left behind. The buildings on the Lualaba's banks had become blurred by distance. "Where are you bringing me?"

"To Kamina." This was obviously a joke. Lisette wore only a light smock and trousers, unsuitable for the mountains. She'd brought no luggage.

Josina pretended for a moment it was the truth. Oxun loved laughter. "But that's far! What of my duties?" She paused as if picturing the route in her head. "Do you have your own aircanoe? How do I not know about it?"

"My own watercanoe."

"*This?*" Josina looked in real disbelief at the small dugout in which they sat. "But there are waterfalls—will it swim up those? Or climb them?"

Lisette patted the tiller she held in her left hand with her right.

"No, not this one. Though its engine is a smaller version of the one powering *Sidonie*."

The queen had long known her sister cared unusually deeply for mechanical devices. Some reports that Josina had skimmed had speculated this machine might prove stronger than it appeared. And indeed they went smoothly and swiftly up the rapids, passing all other vessels, even those without rowers, which were probably powered by waterfire batteries.

They rounded the point and came up alongside a larger boat. In addition to the normal canopy, it had a curious little structure like a spirit house filling its stern. Lisette attached ropes to the dugout's ends and started the crank that lifted it out of the water, then ducked into the house's low entrance for a moment. The heavy growl of a big engine struck the air. She ducked back out of the spirit house, climbed to sit on top of it, and pulled the long lever protruding from the roof from left to right.

Slowly they sailed forward. Still Josina was sure she wasn't being carried away to Kamina, as Lisette had joked. Her sister's confidential air suggested the two of them shared a secret. But what that secret was, she could only guess. Was it connected with *Sidonie*'s engine? In the quickening of the conflict between the king and Everfair's whites, Josina had neglected reports not immediately focused on these troubles. Now she saw with her own eyes that though the boat's length was the usual, that of seven tall men, and its widest width that of two men with their arms stretched to touch fingertips, *Sidonie* was something special.

Where, for example, was the paddlewheel? Standing carefully, Josina walked to where she should have been able to see it. Of course it wasn't there, any more than it had been when she boarded. But something—something loud and issuing a trailing plume of sweetish smoke grey as dagga's—something moved them. Something new and strange. Something with which she should be more familiar. Something which she had no cause to fear: she knew from carefully analyzed auguries that her final hour would remain distant for some years.

The queen could have her sister return them immediately to

Kisangani. Then, however, she would learn nothing. Such as why the invitation had been given.

With a caress, Lisette's fingers released the big lever and clasped what must be the boat's tiller. "Are you going to come up here? Do it now, please—I will need to demonstrate *Sidonie*'s best feature to you soon." Her sister held out a hand to assist Josina onto the little house's wooden roof.

Kneeling as Lisette did, but facing in the opposite direction, Josina leaned over the roof's far side. The water behind them churned around a spinning, many-bladed knife. Only glimpses showed, but Josina knew that gleam, those bright, sharp edges. Longer and thicker than those she'd seen on the engine of the dugout, yet basically much the same.

"She will run on the waterfire batteries or the Bah-Sangah earths. But Chester and I have devised a new system employing palm nut oil which—"

"Is it for this you've lured me away from court? To display your newest fascination?"

"Where else may I talk to you alone?"

The roar of the approaching cascade grew suddenly louder than *Sidonie*'s loud engine. Josina turned and saw that they were very, very close. The wind shifted and wetness wafted across her skin, a cool kiss.

Like a giant woman lying beneath a blanket of hissing lace, the Lualaba's lowest cataract stretched from bank to bank. Along her white curves the scaffolds of the fisher tribes staggered, skeletal lovers.

But—were those black and red poles made of metal? Yes. Part of a new style of fishing scaffold? A man's head appeared, then his chest and arms; he waved at them. Someone she knew? Before Josina could decide, *Sidonie* jerked beneath her and reversed. She fought to keep her balance. Then, with *Sidonie*'s stern pointing upriver, Lisette shouted at her over the rushing water to please take her seat again.

From a bench near the boat's prow, Josina watched her sister lean over the stern as she had done before. She seemed to be tugging at something. Presently, she lifted and set aside what must have been a section of the spirit house's wall. The man on the metal scaffold was Chester! He threw down a coil of rope. It landed where Josina had just been kneeling, a loose end running back up to Chester where he clung to the wet red poles. Lisette shouted once more. Josina couldn't understand what she was saying, but the tone was urgent. She deserted the bench and came nearer to hear better.

Her sister seized her by her arm. "I'm sorry, but I need your help to execute our upcoming manoeuver. Though I am devastated to inconvenience you"—she placed the queen's hand on the tiller—"it won't be for long. You must keep us steady as you can." Again she vanished inside the spirit house.

Josina simply couldn't hold *Sidonie* in one spot. She settled for keeping the boat in the same area—roughly twelve mats in size. Twelve mats of rock-filled foam.

She wasn't going to die. Not here.

In only a few moments Lisette emerged again. "My thanks!" She reclaimed the tiller. "You'd better go back—and hold on!" She seemed to be enjoying herself hugely, an unmistakable grin replacing her earlier hide-and-seek smile.

Another horrible jolt shook *Sidonie*. Josina gripped the bench on either side. She said nothing, yelled nothing. She was not going to die. Not on water. Her destiny had been divined. This wasn't it.

Slanting and lurching in the water like a drunken fish, *Sidonie* backed up the low cascade from the bottom to the top, to the red and black metal poles. There she halted. Twisting on the bench, Queen Josina looked back over the bow. The waterfall was short—only the height of a half-grown maiden—but it was a waterfall, nonetheless. This remarkable boat had climbed it.

The noise of the engine died. "Did you see? Did you *see*?" Lisette came out of the little house crowing with delight, arms spread wide to embrace her joy. "I wanted to show you, and I did! We *could* go to Kamina, all the way—Let me set the anchor, so we may talk."

It took both of them to heave the anchor, a heavy stone, over *Sidonie*'s side. Another breeze, less water-laden, sprang up.

"I have nothing to offer you to eat save this," Lisette said. From a pouch on her hips she produced a metal box. Josina opened it and the lovely aroma of chocolate, too deep to be merely sweet, spilled forth. Hundreds of pieces of roasted and cracked cacao beans were piled up in a tiny, potent mound. Josina would eat a little now, to show appreciation. A good gift.

Wading carefully toward Chester with the rope over her shoulder, Lisette returned shortly with a jug of tamarind and honey, cool from the river, and a precious bottle of *ovingundu,* the mead made by Josina's father's people.

They drank. As promised, they talked. As the queen had expected, their talk was of the conflict splitting the country. A third war loomed in their future.

The king hadn't anticipated that. Who was there to oppose him? The Europeans and Americans were distracted by their plague, the new illness to which many Africans, Chinese, and Bharati seemed immune. Elsewhere in the world, people died by the thousands. So Josina's spies said. Everfair's whites and Christians would have fought in protest of their exile, but lacking foreign support, they shouldn't have any choice in the matter—if General Wilson hadn't so surprisingly taken up the Christians' cause.

"You couldn't have predicted it."

"At any rate, I didn't." Josina knew she must take the blame. "His loyalty is of an excellent quality." As was the *ovingundu.*

"His loyalty! To whom? The other blacks?"

"To whom has he sworn it?"

"To Jesus, it appears."

"No, I think not." The queen was reliably informed that the general served Loango. "Or, if so, he has withdrawn his promise there." She shook her head. "What matters is that many of his fighters will follow him instead of the king. This is dangerous—for the general. He may die."

"It's dangerous for everyone. He won't be alone."

"No. But I will be." She hadn't meant to say that. "Not alone. There is the king. But without you. My sister. You will be gone."

"You can visit—"

"Of course." It wouldn't be the same.

"My queen—"

"Say 'sister.'"

"My sister, I have another present for you." But Lisette held nothing but a full gourd of tamarind. Josina gazed about for an appropriately wrapped parcel.

"I give you *Sidonie*."

"Oh!"

"I wouldn't be able to bring her to New York anyway."

The queen refused to cry. She must not make the land sad. "Thank you!" She took her sister's hand and held it to her heart. "You will leave? You won't stay and fight?"

"That's not what you want me to do, is it? No. As you say, it's dangerous. Too many shonguns. Too many more deaths."

"It's better you're not one of the fighters. Too many will die."

The mead was gone. Josina tipped the bottle upside down just to be sure. She sighed and poured herself a gourdful of tamarind instead. Through the afternoon's haze she noticed fishermen leaving, walking toward the shore. Afternoon? It was later than that; the sun hung low, and faintly over the rapids she heard the evening whistle.

Army against army. More sacrifice. More wounded. The land would suffer. And why? Her husband's spirit father had said there should be no more foreigners. Truly—but couldn't that mean more than one thing?

"We can't let this happen. We must play *sanza* with both men. With them, and all who obey their orders." That no longer included the queen herself. The land had a claim superior to her king's.

The tamarind, like the mead, was gone. That made her explanation of *sanza* on the way back to shore thirsty work.

Arriving once more on the wharf, Josina accepted the ministrations of her ladies and fighters: a seat in a carriage, the tucking of prettily painted cloth about her shoulders against the cool of evening. Her mead-sodden head was soft and rosy as the clouds behind which the sun had sunk—but not so soft she missed the white woman's approach. It was the Poet, Daisy, switching from one side of the vehicle to the other to follow Lisette's face.

The queen shook off the barkcloth and stepped back out onto the roadway, where she could hear the women's words plainly: "You mustn't let me hurt you again, chérie. Ever again! My last letter was meant to heal our rift completely. Let it! And if I write or say something regrettable ever again, let me know—I'm not too old to change!"

"Indeed?"

"Let me change! Let me! Let me not hurt you—"

"My very dear—" Her sister swayed suddenly—due to the *ovingundu,* no doubt—and put out a hand to brace herself. The Poet seized it.

"Say you forgive me! Say you love me still! Say it!"

"If I say so, it's not because you tell me to! And if I kiss you it's because that's what *I* want!" With no thought of their audience, Lisette showed Daisy she meant what she had said. Showed her well.

"Come; we will walk," the queen announced to her attendants. Her bees had returned to their hives on the palace rooftop but not, apparently, before accomplishing their mission. As she left, she heard to her satisfaction her sister's newly melodious voice become muffled, the door to the abandoned carriage shut. She prayed for yet more sweetness to greet its next opening.

Mbuji-Mayi, Everfair, to Mwango, Everfair, September 1918

Undoubtedly King Mwenda's decision to force all whites and foreign blacks to leave the country had been a mistake. Yet the king could not undo it now. He would have to kill any he found who had disobeyed his orders. The moment was as irreclaimable as when he'd unsheathed his original shongo long ago at court. The sixty seasons intervening had taught him wisdom, but not enough. If only he had understood his spirit father more clearly. More quickly. If only there were some way to retract his decree without damaging his authority.

If only he could give up the burdensome blessings of rule and return to his beloved bush.

Flying low on *Lukeni,* passing slowly over the empty town the settlers had called Bookerville, it at first seemed to Mwenda that most must have complied. Piles of unwanted belongings and abandoned supplies occupied the central plaza. Perhaps some people hid in the houses? He had his drummer signal *Brigid*—another name to be changed—to drop a landing party. The fighters swarmed down ropes lowered over the older aircanoe's open sides.

But while they investigated, finding nothing, a renegade aircanoe appeared out of the morning sun to swoop upon the king's command. That must be *Boadicea,* the aircanoe the ungrateful General Wilson had stolen shortly after it received its new closed gondola. Those aboard were armed: out of openings in its sides they shot shonguns, and threw gourds filled with broken palm oil set on fire. The flaming gourds missed *Lukeni*'s airbag, and for the second time the whites' settlement burned.

Well, if they wished to destroy their own constructions the king wouldn't try to stop them. *Brigid*'s landing party had scattered into the bush. They'd find their way back to Kisangani by themselves. The king gave orders to head out for Kamina, the second of this mission's three targets. The caves would be difficult, but using smoke—

A burst of noisy argument at the other end of the steering room roused him from his thoughts. "There's no guarantee we'll get more than a few miles before we crash!"

"What has happened?" he asked, moving toward the shouting men. Loyiki and Kajeje prostrated themselves and Captain Tombo bowed. From the decking, Loyiki explained that several of their airbag's cells seemed to have been "compromised"—cut open by shongun blades, in other words, and leaking. How fast? The men's answers sounded like guesses. He touched their shoulders and bade them stand.

"And *Brigid*? Is there damage there, too?" Captain Tombo asked the drummer to find out. While he waited for a response, Mwenda looked over the map cloths hung on the room's walls.

Loyiki, the spy, filled in missing information. "The terrain is rough between Mbuji-Mayi and Kamina: trees and rocky hills. Our best course is to follow the Lubishi River."

Brigid also reported having been hit. But not as badly, it seemed. The older aircanoe went ahead of *Lukeni,* and King Mwenda watched it appear to rise as the vessel carrying him slowly sank. At last *Lukeni*'s gondola fell so low the steering room's windows no longer showed their companion vessel; instead, green branches framed a smooth blue river.

"My king, we must land soon." Captain Tombo had flown only two other aircanoes. His voice sounded nervous, though his face betrayed nothing of his feelings.

"Yes. Where have you chosen?"

"We're near a hill; a village at its base may provide—"

"Good. Tell *Brigid* to go on to Kamina without us." Mwenda

turned away from the useless window. Taking his goat-hair cloak from a peg by the room's doorless entryway, he left and climbed to *Lukeni*'s forward hatch. He wore his best-designed hand, so he was easily able to undo the fastenings and push up the heavy wooden panel: control *and* strength.

Already they were down far enough he didn't really need the cloak's extra warmth. In front and to the left—the east—he saw a hill's crest. It and the gondola were at about the same height. No doubt this was the spot Captain Tombo had picked.

Mwenda hoisted himself free of the gondola's ceiling. The airbag continued to obstruct his view to the rear. A guide rope threaded its way back along the thickly woven roof. He held onto it and followed it to the engine compartment. Bah-Sangah priests insisted anyone visiting such locations should wear the heavy, clumsy ritual garments, but he would be *on top of,* not *inside,* the little enclosure where the sacred earths exerted their forbidden influence. And for only a moment, he told himself.

But it took Mwenda several moments of straining to catch sight of the aircanoe following them. Washed out by the noontime sun, *Boadicea*'s purple airbag at first blended far too well into the sky's pale blue. Only a glinting window in the gondola gave its position away.

Would it continue following *Brigid* to Kamina?

The hill's grassy slope looked closer and closer as it streamed beneath *Lukeni*'s stern. Mwenda went back inside to brace himself against the gondola's walls.

Thud! Thud-thud-thudduddudd—then there was relative stillness. *Lukeni* was on the ground. Cracking noises announced the settling of the gondola's full weight on joints and joists not meant to bear it. Twice they tilted sharply to port, then starboard, the wind-tugged airbag jerking them from side to side.

The window showed graze-shortened grasses nearby and a distant forest. Captain Tombo sent crew members to assess the "compromise." "What else shall we do?" he asked Mwenda.

"Find out whether *Boadicea* has gone on after *Brigid*." They were acting in the only sensible way, a way that would make it possible to calculate how much weight to dump so as to take off again. Unless—

Screams from above. A horrible light flickered in the window. Kajeje burst through the door. "Get out! They have set fire to us!" Mwenda lost no time leaving, though perhaps some dignity.

Safe on the hilltop, he looked back at the aircanoe's ruins. Fire had engulfed the engine compartment and raced up the lines securing it to the gasbag, which was already ablaze. Fighters scrambled free of the forward and mid-hatches, arms full of weapons and ammunition. Several crewwomen ran past him with sandbags and cloaks, headed for an isolated patch of flames.

Shielding his eyes against the sun, Mwenda saw *Boadicea* circling above, doubtless with more bombs ready to loose if necessary. But the enemy would be easy to evade; all they had to do was abandon the aircanoe and hide. The bush beckoned—but why was *Brigid*'s silhouette growing larger?

Because it was coming back. As *Lukeni*'s crew and passengers retreated into the shadows of the banana trees, the two aircanoes remaining aloft drew toward each other overhead.

"No!" shouted the king. Must so many more die? And at the hands of those who ought to be friends? Yet he had led them to battle—how could he expect them not to fight? "Drummer!" he called. But when the man came, he gave him no orders. *Brigid*'s engine must be running at its fastest and loudest; it would probably drown the drum out.

Quickly the blaze was reduced to charred wood and smoldering heaps of ash. Loyiki guided Mwenda to a spot where the hill fell away so steeply it was easy to see the river valley. Bananas reached up on either side to shelter him while offering an opening in the direction he wanted to look.

The two aircanoes approached one another. Neither tried to get away. They came within a man's length of one another. Closer. Mwenda imagined fighters climbing out of *Boadicea*'s hatches, both sides shooting shonguns, tossing ropes with hooks on their ends to capture the others' vessel. No more bombs? Evidently

Boadicea's commander desired *Brigid* intact. Evidently he was to get his wish.

King Mwenda watched helplessly as bodies fell to the earth. Some used jumpsheets. Some spun and tumbled to their death, arms flailing. Men and women the king had known. Over a hundred.

Eventually the two aircanoes disengaged. But then *Brigid* followed *Boadicea* meekly south.

Defeat was a bitter meal. It spoiled the savor of his voyage homeward through the bush. The women and men of Mwango, the small village at the foot of the hill upon which they'd landed, provided boats to take them back down the Lubishi River to its confluence with the Sankuru and the busier river's engine launches. But Mwenda traveled more slowly than that might have meant, since he insisted on sending out searchers for those who'd leapt or fallen or been tossed from *Brigid*.

At first they found quite a lot of bodies. Then fewer. Animals may have eaten them. Or the king had passed beyond the area of the fighting.

The survivors totaled four hands. Six of them were of the enemy. One of these he was very glad to see: George Albin.

Upon his makeshift throne—a hollow-topped river stone—the king sat in state. Loyiki forced the prisoner to his knees.

"Must he really be bound?" Mwenda asked. "George, will you promise not to escape if you are untied?"

"I give my word. As an Everfairer."

At the king's signal, Kajeje cut the vine tying the white man's wrists together. His arms hung ignored at his sides, though tears of pain welled in his odd blue eyes. "What would you do if I did run? Kill me?"

No. Mwenda would never forget Lily's death during his rescue. The rescue that had cost him his hand. But he sent the prisoner away without another word, and for the rest of the trip said nothing more. He was listening for the instructions of his spirit father. In no other way could he hope to hear how to avert more tragedy.

Kisangani, Everfair, October 1918

Aided by Matty's skills and insight, Fwendi found it easy to organize artistic and untraceable protests of this third and stupidest war. She accomplished much of her work while held within his arms.

At first she pretended reconciliation with him, an explanation for the time they spent together planning subversion. Soon their pretended reconciliation became real. Soon her heart followed its old habits, resuming the soft, swift pulse of love as readily as her flesh and metal resumed their place in Matty's house—and bed.

She accepted his apologies. "Who told you I *wanted* to be married? Great-Uncle Mkoi, when you asked permission?" She laughed and stretched, her brass hand, warm from his embrace, brushing his hair from his face, silver and gold.

"But I ought to have given you a choice, at least." His large eyes studied her worriedly in the dawning light.

"Do it now."

"My love. Will you marry me?"

"Yes! Yes!" She leapt from his bed onto the matting and whirled in circles for joy. "Yes! I will, I will, I will marry you, Matty! Yes!"

Why should she be this happy? Such a strange little man: so sad, so yearning. He must have been born old. Pale skin, flat hair—yet he was her friend, companion to her earliest voyages upon the winds of the world. And now! The adventures they could embark upon, the secrets she could tell him!

But first they must end this war. First there was work to do, such as freeing hostages. Fwendi's star pupil, Mwadi, had discovered at the beginning of the market that her father held George Albin aboard the watercanoe *Sidonie*. Formerly this craft had been owned by Mademoiselle Toutournier. Its plans were available. Mwadi, eager to prove herself capable of doing more than merely listening surreptitiously, of actually conducting an operation, devised a simple strategy. One that ought to work.

So the morning after Matty's proposal, Fwendi left his house bearing herself calmly. Sober clouds obscured the new risen sun; it was almost as dark as before dawn. But not so dark that she missed the shape of the man entering the courtyard as she exited it on her mission.

Had he been watching for her? In that case, Fwendi's departure would have been his cue to attempt access.

The six guards King Mwenda had assigned to Matty stood obliviously in front of the house. Half faced the street, half had their backs to it. On the corner she approached more reliable assistance: an out-of-place flower seller. Mwadi in disguise, as they'd arranged.

Feigning interest in the girl's fat nosegays, Fwendi maneuvered her into the newly installed swing. Somehow they lost their momentum mid-crossing and sat dangling in the intersection, apparently stranded.

At this hour, traffic was light. Fwendi took up the telescoping crook used to pull becalmed swings to the streets' farther sides. She held it ready in case of observers. "There's an intruder. We must change our course."

Mwadi frowned. "Not one of my father's fighters?"

"No. I'm sure. He—he *moved* like a European. Though I didn't get a good look."

Unreasoning fear assailed her. She should never have allowed herself to feel so happy. "I'm going back. Follow me—I may need help." Had she taken too long? Extending the crook, she caught the mooring post and returned their swing to Matty's side of Vuba.

The guards wondered why she'd come back so soon. "I forgot my lubricant!" She spread her metal fingers wide and wiggled them to show the necessity. Inside, she ran up the stairs. Mwadi could find her own way in; she was proficient—

Fwendi stopped. Running made too much noise. Stealthily, she continued down the passage to Matty's room. Ten steps and she heard a thump, a stifled cry. She ran again, faster, not caring who heard, flung the door aside to find poor Matty struggling with a man taller and stronger—

Like the lions who were her ancestors, Fwendi roared and sprang. Tearing with flesh and metal hands, she freed her lover from the other's choking grasp.

Now Mwadi appeared and joined the fight. She had a shongo like her brother's. Blood and shit poured out of the attacker's wounds as he died.

A groan came from the bed's vicinity. Her darling! Fwendi realized she knelt on the sticky red matting, flesh fingers pressed into the white man's throat—though the pulse she'd automatically felt for couldn't have been there. Not with his entrails spilling out on either side of his abdomen. Had she done—that? No: those big slices could only have been cut by Mwadi's knife. Shakily, she attempted to rise to her feet and fell.

But Matty! Crawling, she made it to the bed. He lay naked, as she'd left him, but gasping deeply. Darkening areas on his forehead and cheeks showed where bruises would form.

"Huh—hih—" He wheezed and coughed.

"Here." Mwadi gave her a cup of water from ancestors-knew-where. She held it to Matty's ridiculous moustache with her trembling left hand for a moment, then switched to her slightly steadier right. Neither was clean. He sipped the water down anyway.

A timid knock on the open door preceded Clapham's entrance. He sucked in a sharp breath at what he saw. "I heard—I thought . . . Is anything required?"

"A barrel or shipping crate," said Mwadi. "A sail or something similar to wrap up this fool who attacked your master."

At least one of them was thinking. "And don't let anyone else in here," Fwendi added. "Close and lock the door behind you. Here's the key." She held out the copy from her watch chain.

Fwendi wiped her hands so she could help Matty dress. The water came from the carafe always kept by his bed. Of course.

While she was thus occupied, Mwadi matter-of-factly turned out the attacker's pockets and examined the labels on his clothing, all of it black—even the shirt.

The results were both cryptic and enlightening: no official papers or other clues as to the culprit's identity, but a suicide note in what looked like Matty's hand.

Wheezing, her love denied having written it. The note seemed to puzzle him more than the phial of clear, bluish liquid Mwadi found on the bed beside him. She correctly pronounced it to be prussic acid. Matty agreed with her, and added without apparent rancor that he thought the intruder had meant to make him swallow it. "I knew he was a murderer, but how did he manage to create such a convincing forgery? If—"

"You knew he—you know who this is?" asked Mwadi.

"Of course! I met him several times, following the advice of Mademoiselle Toutournier. We engaged in business. That's—he was Major Thornhill, Christopher J. Thornhill. He must have copied the style of my writing from letters he stole. I don't believe I ever sent—"

"Thornhill! He's the assassin Nenzima warned us about." Fwendi stared down at the dead man. "Yes; the description fits." Though Nenzima hadn't mentioned the stench of perforated bowels.

Clapham returned. Fwendi helped him with Thornhill's remains, which they doubled up, rolled in a length of canvas, and stuffed unceremoniously into a tall basket. The matting they bundled up separately. They lashed the basket's lid in place with a muffler from Matty's luggage.

It was too late now to remain unseen while getting rid of the evidence, as Fwendi preferred. Or too early. After dusk had fallen, they'd be able to transfer it to a canoe unseen. And then, the river and *Sidonie*.

Clapham arranged for food to be brought up to them on trays. Fwendi let Mwadi get the drummers to send their report to Mademoiselle so she could stay with Matty and glare at the phial of poison. The princess returned with a reply from Kalemie: Mademoiselle saw no difficulty with the delay till tonight.

This would be only the second time Mwadi rode animals. She had not progressed far enough yet to process multiple viewpoints without effort. But there was no way to persuade the cats Fwendi used to cross the river's fast-foaming waters.

They dragged the corpse's basket to the kitchen entrance and heaved it into the cart used for market. Fwendi had the better excuse for using Matty's property, so she rode off on the bicycle, pulling the cart, then waited nervously for her student at the wharf.

Everything must go well. Matty had consented to advocate for the Conciliation with other whites; it was to be hoped that, despite his incarceration, George, once freed, would do the same with his wife. She was the chief power behind much of the colonists' opposition. Including General Wilson's.

At last the princess arrived. Together they shifted the basket to Mademoiselle's small, nameless canoe and paddled out a short ways from the shore. Fwendi need not have worried: Mwadi had memorized complete instructions on how to start the canoe's engine, and she shut it off in good time. They reached *Sidonie* without incident, having rid themselves of the basket and matting on their way.

Then they floated on the black water, stars and mist shining silver and grey above. The princess whispered a high, eerie tune, and soon the dim air filled with half-visible white wings. Gulls. Gulls flying in the night. The flock grew, became enormous. Seemingly of its own accord, it mobbed *Sidonie*.

Raucous cries bounced off the flat roof of the canoe's engine house. Was that where they'd hidden him? A tall woman and two men struggled through a door in its windowless side. Screams and shouted orders battled with the gulls' screeching. The birds' wings and beaks struck the wooden walls, the fighters' bleeding arms and heads.

Fwendi shouted above the noise. "George! George! Á moi! Je veut vous sauver!" She grasped her shongun in one hand, stood unsteadily, and hooked hold of *Sidonie*'s low gunwales with the other. She should shoot! But in all this confusion, how to be sure who or what she hit? The gulls were meant to lure the prisoner's guards to *Sidonie*'s bow so that Fwendi might board and untie George and get him safe away. Instead, they looped around nearby, sinking dangerously low or zooming crazily high to disappear from sight.

Fwendi transferred the shongun to her teeth and hoisted herself onto the gunwale with both arms. Not one bit distracted, the thinner of the two men rushed to shove her back off. She aimed and fired. The blade hit him, but he tore it out of his chest and threw it to graze an unlucky bird's belly. The man's wound looked shallow. The poison didn't seem to affect him—had he been previously dosed with an antidote?—but the bird flapped off drunkenly into the night.

The thin man came for her again. All the gulls had gone. Fwendi released her grip on *Sidonie,* dropped back into the canoe, and snatched the paddle from beneath her seat. The river's swirling currents seized the watercanoe and sent it, too, into the darkness. The woman had armed herself. Her shots missed them. Narrowly. Mwadi roused herself as Fwendi paddled furiously to escape *Sidonie*'s searching lights. They had failed. Failed.

The game of *sanza* would have to proceed, regardless.

Kisangani, Everfair, December 1918

Matty laid the Conciliation between them on the low table. "It's decently written," he admitted. "Which of you is responsible?"

Mademoiselle Toutournier slitted her eyes, lifting the corners of her mouth as if delighting in this faint praise. Daisy bristled. "Both of us! It's a collaborative effort."

"Naturally. But someone must have collaborated the most."

"It's of no use, chérie. He won't believe that you are so devious or I so talented as to have contributed equally to such a result." Mademoiselle shook her sleek head as if in sorrow.

"Besides, what does it matter?" She opened her grey eyes wider than it seemed they should go. "All that truly concerns us is your support. You won't withdraw that now you've seen the actual document?"

"Noooo." Matty drew the syllable out long enough to convey nearly its opposite. "This concedes many points." He tapped the Conciliation's three pages one after another. "Everfair's official language is no longer English, we cease to campaign for a national holiday in honor of Mr. Owen's death, and all future immigrants will need to publicly swear allegiance to the throne."

"Not just future immigrants." Mademoiselle sounded proud of that.

"The wording of that clause did impress me as . . . ambiguous."

"Deliberately vague," Daisy said. "We made it so." She lifted her chin.

"Queen Josina has told us she'll be unable to bring King

Mwenda to accept a compact that does not address the language and the holiday," Mademoiselle continued. "We believe we've made the obvious sense of all this acceptable to all sides."

"And what of the obscure sense?"

"No one could call *you* dull!" With a conspiratorial glance at La Toutournier, Daisy leaned forward. "The obscure sense is that once an immigrant has sworn allegiance, he's no longer a foreigner. And any of us may swear, at any time. You see?"

He did see. But the oath that was laid out specified renunciation of one's former citizenship. "Not all will want to do it."

"No," said Mademoiselle. "But the alternative is that none will be able to. It's our best effort."

"Say you'll argue in favor?"

He couldn't do anything else. But he stalled. "There's no mention of the Motes."

"We thought it best to set them aside for the moment." Daisy's expression was painstakingly neutral. "Not to decide about them one way or another."

"Best to set aside our participatory democracy? What would Jackie—"

"Mr. Owen would say we've done what must be done to survive."

"Jackie was a pragmatist," Daisy said. "We could give him a holiday or a statue, but more than anything else—more than the way I wanted to commemorate him—this is the monument he would have wanted us to raise to him. This country is the thing he built, and the Conciliation will save it."

He supposed the Poet was right. If anyone living knew what Owen had been like, it would be she. He shrugged and opened his mouth to make his acquiescence plain. The noon whistle blew. He waited for it to end so he'd be sure to be heard, but it went on and on. It changed notes—how? Impossible—a run of notes, low to high, reversing, repeating—leading up to the familiar melody of their nation's anthem. At last he understood.

He raised his voice. "It's begun. The demonstration—shall we go out? Perhaps we'll be able to see something."

They stood on the front steps. Distantly, from Fina and the neighborhood of the theater, came the sound of voices singing. The Poet frowned. "They've changed my words?"

"Translated them, chérie—and added but one or two more verses."

"What are they saying?" Outside the house one had to shout over the noise.

"That we have had enough. That we need not fight each other to get what we all want." Mademoiselle tucked the Poet's arm in her own. Yes, they had made their peace with one another, as rumor said.

"They sing too fast! It makes them sound—"

"Hopeful?"

"Frivolous!" The Poet descended several stairs, but stopped at the bottom. "Why are they becoming quieter?"

"They march to the palace, to serenade the king and queen. Let them, chérie—let them go."

"No!" Nothing would do but for them to walk up Vuba—the roadway clear of traffic and dry enough—to Fina, and from there to follow in the protestors' wake.

They caught up with the demonstrators at a shrine to the genius loci of the falls, a fish figure of some sort. There was a lull in the singing as the crowd, mostly women, refreshed themselves with coconut juice and pipes full of burning dagga. They wore only loincloths, not the tunics and skirts popular in recent years. Ashes smeared their faces. Leafy wreaths crowned their heads, and many held leafy staffs.

Matty looked for Fwendi and found her, despite the ashes. Atop her loincloth, she'd donned a traditional barkcloth shawl. Her brass hand flashed brightly, even in the shrine's shadow. Did she see him? She did! And once, when she turned his way, she nodded and smiled.

Why the pause here? What were they waiting for? Ah, this must be it, a shrill calliope rolling up Fina under its own power, louder and louder, drowning out their half-voiced singing. Beneath the plants circling the calliope driver's head, Matty recognized the face of Albert—so he, too, was a protestor?

A brief clasp of hands between Fwendi and Albert, and the demonstrators gathered together and continued on their way. Matty did his best to urge the Poet to return to his house—it wouldn't do the demonstrators any good for her to be closely associated with them. Either the music of the calliope made hearing him too difficult, or she was stubbornly pretending not to understand.

The avenue ended at the church. An impressive brick building with white stone columns, it was soon encircled by women and men shaking short leafy sticks at it, chanting what sounded very much like threats.

Fwendi met his eyes again, seeming this time to notice the Poet's presence. She frowned and made shooing gestures, shaking her head.

Suddenly the chants skirled high and the demonstrators moved in. Climbing one another's shoulders, they scaled the church walls. Tiles began to rain down from the roof, tossed to shatter on the surrounding plaza.

This would never do. Taking the Poet's shoulders firmly in his grasp, Matty turned her in the opposite direction and compelled her to leave. He didn't worry about Mademoiselle Toutournier, assuming she'd take care of herself. She always did.

And Fwendi had not yet agreed to let him take care of her. Still, he couldn't resist a last glimpse. His heart stilled, then beat again more strongly. She was walking away, too, in the midst of a small contingent of demonstrators. Walking away from the scene of that trouble.

Although she was walking toward the palace, where she would probably create another scene.

Mbuji-Mayi, Everfair, February 1919

Thomas tried, but without much hope for success. He had never truly known how to calm her down.

"They destroyed a consecrated church!" Vibrating like an angry wasp, Martha sat with both arms stretched out flat on her desk.

A "consecrated church"—was there any other kind? "That was over a month ago," he said.

She made to rise, seeming to find his words a provocation. "Just so!"

With a resigned sigh, Thomas rose also from his extremely comfortable seat. He had no desk on which to prop himself.

Perhaps reminding her of time's passage had been a mistake. Martha missed her young husband, the king's prisoner. It was natural. Though they might be together again very soon, if she'd accept his advice. He tried another tack: honesty.

"This is, after all, King Mwenda's country."

"Is that a fact? Was he not an invader himself but a few years before we arrived?"

"That's true, but—"

"We *won*! You overcame him in battle, destroying one aircanoe and capturing the other—"

"And letting him capture George."

For an awful moment, Thomas thought Martha would cry. She crumpled into her chair—he resumed his own quickly—but when she raised her face to the green light filtering through her office's open windows, it was free of tears. Her jaw was as decidedly firm as it could be for a woman of her age.

"He would hate for me to surrender."

"How do you know that, Martha?"

She raised a sheaf of papers from a basket on her desk. "His letters."

"The king never allowed him to say so!"

"Of course not. But he hasn't said anything to the contrary. We won't quit."

Thomas shut his eyes. Was there nothing else he could say? He opened them. "It isn't quitting. It isn't surrender. It isn't giving up. The Conciliation wasn't even written by the king."

"Oh yes! I know who the author is well enough." Her whole manner came in line with that firm jaw. Straight-backed now, rigid contempt filling her voice, Martha continued. "That French hussy Toutournier. Her interfering fingerprints are everywhere, on every page. Don't defend her! She's a scheming, lying, bold-faced cheat! I've known so for years!"

Thomas had no intention of defending Mademoiselle Toutournier. But to protect the Conciliation, he denied her authorship of it and said that honor was Daisy's.

"Poor Daisy." Martha's contempt for the Poet was a milder sort. "I suppose she wishes not to abandon Lily's grave. Can't she find some way to stay?"

"She has! A way for her to stay and for us all—" He stopped. Shouting would win him no victories. His hands hurt, the skin cracking at his knuckles and wrists, peeling as if they healed from a burn. That was often the case when he fought in Loango's service, whether handling dream bolts or not. This morning he'd neglected to rub them with the oil Yoka provided. The pain irritated him, led him to speak rashly and without heed for consequences. He prayed silently and without words for relief. The act itself brought him peace. He would be answered.

Without making the question an accusation, as slowly and soothingly as he could, Thomas asked Martha what it would take for her to accept the Conciliation.

Her reply was prompt and unthinking. "Guidance from God."

He didn't have to ask which God. For Martha there would always be only one.

A glance out the window showed him Yoka coming up the path. He held the familiar horn of oil: Loango's answer.

"And how will God grant this guidance?"

Martha clasped the wooden cross she wore as a pendant. "I'm not so prideful as to suppose I know that."

Yoka's knock saved Thomas from responding. Accepting the oil and the flimsy explanation for bringing it, Thomas asked his hostess if Yoka could fetch them some tea or chocolate from the commissary. After the acolyte left, Martha complimented Thomas on the gentility of his servant.

"Yoka is much more than that." He wouldn't be angry; it wasn't Martha's fault she was ignorant. Not entirely.

The oil felt good. He continued his efforts at softening her mood. "Let us see if by praying together we two may obtain a share of divine wisdom." Guessing the purpose of the cushions below the portrait of Jesus on the far wall, he helped Martha to them and joined her in kneeling there. He remembered how to bow his head and fold his hands. But in the act of closing his eyes, he surprised a look of suspicion on his companion's face.

"'God is not mocked,'" she quoted. "You follow a heathen path. You can't deny it."

He leaned back on his heels, a little shocked. "But you accepted my help!"

"I accepted your help fighting King Mwenda. This isn't at all the same. I find I'd much prefer to pray without you."

"Then I'll leave."

He intercepted Yoka with the tea and carried it to the guesthouse where Uwimana and Fatou waited. Nenzima had left his side to captain one of the king's aircanoes. He did his best not to grieve over her abandonment, which he hoped would be temporary. If not, well, he would cultivate gratitude for the wives he still had, more than most men.

Was this, perhaps, the root of Martha's issue with his presence?

Jealousy? No. She was obviously dedicated to her husband, heart and soul.

The guesthouse, intended for the families of wounded fighters, rested in the shade of a teak grove. A pair of planks bridged its encircling ditch, the water beneath them low. In a month or so, Uwimana said, the rains would fall more frequently here and fill it higher.

He had barely gotten under the long verandah's thatch when the afternoon's drizzling shower began. "Thomas! Come see!" shouted Fatoumata from the kitchen area. Through the ground floor, a shallow width hung with bundled hammocks, out into the courtyard and up the short flight of steps to where his wives faced each other over their new treasure: a microscope. It had been assembled for the hospital by Chester two seasons—a year—ago.

Nimbly, Uwimana jumped up to offer him her stool. Fatoumata, the eldest, now that Nenzima had left, pushed hers back so he could more easily reach the little table where the shining brass implement stood. An uncovered lamp had been placed beside it.

"What have you found?" he asked as he took his seat.

"We made slides of the ditchwater—so many animals! The hungry worms eat down all the bad ones—those who would grow up to bite us."

"I can't quite—"

"You turn this to make the image clear." Uwimana set Thomas's fingers on a pattern-etched knob. He turned it and the golden circle before his eye suddenly swam with fantastic creatures—tiny dragons with delicate legs and round, swollen heads. As he watched, a relatively larger monster attacked and swallowed a smaller one. "Ah! Yes! It's just as you say!"

"Just as Queen Josina says."

"The queen has a microscope?" He shouldn't have been surprised; her interests were legendarily diverse.

"She sees many mysteries." Fatoumata's breath brushed Thomas's ear. Tearing himself away from the miniature spectacle, he relinquished his seat to her.

"Have we heard any news?"

"No, my dear one. The drums say traders from Mbandaka will come upriver along the Sankuru soon. Perhaps they'll bring word." A circuitous route from Kisangani, but the queen was cautious, and, after all, Thomas was her husband's enemy. Unfortunately. Till the king could be persuaded otherwise.

As the day advanced, the guesthouse's other occupants returned, visits to their ill and wounded relatives coming to an end. Despite the current conflict, the house held only a quarter of the people it was designed for, leaving the entire first story for Thomas and his entourage. When Yoka had returned from his errand to the local clergy, they retreated up the steep staircase. Talk drifting up to Thomas from below sounded less restrained then.

The smells of roasting yams and rich sauces soon drifted up as well. Uwi and Fatou climbed the stairs several times, carrying gifts from the reverent, dishes the people staying here had prepared for them. As his wives served him and ate out of their own bowl, discussing the microscope's revelations and comparing them to what they'd expected, Thomas reflected on what *he* had expected.

The life he lived was wildly unlike his dreams. The country he called home, despite Martha's good intentions and his own, was no Canaan. This was their third war.

But he ate the crisp fried fish and listened to the rumble of contented conversation below, the lilting voices of his wives disputing their discoveries, and thought that all would soon be as it should.

Kisangani to Manono, Everfair, June 1919

Tink made his way slowly among fresh ruins. Most of the palace had been destroyed by demonstrators. Not the cellars, and not the gardens, which flourished, unconfined now by walls on all but one side. Not the royal hives lined against that lone wall. The royal bees seemed unperturbed by the surrounding destruction. One lighted momentarily on Tink's blossom-embroidered sleeve, then flew away in search of less figurative nectar.

Seated on a throne resting under a pavilion roofed in flowering vines, the king was accepting the oaths of his new subjects. George Albin stood on his left, surrounded by fighters. To Tink, he looked ashamed of his capture and defiant in compensation for it.

On Mwenda's right, his favorite, Queen Josina, cradled in her arms a copy of the Conciliation, painted on a folded length of barkcloth. Tink could see everything he needed to from the vantage he claimed at the crowd's front. He watched the principals closely. Three hours into the ceremony, near its end, Martha Albin made obeisance, kneeling quite gracefully for her size and age. The king gestured for her husband to go to her and help her to her feet. Rising, the couple faced the king, who dismissed them.

Soon after, he was the only foreigner left. Dusk was spilling quietly along the ground. The bees slept. Only dampness filled the emptied air. Wordlessly, King Mwenda indicated that the queen should depart, and the fighters and counselors should follow her. Tink and Mwenda were alone.

"Sit down." There was Josina's stool, lower than the king's, and also a cushion at the king's feet. "I don't expect you to salute me properly, since you didn't vow your allegiance."

Tink chose the cushion. "You weren't fooled by the clause about allowing no foreigners to remain."

"I know how *sanza* is played as well as anyone. The words were almost exactly those of my spirit father, in fact." His eyes stared into Tink's. "He is a master of this game.

"*Sanza* teaches us all what we most need to learn. I know this. I know my wise queen. She did nothing I would have forbidden her to do."

Tink nodded without breaking the king's gaze. "Nor have I."

"Yet you neglect to do a thing I wish you would." He pursed his lips. "Perhaps you have good reasons?"

Tink didn't answer. The king might think his reasons for leaving Everfair were good, or he might not.

But Mwenda persisted. "Tell me." He raised his prosthetic hand shoulder-high, rotated it so its piston casings caught the quiet evening light. "For the sake of my lost flesh."

Tink held his head high and steady. He refused to complain about his own loss. His love. "I will still be able to provide you with new versions from abroad."

"But *why*?" Not a challenge, but a cry of confusion. Did the king feel more for Tink than either had realized? "Why must you go?"

He decided to offer at least a facet of the jewel of truth. "My people didn't come to Africa on their own. They were brought against their will."

King Mwenda shook his head. "And so? Of course you may leave when you wish—no one's keeping you. The command put in the Conciliation is not that you have to stay where you don't want to be."

They sat in silence a while.

"Well," said the king, "you'll go, then."

"But I would like the right to return here sometimes. As a favor."

"That seems well within my power. You could come to me. You'd be an ambassador to my court. . . . Yes.

"And of course we will write each other letters." The king seemed cheered by this thought—he smiled, at any rate, and leaned forward to rest both hands on Tink's shoulders. They were near in height, near in age. "We'll be friends."

He had managed not to anger him. That was Tink's first ordeal over. The next morning, he went to the Poet's flat for the second. Rosalie had returned from England earlier that season. She opened the door at his knock.

"May I come in?"

"Mama's away."

"May I come in?" he repeated. "It's to see you, not her."

"I still don't want to marry you."

"That's fine. I didn't expect you to change your mind. May I—"

"All right." The door opened wider and she stepped aside. "You might as well." He followed her into the next room. Beads, pelts, and feathers covered the top of a collapsible table.

"What are you doing?"

"Making masks. What do you care what I'm doing? I'm not her. Lily."

"No. I know." He had always known. "I'm sorry if you thought I thought you were."

"Well, you did." She made no offer of refreshment. Not even water. It would be impolite for him to sit unless she did. There were three chairs, but Rosalie ignored them, so Tink did too.

"I only came to tell you goodbye. I'm returning home with Bee-Lung."

Rosalie looked interested. "Going to China? Macao? To live?"

He'd remembered her interest in his homeland correctly. "To live," he confirmed. "But when I visit Everfair again, would you like me to bring anything back?" He saw her hesitate. "It would be done purely as business. You'd need to offer"—he tried to think of a suitable trade good—"herbs." Bee-Lung could help with choosing those. "Or something else of value in exchange."

"All right. I suppose. I've certainly heard of gems I want, minerals, techniques I'd like to learn. I could probably find the right items to . . . nothing personal?"

He was able to assure her of that.

The closeness the king seemed to crave for, Rosalie abhorred.

Winthrop and Albert took Tink and his scanty luggage to the airfield using a bicycle newly refitted with their latest experimental palm oil engine. As he had expected, the Poet was on duty there.

"Mr. Ho, I understand this will be your last flight out of Kisangani?"

"For some time to come, Mrs. Albin." The formality was stupid, but better than her total silence for eight months after Lily's death. "My base will be in Macao, though I'll make regular trips here—once I've had a few seasons to establish stops along the route."

It was nowhere near the ordeal he'd undergone facing King Mwenda or Rosalie. Things hadn't changed much between them since she'd decided to talk to him again.

Kalala II reached Manono in just under twenty-four hours, counting their time in Kalemie. Bee-Lung didn't come to meet him at the airfield. He found her in her storefront, half the shelves still filled with stock.

"Maybe you'd better leave me here, Little Brother?"

"Ridiculous! Leave you here by yourself?" He took an empty basket from the stack by the back door and began filling it, winding dried grass around the more fragile-looking containers.

"What is there to keep you here?" he asked.

"What is there in Macao to fetch me back?"

Tink could think of a hundred things he missed: the freshness of sea-touched air; the pipa player at the entrance to Camoes Garden; the hill of A-Ma's temple, where they handed out fistfuls of fizzing sparklers on festival day—the childhood from which he'd been stolen. "Our family."

Bee-Lung straightened and held her hands against the low part of her back. "One needn't see Min-Cheng every day. He doesn't change."

That was true. Ever intelligent, but never *too* intelligent, and always supremely successful; their brother had been correctly named.

Scooping a pile of scrolls from a tall stool, Bee-Lung began to bundle them together with a piece of twine. "Really, why do you want to leave?"

"I've found something out about myself. I can't bow to another man."

"Of course. You're Metal Dragon, aren't you?" She set the bundled scrolls in the lid of a grey trunk. "Never mind. I'm going with you, as you see. You go get some dinner in you and leave the rest of this to me." She herself was Earth Dragon, and would prefer to organize her belongings her own way, no doubt.

Tink had his own packing to take care of, too. His house here contained more than the apartment up in Kisangani, but he would take less. Many of the furnishings had been left behind by the Tams. He had no attachment to them. He had asked Mkoi to distribute them, and some things were already gone. His folded clothes had been removed from the wall basket and stacked neatly on the bench holding his notes and drawings.

Those he took. Almost everything else—even his hammock, even the dishes he ate out of that night, he left behind when they boarded *Omukama* the next morning.

Leaving things behind was easy. There would always be more things.

There would never be another love like the one he had lost. And now he was going on not only without her, but without his allegiance to Everfair, the land for which she'd given her life.

Once again, he shared a cabin with Bee-Lung. Once again she stowed many of her precious remedies in their shared quarters. But on *Omukama,* they were located along the aircanoe's starboard side rather than its stern. So for a parting sight of Everfair, Tink went into the common lounge.

The final ordeal. They flew the express to Alexandria. There would be no stop in Kalemie—no stopping till Kampala, unless drums called the vessel down as they'd done at Manono. Only a few hours into their journey, he watched the town and the coast-line of Lake Tanganyika recede.

Roofs: thatch, tin, and tile. Then walls, doors, and windows, a patchwork of dull colors and shadows that fell swiftly behind them, becoming at last a dirty blur on the horizon. That was all there was to see. Nothing beautiful, and not a single dream.

Kalemie to Kalima, Everfair, July 1919

Mornings and evenings, Lisette's rooms let the river's breeze blow through windows on their east and west walls, waking her with its freshness or lulling her to sleep with the sweetness of the intervening garden's jasmine and rose. The school building occupied a peninsula surrounded on three sides by the Lukuga River; no matter which direction the wind came from, it carried a memory of water. And, though quiet, her apartments were never still.

Her bed lay in a small, lilac-shadowed room overlooking the building's courtyard. The largest room, facing the street, was where she received guests and taught, as well as where she wrote and spent most of her day. Her desk did double duty: it held her typing machine and ordered manuscripts, but also her lessons and bell. It had no back: when teaching, she sat at it facing away from the balcony, and when writing, facing toward it.

She closed the balcony doors' white curtains to soften the early sun. They fluttered as if whispering secrets to each other. The heavier cloth covering the dining table to be used in today's exercise stirred only a little.

The last of her students for this class mounted the stairs in the room's center: Nadi. All five had come early. Lisette surveyed them critically as they rearranged themselves on her sofas to accommodate their fellow: suitably coiffed, suitably dressed, suitably restrained in their comportment. So eager! though they did their best not to show it. She remembered how that was.

"Questions before we begin?"

The youngest raised a timid hand. "Will we really be eating these foods?"

"Why not?"

The girl looked to either side. Her companions on the settee didn't meet her gaze, keeping their elaborately styled heads facing forward. She was brave—or Fwendi wouldn't have admitted her—and answered Lisette without their help.

"I've heard the Europeans' food is—unclean. Nasty. Full of illnesses."

"Who told you that? It's nonsense. I myself have eaten with Europeans—I was raised on their food—and I'm fine! And Americans are much the same. Later I'll teach you how to cook for them, since many of you will be hired as domestic servants.

"Now." Lisette nodded at the dinner table set for six. "Take your places. We will assume for the sake of convenience that you've been escorted in properly by gentlemen." She watched approvingly as her students found the cards with their names and waited behind the corresponding chairs. "Mwadi and I will help you to be seated." She rang the brass handbell and her assistant appeared from the closet beside Lisette's bedroom. When teacher and students were seated, the princess assumed the role of parlor maid, ferrying prepared dishes from the closet to the table, pouring grape wine, removing crumbs, remnants, soiled crockery.

The lesson went well. At any formal dinner to which they were invited, these spies would know how to conduct themselves. They left, and she had an interval before her next session. Not long enough to walk to the Lake and back; she could tell so much by the power plant's whistle.

She sat facing the balcony and scratched down a few notes about her latest story: children granted wishes at the whim of a homeless djinn in return for help finding his lamp. Full after the mock dinner, Lisette ignored the summons to luncheon, but then decided to go down anyway—not to eat, but to talk with Fwendi.

No sign of her in the hall—she, too, must have chosen to skip the meal. After checking her office, Lisette found her in the outbuilding housing the school's laundry.

The twin washing machines were silent, though steam rose from one, winding through the grey air to the open skylights high overhead. Empty rods crisscrossed the cathedral-like space, drying racks unemployed outside the long rainy season.

Fwendi sat on the edge of the machines' platform, legs dangling, chin propped on her left fist. Her right hand, a mending set, held a swathe of fabric pinched into pleats against a smooth band, but was idle otherwise. At Lisette's entrance, she started guiltily. "I'm sorry—were you looking for me? I've cleared your schedule for tomorrow, too. Of course you may go. As if you had to ask."

"Naturally I must ask. This is your school, your enterprise." Lisette climbed the short staircase and leaned to look inside the open machine. A dark mass was sunk deep in the sudsy wetness. Not sheets, then. Uniforms, like the one Fwendi now bent to guide between her stitching fingers.

The whir of the hand's gears started and stopped, started and stopped. "You'll admit, though, that it's because of you the queen gives her support."

Lisette admitted nothing of the sort. "It is in her interest."

Finishing the skirt's new waistband, Fwendi got up and put it in the machine. She shut the lid and engaged its plunger to the power shaft. Lisette listened affectionately to the *chunk-chunk-chunk*ing of the washer's operation. But she watched Fwendi, who watched nothing, simply standing at the control panel when she was done with her task, empty hands hanging at her sides.

"You miss him, don't you?" Lisette asked.

"I wish I was Mwadi. I would fly to him tonight."

"He'll be back soon. It's only three hundred miles."

"Three hundred and fifty. Twelve hours for the flight."

"You could have gone with him." Lisette was fairly sure Matty had asked his wife to come with him for *Wendi-La*'s Mwanza premiere. She understood, though, that Fwendi felt she couldn't leave midterm.

Not so, Lisette.

Before dawn she waited below the mooring mast for *Fu Hao*.

According to the drums, the aircanoe would arrive practically on time. Soon the drone of its engine throbbed through the weakening night.

The mast was short. When tied up, *Fu Hao* floated very near the ground. A solid-seeming rolling ladder bridged the gap between the airfield and the new, enclosed gondola for her. As she walked the narrow corridor leading to her cabin, she had to grasp its walls for balance, the floor leaping below her sandals as the vessel dropped its freight.

The cabin was unnecessary; she'd be in Kalima by evening. She could easily have sat with her fellow passengers in the common lounge. The increasing light would display the countryside's rushing mountain streams and verdant orchards—but Lisette had seen them many times. In truth, the trip itself no longer thrilled her—only its end. If she learned to pilot one of the new craft, the aeroplanes fueled by fractionated palm oil, perhaps then her excitement would revive itself. She would be inside the thing's thrumming hull, separated from its motor by only a thin barrier of steel.

She recalled the bicycle she'd ridden so fast, so recklessly as a girl: it had been her friend, her freedom, its black frame and hard rubber tires vital and alive. Where was it now? Where had the sales agents of her parents' forfeited estate sent it? Probably it was no longer in working order. And probably the rubber forming her friend's tires had originated here, harvested in fear and misery by the likes of Mr. Mkoi or Yoka.

A scratching sound upon her cabin door. She opened it to a crewwoman: short, slight, and Bharatese to judge by her precise way of speech. She invited Mademoiselle Toutournier to join the captain on the bridge.

Lisette went. To refuse would not be gracious.

The aircanoe sailed west, toward the Lualaba River. The sun had risen. Beyond the great glass panes of the new gondola's bow, *Fu Hao*'s silhouette crept ahead of them over the plateau like a hunting cat.

Chocolate was offered. Lisette declined as politely as possible. After that, she was left more or less alone, only being introduced to crewmembers as they entered in the course of their duties. She found she was not in anybody's way when she kept near the windows. The Bharati woman lent her a pair of binoculars. Someone else brought her a stool. At intervals she sat, then stood again for a better view of a scene passing under the gondola's belly: a drover with a flock of sheep, a gang of workers digging their way to a dry watercourse—a diversion?

Though familiar, the country changed, always, inevitably. There was a pleasure in perceiving these changes; she was glad not to have missed it.

Twenty-five years she had known Everfair! Almost as long as Daisy. It would be a wonder if either of them had stayed the same; assuredly Lisette had not. Though the country's life might run more slowly . . . No. She thought of the wars, the progress made in weaponry and the healing arts: faster almost than the eye could follow. They flew northward now along the Lualaba, the river's rapids plunging fiercely between slick rocks— Not more slowly, no, but over a much longer time.

The monarchy would not last.

Eventually *Fu Hao* abandoned the Lualaba and entered the valley of the Ulindi River, turning back south and east. Eventually, the little town of Kalima came drifting into sight below: the forges and worksheds. The hotel where she and Daisy had, after so many years, come together once again. The warehouse where she had given up her heart's hope. The little house on the edge of things where Daisy lived now, in exile from the court, minding Lisette's birds and lizards. The airfield with its primitive mast. To which, eventually, they moored.

The fuss with the passenger sling prolonged itself intolerably. Intolerably!

Inwardly, Lisette laughed at herself. How could she be this eager for someone who she was certain awaited her? For someone she knew so very, very well?

But then she was on the ground, understanding that those questions, along with many others, would always be answerless. And then she was once again in the arms of her imperfect love.

Acknowledgments

Writing is a solitary act that expresses the genius of a community. My work has been supported by so many members of my community it would take another book to name them all. Everyone who helped me write the short stories that appear in *Filter House* helped with this book also. To that list add Jaymee Goh, Diana Pho, Dr. Jake von Slatt, Rachel Swirsky, Scott Lynch, Elizabeth Bear, Susan and Bill Gossman, Mary Kay and Jordin Kare, Joe Murphy, Aaliyah Mari Hudson, Bill Campbell, Samuel R. Delany, and the inimitable K. Tempest Bradford. Kenneth Heard looked over Everfair's aircanoes with a researcher's eye. I have heeded his advice as well as I was able. If you notice something wrong with them it's my fault, not his.

I owe much of my inspiration to the author of *King Leopold's Ghost*, Adam Hochschild, and to the brave women and men who stood against the tyrant.

Geoff Ryman asked me why. Michael Swanwick cut his eyes at me. Jim Frenkel bought it. Liz Gorinsky edited it all over the world.

Those of you who donated to the crowdfunders for my sister, Julie, and my mother, June, also helped with this book's creation.

Those of you who wanted *Everfair,* asked for it, pre-ordered it, bought it, and read it are my special friends.

Thank you all.